MOST MEN
DON'T KILL

MURDER IN
BLACK AND
WHITE

MOST MEN DON'T KILL

MURDER IN BLACK AND WHITE

DAVID ALEXANDER

COACHWHIP PUBLICATIONS

Greenville, Ohio

Most Men Don't Kill / Murder in Black and White,
by David Alexander
© 2018 Coachwhip Publications

David C. Alexaner (1907-1973)
Most Men Don't Kill published 1951.
Murder in Black and White published 1951.
No claims made on public domain material.
Cover image: Penguin © Yan Koev

CoachwhipBooks.com

ISBN 1-61646-461-5
ISBN-13 978-1-61646-461-5

MOST MEN
DON'T KILL

For Alice with Love

1

I walked into my hotel room and the naked woman was sitting there in the only easy chair.

I stood for a moment with both the door and my mouth open. I'd been batting around Charley Frayne's bar all evening looking for a girl. Ginny had slapped my face—the side with the scar on it—and I wanted a girl just out of pure meanness. I'd been in a bad mood and I'd had a job to do the next day and the old aching had started in my head, so I'd thought I'd get a girl. Out of meanness, understand. Or maybe because I thought that would stop the aching in my head. Anyway, the only ones who'd come in had played the chill. One or two had taken a drink on me, but after that they'd discovered they had boy friends or husbands or something. So I'd come back to the hotel. I'd only checked in a few hours before.

And there, waiting for me in the easy chair, was Eros' answer to a lustful dream.

A little on the heavy side, perhaps, but Rubenesque, the way I like them. Very long bob curling itself over smooth shoulders. Brown eyes, looking kind of crazy. Lips, fat-pouting, a little too red. And lots of other things. I saw all that in the moment or so I held the door and my mouth open. Then I saw something else, and I closed the door. I closed the door softly.

The funny thing about the brown eyes was they didn't blink. They didn't blink at all. They just kept looking at me kind of crazy. And the funny thing about the fat-pouting mouth was it didn't move but was just slack. You'd have expected her to say something or to blink her eyes or move a muscle when I came barging in like that. But she didn't.

And there was another funny thing.

There was a little stream, red-colored, running down from under her left breast and coagulating itself in the tiny crease that marked the beginning of her abdomen.

All of a sudden I got cold-calm, clammy-calm, like that day I'd got cold-calm on some little atoll in the Pacific. I opened the door again. I didn't open it very far. Then I took the "Don't Disturb" sign off the inside knob and hung it on the outside knob. I closed the door. I didn't have to lock it. The door locked itself.

I walked over and examined her more closely. Under the left breast there was a little hole. Little, but deep. A little, oozing hole, like you might make by sticking an ice pick into a hard-frozen block of raspberry sherbet. Only it had quit oozing. It was just sticky now.

I sat down on the bed. I lit a cigarette and wondered why the hell my hand wasn't shaky. Sometimes my hand got shaky when I tried to tie my shoes. You can't get blown out of an M-4 tank without your hand getting shaky. That's what the doctors told me.

I began to think about things. All the little islands whose names aren't even remembered any more, but which stank with cordite and corpses in the days I knew them. The hospitals that stank with formaldehyde. Skid Row that stank with unwashed men. And now this. There wasn't any stink about this, though. The dead woman, who would have seemed warm and voluptuous if she'd only blink her eyes, didn't stink. She smelled nice. She smelled of expensive perfume.

Before the horrors hit me below the belt and I began to feel too sorry for myself, I knew I had to do something. I tried to think what it was I had to do. Then I knew. I got up off the bed and began to search the room. There wasn't anything in the closet except the old trench coat I had hung there myself. There wasn't anything in the drawers of the dresser except three shirts, three suits of underwear, three pairs of socks, a few handkerchiefs and a manila envelope. They belonged to me. There wasn't anything in the bathroom except my shaving kit, toothbrush and toothpaste. My shaving lotion had a faint, ferny odor to it. It didn't smell a bit like the perfume with which the naked woman had doused herself.

There wasn't even anything under the bed.

The woman sitting in the chair just didn't have any clothes.

I sat down on the edge of the bed again. The cigarette was beginning to burn my fingers. I lit another one off the butt, an old Army habit.

By God, I thought, this is it. This is the prize package, kid. This is the brass ring. First Ginny slaps you in the puss. Now you get a naked dame sitting here with a hole in her heart.

But first there'd been a lot of other things.

There'd been the war and the little islands that we'd come on, roaring from LCT's, with my 50-caliber blasting from the turret and the little men with 25-rifles dying absurdly in our path. There'd been the hospital and some guy with chickens on his shoulders tossing me a heart-shaped picture of George Washington hung on a purple ribbon because I'd forgot to duck. With that and a nickel, we used to say, you could buy a subway ride. Nowadays you need a dime in addition to the Purple Heart if you want a subway ride.

There'd been looking for a job after the war and not getting any. There'd been living in furnished rooms and having the old French key put on the door because I couldn't pay the rent on time. There'd been the 52-20 Club and the time I knocked some twerp off his stool at the unemployment office because he sassed me. I'd told this guy, who had probably been a rear-echelon cook in a service company, that I was a newspaperman and all I wanted was a newspaperman's job. He smirked a fairy kind of smirk at me and said I was a big, husky guy, so why didn't I try bricklaying. That's when I hit him.

I didn't go back for any veterans' unemployment compensation after that. I should have, I guess, because I had a lot of weeks to run. But instead I hit Skid Row.

Now don't think I'm crying in your beer because I hit Skid Row. Some of the nicest guys I ever met outside my own separate tank battalion, which was blown to hell and gone, were on Skid Row. Most of them didn't smell nice and three of them robbed me of a bundle of dough that could have been my passport back to respectability, but there were some nice guys on Skid Row just the same. Guys who would split their last buck and their last crock of muscatel with you.

There was Knotty, the dwarf who wore a monocle, for instance. And Basserty, the jockey who wore a beard and got his name in the papers, but who went on periodical binges. And Killer Carney, the punch-drunk baby sitter. There was the Professor, a rum-dumb nuclear-fission expert, and Shakey, the Shakespearean scholar with a psychopathic hatred of cops. I didn't get to know Polvo, the organ grinder with a dead monkey and George Washington's teeth, or Ebony Black, the gigantic, one-eyed Negro heavyweight, or Tommy Twotoes, the millionaire penguin fancier, until later.

I'm not trying to be lurid in describing these guys. I'm just being brief and factual in presenting a cast of characters who were about to play an important part in the thing that happened to me. You don't always find the real characters, the real dreamers, the real bohemians wearing berets in Greenwich Village. Sometimes you find them wearing peaked caps on the Bowery.

The trouble with me was I'd got myself a dose of shellshock, or combat fatigue, if you wish to use the Army euphemism, along with the crease in my face, that time the M-4 tank caught a Jap mortar lob head-on. They kept me in a hospital for a long time giving me sitz baths and lessons in rug weaving. V-J Day was just something people talked about occasionally by the time I got out. The girls weren't kissing soldiers on the streets any more and weren't asking them what all those pretty little ribbons meant. Most vets weren't even wearing their ruptured ducks any longer. But I got a kind of ironic kick out of wearing the little enamel emblem of the Purple Heart in my buttonhole. With that and a nickel . . .

I was still wearing it as I sat there on the bed looking at the naked woman whose lush body would never give any man any pleasure any more.

The sitz baths and the rug weaving must not have cured me entirely. I was still edgy when I got out. I was impatient of the stupidity of city editors and their excuses for not hiring me. I felt an urge to fist up and throw away the silly forms they gave me to fill out in chromium-glittering advertising and public-relations agencies. Then I knocked the twerp off the stool in the employment place. And once when I was drunk in a bar I smashed a guy just because he was wearing a derby hat.

I'd been on a lot of newspapers in my time, but I was free-lancing in publicity just before the war and couldn't demand a job by virtue of the GI Bill of Rights. I was over thirty years old and would have felt damned silly going back to school to earn ninety bucks a month. The newspapers all gave me the same answers. Five men for every typewriter had come back and had to be hired because they'd been in the service. All the advertising and public-relations agencies ever gave me were a lot of forms to fill out.

I might have got along after a fashion for a while on the disability pension and the princely stipend from the 52-2o Club if it hadn't been for the booze. Instead I made lushing a profession. At first it was bonded bourbon. Then it was bar rye. Then it was draft beer at a dime a copy. And finally it was bottles of sweet wine (guaranteed 20 percent) that could be bought for anywhere from sixty-five cents to a dollar, depending upon the location of the liquor store. After the third time I was locked out of a furnished room and lost all my earthly possessions except the ones I wore on my back or had in my pocket, I started lurching up and down Dream Street.

I'd cashed my state bonus a long time before. By the time the terminal-leave pay came along I had the leaps and the retches so bad I was determined to use all the money in rehabilitating myself. I was going to get new clothes and rent a clean room and start looking for a job again. The terminal-leave pay amounted to quite a bundle in my case. I'd been in nearly four years, most of them in the Pacific, and you didn't get furloughs in the Pacific.

I'd had the check sent to the Red Cross, because I had no permanent address. The man at the Red Cross advised me to go to the nearest bank, deposit the check, and draw out only what I needed for immediate use. But I was half fogged when I got the check and I had Red Eye and Goosey George and the Canned Heat Kid with me. They were all good guys, or so I thought at the time. We went to the bank and some little man told me I should deposit the check so I wouldn't lose my money. But I took the cash. I didn't like the little man. I thought he was just trying to gyp me out of two bucks for a checkbook.

I gave Red Eye and Goosey George and the Canned Heat Kid each a sawbuck. Then we went to the liquor store and bought enough muscky to float the *Queen Elizabeth* on a sea of sweet wine. We started drinking. We sat in a lot of doorways drinking. I woke up in some doorway or other with five bucks in my pocket. They were good guys, all right, those three. They left me five bucks out of several hundred.

At Skid Row prices, five bucks is enough for a three-day bat, with little green men sitting on your shoulder for an added attraction. I looked everywhere for the three good guys and I drank everywhere I looked, but of course they'd gone. I remember that the little green men and I sat down in a lot of doorways and that several cops said, "Hey, buddy, off my beat." And then I remember waking up in Bellevue with a dent over my eyebrow and a lumbar injection attached to my back.

After that they sent me to another government hospital and for a long time I had the old curriculum of sitz baths and rug weaving, plus shock treatments that damn near knocked the teeth out of my head. There was a certain doctor in the hospital. He was a good guy. He got my pension upped a little, and he even helped get me a job. Not much of a job, but a job. It was with something called a research bureau. You went around ringing doorbells and filling out forms. You asked people such questions as whether they preferred green olives or ripe olives or stuffed olives or maybe even the little wrinkled-up olives with a sprig of garlic in them. You got paid according to the number of forms you filled out about people's preferences in olives or brassieres or other articles. That experience got me a job with one of the polls.

What the hell, here I was sitting on the bed in that hotel room and looking at the naked woman with a hole in her heart, and I was thinking about all this. What the hell, you have to think about something, don't you? You can't think about this thing right now, can you?

I got some decent clothes at basement sales out of what I earned. I managed to get something they called an apartment in a cold-water tenement. I didn't quit drinking entirely. I couldn't, it seemed. But I controlled it. I had to have something to do to keep me from drinking. I got tired of going to picture shows. So I joined a veterans' organization. That would occupy my time for a few hours a week, I figured. They had card nights and beer nights in addition to the regular meetings. I met Chet Lassiter at my post of the vets' organization. He'd been a captain of MP's in the Pacific area, and, believe it or not, some MP's were damned good guys. Anybody would know Chet was a good guy. He was taller than I am, and I push six feet, and he was a hell of a lot meatier. It was good, solid meat, too. The kind of meat that makes you know what's behind it if he happens to hit you with a hard-knuckled fist. And Chet knew how to smile It was a good, grinny, broad-mouthed kind of smile that never mocked at people. It just laughed along with them at something that was really funny, and Chet found a lot of things funny in life. He was about ten years older than I was.

Chet and I got to be good friends. We swapped stories about the Pacific fighting. We drank together in saloons. He introduced me to Charley Frayne's place. He also introduced me to Ginny. Ginny did her drinking in Frayne's place. She was by no means one of those female dipsomaniacs who get slobbery and disgusting. But she did a little drinking to drown her sorrows. She wanted to be a dancer and she'd spent a lot of money on dancing lessons and she could dance. But she worked in Vince Parada's Triangle Club and all Vince wanted her to do was strip for the customers.

One look at Ginny and you knew the reason why. Isadora Duncan could dance. But nature had never given Isadora what Ginny had. Ginny was the kind of girl who had only to take off most of her clothes under a blue light to make a nice, comfortable living. I looked at the naked dame in the chair. Ten or fifteen years from now Ginny might look something like that. Only without the hole in her heart, I hoped.

Ginny had the kind of body that could be as stiff and tough as an old-fashioned whalebone corset if she didn't like the man who was trying to put his hands on her, and as soft and pliable as an oil-bathed baby if she wanted to make it that way. She had a mouth that could curse and a mouth that could coo. She could be as tough as a madam with a guy who's only got a buck ninety-five, and she could be a little girl with a snub nose who looked slightly absurd with mascara on her eyelashes. She knew how to dress for the sunlight just as well as she knew how to undress under Vince Parada's blue spots.

I guess I was in love with Ginny. I guess Ginny didn't hate me too much, either. Anyway, I was the only guy who had a key to her apartment. I'd been her guy and she'd been my girl for several months now. I'd enjoyed every minute of it, up to that afternoon. She'd always been soft and sweet with me. But that afternoon she'd slapped me.

Maybe I wouldn't have minded so much if she'd slapped me on the right cheek, the one without the scar. But she'd slapped me on the left cheek, where the flesh is dented in a little zig-zag pattern. I'm sensitive about that scar, although I guess it really doesn't look too bad and some dames have even told me it makes me appear romantic, like the scars of those German posturers who used to give themselves a slash with a razor blade to prove they'd dueled at Heidelberg.

It had been a silly kind of quarrel. I'd said that now I had a regular job and had received my first assignment we could get married and she could quit what she was doing. She'd said, well, we could get married all right, but she'd better keep on awhile at the Triangle until our incomes were more stabilized. I'd said I didn't want a wife who showed everything—or almost everything, anyway—to Parada's drooling customers, even if she did show it under a blue light, and I'd also said that if she couldn't depend on me and wanted an income of her own for a while, why the hell didn't she get a legitimate job just dancing?

That was when she slapped my face. Thinking it over, I couldn't blame her too much. It was her sore point, and I'd hit it on purpose, as a fighter hits a bleeding nose.

I'd got myself to my feet and tried to look very dignified and I'd walked out on Ginny. And then, in a little-boy-I'll-make-you-sorry mood, I'd tried to get myself a dame at Frayne's, where dames weren't usually too hard to get. But I hadn't got one. Certainly, I hadn't got this dame in the chair. She was nice and naked and lushly curved, but I never did go for dames who had holes in their hearts.

I'd had the job for only a few weeks. It was a job with Chet Lassiter. Chet had opened a private detective agency after the war.

He'd done all right until that investigation into the New York divorce scandals came along. Maybe you think about private detectives according to the books you've read or the radio programs you've heard. Tall, lean, irresistible guys or very tough fat boys solving murders. Mostly, in New York, at least, they don't solve murders and are never called upon to do anything very romantic. Most of their cases are very cut and dried. A guy gets suspicious of his business partner and wants him tailed. You tail him, for forty bucks a day, if you aren't underselling. But the big fat, the thing that the private detectives, the private ops, the private eyes, the shamuses—whatever the hell you want to call them—used to live on was the divorce racket. A guy didn't like his wife. A wife didn't like her husband. They wanted to get rid of each other—mutually. But they didn't have the money to go to Nevada or Florida or some other state where the divorce laws are liberal and take into consideration the simple fact of incompatibility. The only valid reason for divorce in New York State is adultery, and that has to be proved.

That was where your glamorous private eye or op or dick came in. He caught you, with malice aforethought, in a hotel room with some girl he'd hired for the purpose. He had his own mousy little private detective or private op or private eye as a witness and he probably had some bribed bellboy to back up the testimony. That's how the private dick earned his fee. The guy and gal got the divorce, the shamus got paid, and everybody was happy.

Chet had become my best friend, and after the investigation into the divorce scandals put the private detective business into an all-time slump, one of Chet's men had left him to operate a chicken farm. Chet offered me the job, provided I'd take a token salary at first plus a bonus for every case I worked on. For a long time there hadn't been any cases, and I'd had difficulty finding anything to do around the office after I'd read "Li'l Abner" and Dan Parker's column in the *Mirror*. Then, a couple of days before,

I'd gone out to Frayne's for a midafternoon shot. I'd met Ginny there and had stayed longer than I'd intended. When I got back to the office, Chet said, "There's news. A client was just in. He left a $200 retainer. I'm turning the job over to you."

"What's the set-up?" I asked, feeling a little trembly about this first assignment in snooping, although I'd had plenty of similar ones as a newspaperman.

"The client's name is Little," Chet replied. "Malcolm Little. I take it he has money. Owns an estate in Westchester. He's around sixty, probably. He's got a wife. The wife is quite a dish. He thinks the wife is cheating. He has reason to believe she'll meet a man in Room 617 of the Sheridan Towers Hotel at five o'clock on the afternoon of the twenty-first. I've already reserved Room 616 of the same hotel for the twentieth under the name of George Spelvin. That will give you a day to establish and orient yourself."

I almost laughed at the alias he'd chosen. It was as obviously phony as Jockey No Boy in the race entries. George Spelvin is the name they use on theater programs when an actor doubles in brass.

Chet favored me with his winning smile. "I told the clerk over the phone I wanted that particular room because I admired the view from the window. The clerk said there wasn't much of a view from the window except a view of a fire escape, so I told him I was queer for fire escapes. I said I'd check in right after noon. You check in some time between twelve and one. Get the layout of the place. Ask the desk clerk if there's been a reservation for Room 617 the next day. Pretend you expect a friend. Try to find out what name was used in making the reservation. That's about all you can do on the twentieth. But I'd better brief you for the twenty-first. We don't know anything about the man who will check into 617. You'll have to spend a boring afternoon. Being bored to death most of the time is part of this business. At the Sheridan Towers they have those inside safety chain-locks on the doors. You hook the chain and you can open the door about a foot. Nobody from outside can open it any further. The man will probably enter 617 early to arrange the seduction scene. You put the chain-lock on your door. Leave it as wide open as it will go. Keep the lights off. Pull the blind down. Sit in a chair near the door, so you can see out the crack. Get yourself a mental picture of anyone who goes into 617 other than the chambermaids and bellhops."

"Do I have to identify the dame the same way?" I asked.

"No," he said, "that's a lot easier. I've got a picture. And it's a dame you're not likely to forget"

He took a manila envelope out of the desk drawer. He took a large photograph of a chesty female out of the envelope. She was quite a dish. She was a dame you wouldn't be likely to forget.

"Take it along with you for checking purposes," he said. He grinned the wide grin. "An old man's darling," he said. "Quite a dish. Maybe not so young as she looks, thanks to the beauty boys, but quite a dish just the same. You and I should have money, Terry."

"Yeah," I said. "And have wives who meet other men in Room 617 of the Sheridan Towers."

On the twentieth, the day I'm writing about now, I did as Chet told me. I checked into the hotel shortly after noon, picking up George Spelvin's reservation. An Italian-looking bellhop took me up and commented upon the fact that I wore the Purple Heart. He said he'd got a gut wound himself in the Bulge fighting. I put away the few clothes and toilet articles I'd brought along. Then I tested the door chain. I could see Room 617 all right through the twelve-inch crack. The hallway was well lighted.

I fooled around awhile, then I went down to the desk and inquired about reservations for Room 617. The clerk was haughty and suspicious and I immediately decided that despite my newspaper training I wasn't too hot at the private-eye business. The clerk wanted to know the name of the guy I expected to register in the room. I invented a name. It wasn't the right name, of course. The clerk examined the card file. He told me the room had been occupied for several days by a J. K. Provost and that the gentleman had thus far signified no intention of checking out.

I called Chet and told him what I'd learned. He said I'd done all right. He said the guy had probably just taken the love nest a few days in advance. He said the guy probably wouldn't even show up in it until the next day. He told me I'd done about all I could do until tomorrow, so I might as well take the afternoon off, see Ginny and have a good dinner on the expense money.

I took his advice. I went down to West Twenty-third Street and saw Ginny. We got to talking about marriage and such matters and it wound up with her slapping my face and me walking out. That was about four o'clock in the afternoon. I went back to the hotel and mooned around and got another of the bad headaches. I left the door on the chain and propped up a chair and turned off the lights and pulled down the blind because I thought maybe the mysterious Mr. Provost might happen around after all and I'd get a gander at him. But after two hours or so I got hungry. I also got the idea it would be fine to spite Ginny by picking up some dame. About that time the phone rang. It was Chet. He asked me what the hell I was doing back there. I told him Ginny and I had had a spat. He told me to go out and eat and drown my sorrows, but not to catch a hangover because the next day was important. The next day, he said, was Terry Bob Rooke's first case.

He'd told me to do just what I wanted to do. Chet was like that. He could sense things and play along with you. He was in something I considered a slightly dirty business, but he was a right guy.

I went to Frayne's and had some dinner and a few drinks and tried to pick up a dame and I couldn't. I came back to the hotel around nine-thirty and got my key from the desk and went to my room and found the naked woman sitting in the only easy chair. I was sitting on the bed now looking at her and trying to figure things out.

I got up and opened a dresser drawer and took out a manila envelope. I took a photograph out of the manila envelope.

There wasn't any doubt about it.

The naked woman sitting in the easy chair was Mrs. Malcolm Little, the dame I was supposed to tail.

She was sitting there as pretty as you please except for the hole in her heart.

2

I had to do something and do it in a hurry. The first thing I had to do was get out of there. I collected my belongings from the closet and the dresser drawers. I stuffed the socks and handkerchiefs and shaving kit into the pockets of my suit and trench coat. I folded the few suits of underwear and the shirts very carefully inside my trench coat. I hung the coat and its padding over my arm, trying to make it look casual. I also tucked the manila envelope containing the photograph under my arm. I hated to leave the brand-new plastic suitcase, but I couldn't very well walk through the lobby with a suitcase without first checking out. And I didn't want to check out. I didn't want to talk to anybody at the desk. And I didn't want any maids or new tenants coming up to the room right after I'd left. They might be surprised to find the room still occupied by the lady who was sitting in the chair.

I nodded good-bye to the lady and walked out. There wasn't anybody in the hall at the moment. I tried the door to make sure the lock had clicked. I left the "Don't Disturb" sign hanging on the outside knob of the door. The key to the room was in one of my pockets along with all the other stuff I was taking with me.

Before I even reached the elevator, I realized what a prize chump I was. I was some private eye, all right. I hadn't even taken the trouble to wipe my fingerprints off the doorknob or anything else. That plastic suitcase was a perfect surface for recording fingerprints. But I didn't go back. I tried to rationalize my actions by thinking that somebody else's fingerprints must be in that room, too, and if I wiped them off I would be destroying the only evidence that could prove my own innocence. But the real reason I didn't go back was that I couldn't stand the thought of doing so. I had to rely on Dutch courage to take me through that lobby with my clothes stuffed in my pockets and draped over my arm and I didn't know how far it was going to carry me. My head was aching like hell again. The little men with the hammers and anvils were playing an overture to madness inside my head. I wanted to get out in whatever air you might be able to find on Broadway.

I tried not to look at the other people in the elevator. I tried not to hurry through the enormous lobby that glistened with modernistic lighting fixtures. It seemed that every person who came within my range of vision was a man wearing a gray hat and smoking a cigarette. I imagined that house detectives were men who wore gray hats and smoked cigarettes. I didn't think house detectives still wore hard hats and smoked cigars.

Finally I was out in the brawling neon night of Broadway. After the crowd had jostled me along a couple of blocks I came to a drug store that sold Toni wave sets to chorus boys who had to curl their hair and safety razors to chorus girls who had to shave their legs. I knew that the drug store had about umpteen telephone booths because its clients came mostly from the theater and theatrical people are great telephoners. I got change for a quarter at the cigar counter and I beat a bleached blonde into an empty booth. I called Chet Lassiter's hotel.

I'd visited Chet's hotel and I knew the fat dame who ran the switchboard in the evenings spent most of her time playing gin rummy with the little drip who served as night clerk. I wasn't surprised that it took her a hell of a long time to answer. No matter who you asked for in Chet's hotel, the fat dame always said, "I think they're out, but I'll see," just to let you know she was going to a lot of useless effort on your account. But I was glad to find she was wrong this time and that Chet was in.

I told Chet there was trouble and I had to see him right away. He asked if the trouble had anything to do with the case and I told him it did and it didn't. I repeated that I had to see him and asked if I could come up.

Chet said he had a little pigeon coming up for a snack and couldn't what I had to see him about wait. I said it couldn't. He said, okay, come on up, but don't stay too long because this was a very particular little pigeon and he had the "Don't Disturb" sign all ready to hang on the door.

I caught a subway up to Chet's hotel, which was in the West Seventies. Chet had the scene all set up in the living room. The lamps were turned down low and the radio was playing soft music. A delicatessen chicken, olives and other stuff were spread out on the table in front of the sofa. On the floor a couple of bottles of domestic bow-wow water were sticking their necks out of a bucket of ice. Chet himself was attired in a suit of monogrammed lounging pajamas of dark maroon and he smelled real pretty of shaving lotion and hair oil.

He said to make it short because the babe who was going to tear the chicken with him might arrive at any moment. So I made it short.

He stood there for a minute gaping at me with his mouth hanging loose and then he said, "How much you been drinking?"

"I had a couple at Frayne's all right," I said, "but not enough for what you're thinking. Besides, when I'm that way I never see naked dames with holes in their hearts. I see little green men with puce top hats."

Chet started striding up and down the room. So did I. They made rooms big in the days when that hotel was built, and we had a good place for striding. Finally Chet stopped striding and stood looking at me, a curious expression on his face.

"I don't want you to get sore, Terry," he said, "but, well, you've told me about the blackouts and about being in Bellevue and the government psych wards and all. Are you sure you're all right, kid?"

"I've got a headache," I replied. "I've got one that's knocking the ears off me. And I've had a few drinks. But . . ."

I fumbled in my pocket through the handkerchiefs and socks and shaving cream until I found the key to Room 616. I tossed it to him.

"But if you don't think I saw the naked dame, drop up and say hello to her. I don't think she'll be going anywhere."

Chet put the key on the table beside the chicken and the olives and the pickles. He said, "I've got to believe you, of course, since you say you're all right. But how the hell did a naked dame get into that room? And where the hell are her clothes?"

"You tell me," I said. "You're a detective, aren't you? But maybe I can offer a couple of suggestions. Since it's the Little dame, the one we were supposed to tail, maybe her clothes are across the hall in 617, where she was planning to meet her boy friend. And maybe your client, old man Little, is the guy who put a hole in his ever-loving wife. Sometimes husbands get upset when their wives visit other guys in hotel rooms."

"Well," said Chet, "there's no use in me going up there now. Things are fouled up enough anyway. The best thing both of us can do is stay as far away from that room as possible for the present until we see which way the wind is blowing. Now, do you think there's anybody at that hotel who might identify you as the occupant of Room 616?"

"There's a bellhop. He saw my Purple Heart and wanted to make war talk. With this scar on my face I'm not too hard to remember. And my fingerprints are around and about. I was in the Army, you know, and it shouldn't take 'em too long to find out from Washington who George Spelvin really is."

"Christ," said Chet. "I try to give you a chance to make a buck and all I do is get you in a jackpot like this. It might be better, kid, for you to take it on the lammister until things start to shape up. If anybody gets nosy I can say that I sent you out of town on some assignment. Meantime, I can start right away finding out whatever I can. I'll have to ditch the pigeon, I guess," he added ruefully. "I don't think you better go back to the flat. And stay away from Ginny. Stay away from Frayne's, too. Look, you used to bum around the Bowery. The Bowery's a hell of a good place to get lost. How about going back down there? I'll see you some place tomorrow after I've had a chance to gumshoe a little."

I thought about it.

"I'm dressed pretty fancy for a Bowery flop," I said. "I'd attract attention. And it wouldn't be easy to buy myself a Bowery wardrobe at this time of night or to get rid of the clothes I'm wearing. I could go down there tomorrow, if the heat's still on. But there's a hotel on Bleecker Street where I might stay tonight. It's sort of a de luxe flophouse. Six bits a night. The Hill, it's called. The Bowery boys go there when they get in the chips. And some pretty well-dressed guys who are dodging wives or process-servers go there, too. I shouldn't attract attention."

"Good enough," said Chet. "Go down there and lock yourself in. Use a phony name, of course. I'll want to barge around tomorrow morning. Where can I see you around noon?"

"There's a ginmill just across the street from the hotel," I told him. "The Hill Tavern. Meet me there. Used to be a village night spot during Prohibition. There's a big room in back with tables nobody ever uses. We can talk back there."

"See you there at noon," said Chet. "You'd better take off before the pigeon flies in. Don't want her to see you here."

"I'm sorry about the pigeon," I said.

"*You're* sorry," said Chet. "Oh, well, I'll give her the bird and a bottle to take home to her furnished room. Go on now. Get lost."

I handed Chet the manila envelope with the photograph of the late Mrs. Little in it. "You'd better do something about that," I said.

He took out the photograph, looked at it admiringly, and said, "Yeah. I'd like to do something about that. But it's too late now, I guess."

The big tile lobby of the Hill Hotel seemed as antiseptic as a hospital except for a few characters who were sitting around on wooden armchairs and benches. There were three guys in front of me at the desk. They were all wined up and argumentative. One of them had a red spot under his eye that must have been a shiner a few days before. The snout of a wine bottle was sticking out of another guy's hip pocket. The clerk was shaking his head and telling them he didn't have any rooms. That didn't discourage me too much. I knew from experience the Hill wouldn't take you when you were drunk and likely to make a mess in your room or come down with a hard case of the screams. The dodge was to buy your key during the afternoon when you were reasonably sober. Then you could sneak in drunk any time you wanted to. You could only occupy a room in the Hill from four in the afternoon until nine in the morning. They spent the rest of the time cleaning and fumigating the premises

The guy with the red spot under his eye was saying, "What the hell, we got money and we want rooms. What're we, anyway, a bunch of crumb-bums, mister? Don'tcha know old man Hill founded this place so it would be a home for homeless men? What're you, anyway, a jerk?"

The clerk winked at me, meaning, "Don't leave, buddy." He said to the three guys, "You got money, maybe, but I ain't got a room. Why don't you try the Waldorf-Astoria or the St. Regis, maybe?"

He turned to me. Obviously he approved of my clothes and my seeming sobriety. He said, "Oh, Mr. Smith. We got your reservation right here." He handed me a key off the rack. He'd called me

Mr. Smith, so that's the way I registered. I handed him a buck and got a quarter change. The three guys were still arguing with him when I went upstairs.

My room was about seven by ten, the same size as all the others. It had a bed, a washbowl, a straight chair and a steel wall locker where you hung your clothes. It was just a cubicle, but it was clean. The boys used to say the Hill was one flop where you never got lousy. They even had facilities for washing and steaming your clothes in the shower rooms.

My room in the Hill wasn't quite as commodious as the one I'd had at the Sheridan Towers, but there was one thing nice about it. It didn't have a naked dame sitting in the chair.

I sat down on the bed and tried to take stock of what had happened to me. But I couldn't make any sense at all out of it. The room at the Sheridan Towers had been just like any other hotel room when I'd first checked in and during the time I'd sat looking out the crack of the door watching 617 across the hall. Then I'd gone out. Ginny had smacked my face, and I'd seen red. I'd kept right on seeing red, walking around with a red haze in front of my eyes and a headache pounding its sledge between my ears. I'd even been seeing red while I was eating and drinking and trying to pick up dames in Frayne's place. And my head had ached like hell. I didn't know how many whiskies I'd had, but I knew I hadn't had enough to make me see things.

Yet I couldn't help wondering if Chet hadn't been justified in reminding me of the hospitals and the drinks I'd had and asking me if I was sure I was all right. I had a strong impulse to go back to the hotel on Broadway and to walk right into Room 616 to make sure that the naked woman really *was* there. But I'd left the key at Chet's place.

I took some codeine that a druggist I knew sold me without a prescription, not because I was a war hero who suffered from headaches, but because he could get an outrageous price from me for the stuff. I went to bed and I went to sleep. I don't think I even dreamed.

I'd set my mind to awaken early. They'd roust me out of the room at nine and I had use for the room that morning. I wakened around seven and had a shower. I didn't shave because a stubble would be consistent with my role of Bowery wanderer. I ate thirty cents' worth of pancakes, margarine, syrup and coffee in the lunchroom attached to the hotel. A block down Bleecker Street was a used-clothing store that opened at eight o'clock, the same time that the bars and most other businesses in that section opened. I went into the store and bought a pair of pants and a coat that didn't match from an old man who had a twitch in his left eye. I also bought a woolen Army shirt that had been dyed blue, and a cap. Next door was an automatic laundry which advertised waterproof canvas bags for half a buck. I went in and bought one of the bags. I went back to the Hill and changed my clothes. I stuffed everything but the suit and trench coat and hat into the laundry bag. I just left the hat in the locker. I wrapped the suit up in a morning newspaper I'd bought. The newspaper hadn't had anything in it about the murder of the naked lady. I hung the coat over my arm.

I turned my key in at the desk and went back to the laundromat. I paid the woman forty cents for a partial dry. She handed me a ticket and told me to take Number Five machine. I stuffed the clothes from the laundry bag into the little porthole of the washing machine, even though most of them were spanking clean. I hooked the bag to the machine. I left the place. After I'd walked a couple of blocks, I tore up the ticket and dropped it in the gutter.

I took a long walk down Bleecker and turned up to Hudson. I found a pawnshop near Tenth. The suit had cost me sixty-five bucks in a basement sale and it was almost new but the uncle would only give me seven clams for it. He said the hock-shop business wasn't what it used to be. I kept the trench coat. I'd bought it in an Army and Navy Store and it was old and nondescript and bore no identification marks. But it was still water repellent and when you're on the bum, on the Bowery, it's nice to have something to keep you dry.

I walked on back to Bleecker. After I'd walked a few blocks I tore up the pawn ticket, too. The only identification I had on me now was my social-security card and a selective-service card stating that I was classed "1-C Disch." I stopped off in one of the little Village candy stores that sell stationery and snuff and shoelaces and nearly everything else, including even candy. I bought an envelope for a penny and three three-cent stamps out of a machine for a dime. I put one of the stamps on the envelope, put my identification cards inside the envelope, borrowed a pencil from the Italian proprietor and addressed the envelope to Robert Lee Lincoln, General Delivery, 90 Church Street, New York City. I liked the name on the envelope better than my own name of Terry Bob Rooke or my other names of George Spelvin and James Smith. I walked along on Bleecker until I found a mailbox. I dropped the letter to my alter ego into the box.

I had a lot of time to kill before meeting Chet at noon. There wasn't much to do but walk around. The nervous feeling of being a fugitive wasn't exactly new to me, although I'd never committed a crime. At least I didn't think I'd ever murdered anybody. When you're on the bum, on the Bowery, roosting in doorways, taking quick gulps from bottles, you get skittish of cops. I'd got over that skittish feeling months ago. Decent clothes, decent food, a job, a girl friend had given me confidence. But now that I was back in my Bowery uniform, I found myself looking apprehensively over my shoulder again and crossing the street to avoid some policeman who probably had nothing more serious on his mind than getting his morning pick-up on the house in some neighborhood bar or shaking down some shifty numbers salesman for a buck or two.

I turned left on MacDougal Street and walked up past Fourth, where Washington Square Park begins and MacDougal becomes

Washington Square West. The tenants in those big apartment
houses that face the park wouldn't stand for any such vulgar name
as MacDougal, I reflected.

I went into the park and watched a couple of old men pushing
pieces around on one of the concrete checkerboards the benevo-
lent and fun-loving city fathers had erected in the park. I watched
gals in slacks and close-cropped hair walking dogs. I watched the
parade of dowager-bosomed pigeons and thought how the verb
"strut" must have been invented for pigeons and Pentagon generals.
A snaggle-toothed kid with freckles hit me smack in the left eye with
water-pistol ammunition and yelled, "Bam! You're dead, mister."

It was an unpleasant reminder. "Not yet, son," I told him, "but
soon, maybe."

The Greenwich Village Outdoor Art Show was in progress and
a little after eleven o'clock the painters appeared and began to
hang their pictures up on buildings and fences that surrounded
the park. I'm just an old art lover, I guess, so I left the park and
went over to look at the pictures the boys and girls were hanging
up. Some of the pictures were simple enough for even a dumb
guy like me to understand—things like dead fish on big platters.
But some of them were pretty bewildering, like the one that had
a lot of dislocated eyes and ears and tonsils floating around on a
background of rusty nails, broken chamber pots and empty whisky
bottles. I stood before one picture for a long time. A kid was also
standing in front of this picture, but our reasons for being fascinated by it were entirely different. It was a picture of a woman
sitting in a chair. She had brown eyes that stared and didn't blink.
She had hair that curled over her shoulders. And she didn't have a
stitch of clothes on.

The guy who was peddling it must have been a real artist,
because he wore a beret and a corduroy jacket. I guess he figured
from my Bowery clothes that I wasn't exactly a patron of the arts,
but he said with some amusement, "I see you like our little lady."

"Yeah," I told him, "but there's something missing. Where's the hole in her heart?"

"What?" he asked.

"Skip it, cousin," I said, and walked off to look at a picture of a green-skinned man with red eyes who seemed to be covered with Japanese beetles. I figured he was probably a wino.

It was getting on toward noon. I walked down Sullivan Street, taking my time, pausing now and then to have a gander at the art work on display. There were quite a few more naked ladies. But none of the others was sitting in a chair. They were just standing around nonchalantly or lying on couches or taking baths in tin tubs.

I turned east on Bleecker and scuttled by the automatic laundry in a hurry because I didn't want them to call me in to get my wash. I went into the Hill Tavern. It still lacked a few minutes of twelve and Chet hadn't arrived. I took a place near the window where I could watch for him. I ordered a shell of beer. There were several other characters standing at the bar, discussing ways and means of getting the price of a day's drinking and a night's flop. Most of them were drinking sherry or muscatel which the Hill sold in short beer goblets for fifteen cents a copy. Some were drinking "Big Boys," a specialty of the house. A "Big Boy" was a shot of whisky that sold for thirty-five cents and looked immense because it was served in a trick glass with a heavy bottom. Actually it contained only about a quarter of an ounce more whisky than a regular shot. A few of the guys were sipping beer very slowly and making frequent trips to the can. I knew that dodge very well, because I'd often practiced it myself. They had a bottle of vino on them. They took a swig of that in the can, then returned to the bar and chased it with beer. It was a cheap way of getting a kick and still enjoying the companionship of other barflies instead of sneaking shots in doorways and alleys.

I was working on my second shell of beer when Chet came in. He sort of sniffed disdainfully, and I couldn't blame him too much because the Hill wasn't shined and scrubbed like Frayne's and the guys at the bar weren't perfumed like the lady barflies who frequented the Broadway bistro. Much to the astonishment of the bartender, to whom a mixed drink usually meant a shot and water, Chet ordered a whisky sour. The poor guy had a hard time finding the ingredients and figuring out what kind of glass to serve it in once he had mixed it.

I told Chet we could go in the back room and talk and the bartender said to switch on the light. The light didn't help much, because it was only a single, flyspecked bulb in the ceiling and the room was very large. During speakeasy days this joint was a Village sucker trap, strictly for the tourist trade. Tables and chairs and a broken-down piano were still standing around and about. On the walls were murals of naked women with wildly streaming red hair. The naked dames weren't sitting in chairs, though. They were dancing around like crazy, drinking from bottles and squeezing big bunches of grapes, and guys with little horns and goats' feet were playing ring-around-a-rosy with them. The plaster had begun to peel off a long time ago and some of the dames looked scaly and leprous. The room was now used mainly as a place where drunks went to sleep it off. There was one lush snoring at a corner table now, his head pillowed on his arms, a half-empty goblet of vino beside him.

We sat down at a table and Chet said, "I did a little barging around last night and this morning and I found out a few things, but they haven't seen the dame in 616 yet. Or if they have, they're keeping it quiet. Probably, though, the 'Don't Disturb' sign's still on the door, so they haven't even tried to get in. The chambermaid will probably begin worrying about the towels and linens late this afternoon and start knocking. Then they'll open up with a passkey."

"What *did* you find out?" I asked.

"Well," he said, "things were pretty mixed up when I saw you last night and maybe I didn't get the timetable straight. I want to concentrate on that now. I think you told me you left Ginny about four o'clock and then you sat around the hotel a while. Now what time did you leave the hotel again and go to Frayne's?"

"Why," I said, "It was right after you called me. As I remember, you called about six, on the button. I might have fooled around for ten minutes or so washing my hands and combing my hair. It took maybe another ten minutes to walk over to Frayne's."

"So you probably got to Frayne's between six-twenty and six-thirty, say?" said Chet.

"That's about right," I replied.

"And how long did you stay in Frayne's?" Chet asked.

"Three hours, at least. Maybe a little longer. I was stalling over my drinks. I had dinner. I propositioned a couple of dames and took the usual time for the build-up. I looked at the big clock over the door when I was leaving. It was just about nine-thirty."

"See anybody you know?" asked Chet. "Talk to anybody?"

"I talked to the dames, like I said. But I didn't know them. One was a big blonde who said she loved her husband. Another was a little brunette. She said she was waiting for her boy friend, but he didn't show up. None of the gang you and I know was around."

The drunk at the table woke up. He saw us and announced, "Gentlemen, I used to play with Eddie Condon. With the other big shots, too. Now I am a wandering troubadour, you might say. If you would care to buy me a glass of wine, I will play for you."

He wore a suit with a checked pattern. It was dirty and rumpled, but it had probably cost a lot when it was new. Chet tossed the troubadour half a buck and said, "Get yourself a drink, but don't bother playing for us."

The drunk headed for the bar and Chet sat looking at me in a funny sort of way, drumming his fingers on the table.

Chet said, "Who served you your drinks, Terry?"

"What the hell is this?" I asked. "Jerry served me before I had my dinner. I bought him a couple of snifters because he said he

had a cold. After I ate, I was up at the other end of the bar and
Charley Frayne himself set 'em up. He asked me about you and
Ginny."

"Who waited on you at the table? Who brought your dinner?"
Chet asked.

"Jesus Christ," I said. "Mr. District Attorney himself, aren't
you? Ray, the guy we always have, waited on me. Ray, the horse
player. He was all hot and bothered because he'd had a ten-to-one
shot at Belmont that got beat a snoot."

Chet picked up our glasses. He said, "I'll get us another drink."
He went to the bar. While he was gone, the drunk came back,
carrying a goblet of wine. He sat down at the piano. I guess he
wanted to give us our money's worth even though Chet had told
him not to bother. He began to play the "St. Louis Blues." The
piano could have stood a little tuning, but all the same you could
tell that this guy knew his stuff.

Chet came back with the drinks. He set a whisky in front of
me. "I was drinking beer," I told him.

"I think maybe you're going to need a shot," he said.

Chet leaned over close to me so he could make himself heard
above the piano.

"I went to Frayne's last night," he said. "I talked to Frayne
himself and to Jerry and Ray. None of them saw you in the place
last night. All of them said you hadn't been there since the other
night when you and Ginny and I had dinner together."

The shivery wail of the blues filled the room. The wild-eyed
dames with red hair and leprously peeling flesh were dancing to
the music.

3

Chet sat there looking at me, waiting to see how I was going to take it. I gulped down the whisky, sent a water chaser after it and coughed a couple of times before I tried to say anything. I shook my head. "It just can't be," I said. "It just can't be."

"No," said Chet, "it just can't be. But that's the way it is. If only one guy had said you weren't there, I'd think maybe he'd just forgotten. But three of 'em, all saying the same thing . . ."

"That Charley Frayne," I said, arguing against my own sanity, "has a memory like Phineas T. Barnum's pet elephant. He could tell you what you were drinking and what colored socks you were wearing on last St. Swithin's Day. And Ray, the waiter, can rattle off the names of all the Kentucky Derby winners since Aristides took the race in 1875 and never miss a one."

The guy at the piano had finished the "St. Louis Blues" and was banging out an old one. It was a crazy thing that had been popular before my time, in the days of Gilda Gray and the shimmy and flappers with rolled stockings and waistlines that reached to their knees.

The words didn't make any sense. No sense at all. And the thing that Chet had told me didn't make any sense, either. Three guys who knew me by my first name had seen me for a period of three hours or more and had talked to me at length about such matters as head colds and my pal and my girl friend and race horses that got beat a snoot at ten to one. Yet a couple of hours later they couldn't even remember seeing me. It didn't make any sense. No sense at all.

"It doesn't make any sense," I said to Chet, and I wasn't talking about the music.

"No," he agreed, "it doesn't make any sense at all, kid, but that's the way it is."

I looked Chet in the eye and asked him, "Chet, do you think I'm lying? Or do you think I'm just plain nuts?"

He regarded me in silence for a moment, as if he were trying to decide.

Then he said, "No, Terry. I don't think you're lying, and I don't believe you're nuts. If you *were* lying, you would be nuts, though, because it would have been damned foolishness for you to lie about being in a place where you're as well known as you are in Frayne's. There's got to be an angle somewhere. Somebody's got to have an angle. But how Charley Frayne or his bartender or his waiter could have one is beyond me. How *all* of 'em could have the same angle in telling a bald lie about an inoffensive character like you makes it even more mysterious."

"Chet," I said, "I've got something to say. I think maybe I could stand another drink before I say it."

"Sure," he said. He picked up the glasses and went to the bar. When he came back with the drinks, I took mine straight.

"So it's like this," I said. "Either I'm lying about being in Frayne's or three other guys are lying for no apparent reason whatsoever. Or maybe I just think I'm telling the truth. Maybe I'm suffering from combat fatigue or shell-shock or delirium tremens. Maybe I'm a character who blacks out and does things like making little holes in the hearts of naked women. And maybe I just imagine I've been doing something entirely different all the time."

"No," said Chet. "You don't believe that yourself, and I wouldn't believe it even if you told me it was true. I know you were in

Frayne's. You aren't smart enough to have made up all those details about what you and other people said and did. I'm no psychiatrist, but I don't think it's the kind of stuff that dreams are made of. I don't think it's what you'd dream you were doing while you were sticking a sharp instrument into the heart of a naked dame, even if you were nuts."

He hadn't touched his fresh drink. He paused now and took a sip of it. "I'm going to figure this out," he said. "I'm going to find out what angle Frayne and Jerry and Ray could possibly have. I'm going to investigate our client, Mr. Malcolm Little, too, and find out something about his late wife's background. But there's not a damn thing we can do until they find the body in that hotel room and the whole business becomes official. Until it does, the best play you can make is to stay lost. Go on down to the Bowery where you'll be just another lost and nameless stumblebum and nobody will notice you."

I had different ideas, but I didn't tell him so. "Okay," I said. "When will I see you again?"

Chet finished his drink and drummed his fingers on the table. "The way I figure it," he said, "they're likely to become suspicious of that 'Don't Disturb' sign and find the body late this afternoon, probably too late for the last editions of the evening papers. That'll probably mean that the story will break for the bulldog editions of the morning tabs that hit the street early this evening. In the meantime I'm going to pay a call and see if I can get a little advance dope, maybe. I'm going to call on my old pal, Lieutenant Romano of the Homicide Squad. Just a social call, of course. If something's already cooking, I'll get it out of him one way or another."

"Then what?" I asked.

"You'd better get in touch with me tonight. Say around six-thirty. Not the hotel, though. I don't want that fat dame on the switchboard listening in. I'll be at the office. Call me there and say you're a client named Jones, just in case."

I agreed. After all, yet another alias didn't mean much in my young life.

Chet left, warning me again to lose myself on Dream Street. I gave him time to get out of the place, then went up to the bar and ordered another shot. I didn't gulp that one. I stood sipping it and considering just how bad a spot I might be in. I knew damned well what Chet meant when he said we couldn't do anything until they found the woman. He meant maybe they wouldn't find the woman. That was a cheering thought. If I hadn't been in Frayne's, if I'd imagined it all, then maybe I'd just dreamed up the part about the naked woman with a hole in her heart, too. Maybe I'd even imagined that Ginny had smacked my face.

If they didn't find the woman with the hole in her heart, all my problems would be solved, even though it would make me appear about as sane as the Mad Hatter on a marijuana binge.

There were a couple of things I had to do, but I couldn't do either of them until later. I wanted to go up to Frayne's. I wanted to see Frayne himself and Jerry and Ray. I didn't for a moment doubt what Chet had told me, of course, but I wanted to hear those guys say the same thing to my face. However, they all worked the night shift and didn't come on duty until around five.

And I wanted to see Ginny. I wanted to see her for the same reason a guy always wants to see a girl he's in love with. But I had an even more urgent reason for seeing her. I wanted to find out about the face-slapping and ask her if I'd looked queer the day before, if I'd acted like one of those schizophrenics in the movies and murder books who might be on the verge of doing something nasty that he wouldn't remember.

I might have gone right up to Ginny's apartment, of course, but I didn't think that would be too smart. The super knew me, and he always sat around with his door open, putting the peek on everybody who came in and went out. He would have wondered at my strange costume. Besides, Ginny seldom got to bed before five A.M. and she was a healthy youngster who liked lots of sleep. She'd be grouchy if I put in an appearance before she had her afternoon Java. Everything considered, I thought it might be better if I postponed seeing her until I'd talked to Chet again and seen the morning editions. That meant I would have to wait and pick her up outside Parada's club after the last floor show, some time around three-thirty in the morning.

I left the Hill Tavern and headed toward the Bowery because that was what Chet had advised and I had nothing better to do at the moment anyway. It seemed a long walk because the callouses I'd acquired in the days when I was ambling along Bums' Boulevard and while walking around ringing doorbells as a poll taker were beginning to soften up.

The Bowery hadn't changed much during my absence. The same cheap shops with the same guys in pink shirts and sleeve garters and Arizona diamonds standing out in front of them. The same rusty garbage cans with their lids ajar, perfuming the streets with the age-old slum odor. The same one-flight-up flophouses advertising the price of eight hours on a hard cot in light-bulb letters. The same unwashed kids squalling through a game of stickball. The same fat old women with beat-up eyes, dangling their mammillary appendages out of the upstairs windows of tenement houses. The same skinny, dark-eyed girls in sleazy silk and too much rouge hurrying to the uptown subway that would carry them to a Broadway movie palace, just as Cinderella's pumpkin coach carried her to the ball, only they were wearing wedgies from Bernstein's basement instead of glass slippers. The same dark, sour-smelling saloons with the neon beer signs winking through the crepuscular grime of their windows. The same cops managing to look mean and bored at the same time. The same pathetic, rum-dumb sad sacks, stumbling and lurching along, their eyes so intent upon the sidewalk that they might be looking for a hundred-dollar bill.

I didn't know any of the bums I passed. The Bowery has a quick turnover. It's a way-station to Bellevue and Rockland State and finally Potter's Field. Yet I seemed to know them all. On the Bowery, it doesn't matter how old or young, tall or short, fat or thin a man might be. Life has slammed them all with a haymaker that leaves them with a smashed-up look, that scrambles their features and bruises their hides, that changes their eyeballs to red-flecked, clouded glass. The stumblebums of any age or size look alike and smell alike on the Bowery.

I walked on down to Grogan's Elite Palace Café and Bar. Here, I knew, the more stable stumblebums, meaning the permanent and semipermanent residents of Dream Street, usually met. I was on the lam, but I had to run into the old-timers, the guys who knew me, eventually, so it might as well be now. On the Bowery you're known only by your nickname, and because I had a scarred face from the war they called me "Soldier."

Grogan's was hardly a palace and it wasn't too elite. The bar was one of those massive, pre-Prohibition affairs of oily-dark wood, with curlycue pillars bulging out at each end. Suds, the bartender, was as massive as the bar. His features were spattered all over his big, ugly face. You could take a jack-o'-lantern and crush it under an M-4 tank and get something better looking. His hands were two hunks of raw, red meat. He looked like a very tough ex-pug, but he was actually a gentle, soft-hearted slob who spent most of his time mothering homeless kittens and listening to tear-jerker soap operas on the radio.

I went up to the bar and ordered a beer. "Hiya, Suds?" I said. "How's Portia facing life these days?" He scrutinized me closely with his little pig eyes and then said heartily, "Well, hiya? Hiya? Soldier, ain't it? I remember, sure. Ain't been around for a spell. Jail or Bellevue? You're looking good, kid."

"Bellevue," I told him. "Any of the old gang around? How about the Canned Heat Kid? Or Goosey George and Red Eye?"

"Them characters," he said disapprovingly. "Them characters got themselves lucky and rolled some lush, I hear. Got a big stake, I hear. They faded."

"Nice guys," I said. "Maybe they're up in the Union League Club drinking Scotch, huh?"

"Maybe they're dead," said Suds. "Trouble with these characters, they get too much gold, they go hog wild. They drink too fast. Bad for the digestion, I always say. Man should drink slow and let it creep up on him. I tell 'em that, but they won't listen. So they drink too fast and get indigestion and you don't see no more of 'em account of they're dead."

Suds poured some milk in a saucer and placed it beside a kitten that was sleeping behind the bar in a box filled with torn newspapers.

"What's the cat's name?" I asked him.

"Stella Dallas," he replied. "You ever listen to that program? Boy, that girl, she has some troubles."

"What became of the other cat, Young Widder Brown?" I asked him.

"Oh, her," he said. "It was kinda sad. That big tom, the one I named Just Plain Bill, he jumped her one day and she died having kittens."

I put money on the bar and ordered another beer. "Have one yourself," I invited Suds. Suds never drank alcoholic beverages. He said even slow drinking gave him indigestion. But on the rare occasions when one of his patrons offered him a drink, he would pour a short milk from the cat's bottle and charge a dime for it. He always put the dime in his pocket instead of the cash register. "To buy more milk for the cat," he'd say.

"Don't mind a short one," he said. He poured out the milk and took my money. When he returned with the change, he said, "Basserty the Beard's back. You know, the jock what goes on periodicals. He got ruled off again, down in Maryland, I think, this time. Got so drunk he fell off a horse right in the paddock, I hear. Shouldn't do a thing like that. Not in public. He's over there in the corner, helping some of the boys figure out a parlay."

I saw three or four of the guys clustered around a table, with Basserty the center of attention. They had spread out in front of them a *Racing Form* and an Armstrong scratch sheet that they must have pooled their nickels and pennies to buy. They were intent upon what they were doing and what Basserty was telling them.

Basserty had the dubious distinction of being the only jockey on the American turf who wore a beard. It was about the only distinction he did have, for he seldom rode a winner. He was nearing fifty, which is a very ancient age indeed for a jock. He weighed about 1o5 pounds when he was soaking wet with sweet-wine sweat. He rode around the half-milers of the leaky roof circuit for the most part, when he was riding at all, but his age and the beard had gained him a certain measure of fame in the sports pages and he occasionally got mounts at one of the big tracks. His life was very well ordered. He would ride wherever he could, live frugally and save his money for six months of the year. For the next six months he'd get drunk and hit Skid Row. When his money and his credit were gone, he'd return to the tracks, get a stake from some source, wheedle the stewards into reinstating him, and work at riding and exercising horses again. He'd been following this schedule for years.

I picked up my beer, walked over to the table and stood around waiting for somebody to recognize me. Basserty was saying, "I'm tellin' ya, they ain't gonna beat this horse Sober Sides in the fourth. I rode his daddy, Deacon Smith, his name was, and there was a horse that could really take it on the Bill Daly. Look here in the *Form* now. This Sober Sides, he worked six furlongs in one-twelve and a fraction. Why, I'm tellin' ya, these here two-year-olds won't run a race that fast."

Knotty, the dwarf, screwed his monocle tightly in his eye and peered at the entries in the scratch sheet. He shook his oversized head vigorously. "Naow, chums, naow," he said. "I definitely do not like the name of the bloomin' steed. Too depressin'. Son of Deacon Smith, you sye? Knew a deacon's son in h'England once. Came to no good end Came to a bloody bad end, in fact. Hanged by the neck and all that, y'know."

Knotty was a stubborn and opinionated little character. He pretended not to regard himself as a dwarfed, misshapen accident of Nature. He said he came from a long line of dwarfs, all of whom had entertained the crowned heads of Europe in their day. "Circus clowns, y'know, chum. Only real comedians there are, rahlly." His accent was as phony as a seven-dollar bank note issued by the Confederate States of America, but he swore he was an Englishman educated at Cambridge. Because the other drifters kidded him so much about his pretended antecedents, he once bought a monocle in a novelty shop. This, he believed, proved his British heritage beyond any shadow of a doubt. He screwed the monocle into his eye at the slightest excuse.

Another of the engrossed handicappers, Killer Carney, the punch-drunk baby sitter, suddenly discovered my presence.

"Hey, guys!" he bellowed. "Hey! It's the Sober! Hiya, Soljer? Where ya been, boy?"

"Hello, Killer," I said. "How's the baby-sitting business?"

"Aw," said the big goon with the fist-mangled features, "I still got plenty of clients. But they ain't no money or no future in it. I do it just for fun, mostly, but sometimes one of the ladies, she gives me a pint of wine or a feed or maybe a little change."

It was true enough that the Killer worked at baby sitting almost entirely as a labor of love. At some time, many years before, the broken-down old heavyweight's wife had died in childbirth and the baby had lived only a few hours. The Killer was queer for kids and the East Side urchins knew it. He would even go without his vino and suffer through the shakes in order to buy candy or bubble gum or water pistols for the grimy youngsters who formed a vociferous cortege around him every time he walked down the street. It was nothing unusual for him to be summoned from a ginmill or a flophouse because an emergency had arisen in the life of Mrs. Levinsky or Mrs. Murphy or Mrs. Caposella and his presence as a baby sitter was urgently required. At such times the boys usually took up a collection to buy him a crock of wine, so he'd have something to steady him through the next few hours. But the Killer never got drunk on the job or neglected his duties. He was very conscientious about his baby sitting.

Jockey Basserty looked up from the scratch sheet and greeted me. "Never ask questions of a returning prodigal," he admonished the Killer. Basserty was wearing a checkered cap, a soiled two-color gabardine sport shirt, stained riding breeches and boots. The costume made his shriveled body seem ludicrously childlike in contrast to his seamed old-man face and his bristling beard.

"We're figuring out a three-horse parlay that's sure to pay the limit," he informed me. "Maybe you'd like to declare in the pool."

Knotty adjusted the monocle and looked me over carefully. "The Soldier's lookin' bloody pros'prous," he declared. "'Ad 'imself a bawth and 'e's sober as a bloomin' 'oot-h'owl. What I sye is, let the Soldier pick the blawsted third beast for us. Fresh viewpoint and all that, y'know."

He handed me the scratch sheet. One name leaped out at me: *Unlucky Lady.*

"Well," conceded Basserty grudgingly, "she's out of a good mare and she's got a bit of early lick."

I tossed a dollar in the pool and the Killer clumped out to place our bet at Dago Dave's poolroom.

The boys appeared to have plunged all their available capital on the parlay. I suspected that each of them had some change stashed away against the awful moment when he couldn't possibly get the drink he needed without buying it himself. But I could sympathize with such hoarding. I sat down at the table and bought them rounds of vino for the rest of the afternoon. I stuck to beer myself. I knew what that sweet wine did to a man, and I had things to do.

The Professor and Shakey came into the bar. When they sensed that I was springing for the vino, they came over and greeted me effusively. I didn't mind. The Professor was a harmless screwball with the biggest, craziest eyes I ever saw. He was supposed to have been a professor of physics at some university once. Maybe he was. He always carried a battered old brief case around with him. It was filled with scraps of paper on which the Professor had computed endless rows of figures. Nobody but the Professor knew what the figures meant, although he often tried to explain what he called his "formulas" to the other boys.

Shakey didn't get his nickname because he had a shaky hand. A shaky hand is hardly a distinction on the Bowery. When Shakey was in his cups, which was most of the time, he insisted upon quoting Shakespeare. He kept a well-thumbed copy of the Bard's works tucked into the waistline of his pants, which were secured by a piece of heavy twine instead of a belt. Besides being a student of Shakespeare, Shakey was a cop-hater. He didn't just dislike or resent cops in the resigned way that most of the boys did. He hated them. He wanted to destroy them all in as painful a manner as possible. The Professor held that cops were merely a necessary evil of our social system and that some of them were even good guys, and his complacent attitude drove Shakey mad.

"How, now! Good morrow, sir!" cried Shakey, who seemed delighted about something. Dropping the Shakespearean form of address, he said, "You been away, Soljer, and you didn't hear the good news. You remember that Wop cop, Turrone? Coupla other Guineas caught him one night. He'd framed their little sister on a street-walking charge. They cut his ears off. Sliced 'em right off, like they do in Sicily. 'Friend, Roman, countryman, lend me your ears,' they said to him."

"Nothing of the sort," said the Professor. "You shouldn't bear false witness like that, my friend. Turrone was merely transferred to another precinct."

The Professor informed me he had just sold the formula for a synthetic atom bomb to the Israeli government for a mere ten thousand dollars. He said he had to go uptown that afternoon to collect the sum due him and that he dreaded the subway trip.

Suds came over to the table and said that if we wanted further drinks to order them now because "Stella Dallas" was about to come on the radio and he would brook no interruptions during the program. I ordered another round. The Killer went down to Dago Dave's again to get the race results. He returned to say that Unlucky Lady was the only horse in our parlay that had won.

Kerrigan, the cop, came into the bar. He was a big, fat, good-natured guy who only wanted you to keep out of his way when you were in a mood for making trouble. He'd even let you sleep it off in doorways without clubbing your feet. He went into the back room and in a minute Suds followed him, carrying a shot. Shakey had begun to make hissing sounds as soon as Kerrigan entered the saloon. "Kerrigan! Cops!" he said, and spat on the floor.

It was nearing five. I had to get to Frayne's place. I rose to go.

The Professor laid a restraining hand on my arm and said, "My boy, I wonder if you could spare me subway fare for a few hours? Have to go up and collect that ten thousand, you know."

I gave him a dime. He looked at it and seemed chagrined. "My boy," he said, "don't you know the subway fare's no longer a mere nickel? How do you expect me to get back from uptown?"

"I thought you were collecting ten grand uptown," I said.

"I am," he replied. "I am indeed. But certainly you don't expect me to offer bills of such denomination to a subway money-changer."

It was a good answer, so I gave him another dime and left the place.

I don't know why I noticed the truck parked outside Frayne's except it was a funny time of day to deliver ice. The name "Inter-City Ice Co." was painted on the truck.

I went inside Frayne's a couple of minutes after five. The night shift had just come on. There wasn't much of a crowd in the place. Frayne was still buttoning his white coat. I stood at the end of the bar and waited for Frayne to notice me. I saw him looking at me out of the corner of his eye. I guessed he didn't recognize me in the Bowery outfit I was wearing. I also guessed he didn't want a guy dressed like that standing at his bar. I waited until he ran out of glasses to polish. Finally he came up and leaned over the bar so he could talk to me without being overheard.

"What's the idea of coming in here in that get-up?" he asked. His voice wasn't pleasant.

"Because I want an answer," I said. "A straight one."

"What answer?" he growled. "I'm fresh out of answers. Why don't you dust, like a good boy?"

"I want to know if you saw me in here last night," I said. "I want to know if Jerry and Ray saw me, too."

He looked me straight in the eye. "Listen hard so you'll hear the answer," he said. "I already told your partner. I didn't see you because you weren't in here. Jerry didn't see you. Neither did Ray. Satisfied?"

"No," I said. "I want to hear Jerry and Ray say it too."

Frayne flicked his head at Jerry. Jerry walked up to the bar, trying to look casual.

Frayne stuck a thumb in my direction. "Did you see this guy in here last night?" he asked.

Jerry shook his head. "Nope," he said. "Haven't seen him since last week. Why the funny clothes?"

"Never mind the clothes," said Frayne. "Call Ray."

Jerry went to the back and spoke to Ray. Ray came up, a napkin over his arm and a scratch sheet sticking out of his pocket.

"You see this gentleman in here last night?" asked Frayne.

"Mr. Rooke?" asked Ray, looking curiously at my clothes. "Why, no. Haven't seen him since he had dinner here the other night with Mr. Lassiter and the young lady."

"Satisfied?" asked Frayne.

"No," I said. But there was nothing I could do about it.

"Look," said Frayne. "I can go along with a gag, but there's a limit. I don't know what trouble you're in, but I don't want any part of it. You got your answer. Now get out, please."

I got out. I was dazed, like a guy who's taken too many on the button. I was punch-drunk, like Killer Carney, the baby sitter. Why in hell should those three guys lie in their teeth like that? There wasn't any answer. Or maybe they weren't lying. That was a really terrifying thought. If Frayne and his men weren't lying and if the naked woman with the hole in her heart was found, what did that make me?

Maybe because of the fact that my brain wasn't working, my body made its needs felt. I hadn't eaten since breakfast early that morning and I was hungry. I walked over to Ninth Avenue where they wouldn't mind my informal apparel and went into a lunch counter. I ate some greasy corned beef hash with an anaemic-looking fried egg on top of it and drank three cups of black coffee. After I'd eaten I walked across Forty-second Street and took a seat in Bryant Park, back of the Public Library, until it was time to call Chet. I noticed that since they'd planted flowers and shrubs and prettied up the place not many bums were parked there. Most of the people around me were fairly well dressed. I guess bums can't stand prettiness. Too much of a contrast.

At six-thirty I went into a cigar store and called Chet at the office. When he answered I said I was Mr. Jones, feeling kind of silly.

"Oh, yes, Mr. Jones," said Chet. "Where are you? I want to talk about that case with you."

"I've been downtown like you told me," I said. "But I'm on Forty-second Street now. Where will I meet you?"

"How about the place we met this morning?"

"Okay by me," I said.

I took the Sixth Avenue subway down to Washington Square and walked over to the Hill Tavern. Chet was standing outside the place, waiting for me. We got a couple of drinks at the bar. Chet again ordered whisky for me. We went into the back room. The same damned piano player was there strumming the keys. He was glassy-eyed drunk by now. Some of the boys who must have got a stake were sitting around him, feeding him wine and calling out their selections. One old guy who had the weeps kept calling for "Hearts and Flowers." When the others didn't have a selection, the piano player knocked out "St. Louis Blues" of his own accord.

We sat at a table as far away from the piano as possible.

Chet said, "Well, I paid that little visit on Romano. The call came in just as the lieutenant and I were cutting up old touches. They found Mrs. Malcolm Little just after five o'clock this afternoon. Romano let me go along to the hotel with him just for the ride."

"So they found her," I said dumbly.

"Yeah," replied Chet. "Only they didn't find her like we expected them to."

"You mean she wasn't really dead?" I asked.

"Oh yes," he said. "She was dead, all right. Nice little hole right in the heart. But she wasn't sitting in a chair, like you said. She was lying on the bed."

"What?"

"She was lying on the bed," repeated Chet. "And the lady wasn't naked. She was fully clothed, in fact. Right down to her girdle. There was quite a lot of blood on the dress where the weapon went through. Too bad. Expensive dress. Hattie Carnegie label, Romano said. I wouldn't know where the girdle came from."

"But Chet . . ."

He cut me short. "Yeah, I know," he said. "It can't be, but it is. And there's more to it, so keep listening. Some of the clothes were hung up neatly in the closet of Room 616. Others were still in her suitcase and in the drawers. Another suitcase was empty. A plastic suitcase. The only really good fingerprints they found were on the plastic suitcase."

Chet paused and wet his whistle. I tossed off my own neglected drink.

"They found out her identity as Mrs. Little easily enough," Chet continued, "from cards in her pocketbook. She was also identified as the dame who registered as Mrs. J. K. Provost in 617 that morning. J. K. Provost had been at the hotel for a week, but he'd flown the coop, bag and baggage. The cops want to question Mr. Malcolm Little. Maybe they already have. I hope he doesn't spill about hiring us to tail his wife. It wouldn't make Romano like me much."

The piano player was again banging out "St. Louis Blues." I thought that every time I had a nightmare I'd hear that weepy wail and see naked, dancing women with flaming hair.

Chet was saying, "And there's one more thing. The medical examiner was pretty certain about the time of death. He swore she'd been dead for at least twenty-four hours."

"But, Chet," I said, and my voice was louder than I'd meant it to be. "That means she was dead by five o'clock yesterday afternoon. It means . . ."

"Yeah," said Chet. "It means you were sitting right there when the dame was killed."

4

The piano player had a fresh goblet of wine. He had switched to "Hearts and Flowers" at the request of the weepy old man. It was funny as hell to be sitting there wondering if I was a murderer to the tune of "Hearts and Flowers" while the peeling, naked, red-haired women danced all around me.

Finally I said to Chet, "Suppose I should go up to the Vets' Administration, see a doc I know? Suppose I should tell him just what I think I did and just what actually happened? Have him get me hospitalized, put under observation?"

Chet thought about it. At last he said, "Of course, that would put you in the clear as far as the cops are concerned. But suppose they don't turn up anybody else who might have done the job? What would they do to you then?"

"Put me in a locked ward at some hospital," I said. "Throw the key away, I guess."

He shook his head. "That wouldn't be nice," he said. "Not nice at all. I'll get us another drink."

He picked up our glasses and went to the bar. The piano kept thumping, slightly off key. The crazy, leprous women kept dancing around and around.

Chet returned with the drinks. He took an experimental sip, wiped his mouth on the back of his hand. He said, "Let's look at it the other way. The whole thing's too fantastic, but let's say that everything happened just the way you think it did. If you had blacked out and done a murder, maybe your subconscious or whatever you call it would try to build up a defense mechanism, an alibi. But the alibi of being at Frayne's wouldn't be any good because the dame was killed more than an hour before you say you got there. Maybe several hours earlier. And you say you remember being right in the room at the time she was being killed. I don't pretend to know the angle of Frayne and his boys, but we'll skip that for a minute."

He took another sip and lit a cigarette. "You didn't know the woman," he continued. "I know you were at the hotel solely because you were working on a case in which the woman was involved. The woman didn't register for 616. She registered for 617 as Mrs. Provost. And there *was* a Mr. Provost. He'd been in 617 for a week and he's lammed. There must have been a reason."

"I wonder how the guy got out of the hotel without his baggage?" I said, remembering my reason for leaving the plastic suitcase with the telltale fingerprints behind me.

"That shouldn't be too hard in a lobby as crowded as the Sheridan Towers'," said Chet. "And he was probably traveling light, anyway. So we have the mysterious Mr. Provost as a suspect. And then there's Mr. Little. We know he was jealous of his ever-loving wife, and damned suspicious. He wouldn't have hired Lassiter, Private Investigator, otherwise. With a dame like that there might have been a lot of other men, too."

He took an extra-big sip and finished his drink. My own was still untouched. I took it at a gulp. I tossed some water after it to put out the fire. Chet went through the motions of grinding his cigarette out very carefully in the ash tray.

"I'm not even going to consider all the questions you want to ask right now, because I don't know the answers," he said. "How did the dame get in your room in the first place? How did a dead woman get up off a chair and lie down on a bed? How did a dead woman who was naked get herself fully clothed? How did her clothes and baggage get in your room? No, I can't answer any of 'em right now. So it's up to me to make like a sleuth, and it's up to you to get lost. Go on back to the Bowery. I'm going to do everything I can. I don't want you to get in touch with me at the office or the hotel. If they find out my connection with this, they may tap the wires. Is there any place I can reach you about this time tomorrow?"

I told him that Grogan's Elite Palace Café and Bar had a phone and he could call me there and ask for "Soldier."

"Do they have a name like that in lights?" he asked. "Anyway, we'll look up the number in the book on the way out. You'll be needing some cash, maybe. I brought some along."

"I've got some of the expense money left," I told him. "I didn't bother to pay the hotel bill when I left the Sheridan Towers."

"There's a hundred in small notes in this," he said, handing me an envelope. "It should take care of an emergency."

"On the Bowery," I said, "that will buy little pink women with yellow sunbonnets to match the little green men with puce top hats." I pocketed the envelope.

We stopped at the telephone booth and Chet thumbed through the book until he found the number of Grogan's fancy-named saloon. He jotted it down. "Be there between seven and eight tomorrow night," he said. "I'll want twenty-four hours for prowling around."

I started to leave with him but he told me to get another shot and stall around until he was out of the place. I felt as if I could use another shot. I had it at the bar.

I was hardly conscious of my aching feet during the walk downtown. My brain was too busy whirring round and round with riddles to register any other sensation. I couldn't help wondering if I were really sane despite the critique of pure reason Chet had just read me. I knew I'd been in a state when I'd returned to the hotel after playing the role of He Who Gets Slapped. I'd been in a state of red anger at Ginny and at the world at large. The doctors had warned me against giving way to any emotional crisis, especially against becoming angry. But I can't help getting angry when somebody slaps my face, even though that somebody is a dish like Ginny. After I'd become angry I'd got the headache, and that in itself was a danger signal. Frankly, I didn't remember much of anything about that trip from Ginny's apartment to the hotel. I didn't remember much of anything about that phase of the afternoon which might well be the time that Mrs. Malcolm Little was being murdered.

I wondered if I could have killed the woman while the red fog of anger still hung over me, while my mind was in a semi-blackout. I tried to remember if I'd taken a subway or a bus or a taxi from Ginny's place to the hotel, and I simply couldn't be sure. Maybe I had even walked the distance. I wondered if it were possible I had met the woman in the hallway of the hotel and lured her into my room on some pretext. After all, she had had a room just across the hall. Perhaps I'd transferred my anger at Ginny to the woman and had killed her in a fit of insanity. But what weapon had I used? I didn't even carry anything as lethal as a penknife or a corkscrew.

I had definitely seen the woman dead, and they had found her dead. But I had seen her sitting in a chair in the nude and they had found her lying on a bed fully clothed. I must have seen her nude, I thought. I could remember the more interesting details of her anatomy very clearly indeed. Or maybe I was some kind of sex maniac and sadist when the spells came over me. Maybe I'd stuck a pointed instrument in the woman's heart and stood there admiring my handiwork and mentally stripping the woman, just imagining all those voluptuous anatomical details. Maybe she *had* been sitting in a chair and I'd picked her up and placed her on the bed because a bed is more closely associated with the sex impulse than any other article of furniture.

But even looking at it the worst way, from my own point of view, there were a lot of things that needed explaining. The absence of a weapon, for instance. And I couldn't convince myself that I hadn't searched the room in an entirely sober frame of mind. There simply had been nothing belonging to the woman in the room. Nothing but her own body. And there wasn't any life left in that.

By the time I hit the Bowery the night editions of the morning tabs were out. It was there, all right, smack on page one. I took the papers I'd bought into Grogan's Elite Palace Café and Bar to read all about it. Sad Eyes, the night bartender, was on duty. He was a stooped, skinny guy, with a long, corded neck and an acrobatic Adam's apple. His eyes were enormous and rheumy and never seemed to blink. The guys I'd been drinking with a few hours before were still at the same table, but I didn't join them right away. I went to the end of the bar, spread the papers out in front of me, and ordered a beer. The facts in the two stories were practically identical:

MILLIONAIRE'S WIFE FOUND
MURDERED IN HOTEL ROOM

Mrs. Malcolm Little, wife of the millionaire Wall Street broker, was found stabbed through the heart in a sixth-floor room of the Sheridan Towers Hotel, Broadway near 51st St., late yesterday by a chambermaid who entered the room with a passkey despite the fact that a "Don't Disturb" sign had been posted on the door all day. The maid, Adele Wilkins, 112 Parsons St., Brooklyn, stated that she had knocked on the door several times during the afternoon without receiving a response and that just before going off duty she had become suspicious and asked the housekeeper's permission to open the room.

Mrs. Little was well known on Broadway a few years ago as Danise Darlan, a night club entertainer. She was married to Little, partner in the brokerage firm of Leopold, Little and Kittredge, in 1944. Police last night were seeking the husband of the murdered woman for questioning at his country estate near Tarrytown. Last evening servants stated that Little had presumably spent the day at his Wall St. office and had not returned to the estate.

Mrs. Little's body was found lying on the bed of Room 616 of the hotel. Police say that she had been stabbed through the heart with a weapon similar to an ice pick. Dr. John P. Garson, medical examiner, stated that the woman had been dead for at least 24 hours before the body was discovered.

According to the hotel management, Mrs. Little registered for a different room, Room 617, on the morning of the 20th under the name of Mrs. J. K. Provost. Identification was made through cards, letters and a driver's license found in the murdered woman's purse.

A J. K. Provost had occupied Room 617 for the past week. According to police, he has disappeared without checking out of the hotel or leaving any trace of his identity. Police have no adequate description of the man who registered under the name of Provost except that hotel employees recall that he was "tall."

Mrs. Little's baggage, clothing and effects were found in Room 616, which was engaged about noon of the 20th by a man registering as "George Spelvin." (George Spelvin is a name used on theater programs for actors who play two parts.)

A bellboy, Anthony Sallucci, of 5718 Speed Ave., the Bronx, described "Spelvin" as a tall man with a scarred face who wore the emblem of the Order of the Purple Heart. Police believe that fingerprints on an empty plastic suitcase found in Room 616 may lead to the apprehension of "Spelvin." No other trace of the man's occupancy was found in the room.

Benjamin Ellsworth, room clerk, who resides at the Sheridan Towers, stated that Room 616 had been reserved over the telephone by a man who said he "liked a view of fire escapes."

When the woman's body was discovered it was gowned in street attire that bore the label of an exclusive dressmaker. Robbery has been ruled out as a motive for the crime. Valuable jewelry and a large amount of cash were found among Mrs. Little's effects.

Police believe that the murderer was well known to Mrs. Little and that he struck without warning. The dead woman's clothes were not mussed and there were no signs of a struggle.

Police have not found the murder weapon.

That was about all except the names of police officers conducting the investigation, including that of Chet's pal, Lieutenant Romano. The only thing really new to me was the statement of the bellhop who had conversed with me about the belly wound he got in the Bulge fighting. So now I was a marked man in more ways than one. Old Scarface Spelvin.

I read over the stories in both papers a couple of times. I saw the Professor lurching in my direction and I turned hastily to the race results. The Professor was carrying a hell of a load and most of it wasn't erudition.

"Soldier, my boy!" he exclaimed. "Back from the wars, are you? Come to the table, my boy. Come tipple the evening away with us. Drink down the blood of old, old memories, drowned in the ruddy wisdom of strong wine. But, ah! I forget. My just indebtedness, sir. My just indebtedness to you of twenty pence, with interest, sir, with interest."

He bounced a quarter on the bar in front of me. "Thanks," I said. "You must have collected that ten gees."

"No, my boy," he said, "I didn't. Too bothersome a trip. Much too bothersome. Besides, ten thousand ducats are a mere bagatelle. By week's end the Israeli government will offer me twice or thrice the sum for my precious formula. You'll see, my boy, you'll see. What need have I of their tawdry gold this night? After you left us, that eminent hippologist, the bearded Basserty, selected a steed that won at twenty pieces of eight for every one invested. We pooled our funds, so to speak, so temporarily we are masters of our fate and finances. Come, my boy, and share our corporate good fortune."

After this lengthy speech the Professor seemed ready to fall on his face, so I took hold of his elbow and escorted him to the table. As I led him away, Sad Eyes shook his head lugubriously and said, "Big woids. Some day dey'll choke him to deat', dem woids."

Before the Professor collapsed in his chair, he waved his arm imperiously toward the bar. "Refreshment!" he commanded. "Refreshment for all, you sad-eyed, surly boniface!"

Knotty, the dwarf, had fallen sound asleep in his chair, but through some freak reflex of the facial muscles his monocle was still screwed tightly in his eye, giving him the appearance of a baleful, gnomelike Cyclops. Killer Carney was reliving old ring battles and tears were streaming down his grizzled cheeks.

"They told me to take this dive, see?" he was saying. "It was the only way I could get the fight. I could of took him easy in that fourth round and maybe had a chanct at the champ. But my wife was having the baby and I needed the dough, so I dived in the seventh. This other guy, he couldn't even make it look good. I had to take the count on a left jab to the shoulder. Them sportswriters, they crucified me. They nailed me to the cross. I never got nothing after that but club fights in the sticks. And there wasn't no use in taking the dive, after all. It didn't even pay for my wife and baby's funeral."

Basserty was snarling through his beard. "Sportsmen!" he said. "In the ring or on the race track, it's all the same. Five thousand horses I've ridden in my day. Maybe more. 'Give him a easy ride, Basserty,' these gentlemen, these sportsmen tell me. Or, 'He ain't hardly up to a race. We're tightening him up a bit, so don't ride him out.' Or, 'We ain't betting today, Basserty, so don't cross us up.' So the day they're out to win some other boy rides and the suckers cheer him and old Basserty's lucky to have so much as a two-dollar ticket on his nose. Three times they ruled me off for what they call incompetence. And all I did was follow riding orders."

Shakey had his volume of Shakespeare open in front of him, but he was obviously too bleary eyed to read it. "They're like cops," he declared. "Like dirty, rotten cops. They won't give nobody a chanct." Suddenly he discovered the headlines in the papers I'd laid on the table. "Murther!" he cried. "Murther most foul!"

He drew one of the papers toward him and tried to read the story but the small type was too much for him.

"I bet the stinking cops have got some poor bum they call a suspect down in the sweat-box right now," he said. "Some poor guy what didn't do nothing worse than hustle flop money while a cop was looking. They got a big, bright light shining right in his face, blinding his eyes. They're hitting him with rubber hoses and twisting his arms and pulling his fingernails out with pliers and laughing when he screams. I can just see the bastards slobbering and laughing."

It wasn't a pretty picture that Shakey was painting, even if it was imaginary, and in my present mood I didn't like it. But Shakey was all wound up and was relishing his gory descriptions.

"I knew a bunch of cops once what accused some poor bum of murder. They got a dentist to work on him. This dentist, he drilled holes in all the poor bum's teeth, right down through the nerve. Drill got so hot, the poor bum's teeth started smoking. The cops just slobbered and laughed and invited all their friends in to see the fun. Poor bum blew his top. Saw him out to Rockland State, last time they had me there. He still had holes in all his teeth and they ached him all the time. Face was so swole up he looked like he had a couple cantaloupes in his cheeks. Cops!" Shakey spat on the floor.

The Professor flourished his glass. "A toast!" he cried. "To the police! To the sterling defenders of public morals!" He drained the glass, a good deal of the wine spilling down his chin, slumped in his chair and went quietly to sleep.

"I wisht I had a baby to sit with," said Killer Carney.

Somebody had brought me a goblet of muscatel instead of beer. I knew the stuff was poison to me, but I drank it anyway. I was a man with murder on his mind and it didn't seem to matter much what I drank. The boys continued to buy rounds of drinks. They wouldn't let me pay for any. The wine was smooth going down and it started a fire.

"You bought this afternoon," said Basserty, "and we got lucky after you left."

"I quoted Shakespeare," declared Shakey. "I said, 'A horse, a horse, my kingdom for a horse,' so old Basserty, he comes up with one."

"What's the good of money?" asked Killer Carney. "I got money onct for taking a dive and it didn't even pay for the funeral."

"'My purse, my person, my extremest means lie all unlock'd to your occasion,'" Shakey quoted from *The Merchant of Venice*.

It was a weird evening. Knotty and the Professor snored peacefully. Shakey muttered of the villainy of cops and quoted the Bard. The Killer ducked and punched his way through forgotten fights. The bearded Basserty rode down the stretch again, flailing his whip against the flanks of horses that had long been dead.

Shakey grew tired of listening to the others' tales of the slings and arrows of outrageous fortune that they had endured. "'Griefs of mine own lie heavy in my breast,'" he quoted from *Romeo and Juliet;* then, to show his versatility, he switched to *King Henry IV.* "You know what we are?" he inquired. "We're 'slaves as ragged as Lazarus in the painted cloth.'"

Once the Professor awakened. "Silence, you smirking clown!" he bellowed at some imaginary presence.

The roar roused Knotty from his slumbers for a moment. "Clowns?" he mumbled. "Clowns the only actors. All my ancestors clowns. Made kings and queens and little children laugh."

They drank and slumbered and muttered. But always for me there was another person present. A woman who wore no clothes. A woman who did not blink her eyes.

The night flowed swiftly on a sea of wine. The face of a clock seemed to float toward me and I saw that it was nearly three. I must leave, I thought. I must see Ginny.

"I am a soused gurnet!" Shakey shouted.

"What's a gurnet?" the Killer asked.

"I looked that up once," said Shakey, looking wise. "A gurnet is a fish what lived in Shakespeare's time."

An overabundance of drink had had a strange effect on Shakey.

It seemed to have given him second sight, to have washed the film from his eyes. Now he was avidly reading every word of the murder story.

Suddenly Shakey said, "Hey! Hey, guys! The bird what killed this dame had a scar on his face!"

He brushed his fingers lightly against my cheek. "'Out damned spot! out I say!'" he cried.

I got to my feet, leaning heavily on the table for support. A wine glass tottered from the table and splintered on the tile floor. The Professor awakened again from his troubled sleep.

"Hey!" persisted Shakey. "Soldier's got a scar on his face! You kill that dame, Soldier?"

"No," I told him. "I only murder naked dames. This dame had her clothes on."

"What Freudian fancy is this?" asked the dazed Professor.

"I don't know, Professor," I said, "but I've got to get some air."

I walked toward the door. My legs felt numb and my head was spinning. I knew that I was staggering.

"Hey, Soljer," Sad Eyes called after me. "Dontcha pass out outside the jernt now."

Somehow or other I managed to get to Fourth Street, where Vince Parada had his sucker trap and where Ginny peeled for the uptown and out-of-town customers who were slumming in the Village and paying a stiff cover charge for the privilege of seeing how the other half allegedly lives. I know I walked part of the way, trying to blow the wine fumes out of my head, and that I was riding a subway at one stage of the journey. I also remember hailing a cab but the heap jockey wouldn't take me, partly because I looked drunk and partly because I didn't look as if I had the fare. That made me laugh, since I had over a yard in my pocket.

A huge photograph of Ginny wearing a G-string and a filmy brassiere hung outside the Triangle Club. It was only a little after three and I knew Ginny wouldn't be coming out for a while, so I stood around looking at the picture. A cop came along and touched me on the shoulder.

"Okay, bud," he said. "You had your thrill. Get moving."

I'd had my thrill, I thought. I started laughing again as I had when the heap jockey refused me as a fare. If the cop only knew, I thought. I wanted to tell him Ginny was my fiancée and she was just as pretty with all her clothes on. The cop didn't like my laughing. He said, "What the hell's so funny? You a comedian, maybe?"

"The lady hasn't got a hole in her heart," I told him. It must have been the sweet wine that made me say a fool thing like that to a cop. Me, a marked man whose description was in the papers, standing there talking to a cop, with the lights of Vince Parada's neon sign winking over the scar on my face.

"You're another one of them goddam winos," said the cop. "Why don't you get moving and find a nice, quiet doorway off my beat?"

I wanted to tell him that I was a murder suspect and that maybe they'd give him something nice like a couple of complimentary tickets to the Policemen's Ball if he took me in. But I didn't tell him that. Instead, I got moving. I moved in a very limited area, though, because I wished to keep the Triangle Club in sight.

Sweet wine does funny things to a man, especially if he helps it along with a few whiskies and a few beers. All of a sudden I felt weak. It seemed somebody had turned on a faucet that made every pore of my body spit sweat. I began shaking and jerking like a burleycue babe doing the bumps. My tongue was cottony as a caterpillar's cocoon. Something slammed up from the pit of my stomach and hit my gullet like a fist. I tried to vomit, but I couldn't.

Just then I saw Ginny coming out of the club and it jolted me out of the spell. I was still clammy with sweat, but I wasn't weak any longer. If I'd been in any condition to analyze myself, I'd have recognized the danger signals. I was angry again. The old red haze was back.

Because Ginny wasn't alone. A big guy was with her. The guy wasn't young any more, but he was handsome. Tall, dark and handsome, the way lady novelists of the Victorian era used to describe suave villains. He was dressed in dinner clothes and a black felt hat. He was built like a fast light-heavy.

He and Ginny stood there in the light of the Triangle Club's neon sign and I could see them very clearly, even at a distance. They seemed to be on very intimate terms. The guy was holding her hand. He was leaning close to her, as if he were whispering sweet nothings in her ear. The guy was Vince Parada, who owned the club. I knew him, but we weren't exactly chummy. During Prohibition he'd operated a swank society speak called the Three Ring Circus. In those days it was fashionable for thrill-seeking debutantes and bored society women to go for racket guys, especially the ones whose features were still intact, like Parada's. He had been a figure in several scandals and divorce suits.

The neon sign winked off for the night. But I was still looking at the world through a red-colored haze. It occurred to me that this was the guy who paid Ginny a weekly salary to take her clothes off in public. I didn't even think about the spot I was in or consider the fact that I shouldn't attract undue attention to myself. I walked slowly toward Ginny and the guy, keeping to the shadows. When I was a few feet away from the guy, I lunged. I started a haymaker somewhere back in the Honan Province of China. It was the kind of punch that Firpo threw the night Dempsey landed in the press box. Mr. Vincento Parada, pretty dinner jacket and all, lay down on the sidewalk.

Ginny gave me a startled look. She recognized me and in that split second stifled the scream that was already throbbing in her throat.

She looked at the prone Parada, saw he was out, said, "Beat it. Quick. The apartment."

I came to my senses and started running. I ducked into an alleyway. After a few minutes I peeked out of the alley. A cop was helping Vince to his feet. It looked like the same cop who had interrupted me while I was admiring Ginny's picture. Keeping close to a building, I sneaked out of the alley. I hurried down the street in the opposite direction from Vince and Ginny and the cop. I turned a corner. I turned a lot of corners. I kept on turning corners until I'd lost myself in the twisted maze of the Village's little streets. I took an azimuth on the women's jail on Greenwich and went to the Sheridan Square subway station. At that time of morning you wait a long time for a subway. Socking Vince and darting through the Village streets had sobered me up. I was shaky again. I kept looking over my shoulder, expecting to see a cop. But a guy wearing overalls and carrying a lunch pail and another guy wearing dinner clothes and carrying a load of liquor were the only persons who came into the station.

A local finally roared along. I took it up to Twenty-third Street.

I walked west until I came to Ginny's apartment house. It was one of those brownstones that had been remodeled when they built the London Terrace Apartments years ago and the neighborhood had taken on a touch of class. I mounted the stoop and unlocked the door as quietly as I could. I tiptoed up two flights of stairs. I had the feeling that maybe they already knew I was the hunted scar-faced man and that Ginny was my girl. I thought maybe a whole room full of cops would be waiting for me. I had a key, but I tapped lightly on Ginny's door in case she'd beat me home. She opened the door.

She was wearing a loose-fitting crash wrapper that hung to her ankles. She'd cold-creamed the rouge off her face. She'd let down her hair. Her hair hung to her shoulders in a long bob, like the hair of the naked woman who'd been sitting in the chair.

Most women look pretty sloppy in loose wrappers, after they've wiped off the war paint. Ginny didn't. Her unrouged face with its button nose and big eyes had an appealing, little-girl look. But you knew that what was under the wrapper belonged to a full-grown woman.

Ginny closed the door softly and locked it. She said, "You poor, jealous jerk."

She had anticipated my needs. She had a big slug of whisky poured into a glass. She handed the glass to me. I drank the whisky down without a chaser. For a minute there were crickets inside my skull. Then the shaking and sweating stopped.

"Those are pretty clothes you're wearing," said Ginny. "Brooks Brothers?"

"Had 'em made in London," I said. "Bond Street."

"Aren't you in enough trouble?" she asked. "Every cop in town is looking for a guy with a scar on his face. So you have to sock Vince Parada who knows all the cops by their first names."

"Did he recognize me?" I asked.

"No, thank God," replied Ginny. "He never knew what hit him. I told him it was some drunken bum. I guess I told the truth."

"What makes you think the cops are looking for me?" I asked.

"I read the papers," said Ginny. "Especially the tabs. They print pieces by Winchell and Sullivan. Sometimes one of them mentions me. So I gather from what I read that the cops want to talk to Mr. George Spelvin, Room 616, the Sheridan Towers Hotel."

"Why do you think that's me?"

"Elementary, my dear Watson," she said. "You wrote it down."

She tore a sheet from the pad beside the telephone and handed it to me. On it, in my handwriting, was scrawled "Geo. Spelvin, Rm. 616, Sheridan Towers." I'd jotted it down that afternoon she'd slapped me, before we had the fight, in case she wanted to call me. I tore the paper up in little pieces. I ripped a couple of more sheets off the pad in case the pencil had left an impression, and tore them up, too. I went into the toilet and flushed the torn paper down the stool.

When I came back into the room, Ginny said, "Were you really shacking up with the dame? Did you kill her?"

"You tell me," I said. "I don't think so, though. I think somebody was sticking a shiv in her about the same time you were slapping my face the other day."

"I'm sorry about slapping you," she said. "But you shouldn't needle me about the way I earn a living. I don't like showing it to 'em till they drool, either. But I *do* like to eat."

She poured out another drink and handed it to me. "Sit down and sip this one," she said. "And tell me what really happened."

I sat down and sipped. I told her what I thought had happened. I put in all the details I could remember. After I'd finished, she said, "It's a funny yarn, all right."

"Yeah," I said. "I'm laughing."

That little-girl look of Ginny's was too much for me. I wanted to kiss her. Wanting to kiss her made me jealous again.

"What the hell were you letting that cheap mobster maul you for?" I asked.

"He wasn't mauling me," said Ginny. "He was just holding my hand in a nice, friendly manner and telling me his troubles. He's got the same troubles you have, in a way. Mrs. Malcolm Little."

"What?" I roared.

"Keep your voice down," said Ginny. "The neighbors. When she was Danise Darlan she worked for him at the old Three Ring Circus. It was after Repeal, of course, when the place went legal. Not so very long ago. Vince and Danise were that way at one time, it seems. He's all upset about them shoving her beautiful body in an icebox at the morgue. Vince is sensitive."

"Listen," I said. "Has Vince been acting strange the past few days? Has he seemed to have something on his mind?"

"I wouldn't know about the past few days," she replied. "He just got back tonight. He's opening a place in Miami this winter. He's been down there looking things over for the past week."

"Was he sunburned?" I asked. "Did he bring back any palm trees to prove he'd been in Florida?"

"He uses a sun ray lamp anyway," Ginny replied. "I didn't see him carrying any palm trees around. What are you getting at?"

"Just this," I said. "Mrs. Malcolm Little, or Danise Darlan, if you prefer, registered for Room 617 at the Sheridan Towers as Mrs. J. K. Provost. A guy named J. K. Provost has been occupying Room 617 for the past week."

"Maybe you've got something," she said. She puckered up her brow thinking for a moment and then she added, "Maybe you've got more than you figure. Vince is queer for tools. He keeps a whole chest of gadgets at the club. He's always mending things around the place. It's sort of a standing joke. And he carries a little case of miniature tools around in his pocket, kind of like a Boy Scout who believes in being prepared. Some of the tools have sharp points. They could make a nice hole in a woman's heart."

"Honey," I said, "I'm going to tell all this to Chet. He used to be a real cop, and he's investigating this on his own, because I'm involved and so is he, in a way. He's got a line into Headquarters through a pal of his named Romano. He can get the Miami alibi checked. In the meantime, play up to Vince yourself. Try to draw him out. He might spill something."

"I'll probably have to let him maul me if I do," she said. "I'm kind of particular about who I let maul me."

"How about me?" I asked.

"You can kiss me good night," she said. "Then you go to sleep on the couch. You look dead."

I kissed her more than once. Then I went to sleep on the couch.

It was after six o'clock in the morning when I reached the Bowery. A big sign read:

THE CASTLE
Rooms-50c

The flophouse was just up the street from Grogan's Elite Palace Café and Bar. When you were in the chips on the Bowery they said you were playing the Palace and the Castle, meaning you had both drinking and flop money.

I went up a flight of stairs and entered the dingy lobby. I woke up a fat guy with a wart under his eye who was sleeping at the desk. I told him I wanted a room. He said, "Look, bud, you ain't got hardly a hour left on the night shift. Why don't you come back at nine and go on the day shift?"

The Castle kicked its night lodgers out at seven-thirty in the morning. Between seven-thirty and nine they gave the place a sketchy cleaning. At nine they let the day lodgers in.

"Suppose I pay you for night and day both?" I said.

He scratched his head. "Well, we got some empty rooms," he said. "I guess I could tell 'em not to wake you up."

I handed him a buck. He said, "It don't seem exactly fair, though. Tell you what, I'll charge you six bits." He handed me a quarter change and a key to Room 202.

"Thanks, pal," I said.

I walked toward a stairway. On the walls by the stairs there was an arrow pointing upward and the word, "Rooms."

The room didn't seem as big as the one I'd had at the Hill and it wasn't by any means as clean. I examined the bed carefully for any telltale brown spots that might mean bugs. I didn't find any. I stripped and lay down. I was feeling good. Being with Ginny always made me feel relaxed and sort of proud of myself. I'd had a couple of parting shots of Ginny's whisky, too, but that wasn't all that contributed to my sense of well-being. I could see my way out of the mess now. I felt sure that Vince Parada and J. K. Provost were one and the same. It was cut and dried. Vince even carried the murder weapon around with him. All we had to do was prove he wasn't in Miami. I had an urge to call Chet right away and tell him the good news so he could start things rolling. But I thought I'd better wait until he got in touch with me that evening. I was thinking pleasant thoughts when I fell asleep.

When I awakened it was after noon. I didn't have too bad a hangover. I figured I didn't even need an eye-opener too urgently. That was a good thing, since I didn't have one on me. But I did have another craving. I wanted a cigarette. I fumbled through my pockets and all I found was a crumpled, empty package. I explored the pockets of my trench coat on the off chance I'd find a loose butt. My hand plunged through a big hole in the lining. It came in contact with something that felt like a little wooden cylinder.

It took some extracting, but I finally fished the thing out. Instead of one cylinder, it was two half-cylinders screwed together. It was varnished bright yellow. The name "Inter-City Ice Co." was printed on it in red letters. The name seemed familiar. Suddenly I remembered where I'd seen it before. On the ice truck parked outside Frayne's.

I unscrewed the thing. One half of the cylinder was the handle of an ice pick. The other was a sheath. The steel pick was sharply pointed. Something had stained the pick. Something brownish had dried on it. Something that had been kind of gummy.

Something like blood.

5

I sat on the edge of the cot looking at the thing in my hand. The sharp thing with a stain. The thing that might have been stuck in a woman's heart. I had a peculiar feeling that I had seen it and handled it before. It wasn't just the fact that I remembered the name of the ice company because I had seen it on a truck. The thing itself seemed familiar. But I had no idea how it had got into my pocket. Or rather into the lining of my coat.

I tried to identify it by association. I had seen the ice truck in front of Frayne's. So maybe the ice pick had come from there. But that really led me nowhere, except to the remote possibility that someone had slipped the thing into my pocket while I was standing at Frayne's bar. You had legitimate use for an ice pick only if you needed to crack ice. You cracked ice only if you had an old-fash-ioned icebox instead of a refrigerator. Ginny, I suddenly recalled, had an old-fashioned icebox. It had a pipe under it to serve as a drain. I had cracked ice the afternoon that Ginny slapped me. I always liked my own liquor straight, but Ginny liked a highball. So I had cracked ice and I had used an ice pick. I remembered now that it was an ice pick exactly like the one in my hand. Maybe it was the same ice pick. That had been the afternoon I got sore, the afternoon the red haze swam in front of my eyes. The afternoon the woman was murdered.

I had to phone Ginny right away. She couldn't have had the dozen or so hours of sleep she usually liked. She'd be grouchy, but I had to talk to her. I had to find out. I hurried into my clothes. I ran down the steps to the lobby and tossed my key to the clerk. It was a different clerk. He said, "You checking outta a day bed already?" Then he saw the number of the key and said, "Oh, you're the guy what took the special rate."

I did want a drink now. But I didn't want to run into the crowd at the Palace. I went into a small, dark bar next to the flophouse and ordered a double shot of whisky. The place had a telephone. I dropped a dime in the slot after I'd swallowed the shot and dialed Ginny's number. It took her a long time to answer and when she finally said hello her voice sounded sleepy.

"It's me," I said. "The jealous jerk. The drunken bum. Sorry to wake you up, but I've got to ask you something."

"I'd think you would be sorry," she said. "You just left here a few minutes ago, didn't you?"

"More than six hours ago," I replied. "It's almost one."

She said, "I haven't had enough sleep for a working girl."

"Listen, Ginny," I said. "You know that little ice pick you have in the kitchen? The one with the two wooden parts that screw together?"

"What?" she said. "Ice pick? Are you drunk again? Oh, Terry, you don't mean it was *that* ice pick . . ."

"I want to know where you got it," I said.

"Let me think," she said. She sounded wide awake now. "Oh, I know. I got it at Frayne's. I was in there one day and the ice man gave Frayne a whole handful of them. Kind of an advertisement, I guess. I asked him for one."

"Have you got it now?" I asked.

"I—I think so. The last time I saw it was the other day when I was making a highball for . . ."

She paused, then said, "I keep it in the drawer of the kitchen table."

"Who were you making highballs for?" I asked.

"Why, for you, I guess."

"No," I said. "I don't drink highballs. I don't even take ice in the water chaser."

"Well, it must have been that day you were up here and made highballs for me, then. The other day when we had the fight."

"Look and see if the ice pick's still there, Ginny," I said.

She said, "Hold the phone." She was gone so long I had to put another dime in the slot to keep the operator from disconnecting me.

Finally I heard her voice again. She said, "Terry? It isn't there. I always keep it in the drawer of the kitchen table, but I looked everywhere else it could have been, too. If it's here, I just can't find it."

You might not think a strip teaser would be a good housekeeper. But Ginny was. A place for everything and everything in its place. She even bawled me out for throwing my clothes on the floor instead of hanging them up when I slept on the couch. If the ice pick belonged in the drawer of the kitchen table, she would put it back there. And it wasn't there now. It wasn't there because it was in my pocket.

I said, "Well, that's that."

"What is it, Terry?" she asked, and there was concern in her voice. "What's this all about? I want to know."

"I can't tell you over the phone, kitten," I said, "but don't worry."

"Terry, darling," she said, "whatever it is, I know you didn't do anything wrong. I love you, darling. I want to help."

"There's nothing much you can do right now," I told her. "Except maybe make like a lady Sherlock with our friend Vince. If the cops *should* call on you, you haven't seen me since the other afternoon. We had a fight and you haven't seen me since."

"All right, Terry," she said, "but when *am* I going to see you again?"

"I don't really know," I replied. "Maybe I can have Chet check with you, or call you myself. And I think they let you have visitors in the death house."

"Terry! Don't . . ."

"'Bye now, kitten," I said. "Don't let your G-string slip." I hung up.

I felt kind of funny. It was the first time that Ginny had said she loved me, right out like that. Of course, I had reason to suspect she might, right off the old past performances, as Jockey Basserty would say. But, verbally, at least, our love-making had consisted largely of wisecracks. Despite the thing in my pocket, despite my doubts about my sanity, what Ginny had said made me feel good in a foolish sort of way.

But almost at once my feeling of elation changed to one of suspicion. Ginny had started to say she was cracking ice to make highballs for somebody, but she had choked up before she told me who it was. She hadn't cracked any ice the day I was up there. I'd attended to that department myself. I wondered if she'd been cracking ice to make a highball for Vince Parada, if he'd been in her apartment as well as the Sheridan Towers during the time he was supposed to be in Florida. Ginny might have told him about me being in Room 616, or he might have seen what I'd written on the telephone pad and figured out a way of making me the fall guy. Of course, he couldn't have seen the pad until after the woman was killed, because it was during the time of the murder or directly preceding it that I had been at Ginny's place and had written on the pad. Maybe he'd had the body hidden some place and had dragged it into my room after he'd seen the pad, perhaps during the time that I was in Frayne's place. Only Frayne and his boys swore that I hadn't been in the Broadway ginmill.

There was one thing I couldn't explain away. The blood-stained ice pick in my pocket. Vince Parada had had no opportunity whatsoever of putting it there.

Unless . . .

And that possibility hit me a nasty one below the belt.

Unless he had put it there by proxy. I'd slept in Ginny's place last night. Ginny had picked up my clothes that were strewn all around and hung them neatly on a chair while I was asleep. It would have been easy enough for her to slip the ice pick into the pocket of my coat.

I'd done all this thinking that didn't lead me anywhere except to another unpleasant possibility while I was taking another drink in the little bar next to the flophouse. I didn't want to stay there any longer. The place smelled even worse than most Bowery joints. Probably that was because of the perfumed-air device they used, which stank worse than the smells it was meant to cover.

When I left the place, Sanitation Department men were tossing the contents of waste cans into the maw of one of those big garbage-grinding trucks that make more noise than a platoon of tanks going into action. I figured the little ice pick in my pocket was too hot to hold. I took it out of my pocket and tossed it into a garbage can that the Sanitation men hadn't emptied yet. I stood around to make sure they didn't skip it. They didn't. They emptied the can into the whirring mechanism of the grinder and I guess the ice pick was chewed up along with the other junk.

I bought the afternoon papers at a corner stand. The only thing new about the murder was in their follow-up leads. Mr. Malcolm Little had voluntarily surrendered to police when the story of the murder broke. He had first heard of it over his radio in a room at the Harvard Club, he stated. He said he was staying at the Harvard Club because his wife had intended to spend a few days in town shopping and he did not wish to remain at his country place alone.

He was very much surprised to learn that Mrs. Little had gone to a Broadway hotel and registered under an assumed name. Usually, it seemed, she registered under her own name at the Plaza or the Pierre. Mr. Little stated that on the day of the murder he had remained in his brokerage office until three o'clock, having had lunch sent in from a nearby restaurant. These facts were verified by his partners and employees. During the crucial hours between three and five, he said, he had been taking a constitutional about the city streets. He had walked all the way up to the Harvard Club from his downtown office, and had made only one stop, at a tobacconist's on lower Broadway. He had reached his club some time after five and had gone to his room. He had not heard of the murder until he listened to a nine o'clock news broadcast the following night. He had immediately telephoned his lawyer, who accompanied him to police headquarters.

Mr. Little, the paper said, had been questioned at some length, but he had not been detained by the police. The police had failed to unearth either Mr. J. K. Provost or Mr. George Spelvin. A man with a scarred face had been picked up by police in the neighborhood of the Sheridan Towers and had been questioned, but Anthony Sallucci, the bellboy, had failed to identify him as the occupant of Room 616.

The fact that the cops were picking up just anybody who had a scar on his face gave me an idea. I went into a drug store and bought gauze and adhesive tape. I also bought the forgotten cigarettes. I had to eat something, so I entered a big, noisy cafeteria that was filled with dirty men. I went into the can and put a bandage over the scar, sticking it on with adhesive tape. Then I joined the line at the counter and got a tray of food.

I had nothing to do until seven o'clock that evening except to stay out of the clutches of the cops if possible. I strolled around the streets with the other drifters. I saw the Professor and Shakey sitting in a doorway on a side street.

They looked terrible, the way only bums on the Bowery with a hangover can look. They had evidently spent all their winnings of the day before. They had about an inch of wine left in a pint bottle and they were having a heated argument over who was entitled to the final gulp. I settled the argument by taking the bottle away from them and drinking what was left myself.

"He who steals my wine steals trash!" declared Shakey. He noticed the fresh bandage on my cheek and said, "Hey, what happened to you? Some stinking cop socked you just for fun, I bet."

I told him I'd got in a fight and showed him the bruised knuckles of the hand that had landed the haymaker on Parada. I was glad he didn't remember his suspicions of the night before that I might be the scar-faced man they were seeking for murder.

"You ain't got any cabbage, have you, Soldier?" Shakey asked. "We could use another pint."

"To think," said the Professor, sighing, "that I might have had ten thousand dollars in my tattered jeans if I had only made that trip uptown. Ah, well, it was a pleasant evening."

I told them I'd take them over to the Palace and buy a fancy drink instead of a pint of belly wash. By the time we arrived at the saloon, Suds had already listened to the "Big Sister" and "Ma Perkins" programs and was about to tune in "The Second Mrs. Burton." I told the boys they could order the best in the house.

Shakey thought he'd like to have a whisky sour.

"I ain't got no fruit," said Suds. "Besides, it takes too much time to make and I'm listening to the radio."

"Let's try a milk punch," suggested the Professor. "Invigorating and nourishing."

"Nah," said Suds. "The milk is strictly for the cat."

We compromised and had straight whisky with a water chaser.

Basserty came in looking as tough as Shakey and the Professor. I bought him a shot to straighten him out.

He asked me if I had the price of an Armstrong and a *Form*. He couldn't stand to start a day without handicapping the horses, even though he had no money to bet them. And he'd already missed the early races. I gave him money and he went out and bought the racing sheets. While he was gone, the Killer came huffing and puffing into the place, accompanied by Knotty, the dwarf. Knotty was almost in tears because he'd lost his monocle while he was drunk. I bought the two of them a drink and slipped Knotty a buck so he could buy himself another monocle down at the novelty store.

When Basserty returned with the racing papers, I glanced over the scratch sheet. My eye lit on a horse in the third at Pimlico. Its name was Hidden Thing. I handed the Killer a couple of bucks and told him to go down to Dago Dave's and invest it on Hidden Thing. Basserty looked the horse up in the *Form* and said he didn't appear sharp enough to win.

"You don't know how sharp that Hidden Thing is," I told him

The Killer complained that he only had a few minutes to get the bet in and didn't know if he could make it. He had plenty of time, actually, but he wanted to make it look difficult so it would seem he had earned the drink I bought him. He said he'd wait at the poolroom for the result.

When the Killer returned, his big, battered, silly face was one large grin. "Hey, guys!" he bellowed as soon as he entered the doorway. "That Hidden Thing wins and pays $12.60. We got drinking money." He declared himself and the others in as a matter of course.

We sat down at a table and switched to wine by common consent. A wino likes a few whiskies when he's in the chips, but he can't stand too many. I went easy on the Sneaky Pete, though, because I knew what it could do to me. It made the red haze come in front of my eyes. It made me sock guys like Vince Parada. And maybe it even made me stick ice picks in naked women.

I placed a couple of bets for the corporation on horses that Basserty picked by their form, trials and breeding instead of by their names, and we ran out of the money. Then Shakey insisted that two beetles named Cop Fighter and Hamlet's Ghost couldn't lose. I warned him that cop fighters never won and that Hamlet's Ghost was a dead one, but I made a parlay for him anyway, and both of those lost, too. After he'd consumed enough vino to make him ambulatory, Knotty went out to replace the monocle with the buck I'd given him. "H'I simply feel nekkid without h'it, y'know," he explained.

The Professor had Killer Carney seriously worried over his income taxes. The Professor maintained that since the Killer had received cash and other valuable assets from the ladies of the neighborhood for his services as a baby sitter, he was a working man and must fill out a return. He offered his professional services as a mathematical wizard in assisting the Killer to make out his tax properly.

What brow the Killer had was furrowed with anxiety.

"Well," he said, "Mrs. Danowsky, she usually gives me four bits for sitting with her son, Kosciusko Danowsky, on account of he is a problem child. And Mrs. Clancy gives me a feed for sitting with her boy, Eamon DeValera Clancy. Mrs. Cassellini stakes me to a pint of homemade wine because her little girl, Galli-Curci Cassellini, likes to see me make funny faces."

The Professor shook his head portentously and said that the Killer had better keep stricter account of his sources of income if he didn't want the government agents after him for tax evasion.

I stayed in the Palace, taking my wine slowly and letting it creep up on me in the manner that Suds recommended. I had to stay somewhere away from the cops. Kerrigan was the only cop who ever came into Grogan's place and he had never been known to make an arrest. Later that afternoon we all had to speak in whispers while Suds listened to his favorite soap opera, "Stella Dallas."

Knotty disgraced himself during the program by entering noisily and inviting attention to the new monocle which was screwed into his eye at a rakish angle. Suds wouldn't speak to him for the rest of the day.

Suds came over to swipe the wine rings off the table and collect our glasses. "That Stella Dallas," he said. "She's in another jam already. Just yesterday they had her all tied up and gagged and sitting helpless in a chair. And now she's in another jam already."

"Yeah," I said, "it's not nice for a lady to be sitting helpless in a chair like that."

My dinner consisted of a corned beef sandwich, which was the only thing on the menu of the Palace and which gave Grogan the excuse of calling his place a café as well as a bar. Right around seven o'clock, after Suds had fed the cat and gone off duty and Sad Eyes had taken over, the telephone rang. I was so sure it was Chet calling me that I half-rose from my chair. But Sad Eyes said that the Killer was wanted on the phone. The Killer said, "I knowed it, I knowed I'd get a baby-sitting job tonight," and hurried to the booth.

When he finished the conversation he was fairly blubbering with excitement. "Hey, Sad Eyes! Sad Eyes!" he called. "You got the special bottle? You got it, ain'tcha?"

"What special bottle?" asked Sad Eyes sourly.

"Why, Tommy Twotoes' bottle," said the Killer. "He's a-coming down tomorrow. He's coming here to see us. He just runged me up on the telephone. He's a-coming down and he wants me to have the boys here."

I had only met the fabulous Tommy Twotoes once and I didn't like to remember that experience. Tommy Twotoes was a Bowery god. Many years ago, around the turn of the century when he was still a punk kid, he'd played the Skid Rows of a dozen towns from San Francisco to Boston. Now in his late sixties, he was a retired millionaire. He had drunk so much during his long and fantastic career that he had become a bloated, crippled caricature of a man. He must have weighed around three hundred pounds. His jowls were flabby, pendulous sacs. He was so completely bald that even his eyebrows had disappeared. Encroaching layers of fat almost obscured his eyes and even at a short distance his face appeared to be a pallid, featureless blob except for the rose-tinted, porous nose. He was in the advanced stages of alcoholic neuritis and walked like a semiparalytic or a tottering child, putting one foot in front of the other painfully. His head was hunched down between his shoulders at a grotesque angle.

Tommy Twotoes knew most of the permanent and semipermanent vagrants of the Bowery and made a point of visiting them periodically as a kind of memorial of the days, half a century before, when he had trod such streets himself. On such occasions he would set up drinks for all and sundry, stake the boys to a week's flop and drinking money and listen to their troubles like a kindly and understanding father. In special cases he would take some of the boys back to his estate on the Hudson for a week or so. From time to time a few of them had been put to work in various capacities on his household staff.

The day I'd met Tommy Twotoes I'd about hit bottom. I was sick-drunk and mean-drunk on sweet wine. The old red haze was hanging over me and I hated everybody. I looked upon the grotesque old man as an interloper from another world, come to Skid Row to taunt and patronize its unfortunates. I'd sounded off against him, and I guess it was pretty much like one of the comrades in Union Square sounding off against the capitalists. I'd become so insulting that his gigantic body servant, Ebony Black, would have lowered the boom on me if Tommy Twotoes had not intervened.

That was the only time I'd ever seen Tommy Twotoes, but I knew his story well from my newspaper days. Some sports columnist was always reviving it for a Sunday feature. His family had gone under the name of Tuthill for generations, but in one way or another Tommy discovered that he had a small amount of Indian blood and that the family name had originally derived from a brave called Two Toes. He promptly adopted Twotoes as his legal name. He became the outstanding sports promoter of his day and branched out into the theatrical entertainment field. Once he had promoted the matches of such men as Tommy Burns, Jack Johnson, Stanley Ketchel, Bat Nelson, Ad Wolgast, Frankie Erne, Abe Atell and Johnny Kilbane. Then he had opened a race track just across the border in Mexico and had offered the Twotoes Stakes, the first $1 00,000 race in the history of the world. Furthermore, instead of presenting the winning owner with a handsome trophy he had presented the winning horse with a solid gold water bucket on the theory that the horse, not the owner, did all the work. He had owned theaters and night clubs and a motion picture studio and it was rumored, but never proved, that his was the capital and the master mind behind the most successful ring of Prohibition rum runners.

Upon his retirement years before, he had stated:

"I have always conceived it as my mission in life to expectorate in the complacent face of conventionality and to corrupt the morals of my fellows by offering them the opportunity to witness such bestial spectacles as prize fights and affording them the chance to gamble upon race horses, leer at seminude women and drink strong spirits."

The accomplishment of such a mission, he added, had proved highly profitable.

In view of my behavior the last time I had seen him, I doubted that Mr. Twotoes would welcome me at his open house the next day and I planned to avoid the Palace if possible. Perhaps, I thought, I would be in jail by then, anyway. Most of the other boys, however, were highly enthusiastic over the prospects of the free load that was in store for them. Each of them put the bite on me for a quarter or two on the assurance that they would pay me back as soon as Tommy Twotoes had staked them.

The Killer was still bumbling around telling the boys of Tommy Twotoes' impending visit when the phone rang again. Sad Eyes came out cursing this time. "A goddam social sekketary I'm getting to be," he complained. "They want the Soljer now."

It was Chet, of course. He said, "Hello, is this Soldier?"

"This is George Spelvin Jones," I replied.

Before he could tell me of any developments, I admitted that I had disobeyed his instructions and visited Ginny and blurted out the story of Vince Parada, his connection with the murdered woman, and the fact that he had been away from his club for a week before the murder. I laid it on as thick as possible. I didn't tell Chet about having socked Parada the night before. I wasn't too certain about my own sanity and I didn't want Chet to doubt it, too. If he did, I wouldn't have anybody working for me. And the Lord knew I needed somebody. Somebody big and tough and dependable like Chet. So I didn't tell Chet about finding the ice pick, either. I was holding out on him, and maybe that was wrong. But in my addled state of mind, in my confusion over the part that Ginny might have played in framing me, it seemed the best thing to do at the moment.

When I let him get a word in edgewise, Chet said that he was glad we had another suspect because the cops were always inclined to handle a citizen of Mr. Malcolm Little's prominence with kid gloves. He said he'd get in touch with Lieutenant Romano right away and have Parada's Miami alibi checked. Then he told me his own news. It wasn't good.

"Kid," he said, "they worked a hell of a lot faster than I ever thought they would. The identification of your fingerprints came through from Washington this afternoon. The cops have already thrown a dragnet out, as they say in the books. They're looking for Terence R. Rooke, war veteran, height five-eleven, weight 173, hair brown, eyes blue. They know you're a former newspaperman and they even know you've been in government hospitals. I don't think they've traced you to the agency yet, though. If they have, Romano held out on me. Of course, they know about the scar from the bellhop. So keep under cover. Stay down there for the present. Stay lost."

Chet went on to say that Little had no real alibi for the time of the murder and that he might bust the case wide open by telling Romano that the man was suspicious of his wife, knew of her assignation at the Sheridan Towers and had hired a shamus to tail her. He said he didn't want to tell Romano that right away, though, because it would involve me and besides he was saving it for his ace in the hole when the going got really tough.

Chet said we'd better check again soon. He planned to inform Romano of the Parada angle as soon as he hung up. He said he could tell Romano about Vince without revealing the source of his information. He thought the lieutenant might question Vince at the Triangle Club that evening and that maybe a report from Miami would come through by morning. He said he'd call me at the Palace at noon the next day. I told him I would be there. I'd forgotten all about wanting to dodge Tommy Twotoes.

"There's one good thing," Chet added. "At least I think it's good. Romano's not giving out anything to the papers about the identification of the fingerprints. He doesn't want to put the suspect on his guard, he said. So there shouldn't be anything about you, under your right name, in the newspapers for a few days, anyway."

Chet was so wrong about that, I discovered a short while later when the tabs were out. Some smart boy on the *News* had got himself a beat and a by-line. He must have been a Johnny-Come-Lately, because I knew most of the old-timers on the police beat and I didn't recognize his name, which was Ted Phelps. His story read in part:

Police yesterday refused to confirm or deny an anonymous telephone tip received by the *News* which stated that a war veteran who has been treated at government hospitals for a face wound and nervous disorder is being sought in connection with the brutal murder of Mrs. Danise Little in the Sheridan Towers Hotel on Monday. Information received by this newspaper was to the effect that identification was made through fingerprints left on a plastic suitcase in the room where Mrs. Little's body was discovered.

The *News's* informant stated that the fingerprints have been identified as those of Terence R. Rooke, described as being five feet, 11 inches, with brown hair and blue eyes. The man who registered for the murder room gave the name of George Spelvin. A bellboy, Anthony Sallucci, stated that "Spelvin" had a scar on his face and that he wore the emblem of the Purple Heart, a decoration given to men who were wounded in action in the war.

Rooke is believed to be a former newspaper and publicity man who was employed on several metropolitan dailies as a reporter before the war.

There was another column or so of rehash on the murder itself. I knew damned well from experience that no reporter would write a story like that and no editor would pass it merely on the authority of an anonymous telephone call. There was something behind it and I thought I knew what it was. It was the old you-scratch-my-back-and-I'll-scratch-yours business. When a cop comes up for promotion it's nice to have a friend who writes little pieces for the paper. That friend will mention the cop favorably, maybe, and spell his name right when he's working on a case. And the best way for a cop to win friends and influence people on newspapers is to give them a little exclusive information. It had to be Romano himself or somebody in his department who had passed that tip to the reporter, Ted Phelps, with the understanding that the source of his information would not be revealed.

The fact that the cops had already traced me back as far as my newspaper days showed that they were getting close and were wasting no time in their investigation. They must want me and want me bad. I wondered how long it would be before I was connected with Chet. Romano wouldn't like Chet then and we'd lose an invaluable contact at Headquarters. We'd lose it anyway if Chet went in and told his story this late. Or if Mr. Little spilled his guts about hiring Chet's agency to put the peek on his ever-loving wife and her mysterious boy friend, Mr. J. K. Provost.

I went back to the table and sat down and drank for a while. Several hours of wine-bibbing had taken the edge off Shakey's hangover and brightened him up. He showed a renewed interest in the bandage I was wearing.

"'We talk here in the public haunt of men,'" he said, quoting the Bard again. "Say," he added, "that mother-slugging cop socked you right on the scar, didn't he?"

I told him the guy who hit me wasn't a cop. He wouldn't believe me, though, because he thought only cops went around socking innocent bystanders. He began to read the tabs I'd bought. He read the comics and cussed out Dick Tracy and Kerry Drake because they were cops. He turned to the news section and read Phelps' story. Suddenly he became excited.

"Hey!" he cried. "I bet the cops did pick you up last night and beat you over your scar with a rubber hose! It says here the guy they're looking for in that murder was a soldier. Hey, you didn't knock that dame off, did you?" He grew grave and lapsed into Shakespeare again. "'Truth will come to light; murder cannot be hid long,'" he declared ominously.

I got up from my chair. A Western Union messenger boy came into the saloon. He seemed startled when he saw the kind of place he was in. He walked up to the bar and spoke to Sad Eyes. I could tell by the way Sad Eyes' Adam's apple was bobbing up and down that he was answering the messenger boy.

Shakey closed one eye so that he could take a dead sight on the messenger boy with the other. "That's the first damn midget cop I ever saw," he declared.

"Hey, Soljer!" yelled Sad Eyes. "You gotta telegram! What the hell happens next in this jernt? I'm a goddam social sekketary."

The telegram was addressed to "Soldier," care of Grogan's Elite Palace Café and Bar. I signed for it. The messenger boy hung around, so I gave him a quarter.

He seemed surprised. He wasn't as surprised as I was, however, when I tore the telegram open. The message read:

URGENT YOU MEET ME MY APARTMENT
NINE-THIRTY. IN DANGER
                                            GINNY

I looked at the clock. It was eighteen minutes to nine. I got Sad Eyes to change a quarter and went into the phone booth. I dialed the number of Ginny's apartment. I could hear the muted ringing of the phone. There was no answer. I hung up, waited a second, and deposited another dime. I called Vince Parada's Triangle Club. The phone was in Parada's office. One of Parada's mugg hangers-on answered gruffly. I asked for Ginny.

He said, "The dinner show's on. We can't call no performers to the phone while the dinner show's on. Call after nine."

The dinner show ran until nine, I knew. But Ginny's turn was usually over before that time. If Ginny was appearing in the dinner show, she must be all right so far. Probably the danger she feared wouldn't arise before nine-thirty. I thought about going to the club to pick her up. But it was a quarter to nine by now. If she left right after her number in the dinner show, I would almost surely miss her. I decided to go to the apartment instead. I hurried toward the door. The boys were eying me curiously. The Killer called after me, "Hey, Soljer! Somethin' happen? Somebody dead?"

Somebody being dead wasn't a comforting thought. I caught a cruising cab and figured I was lucky, because there aren't too many cruising cabs in that section of the city. But once inside I thought I was a fool for not taking the subway to avoid traffic and stoplights. I thought the heap jockey was taking hours. Actually, we arrived at Ginny's address on Twenty-third in a little more than twenty minutes.

It was hardly possible that Ginny could have arrived home, but I raced up the two flights of stairs. I unlocked the door without knocking. The apartment was dark. I reached for the light switch by the door. I flicked the button and nothing happened. The ceiling bulb must have been burned out. I started to grope my way through the darkness toward a table where I knew a fat-bellied lamp was standing.

The guy who dropped the atom bomb was an expert marksman. The missile hit me a bull's-eye on the back of my head. For a second I saw all the weird, unearthly swirling and billowing and brightly colored things that the people of Hiroshima and Nagasaki must have seen the instant the big bombs fell. Then I hit the floor and I no longer saw anything at all.

When my mind clutched feebly toward returning consciousness, whole years of my life were blotted out. I was back on one of the little islands whose name nobody remembers any more. I had just been blown out of an M-4 tank. I was crawling on my belly. My head was a great bulge of pain. My neck felt as if it were broken.

Only I wasn't crawling. I was being dragged. Then I was lying still and someone was bending over me. It was the ghouls, I decided, the Graves Registration boys. They would clip off one of my dog tags for identification on the casualty lists. They were going through my pockets. I was too weak to resist them. Hell, I thought. I'm not just weak. I'm dead.

There was a nerve-rasping, screeching sound. It sliced like a sharp tool into the great, throbbing hurt of my head. I knew that sound. A window in Ginny's apartment made that sound when you raised it. I wasn't on the little island any more.

I was in Ginny's apartment. But Ginny's apartment was no longer a nice, safe, pleasant place.

Somebody was lifting me up. They were strong. Maybe there was more than one of them. I could see nothing in the darkness. My head was too painful and muddled to permit of clear impressions. I was being propped up against something. The something ended at my waist. Above that there was nothing. There was night air on my face. It revived me some. Below me there was a concrete areaway. Three stories below me. There was a pressure against my shoulders. The solid support against my legs and hips seemed to be moving away from me.

Instinctively I fought for a foothold. I got my feet propped against a baseboard. I lunged. At the same time I struck out blindly, using my arm like a cudgel, the side of my hand like the blade of a cleaver. It was a jiujitsu blow they'd taught me in the Army. The side of my hand hit something hard. I thought my hand was broken. Somebody grunted and stumbled. I lunged forward again, away from the open window, and fell flat on my face. The heavy shadow was coming toward me, slowly, carefully. I could hear breathing in the taut silence of the pitch-dark room. I made a supreme effort despite the aching of my head and the sour sickness of my belly. I got to my knees and sprang toward the shadow. I missed. I was flat on my face again in the darkness.

The shadow didn't make another try for me. It fled across the room. A door opened and shut. I staggered to my feet. I bumped up against something and knocked it over. I plunged out into the lighted hallway.

The shadow was gone. I could hear footsteps clattering down the stairs. I went to the head of the stairs. Vertigo overcame me. I fell down. I didn't stop rolling until I had tumbled half a flight. I lay on the stairs for a while, panting like a flushed animal. The house was very still. There were no longer any clattering footsteps. I remembered that the superintendent's door had been closed when I entered. He must be out of the house. I crawled back up the stairs. The door to Ginny's apartment was open. I went in and found the table lamp. I switched it on and collapsed in a chair. I sat there for a while holding my head between my hands. Then I looked around.

The room seemed just as usual except for an overturned end table. There wasn't any bulb in the ceiling light fixture. The bulb lay on the table beside the fatbellied lamp I had just lit. The only clock that Ginny owned was a dollar-ninety-eight alarm clock. It stood on the mantel. In the center of the dial was a painted figure of Mickey Mouse. Mickey Mouse's white-gloved hands pointed to the time. It was just nine-thirty-seven. Ginny was seven minutes late. The telegram had said nine-thirty. The thought made me laugh. Ginny hadn't planned to meet me at nine-thirty or nine-thirty-seven or any other time. She'd sent her boy friend instead. She'd told Mr. Parada, the suave, sleek Mr. Parada who caused the ladies' hearts to go pitty-pat, about my socking him the night before. She must have also told him about my suspecting him of the murder of Danise Little. Mr. Parada had arranged for her to send the telegram. Then he, or some of his boys, or maybe both, had formed a reception committee.

It didn't make sense, of course, Ginny turning suddenly on me like that. But nothing in this screwy business made sense. And it seemed to me that figuring Mr. Parada and my ever-loving girl friend as confederates explained a lot of things. It explained why Ginny had put that little ice pick in my pocket, for instance.

Thinking of my pocket reminded me that whoever had clouted me and had tried to toss me out of a third-story window a few minutes before had been going through my pockets. I felt for my money, and laughed bitterly at my foolishness when I found it intact. They hadn't been out to roll me. They had been out to murder me. In the pocket of my trench coat—the pocket without the hole—I felt a piece of paper. I thought at first it was the telegram I had received from Ginny. But it wasn't the telegram. The telegram had completely disappeared. It was a folded piece of paper. On the paper there was typing. The typing read:

```
To Whom It May Concern:
I can't take it any longer. I mur-
dered the Little woman in a fit of
insanity. The war caused it all. My
name is Terence Robert Rooke. I was
George Spelvin, the man in 616 of
the Sheridan Towers Hotel.
```

There wasn't any signature, but this touching little missive about explained everything, I thought. Ginny and Parada were in love. Parada's old girl friend and Ginny's boy friend had stood in their way. So they'd planned to get rid of them both. Parada had killed Danise and framed me for the murder. Then he was going to fake my suicide. Only I was still alive.

Suddenly it occurred to me that I might not be alive for long if I stayed where I was. Parada or his boys might be coming back. But there was something I had to do before I left the apartment.

Once upon a time Ginny had decided to quit strip-teasing for a respectable profession like stenography. She'd bought a little portable typewriter for practicing. I went to the desk and took the lid off the typewriter. I put in a sheet of paper. It was the same kind of paper as that on which the suicide note had been written.

I typed "Now is the time for all good men to come to the aid of their party." The sample matched the type letters on the suicide note perfectly. Before I left I set a match to the suicide note and flushed the charred paper down the toilet.

I don't know what led me to go down to Vince Parada's Triangle Club. The red haze was in front of my eyes again. Maybe I just wanted to smash Parada. Maybe I was intent upon killing Ginny. My head was reeling and my legs were wobbling. But somehow I got down to Fourth Street. Jocko, Parada's doorman, stopped me. He had gone off duty by the time I'd reached the place early that morning. I knew him fairly well. He was a big, dumb goon who had done a stretch for bootlegging before Repeal. He mistook my dizziness for drunkenness.

"Look, Mr. Rooke," he said, "you can't go in all drunked up like that. Besides, look at them clothes you're wearing. And you're hot with every cop in town."

"I've got to see Ginny," I said stubbornly.

"You can't see her nohow," he replied. "She and the boss, they left together, right after her turn in the dinner show. They was in a hurry, it seemed like. And they ain't come back. Look, fellow, I been hot with the cops myself. I know what it's like. There's one up and down this street every few minutes. Fade, won'tcha, Mr. Rooke? And I'll forget I even seen you."

I faded. I couldn't think of any better place to go, so I went back to Grogan's.

As soon as I went in, Sad Eyes stormed at me. "You!" he said. "You think maybe I ain't got nuttin' to do but take your social messages? You think maybe I'm your sekketary? Some pal of yours, he's been calling up all night. Here, I got the message. He wants you should call him back."

He fumbled in his pocket, his Adam's apple jumping up and down with annoyance. He handed me a smudged piece of paper. On it was scrawled "Call Chet hotel."

I didn't call at once. I needed a drink. Besides, nothing that Chet had to tell me could be any worse than the thing I already knew. I had a double whisky Then I went back and made the call. The fat operator went through her usual routine of telling me that Chet was out, but he answered the phone.

"Terry!" he said. "I've been trying to get you all evening. Listen, Terry, Ginny called a little after I talked to you. She wanted to know how to reach you. Said it was urgent, but wouldn't say what it was. I didn't want to give her the address, but she insisted and I finally did. Did she get hold of you?"

I stalled for a minute. I couldn't tell him about Ginny leading me into the trap. There was something too final about telling him. If I put the thing into words, I felt I was condemning Ginny with no chance of reprieve. There couldn't possibly be an explanation for the thing she had done, but still I couldn't tell Chet about it.

So I said, "Oh, yeah. She got in touch. Nothing important. She was just worried about me."

"Listen, kid," said Chet urgently, "be careful. They're after you. I don't mean just the cops. Somebody's after you and they mean business. Stay hid, kid, and don't trust anybody. *Anybody*, understand?"

I told him not to worry, I wasn't in a very trusting mood at the moment. He said he'd call the next day as we'd agreed, and hung up.

I picked up another hooker of rye at the bar, went over and sat down with the boys. I could see the question marks in all of their eyes, but I didn't volunteer any information. Finally Shakey saw the duck egg on the back of my noggin and could contain himself no longer.

"I see them cops has been beating you up again," he said. "Them stinking Cossacks."

"I fell down," I said. He looked doubtful, but on Skid Row it isn't good taste to ask personal questions. Too many people have too many things to hide.

Finally I decided the safest place for me was bed. I went to the Castle again. The fat clerk with the mole under his eye remembered me and said, "You want the same room again? Two hunnerd and two where the walls are talking to you? You didn't find nothing in there, did you?"

That gave me a start. I remembered the ice pick. I said, "Find anything? What the hell do you mean?"

"Oh, little things that crawl around," he replied. "You shouldn't of found none. The place was exterminated just last week."

I told him it was a fine room and I hadn't found anything. I paid him and took the key. I went to the room and stripped off my clothes. I flopped on the cot and before long I was dreaming that I was manning a 50-caliber in an M-4 tank that was chasing a bunch of naked women. Some of the naked women looked like Mrs. Malcolm Little and the others looked like Ginny.

Some time after midnight I was awakened by a knocking on my door. I lay still for a minute, making sure that this wasn't just part of the dream. It wasn't. The knocking was repeated. I'd written my name down as Jones. Nobody could have traced me here by that.

I must have been followed. The ones who were after me had me trapped again. I'd been foolish to go back to Grogan's. This time they weren't likely to leave the job unfinished. Or maybe it was the cops who were hunting for a man with a scar on his face. They could have described me to the room clerk. He'd seen the scar when I'd registered before, and the bandage wasn't much of a disguise.

I crept to the door in my bare feet and listened. I heard the clerk's muffled voice saying something to somebody. There was more knocking. I jumped into my pants. I wasn't going to be caught with my pants down actually as well as metaphorically. I looked out the window and thought of taking the fire escape. There were still quite a few people on the street. And there was a cop right under the window. He might have been posted there in case I took to the fire escape.

The fat clerk was calling, "Hey, fella! Wake up! It's your friend. He says he's gotta see you."

What friend? Chet? He didn't know where I was. But he might have gone to the Palace and the boys might have told him I would probably sleep at the Castle. I didn't think it was a friend, though. I thought it was the ones who were after me. Or the cops.

There was another voice. "Hey, Soljer! It's the Killer, Soljer! Lemme in!"

I opened the door. The Killer was sweating and excited.

The fat clerk said, "You know this guy? He come barging in. Said he had to see the guy with a bandage on his puss. I didn't want to call you, but he said it was important."

"It's okay," I told him. The fat clerk went away.

"Hey, Soljer," sputtered the Killer. "Tommy Twotoes called up again. I been looking all over for you. He called me up at Grogan's from some big hotel he's staying at in town. He's comin' down tomorrow. About noon, he said."

"So what?" I said. "I knew that already. You wake me up to tell me that?"

"He wants to see you, Soljer. He asked me if the guy they called the Soljer had been around, the one what bawled him out the last time he saw him, and I said you had. He said be sure and have you in Grogan's tomorrow. Today, I mean, 'cause it's already after midnight, ain't it? He says it's important."

"Hell, he doesn't even know me," I said. "He must have meant somebody else."

"He meant you, all right. He knows you. Tommy Twotoes don't forget nobody. You better be there, Soljer."

The Killer can become very melodramatic at times. "You better be there, Soljer," he repeated portentously. "Maybe it's a matter of life and death."

6

Tommy Twotoes, benefactor of the Bowery, didn't arrive at Grogan's Palace promptly on the stroke of noon, but a telephone call did. When Suds summoned me to the phone I was sure it was Chet calling, but I was mistaken. A woman's voice answered my hello. I knew the voice, of course, but I was so dumb-struck with surprise that I asked, "Who the hell is this?"

"It's Ginny, you idiot," the voice replied.

Since she was putting on the innocent act, I decided to play it cozy, too.

"How in hell did you get this number?" I asked her.

"From Chet," she replied calmly, and I had to give her credit for the performance she was staging. "He didn't want to give it to me, but something's come up and I wanted to tell you about it myself."

I gave her an opening. "Why didn't you send me a wire last night?"

She must have anticipated that one because she had an answer ready. "Why should I?" she asked. "He said you wouldn't be there until noon today. Don't worry. I'm calling from a booth, so the line's not tapped."

The sheer cold cheek and self-possession of the girl who had lured me into a death trap only a few hours before left me speechless for a minute. I hesitated, then I said, "Something important about Vince?"

"Maybe," she replied. "I just don't know. You remember that picture of you I had? The one in uniform? Well, when we had the fight the other day I was so mad I took it down and stuck it in a bureau drawer. Then you came around the other night and we made up and I took it out again and put it on the little night stand by my bed. And now it's gone. I can't find it anywhere."

"What the hell?" I said. "Who'd want my picture?"

"The cops, maybe," she replied logically enough. "Or the newspapers."

"But how could they get it?"

"Maybe someone stole it and gave it to 'em," said Ginny.

"But who could have done that?"

"Vince Parada, maybe. He was up in the apartment yesterday afternoon. I missed it right after he left."

"What?" I roared. "You let that cheap mugg up in your apartment?" I thought I sounded jealous, convincing. I thought I was putting on a pretty good act myself.

"Keep your water cool, sonny," she said. "You wanted me to pump him, didn't you? Besides, he didn't come by himself. Gert, the torch singer at the Triangle was with him. She's sweet on Vince. We sat around and had highballs. I didn't have any pick, so Vince had to crack the ice with one of those little tools he carries around with him. It was just like an ice pick. It worked fine. I tried to make Vince talk, but I didn't get very far. Then they left, and I felt lonesome. I wanted to kiss your big, ugly puss. I'm just a silly little girl, I guess. But when I looked for the picture, it wasn't there. It wasn't anywhere."

"If Vince took the picture, he had to go in your bedroom," I said. "What the hell was he doing in your bedroom?"

"Not what you think, you dope," she replied. "I told you there were *two* women there. I don't think Vince is that good. He had to go through the bedroom to get to the bath."

"Oh," I said. "So that's that."

"Chet said he'd call you," said Ginny. "He acted as if he might know something about Vince."

"Don't try calling me here again," I told her. "If the cops have my picture or if somebody's going to publish it in a newspaper, I'll have to get a new address."

I didn't want Parada's goons looking for me at Grogan's.

"Honey," she said. "Be careful. Keep your nose clean."

"I'm not worried about keeping my nose clean," I said. "I'm worried about keeping my seat from getting hot."

I thought Ginny must have been very puzzled over my not coming right out about the telegram and the murderous attack on me in her apartment.

About ten minutes later I had another telephone call. This time it was from Chet. I told him about the disappearing picture.

"What do you make of it?" I asked.

"I make Parada," he replied. "He knows the heat's on him. He suspected it would be yesterday. If some paper runs that picture of you and you get picked up it will help to take the heat off him. I just left Romano. He picked Parada up at his apartment early this morning. Romano questioned Vince and got the Miami alibi. He's not holding him, but he's put on a twenty-four-hour tail. Romano checked Miami. Parada registered at a Beach hotel, all right. On the fifteenth. He's still registered there, in fact. Never checked out. Left his baggage. But he hasn't slept in the room since the night of the nineteenth. That would give him plenty of time to fly back and chill the dame on the afternoon of the twentieth."

"Maybe we're getting somewhere," I said hopefully.

"Yeah, maybe we are," said Chet. "And there's more. Romano had been holding out on me. They found a plane ticket in the dame's bag the day she was discovered dead. It was a ticket to Miami. She was supposed to leave yesterday. Only she couldn't on account of she was slightly dead."

"Jesus Christ," I said.

"No," said Chet. "Not Jesus Christ. Vince Parada. There's quite a difference. Vince could have registered at the Sheridan Towers easily enough on the thirteenth as J. K. Provost, then taken off for the South. He could have flown back under pretext of meeting the woman and taking her back with him, and killed her instead. Don't ask me why, and don't ask me about all that hocus-pocus of changing rooms, undressing her and dressing her again and moving her from a chair to a bed. I don't know, but it'll all come out in the wash. Anyway, it looks like Parada. He's a three-to-five shot in my book."

Chet said that if Parada was smart, he'd send the picture to the same reporter who had broken the fingerprint identification story. In that case, the photograph wouldn't be published until the *News* was on the street that night. He said he'd better not call me any more at Grogan's and if I could find a better hideout to do so. He gave me the number of the pay telephone in the lobby of the building where he had his office. He told me to call him there the next day at noon. He said he'd be waiting for the call.

The next event that occurred at Grogan's Elite Palace Café and Bar that day was the grand entrance of Tommy Twotoes, the Bashaw of the Bowery, and his retinue. The saloon was full by the time he arrived and the boys had been waiting around with a general air of repressed excitement. Basserty and Knotty and the Professor and Shakey were all assembled and so were a great many others. Some I knew by sight. Others I couldn't remember having seen before.

Killer Carney had been posted outside as a lookout and he came dashing into the place fairly bubbling over with the important news.

"He's a-comin'!" he yelled. "He's a-comin', fellows!"

Everybody in the ginmill but Suds and me dashed to the door, overturning chairs and stools and even leaving unfinished drinks on the bar and tables. It's unheard of for anybody on the Bowery to leave a half-finished glass of Sneaky Pete behind him unless he is very excited indeed. I have even seen a guy finish a shot before running from the cops.

I watched through the window as the huge Rolls-Royce town car drew up to the curbing. The Rolls-Royce job must have been at least twenty-five years old, but it was still plenty impressive. It had been polished until it sparkled like the hearse in an Italian funeral procession. The high-pitched rear end of the vehicle with its glistening glass resembled a big, square showcase. The gigantic, one-eyed Negro, Ebony Black, was the chauffeur. He sat in the uncovered driver's seat and he really looked majestic, for he was wearing purple livery. He had been a heavyweight in Tommy Twotoes' stable of fighters and it is probable he might have beaten 'em all if the champions of that time hadn't remembered the black panther, Jack Johnson, and drawn the color line, less because of race discrimination than because of the fact that such contenders as Harry Wills and Ebony Black gave them a hard case of the jitters. Tommy had named the big Negro Ebony Black, a precursor to such fantastic ring names as Kid Chocolate and Violet Ray.

Beside the giant chauffeur sat a runt of a man named Polvo, who was clad in corduroy breeches, a checked shirt and a hat with the brim turned up on one side. He also wore gold earrings. I suppose he was acting as the eminent Mr. Twotoes' footman. Polvo was quite a character in his own right. He came originally from one of those Balkan states that get their names changed after every war. He had been an organ grinder on the Lower East Side until his monkey, General Lafayette, had died on him. Up to that time Polvo had been a fairly stable citizen as Bowery characters go, except for a sneaking suspicion he entertained that he was a reincarnation of George Washington. When his gums shriveled and his teeth fell out, Polvo had even had a dentist manufacture him a set of "sea-horse ivory" dentures, because those were the kind of false teeth that George Washington wore. (I was to learn a great deal about these extraordinary teeth and their history later. Washington's dentist fashioned his teeth from the tusks of the walrus and hippopotamus, which in those days were known as sea horses. The upper and lower sets were hinged together by springs and had to be held in the mouth through contortions of the facial muscles.) Polvo's teeth were duplicates of Washington's and must have been just as uncomfortable as those worn by the Father of his Country. The teeth were as ghastly as recently scrubbed tombstones and gave Polvo's dark, wrinkled face an eerie look when he wore them. He usually inserted them solely for the sake of appearance and took them out whenever the necessity of eating or talking arose.

Polvo and General Lafayette had been very close, and when the monkey died the little organ grinder went on the bum and the booze. Finally, Tommy Twotoes had rescued him and given him a job.

The arrival of Tommy Twotoes' town car brought great agitation to the street. Squalling kids were making a concerted rush for Grogan's. The bums who made up the reception committee were practically bent double in homage to the Great Personage. For a while it looked as if they'd have to call out the police reserves to make a path for Tommy Twotoes.

Getting the crippled and bloated old man out of the car was a job of work in itself. Ebony Black and Polvo posted themselves on each side of the door to assist their boss, but when Polvo began to crumple under the man's weight, Killer Carney went to his aid. Flanked and supported by the two old heavyweights, with little Polvo blazing a trail through the assembled bums and onlookers, Tommy Twotoes made his way into the saloon, nodding benignly and waving his hands at those who greeted him, an ancient potentate bestowing blessings on his subjects.

Even Suds rose to the occasion. He had found a slightly faded red ribbon somewhere and had tied it in a bow around Stella Dallas' neck. When Tommy Twotoes made his entrance, Suds sang out a little speech that he must have been mulling over in his mind: "Welcome to Grogan's Elite Palace Café and Bar, Mr. Twotoes, sir! We have your special bottle ready."

Suds unlocked a cabinet at the rear of the bar and brought forth a squarish bottle of blue crockery. On the crock was printed:

Special Reserve
Marley-le-Duc, France
M. Tommy Twotoes

These special crocks from famous vineyards in France, inscribed with the purchaser's name, were imported widely by rich Americans before the war and the vintners began the profitable business again soon after Germany's surrender. Tommy always left a few bottles on hand at Grogan's against his visits. He paid the bartender the regular price of a pony just to pour his own brandy into a glass for him. Every Christmas he sent a few cases to Grogan's to be distributed among the boys and for the next few days Bowery bums would be drinking finer brandy than many millionaires.

Tommy Twotoes inspected the bottle that Suds was holding aloft and inquired, "How many of these do you have on hand, my friend?"

"Only five, Mr. Twotoes," Suds replied.

"You'd better fetch a case from the car," Tommy told Ebony Black. "I wish every gentleman here to sample my brandy unless he prefers other poison. But first you and the estimable Killer will conduct me to a table."

The two old fighters placed the three hundred flabby pounds of Mr. Twotoes tenderly in a chair at the biggest table in the room and Ebony Black left to get the case of brandy. There was a kind of respectful clamor among the boys to gain a place at the table. The Killer crowded into a chair at the Master's right and the cocky little Polvo, making like a bodyguard with menacing glances at the others, took the chair to his left. The Professor, Basserty, Shakey and Knotty also managed to acquire places of honor. Tommy Two-toes signaled Suds for drinks all around and I'm damned if some of those guys didn't prefer fifteen-cents-a-glass Sneaky Pete to the priceless brandy he was offering them. Tommy and a few of those closest to him had their drinks served in brandy snifters, but Grogan's supply of such fancy items was strictly limited and the others drank from shot glasses, wine glasses, highball glasses and even beer shells. The few bottles of Twotoes Special that Suds had on hand were just about exhausted by the first round, but Ebony Black came in bearing reinforcements and the cheerful news that there were more replacements in the trunk of the town car.

I had been lurking in a dark corner, but Tommy Twotoes spied me suddenly and beckoned. I went over to the table somewhat hesitantly and somebody found me a chair.

"Welcome, Soldier," Tommy Twotoes greeted me. "I am happy you could attend our little conference of untrammeled minds and limitless thirsts."

"The Killer said you wanted to see me," I replied. "I guess it's about the last time we met, although I hardly thought you'd remember it. I was out of line, I guess. I'm sorry if I offended you. I was pretty drunk."

"And today you are most disgustingly sober," he said. "A condition that we will attempt to rectify with the nectar of grapes warmed in the sun of southern France. I have found that the nectar, applied internally, accomplishes small miracles. And I do not like apologies, Soldier. A man speaks his mind, whether he is drunk, demented, sober or senescent, and that I admire. However, I think I should explain myself to you. That is one reason I wished to see you. The other reason is more important, even. We will speak of it later, and in private."

"There's no need for you to explain yourself to me," I told him.

"I feel called upon to do so, nonetheless," he insisted. "You accused me of patronizing men that I am proud to call my friends. Soldiers of misfortune, perhaps they are, but men of strong minds, true bohemians, gallant dreamers, admirable anarchists who flout the outworn moral codes and social strictures and find a Nirvana of their own in gutters when a bottle's near to hand. Patronize them, sir? By the belching belly of Bacchus, never! I salute them. I envy them. Half a century or more ago I was one of them. I still am, in spirit. I like them. I enjoy their company. I try to help them in my own peculiar way."

"You helped that bloody Polvo, all right," declared Knotty, the dwarf. "That Polvo was low as a bloomin' whale's droppin's when you picked him up."

"It was after General Lafayette died," Polvo apologized. "He died right in my arms. I was all broke up."

"Take out George Washington's teeth so you can enunciate more clearly," Tommy Twotoes instructed Polvo. "The redoubtable Killer is right. You had become a mission stiff. There is nothing lower."

"A mission stiff is even lower than a cop," put in Shakey.

"It was like I was George Washington and you come and took me out of Valley Forge," said Polvo, who had removed his false teeth.

"You faced a far worse fate than merely freezing in the snow," Tommy Twotoes declared. "You were on the very brink of being reformed. A fate worse than death. However, you have repaid me fully."

He addressed his intent and respectful audience. "Polvo," he said, "is an excellent chef. His shish-kebab is noteworthy, which leads me to believe my modern reincarnation of George Washington may have a dash of Armenian in him. Proving our country really is a melting pot. My late lamented chef had died of drinking cooking sherry when the best liquors of the Continent were available to him." Tommy Twotoes shook his big head sadly and the flabby jowls trembled with the movement. "A man may drink all sorts of vile liquors," he said, "but once he resorts to cooking sherry, the fires of the crematorium begin to glow red for him. Fortunately, the good Polvo has filled my departed chef's place quite adequately."

"I take good care of the penguins, too, I do," said Polvo.

"What?" I asked in surprise.

"Penguins," said Tommy Twotoes. "*Spheniscidae.* Some wealthy men cultivate blondes in penthouses. Others cultivate orchids in hothouses. I cultivate penguins in coldhouses. Penguins are most delightful birds and the study of them is highly instructive. They exhibit all the more villainous mores of the human race. They are complete egoists and their behavior patterns are decidedly unchristian. The study of penguins might help you to solve your problems, Soldier."

"What problems?" I asked suspiciously.

Tommy Twotoes' little eyes regarded me steadily from their folds of flesh for a minute. I felt as though I were being stripped naked. Finally he said vaguely, "Oh, we all have our little problems, don't we?"

Having disposed of my problems, Tommy Twotoes returned to the penguins. "Unfortunately," he said, "I have been unsuccessful in discovering a method of making penguins breed in captivity, even though authorities on the *Impennes* order insist that they are the most maternal and paternal of all birds—"

"Maybe them vitamins will work on 'em," said Polvo hopefully.

"Hormones," corrected Tommy Twotoes.

"Yeah," said Polvo. "It was last week we give 'em the vitamins."

Suds was kept so busy refilling glasses and uncorking fresh bottles that he had no time to listen to his soap operas, although he cast a wistful glance at his radio occasionally. After Tommy Twotoes had assured himself that all his guests were being served promptly, he turned to me again.

"Before the subject of mission stiffs and penguins arose," he said, "I was saying that I attempt to help my good friends here in my own peculiar way. Unfortunately, my own peculiar way is looked upon askance by the constituted authorities of our social system. In my estimation, true charity does not consist in giving a man what you believe he needs. It consists in giving him what he wants. Few of these men want such usual relief handouts as soup, sandwiches and fumigated clothing. They do desperately want enough alcohol to keep them alive. This I try to supply them from time to time. It has long been my fondest desire to establish a chain of clubhouses on the Skid Rows of the nation wherein duly accredited bohemians, or bums, if you prefer the vulgarism, may quench their thirst without cost and have clean beds on which to sleep off their drunks. I have tried hard to make provisions for such a worthy foundation in my last will and testament. But my attorneys assure me it is out of the question. They maintain that Civic Virtue would rear its ugly head and overrule any such bequest I might make and that eventually my estate would be deflected to the support of missions and the type of welfare societies that I abhor. This would constitute the foulest sort of knavery, of course, but I am assured it could be legally accomplished."

Tommy Twotoes shook his head and the flabby jowls trembled again. He said, "I won't have that! And so I do the best I can during my lifetime. I visit my friends in their native haunts and together we look upon the wine when it is red. Or I have groups of the boys visit me at my estate, where we drink good liquor, eat good food and make good talk for a week or so. It is a poor thing, but it is the best that I can offer."

"Maybe you don't like apologies," I said, "but, by God, I'm sorry for the things I said to you the last time we met. You are a man of noble impulses."

"You do me too much honor, sir," he replied. "Or else you insult me. Men of noble impulses are usually deadly bores."

Suddenly he turned to the boys and inquired, "Does any of you have a good singing voice? I need a man to sing to my penguins. Perhaps good singing might encourage them to breed. During Scott's last expedition to the Antarctic in 1910, his men discovered that singing delighted their penguin audience. The penguins came to expect the explorers to sing at a regular hour every evening and would assemble immediately after dinner for a concert. However, penguins are severe critics. One of the men of the expedition sang flat and the penguins would invariably scream him down before he had finished half a bar."

"I sing pretty good," said Killer Carney eagerly, anticipating an invitation to Tommy Twotoes' baronial acres. "Mrs. Sapoloukos' little girl, Circe, likes the way I sing her to sleep when I'm a baby sitter for her."

"Fill the glasses, Suds!" called Tommy Twotoes. "The Killer is about to burst into song."

The glasses were refilled, and after clearing his throat a few times, the Killer began to render a song about the misadventures of a drunk who fell into a garbage can.

The Killer choked on alcoholic phlegm in the middle of his rendition, and Tommy Twotoes shook his head sadly.

"No, Killer," he said. "Your talents lie in other directions, I fear. You were a doughty battler in your day, you are a tosspot of no mean accomplishments and your reputation as a baby sitter is of the highest. But I'm afraid your singing would be most unfavorably received by my penguins."

"Maybe if they had some little penguins I could come up and baby sit 'em for you," suggested the crestfallen but still hopeful Killer.

"As I've remarked," said Tommy Twotoes, "my penguins have thus far refused to breed in captivity, even though I have gone to great expense and considerable pains to have a miniature Antarctic constructed for them on my estate. But even if a sudden wave of rutting should sweep through the rookeries and the birth rate surpass that of the Lower East Side, I doubt they would require the services of a baby sitter. They are fiercely and possessively maternal and paternal. Sometimes barren penguins even attempt to hatch rocks."

All of the boys immediately began to hint for invitations to Tommy Twotoes' place, each constituting himself a penguin authority.

It was evident that the Professor had known of Tommy Twotoes' penguin rookeries and had done a little reading up on the subject. He said, "My own studies have been devoted mostly to the field of physics, particularly to nuclear fission, in recent years. But I have a smattering of ornithology. Any well-rounded scientist must have." The Professor shrugged modestly. "I would welcome the opportunity to observe these intriguing birds of yours at first hand," he hinted.

"My pater was a clown," said Knotty, the dwarf, screwing the monocle securely in his eye. "A bloody good one, too. Used a parrot in his act. Used to study the parrot when h'I was a shaver. Cawn't imagine there's much difference between a parrot and a penguin, rahlly. Both bloomin' birds, y'know.

Basserty, the Beard, said, "I know a lot about animal psychology. Had to, as a horseman. Birds are just animals with wings, I guess. Often wished some of the horses I rode did have wings, in fact. We had an old mare at a farm near the Timonium track in Maryland once. Well-bred thing, but she was stud-shy. So scared of a stallion we couldn't breed her. Then we tried putting ginger in her fodder and she had a foal every year, regular as clockwork. You let me come up and feed those penguins of yours a little ginger. That's what they need."

"If them penguins like singing, they must like poetry," declared Shakey. He fished in the waistline of his pants and brought out the volume of Shakespeare. "You ever read 'em Shakespeare's sonnets? Or 'Venus and Adonis'? There's some pretty hot stuff in them pomes. You let me come up and read Shakespeare's pomes to your penguins and maybe it'll give 'em ideas. Maybe they'll start breeding like rabbits."

Poor Killer Carney, who had failed in his audition as a singer and whose services as a baby sitter for penguin chicks were not required, appeared very dejected.

Tommy Twotoes again turned his attention to me. "Soldier," he said, "you look to me as if you'd have a good baritone voice. Why don't you come up and sing to my penguins?"

"How can you tell a man's singing voice from his appearance?" I inquired.

"It's a Twotoes adaptation of the Lombroso theory," he explained. "Tenors and bassos are usually either squat, heavy men or tall, broad-shouldered heavyweights. Baritones, as a rule, are the rangy type, with determined chins. Best baritone I ever knew was a light-heavyweight contender I used to manage."

The fact of the matter was that I had sung a fair baritone with my college glee club. Tommy Twotoes' offer was tempting. I could hardly think of a more comfortable hideout than a millionaire's estate with a well-stocked cellar. However, I remembered that within a few hours my picture might be plastered over page one of a tabloid and I didn't imagine Mr. Twotoes would be willing to harbor a murder suspect, despite his unconventional outlook on life.

"Sorry," I told him. "I must be the exception that proves the rule. I used to sing a very elegant soprano in the boys' choir of my church, but then my voice changed and I lost my religion when I couldn't earn a dollar every Sunday. I'm afraid you'll have to engage another minnesinger for your penguins."

"Why don't you come up and visit me anyway?" he pressed. "Perhaps you may rediscover the dulcet soprano of your callow youth. I feel sure my penguins would react favorably to a good

soprano voice. However, I must ban church music from your rep-
ertoire. Penguins, as I have stated, are distinctly unchristian. Polar
explorers have discovered they prefer the bawdier type of ballads.
In any event, I think you should come up with me. My place
would furnish an ideal retreat for you at the present time."

I regarded the gross, flabby man with suspicion. "Why do you
think I require 'a retreat at the present time'?" I asked.

"Later, Soldier, later," he replied. "I told you that I wished to
speak to you in private."

By the time the case of brandy that Ebony Black had brought
from the car was exhausted and the giant Negro had been sent for
another, many of the boys had passed out cold. They were draped
about Grogan's Elite Palace Café and Bar in various grotesque
poses and the cacophony of their snores rose and fell in the room
like an amplified chorus of gargantuan mosquitoes. Tommy Twotoes' brandy was much too rich for the enlarged livers of most of
the winos and smokeheads who had partaken of it.

Mr. Twotoes himself showed few effects of the liberal libations
he had consumed. He lectured me at length upon Clausewitz'
theory of warfare, with sidelights upon the tactical maneuvers of
Stonewall Jackson, evidently believing I was a military expert because I'd fought in a war and they called me "Soldier." He and the
Professor dealt with the obscurer phases of nuclear fission. The
Professor was even encouraged to explain the Einstein theory in a
few well-chosen words. "A man standing on a corner and a man in
a moving car both see a stoplight change at the same instant," he
said. "That's all there is to relativity."

The old man needled Shakey by expounding the theory that
the Baron Verulam, Sir Francis Bacon, was responsible for all the
plays ascribed to William Shakespeare. He argued with Basserty
over the merits of the Bruce Lowe System of classifying race horses
into numbered thoroughbred families. He entertained Knotty, the
dwarf, with a scholarly discussion of the evolution of circus clowns

from medieval court jesters and miracle play buffoons. He had just launched into a biographical sketch of Jack Broughton, the father of English pugilism, for the benefit of Killer Carney and Ebony Black when Kerrigan, the cop who never arrested anybody, came into the saloon for his afternoon shot on the house.

Officer Kerrigan looked with surprise upon the dozing drunks who made a stertorous waxworks of Grogan's grog shop. Then the red-faced policeman discovered Tommy Twotoes and hurried to our table, beaming as rosily as a stoplight. Shakey, the cop-hater, began to make menacing sounds in his throat as Kerrigan approached the table.

I felt damned uncomfortable as Kerrigan extended his hand and greeted Tommy Twotoes with bumbling effusiveness. Of course, I knew of Kerrigan's reputation as a cop who only walked his beat because that was the shortest distance between saloons where he could free load, but I felt damned awkward just the same. I tried to make myself as small as possible and to avert the side of my face that had the scar concealed under a bandage. Out of respect for Shakey's prejudices, Tommy didn't offer Kerrigan a drink, but I saw him slip the cop a bill surreptitiously. It looked like a sawbuck.

I didn't like the few remarks that passed between Kerrigan and Tommy Twotoes, either.

"Well, Officer Kerrigan," said Tommy. "Have you apprehended any murderers recently?"

"Aw, I don't bother none of the boys unless'n they do something real bad," replied Kerrigan. "Do I, boys?"

Nobody answered except Shakey, who growled something that sounded like "stinker."

"Perhaps I can put you in the way of arresting a murderer before long," said Tommy Twotoes jocularly.

"You just point him out to me and I'll oblige by putting the bracelets on him," promised Kerrigan.

"Officer Kerrigan, you're an ornament of the forces of law and order," Tommy Twotoes declared.

"Thank you, sir!" exclaimed the bedazzled cop. "Thank you very much indeed!" He made his way to his private free-loading room in the rear.

"Ornament of law and order!" sneered Shakey. "I seen that son of a bitch kick a poor old bum to death with his big flat feet onct. Over on Delancey Street, it was. Poor old bum was over eighty. All he was trying to do was brace a guy for a shot of Sneaky Pete. That Kerrigan stomped on his face till his teeth bounced on the sidewalk like poker dice. Then Kerrigan ground his heel in the old bum's eyes till the eyeballs come squirming out of the sockets and run right down his cheeks like a coupla aggies in a game of marbles. Ornament of law and order!"

"Now, now, Shakey," admonished Tommy Twotoes, "you wouldn't have us believe that our gentle friend Kerrigan is like the Marquis de Sade, would you?"

"I don't know what a marky sad is," said Shakey. "But Kerrigan's worse."

The maligned Kerrigan came out of the back room, wiping his mouth on the heel of his hand, waved to Tommy Twotoes and left Grogan's for the next call he had to make in the line of duty and refreshment.

"Now that Officer Kerrigan has vacated his private office, I think you and I will make use of it, Soldier," Tommy Twotoes said. "If you will assist me to my feet, gentlemen . . ."

Ebony Black and Killer Carney hoisted the heavy bulk of Tommy Twotoes and led him through the curtains of the back room. I did not follow at once. I sat there watching the two big men escort the old millionaire across the saloon and wondered just what the hell he had to say to me that couldn't be said in public.

Ebony Black and the Killer returned to the table after they had deposited Tommy in the back room. Ebony Black spoke to me. "The boss wants to see you," he said. That was all he said. He spoke softly. His voice was even musical in a deep-throated way. But somehow I detected a menacing undertone in it. Ebony Black seemed to be saying that I could go under my own power or be carried. I went to the back room.

Tommy Twotoes hadn't bothered to go through the physical convolutions that were necessary to seat himself. He stood braced against a heavy table.

He said, "Well, Terence R. Rooke, how does it feel to be a fugitive from justice?"

7

I stood for a long minute just looking at him. There was a lot of him to look at. I couldn't think of anything to say. Finally I said something very original. I said, "I don't know what the hell you mean."

There wasn't even a flicker in the little eye-slits of his doughy face. He said, "You know quite well what I mean, Terence."

"My name's Soldier, not Terence," I told him.

"I should have preferred to discuss this matter in the privacy of my study," he replied. "It is soundproof. But I failed to persuade you to visit me at my home. However, since Ebony Black is standing guard outside, we are not likely to attract eavesdroppers. Perhaps now you will accept my hospitality. The alternative might prove most unpleasant for you. For the present, suffice it to say that I never forget a face. I was on the sixth floor of the Sheridan Towers Hotel on the afternoon of the twentieth. I saw you. I knew that I had seen you before, but the clothes you were wearing distracted me. I could not place you until I read a story in the paper last night. About a war veteran. With a scar on his face. Then I remembered the man called Soldier. The one who had spoken his mind to me. I remembered that I was coming here today. I had already called the Killer to tell him so. After I read the newspapers, I called the Killer again."

"You talk like a man with a hole in his head," I said.

"No, Terence. I don't talk like a man with a hole in his head. But I am thinking of a woman with a hole in her heart."

"You don't make sense," I insisted desperately. "What's your angle? Why should you want me to come to your home with you?"

"Perhaps I merely like your company," he said. "Or perhaps I wish to hear your story."

"I haven't got any story."

"You can't sing baritone. You have no story to tell me. Still, I crave your company, Terence. Again I proffer my hospitality. Will you accept it, or shall I leave you here under the guard of Ebony Black while I dispatch one of the boys for Officer Kerrigan? He might be interested in meeting George Spelvin, you know."

I'm not too bad with my mitts and I learned a lot of dirty stuff in the Army. Ebony Black must have been nearing sixty, but I still had no desire to tangle with the one-eyed colossus. The other boys liked me well enough. But I knew if it came to a showdown they'd do anything that Tommy Twotoes told them to do. I figured I was outnumbered. I'd have figured I was outnumbered if I'd only had Ebony Black to deal with. I gave in.

"I accept the kind invitation of Mr. Tommy Twotoes with pleasure," I said.

"Excellent!" said Tommy Twotoes heartily. "Polvo and Ebony Black and I will do our best to make your stay with us a pleasant one. And now I must return to my guests or they will deem me wanting in courtesy. If you will be good enough to range along my port side and summon Ebony Black to convoy me to starboard . . ."

I called the one-eyed Negro and we propelled the man-mountain back to his table. Sad Eyes had come on duty for the evening, but Suds agreed to stay for a while to help out, doubtless anticipating the fact that Tommy Twotoes would tip him heavily. Since Suds had refused alcoholic beverages, Tommy had sent out for a case of milk, which Suds and the cat, Stella Dallas, split between them.

Bums from remote sections of the Bowery and other Skid Row neighborhoods had heard of the free load through the grapevine and more customers were pressing their way into Grogan's ginmill every minute. Besides, the boys who had passed out earlier had begun to wake up and were starting all over again. All in all, it was a gala evening at Grogan's Elite Palace Café and Bar.

Tommy Twotoes said, "Ebony, I think it's time we ate. You made arrangements with the caterers, didn't you?"

"Yes, boss," replied Ebony Black.

"Call them and tell them we are ready to have them serve," Tommy instructed the old heavyweight.

"No doubt some of the boys will object to solid nourishment on constitutional grounds," said Tommy Twotoes, "but I have found it best for a drinking man to eat and I have selected viands that may tempt the delicate appetites of my guests."

After a while a small truck pulled up at the door of Grogan's. It bore the name of one of the swankiest caterers in the city, a concern that usually laid out the fodder for such clambakes as debutante balls and receptions for visiting royalty. Two very supercilious waiters clad in tails and white ties accompanied the truck. They obviously didn't like the smell of Grogan's creep joint, but they went through the motions of serving the food with a demeanor that was eminently correct.

Tommy Twotoes had ordered the boys a very fancy free lunch. I can't remember all the items on the menu, but there was fresh caviar, crème vichysoisse, lobster Newburg, broiled squab with wild rice, and asparagus hollandaise. Knowing a drunk's allergy toward sweetmeats, Tommy had ordered a ripe old cheese instead of dessert. The caterers also supplied the champagne, since Grogan's never had any calls for such a sissy drink. They had evidently expected the saloon to have coolers, however, for they hadn't brought any along with them, and it was necessary for the haughty waiters to chill the bubbly in mop buckets that Suds and Sad Eyes brought out of a storage closet.

Despite the food, I was beginning to get pretty drunk. Maybe it was just as well. Cops kept sticking their noses into the place to see what the hell was going on and to gorge themselves on the free lunch, and I didn't even mind them, although they set Shakey to snarling. And if my nervous system hadn't been quieted down by copious quantities of brandy and champagne, I would have jumped out of Tommy Twotoes' car a short while later and dashed down Broadway, bowling over the pedestrians in my path.

At some point of the evening, an old man came in selling newspapers. Tommy Twotoes bought both the morning tabs and told the old man to keep the change from the five-dollar bill he handed him. He left the newspapers folded on the table beside him, but I managed to sneak a peek at the *News* when he wasn't looking, and it was there, all right. The picture of me was captioned "EXCLUSIVE PHOTO OF MURDER SUSPECT" and underneath there was some small type stating that the photograph was copyrighted by the *News*, and I wondered how in hell a paper could copyright a picture of me that had been taken from my girl's bedroom—even if it had been taken with my girl's permission. There was so much going on that nobody paid any attention to me. I slipped the paper back under the *Mirror* so that my picture would be covered.

The caterers cleaned up the remains of the feast and took themselves off. Finally, even Tommy Twotoes' seemingly inexhaustible supply of blue-crocked brandy began to run low.

"It is growing late and I am growing old," said Tommy Twotoes. "Polvo, do you have the satchel?"

"Right here," said Polvo eagerly, producing a brief case and drawing himself up importantly to his full height of about five feet. He inserted the sea-horse ivory false teeth that were modeled after George Washington's, so it was evident that he was about to act in an official capacity.

"Just a moment," said Tommy, raising a restraining hand. "Before we begin, I have an announcement to make." A hush came over the room, except for occasional snores from those who had succumbed to the torpor induced by heady brandy and rich food.

"The Soldier has kindly consented to visit me," continued Tommy Twotoes. There was a little mumbling of disappointment among those who had not been invited. "He will accompany me tonight in the town car. But I have a special job for a few of you others." This announcement brought a murmur of excitement and renewed hope. "I have chosen the Killer, Basserty, the Professor, Shakey and Knotty for this special assignment. Ebony Black will pick them up here tomorrow morning, promptly at nine. You will bring the station wagon, Ebony, so our guests will not be crowded. Now, if you please, Polvo, we will proceed with the dispensation. Killer, you and Ebony Black will act as sergeants-at-arms."

The Killer took his place beside Polvo and the giant Negro, fairly bristling with the responsibility bestowed upon him. "They won't none of these bums get no second helpings with me, here," he assured Tommy "I know 'em all, I do."

A single-file line began to form in the saloon. It reached in serpentine fashion from the table at which we were sitting clear out into the street. The slumberers awakened suddenly as the line began to form as though some psychic alarm clock had jangled in their sleep-sodden heads. Polvo opened the brief case dramatically and began to extract its contents. The brief case was filled with crisp new ten-dollar bills. Polvo stacked them in neat piles. As each of the boys passed by, under the watchful eyes of Ebony Black and the Killer, he was handed one of the bills. Each tipped his cap or battered hat as he received the money and said, "Thank you, Mr. Tommy," or "Bless you, Mr. Tommy," or made a tearful and more emotional acknowledgment of the gift.

After the long line had finally passed the pay-off table, Suds and Sad Eyes were kept busy enacting the role of bank tellers.

Several of the boys who had reached a stage of drunkenness where they were afraid of being rolled but who were still cagey insisted upon depositing all or part of their windfalls for safekeeping. The bartenders jotted down the amounts and the names of the depositors in Grogan's Security Company.

As Tommy Twotoes was assisted to his feet preparatory to leaving the saloon, Killer Carney jumped on the table and called, "Hey, fellas! Three cheers for Tommy Twotoes!"

A stranger cheerleader never gesticulated in front of a more grotesque audience. The rah-rah-rahs resounded in Grogan's Elite Palace Café and Bar, though some of them were little more than alcoholic croaks. The Professor, who claimed to be a Princeton graduate, added a "sis-boom-rah-Tiger" of his own accord. The reception tendered by Mr. Tommy Twotoes to the Bowery's bohemians thus ended on a note of academic ebullience.

During the ride uptown in Tommy Twotoes' town car I suddenly became sleepy. The mellow brandy and the rich food must have hit me like a delayed action bomb. I didn't even consider my peculiar situation. My fate, which hitherto had rested with luck and Chet Lassiter, was now in the hands of the world's most eccentric millionaire, an unconventional and unpredictable alcoholic whom I hardly knew. For the moment, however, I felt only delightfully drowsy and glutted and the small, insistent voice of worry within me was completely stilled. I was entirely content to sink down on that portion of the upholstered seat cushion that wasn't occupied by Mr. Twotoes' gargantuan bulk and to let the pleasant torpor wash over me.

The car stopped and drew up to a curbing after a short drive. Tommy Twotoes flicked on the light in the back seat and looked at the front page of the *News* he had purchased. He said, "The photograph of you is rather a good likeness, Soldier, but it must have been taken before you got the scar, unless, in your vanity, you had it retouched."

I didn't answer him because something more urgent was occupying my entire attention.

"This is the Sheridan Towers!" I exclaimed.

"So it is," replied Tommy Twotoes calmly. "But there is no need for you to be nervous, Soldier. I have been accused of many things, usually with entire justification, but the police have never yet suspected me of harboring men wanted for murder. I am still registered at this hotel, you see. Polvo and Ebony Black have gone inside to collect my baggage and to check me out."

Tommy Twotoes switched of the light and at almost that exact moment someone opened the door of the town car and stuck his head inside. I jumped like a two-year-old colt that has been hit with an electric battery. Tommy Twotoes placed a reassuring hand on my knee but I was already shaking with fright and beaded with sweat. The man's head was turned toward Tommy, who, fortunately, was sitting on the side nearest to the curbing. The man's sculptured, heavily defined features reminded me of the profile on an ancient Roman coin that had been in the collection of an uncle of mine when I was a child.

"Well, Tommy!" said the man. "Knew it must be you when I saw the rig. It's one in a million. Why don't you turn it in on a new bicycle?"

"If it isn't Lieutenant Romano of the Homicide Squad!" said Tommy

I averted my head so fast I almost broke my neck. I didn't want to attract undue attention to myself, but I faked a coughing fit so I would have an excuse for covering my face with a handkerchief. Thank God, the bandage-covered scar was on the side of my face that was turned away from the detective. Romano regarded me curiously. It was almost dark, but I felt as though they had me under the big light in the goldfish bowl where suspects are paraded in the police line-up.

"I see you're taking one of the boys home with you," said Romano. He spoke pleasantly enough, but I thought I could detect a menacing edge to his tone.

"Yes," replied Tommy. "He sings baritone. He is coming up to sing to my penguins. My penguins ark at baritones like schoolgirls squeal at certain sickly tenors."

"How are the penguins?" inquired Romano.

"They stubbornly refuse to propagate their kind," Tommy Twotoes answered. "We have tried hormones, vitamins and an assortment of nostrums, even including illicit cantharides, or Spanish fly. All to no avail. The males remain as impotent as the Nubian eunuchs of an ancient queen and the females as frigid as a statue of a spinster hewn in granite. I am beginning to despair."

"Maybe you got a bunch of queers," suggested Romano.

"It is possible," replied Tommy. "I am thinking of engaging the services of a psychiatrist for my birds."

There I was, sweating with the kind of terror I hadn't known since the Japs came howling at us in a banzai charge on Los Negros and these two smug bastards were casually discussing the sexual shortcomings of penguins in captivity.

"You staying at this hotel, Tommy?" asked Romano, making an absurd attempt to sound as if the question were of little or no importance.

Tommy Twotoes chuckled.

"Lieutenant," he replied, "let's not be so heavy handed. It doesn't become an officer of your intelligence. You doubtless know quite well that I've been staying here. On the sixth floor. I even registered under my own name."

"Too bad about Danise," said Romano, quite unperturbed by Tommy's admonition. "Old flame of yours, I seem to remember."

"The last, and in many ways the most desirable, of an old man's darlings," said Tommy Twotoes. "And unless recollection fails me in my advancing years, she was also an acquaintance of yours, Lieutenant."

"Oh, yeah, I knew her," Romano replied.

"As did every rugged and virile male of Broadway," said Tommy. "Danise, I fear, had a regrettable weakness for rugged and virile males."

"Yeah," said Romano. "I found that out. Well, I gotta shove off and talk to a editor. Probably he won't say anything, but I gotta talk to him anyhow. The *News* run a picture of this jerk which maybe stuck a sharp instrument into poor Danise. I'd like to know where they got hold of this picture."

"If you want me for further questioning, you'll find me at my place up the Hudson," said Tommy. "I'd be very much interested in learning where they got that picture, too."

"Now why would I ever want you for questioning?" asked Romano innocently. "But maybe I might come up just to chew the fat about old times on the Street and drink some of that fancy brandy of yours. And to tell you about the picture if I find out anything myself."

"You do that, Lieutenant," Tommy Twotoes said.

Before I could recover sufficiently from the shock to say anything, Polvo and Ebony Black arrived with the baggage. While they were piling it in the luggage trunk that had recently held the cases of French brandy, Tommy Twotoes opened the glove compartment and produced a blue crock. He found a metal drinking cup in the same compartment and poured me a healthy slug.

"I think you need this, Soldier," was all he said.

I had to hold the cup in both hands to get it up to my mouth. After I'd swallowed the brandy, I blurted, "What the hell are you trying to do to me?"

"Nothing, Soldier, nothing," he said soothingly. "Our meeting with Lieutenant Romano was purely accidental, an eventuality I had no means of foreseeing. But perhaps it is just as well. He showed little interest in you, even though he must have seen your photograph only a short while before. That means you will not be too readily identified through the photograph alone."

I was by no means placated. "God damn you!" I flared. "You knew the murdered woman. She was your mistress once, from what that copper said. You were in the hotel when she was chilled. On the same floor. Maybe you killed her. Or maybe you had the big Negro or the little greaseball who wears George Washington's teeth stick an ice pick in her heart."

"That might easily have happened, of course," Tommy Two-toes said. "Even Lieutenant Romano, one of the numerous Broadway cops I used to pay off when I was interested in the operation of speakeasies, seems to suspect that something of the sort might have occurred."

"There's something phony about your wanting me to come up to your place," I continued. "I'm drunk, but I can still figure angles. I'm hot with the cops. They want me. It's going to be nice for you to have me around so you can produce me the minute the bloodhounds start yapping too close to your heels. I'm not having any, Mr. Twotoes. I'm passing the deal. I'm leaving right now."

I reached for the door handle but at that second Ebony Black started the car. I fell back against the seat cushions, and Tommy Twotoes put a restraining hand on my knee.

"Don't be too hasty, Soldier," he said. "I don't think you'd get far if I set Ebony Black after you. And a chase would create a most undesirable commotion on such a crowded thoroughfare. You may have good reason to suspect that I killed Danise, or that I had her killed. But proof of the fact is lacking. And proof of the fact that you did not kill her is lacking, also. If I were responsible for Danise's death, it would be my nature to conceal my guilt in every possible way, even perhaps to making someone else the scapegoat. But try, for a moment, to assume that I am not responsible, that

I am an old man who treasures the memory of his last sweetheart, who is shocked by her brutal murder, and who is determined to use every recourse at his command to make the guilty person pay. That is another way of explaining why I desire your company and wish to talk to you in private. Guilty or innocent, you must know many things I want to know. I intend to find them out."

There was a long silence. Ebony Black drove the ancient town car very slowly up Riverside Drive, but I did not try to escape from it again. I tried to think, but I was befuddled. It wasn't only the drink. It was too many suspects. Up to now, Vince Parada had been Exhibit A in my mental rogues' gallery. For personal reasons he still was, of course. But there was Malcolm Little, the woman's husband, who perhaps had the best motive of all and who had no witnesses as to his whereabouts at the time the murder was committed. There was the mysterious, ghostly Mr. Provost, who had occupied Room 617 and who had disappeared into thin air about the time of the murder. And now there was Tommy Twotoes and his two ill-assorted henchmen, the gigantic, one-eyed Negro and the undersized Slav who wore George Washington's false teeth.

Also, of course, there was myself, Terry Bob Rooke, a shell-shocked guy who got a red haze in front of his eyes at times and who could not account satisfactorily for his actions during the all-important afternoon hours of the twentieth. I thought of something that Clarence Darrow had once said. The great criminal lawyer had remarked that most men haven't killed anybody but that they have read obituaries with pleasure. I was one of the men who had killed. Strictly in the line of duty, of course. The great majority of soldiers go through a war shooting their guns and throwing their grenades and never knowing for sure if they've hit anybody in the wild confusion of battle. But there was a lot of in-fighting in the Pacific. Close-up stuff. When you were spraying bullets out of a 50-caliber gun and little men just a few yards in front of your tank began to fall down and various parts of their anatomies began to fly through the air with the greatest of ease, you were pretty certain of the fact that you and nobody else was responsible for their sudden demise.

I thought that maybe there is a certain sadism latent in all of us and that once we've tasted blood it's hard to slake our craving for it. Maybe the urge for killing swept over me during the spells, the temporary blackouts that came after I'd been angry or gone through some emotional conflict. How else could I account for the fact that I had imagined the woman with a hole in her heart was sitting in a chair completely naked when actually she was lying on a bed completely clothed? How else could I account for the fact that I'd searched the room for her luggage and clothes and found none, when her belongings were all over the place?

But I hadn't imagined the events of the night before. I had a lump on the back of my noggin that testified to their reality. The night before somebody—with the connivance of my girl friend, it seemed—had tried to murder me.

I was too drunk and sleepy and confused to think things out. Suddenly it seemed to me that the flabby bulk of the silent old man beside me emanated strength and power. I had placed my fate completely in his hands, and, for the moment at least, I was content to let it rest there. I was like a sick man who submits fatalistically to the ether and the surgeon's knife

At length Tommy Twotoes said, "You must bear with me, Soldier. I am known for my idiosyncrasies, but oftener than not there is a method in my madness. The sporting press, for instance, adjudged me quite insane that time I gave birthday presents to fourteen hundred horses."

I suppose he had intended to rock me out of my reverie, and he was entirely successful.

"You what?" I asked incredulously.

"I presented fourteen hundred horses with appropriate birthday presents," replied the old man, chuckling at the memory. "It created quite a sensation and caused a great deal of comment. That was what I was seeking—publicity. It was quite a long while ago when I was operating the race track in Mexico. My general manager, Judge Andy Boots, who was quite a character in his own right, and I were celebrating New Year's Eve with some excellent brandy that had just come in on one of the ships in my rum fleet. We were at a border town in the States. When the clock struck midnight and the bells began to clamor and the sirens to shriek, I said to the Judge, 'Andy, do you know what day this is?'

"He replied accurately enough, that it was New Year's, 1925. 'Andy,' I told him, 'you are both drunk and ignorant. This is the birthday of every horse at our race track, and it behooves us to do something about the matter.'"

Tommy poured two metal cups of the brandy from the blue crock and passed one to me. Evidently he was offering a toast to old and pleasant memories.

"You see," he explained, "all American thoroughbreds have their official birthdays on January first, regardless of the date they were foaled. It is a matter of convenience in arranging races for the various age divisions. There were about fourteen hundred horses, including lead ponies, at our track, and I instructed Judge Boots to obtain a pound of lump sugar for each and every one of them as a birthday present. Andy protested that it was quite impossible to procure fourteen hundred pound packages of sugar lumps at that hour of the night. I replied that I employed only men who could accomplish the impossible. Andy aroused wholesale and retail grocers for miles around from their connubial couches on that well-remembered evening and by morning we had the necessary number of gifts, all neatly wrapped in tissue and tied with blue ribbon for colts, geldings and stallions, pink ribbon for fillies and mares "

Despite my anger and my generally addled state of mind, I couldn't help laughing. Tommy Twotoes said, "So you see, my methods are highly unconventional, but at times they bring results. I suggest that despite your suspicions, which are not entirely unwarranted, you should trust me. We have a tedious drive before us. I won't allow Ebony to proceed at more than thirty miles an hour. Having thus far survived the ravages of a misspent life, I have no intention of being killed in a traffic accident at this advanced age. I suggest you try to sleep, Soldier, and refresh yourself. I will keep you awake for most of the night after our arrival. I intend to talk to you at some length, regardless of your own desires. I feel it is my duty to protect you from yourself—and, perhaps, from others."

"What others?" I asked.

"I am not prepared to state their identity until we have had our talk," he replied. "But it is fairly obvious that if you are guiltless, there must be certain well-directed forces working against you. The corpse was found in the room you were occupying. You were identified to a newspaper by an anonymous source. Your picture was sent to a newspaper. I told you a while ago that there might be a parable for you in the unchristian lives led by penguins."

The old man was obviously enjoying his recital, although I failed to see what relation the habits of penguins had to my peculiar and precarious situation.

Tommy Twotoes continued: "When the penguin flock goes down to the sea to bathe or to seek food, they appear to the casual observer to be the most friendly social group imaginable. They chatter gaily of how fine the water is going to be and speculate upon the dainty morsels that are in store for them once they have taken the plunge. They concentrate upon some weak-minded penguin and try to persuade him to take the first dive. This expendable penguin thus becomes bait for any sea leopards, their hereditary enemies, that may be in the vicinity. If he is not devoured, the others risk the plunge. If the weak-minded penguin cannot be persuaded through flattery or cajolery, the flock passes a conscription act, and he is immediately shoved into the water. Often his mate and his friends are the ringleaders in forcing such foolhardy heroism upon him."

I couldn't see him in the darkness but I felt that the little slits of his eyes were regarding me shrewdly.

"Your little lecture seems to indicate that it is dangerous for a person to trust anyone else, although you have just suggested that I should place my trust in you," I said.

Tommy Twotoes chuckled. "You are beginning to comprehend the Parable of the Penguins," he said. "Now I think you should try and go to sleep."

I dozed fitfully for the rest of the journey. When I awakened it was midnight and we were passing through the silent streets of Tarrytown. The car turned onto a road which wound up a bluff that overlooked the moon-silvered river. I could see a towering structure looming darkly against the sky, like some turreted castle of the Middle Ages. I thought at first that this was Tommy Two-toes' home, but I soon learned that it was his penguin rookeries. The house itself was a low, functional modernistic building that might have been designed by Frank Lloyd Wright, and it appeared insignificant beside the tiered rookeries where Tommy Twotoes' persistently sterile penguins dwelt.

As the ancient auto chugged and clattered up the driveway of the estate, a wild, unearthly clamor ripped the night. The penguins were ark-ing their protest at having their rest disturbed by unseemly noises.

"My poor birds," said Tommy Twotoes. "It is thoughtless of me to interrupt their slumbers at such an hour. Fortunately, my nearest neighbor is my good friend, the bereaved Mr. Malcolm Little, and his estate is half a mile from here."

I laughed bitterly. "A guy should never go to a zoo when he's intoxicated," I said.

"You speak in riddles, Soldier," Tommy said. "What is the meaning of that remark?"

"He might stick his head in the lion's mouth," I replied.

Tommy Twotoes' house proved to be as extraordinary and contradictory as its incredible owner.

"I don't particularly admire modern architecture," he explained. "My own taste inclines more toward the baroque and rococo. However, the house which this architect designed is eminently adaptable to the use of a crippled old man. The man who designed it employed gradually rising ramps instead of stairways to reach the different levels. I found, however, that there were some days on which even the ramps were a problem, so I had an escalator installed. The architect was aghast at the addition. He regarded me as the type of man who might pencil a mustache on the Mona Lisa. He even sued me."

The first thing I noticed at Tommy Twotoes' house was the sign on the front door. It was a little metal sign and it read "Repeal the 18th Amendment." Since the Eighteenth Amendment had been repealed in 1933 and since Tommy Twotoes' fortune had been made by Prohibition liquor as well as horses, fighters and half-clad girls, the sign seemed somewhat incongruous.

I suppose the interior of the house in its pristine state had been a shining example of the modern architect's aim of creating a machine to live in. Now it resembled nothing so much as an unclassified version of the Sears-Roebuck catalogue with a lot of typographical errors. I had never seen such a wild jumble of unrelated objects even after an air raid. The hallway was dominated by the sinuous bulk of the escalator and in the wan glow of the single night light I had the unpleasant impression that this mechanical stairway was a huge dinosaur lurking in the shadows and arching its neck.

Ebony Black switched on some lights and I began to discern other things—more things than I could possibly enumerate from memory. There was a totem pole that doubled as a hall tree, for instance.

Tommy Twotoes was saying, "You see, I am the bane of interior decorators. I dislike interior decorators. They cut their hair too long. I surround myself with things that are useful to me or that mean something to me. The totem pole, for instance, is a relic of my youth, when I panned for gold in Alaska. It also has a sentimental association, because the second face from the top resembles my great-uncle, who was a Baptist preacher."

On the walls near the totem pole hung a pair of boxing gloves once worn by the great Negro fighter Sam Langford, a bat that had belonged to Ty Cobb, a set of racing plates that had once been shod to the ground-devouring hoofs of the gallant gelding, Exterminator. All were duly labeled, like exhibits in museums. On another wall was an oil painting of heroic size and touching theme. It depicted a family of the Victorian era picnicking in sylvan surroundings beside a little summerhouse that resembled a miniature Greek temple. A young man wearing curly sideburns and a Prince Albert coat was surrounded by his adoring family. His wife was a pale, angelic creature in hoopskirts and his child a doll-like moppet with enormous eyes. A silky collie dog gazed worshipfully at his master. A brass plate attached to the ornate gilt frame proclaimed that the title of this work was "Reward of Virtue." Beside this painting was a colorful three-sheet poster on which was lithographed the likenesses of a number of high-kicking, buxom ballerinas of the late Billy Watson's Beef Trust. To this was attached a printed sign which read "The Reward of Vice."

Tommy Twotoes saw me examining the oil painting of the Victorian family curiously.

"That is also a pleasant souvenir of my youth," he said. "I once played the piano in a Barbary Coast bawdy house. The madam was a sentimental lady with a great respect for the homely virtues. That painting hung in the place of honor, directly above the piano, in the parlor of her sporting house."

I entered the living room, crossed a deep-piled Persian rug and ran an obstacle course of Early American cobbler's benches, Turkish ottomans, Victorian whatnots, Russian samovars and Japanese screens to find a seat in a Chinese throne chair that was inlaid with mother-of-pearl and flanked by a Duncan Phyfe coffee table and something that looked like a Biedermeier hope chest. In addition to the items enumerated, the room contained Empire love seats, a Grand Rapids mission library table, zebra-wood credenzas that were extremely *moderne*, slim-legged gilt Regency occasional chairs, marble-topped brass stands holding potted plants, and a huge, overstuffed article that appeared to be the result of cross-breeding an easy chair and a divan. This latter had been especially designed, I learned later, to contain the imposing bulk of Mr. Twotoes. The fourteen large and small tables in the room were littered with such things as ogreish African wood carvings, ivory Japanese back scratchers, gaily painted Toby jugs, Dresden shepherdesses, vases of flowers, beer mugs, wine glasses, decanters, ash trays and cigarette boxes of precious and semi-precious metal, china, glass, pottery and plastic, book ends fashioned in the shape of penguins, Rodin's "Thinker" and Grecian discus-throwers, and busts of such assorted characters as John L. Sullivan and William Shakespeare. The walls were covered from floor to ceiling with Aubusson tapestries, cuckoo clocks, Mexican sombreros, Moslem prayer rugs, Japanese kakemonos, Spanish shawls and pictures that varied from original pen-and-ink sketches by Milt Gross to excellent reproductions of paintings by DaVinci, Delacroix and Dali.

I sank down into the inlaid throne chair in utter bewilderment, but Tommy Twotoes, who was supported into the room by Ebony Black and Polvo, said, "Don't make yourself too comfortable, Soldier. I wish to interview you in the study."

Polvo touched an ornamental knob in the woodwork and a tapestry-covered panel opened silently, revealing another room.

Tommy said, "When I was a kid, I always wanted to have a house with a secret door. Now I have one. Just one of the rewards of a misspent life."

Polvo switched on a light. The study was by no means as startling as the living room. It contained the usual furniture, including a desk on which a gold-plated typewriter was sitting and another junior-size sofa that had been especially constructed to support the master of the house. The walls were lined with bookshelves and hung with framed photographs. Mr. Twotoes appeared to have a catholic taste in literature. There must have been a sentimental streak in the old man, or else a sly sense of the ironic. A beautifully bound edition of Alice Hegan Rice's *Mrs. Wiggs of the Cabbage Patch* rubbed shoulders with weighty tomes dealing with Napoleon and his campaigns, books on polar exploration and penguins, Clausewitz's complete ten-volume treatise on war, and Dr. Bernhard Wolf Weinberger's scholarly work, *An Introduction to the History of Dentistry,* from which Polvo had drawn the specifications for the replicas of George Washington's false teeth which he wore on state occasions.

All of the photographs depicted a slim, alert and fashionably dressed man in the company of once-famous fighters, jockeys and theatrical figures. As Tommy was settled down into his special chair by his two lackeys, he noted me peering curiously at the photographs.

"Yes, Soldier," he said, "that was I, to use the grammatically correct though somewhat awkward pronoun. Before my long illness some dozen years ago I was a beau in appearance as well as inclination."

I seated myself. Ebony Black placed a blue crock of the special brandy and glasses conveniently to hand. Tommy nodded at him. "You and Polvo may go to bed," he said. "The Soldier can assist me to retire when the time comes."

Ebony Black said, "I'll be waiting up for you."

"You will go to bed," repeated Tommy sternly. "That's an order."

The gigantic Negro looked at me suspiciously out of his one eye.

"I'll be waiting up for you," he said again doggedly. Ebony Black and Polvo left the room. The secret panel closed noiselessly behind them.

Tommy shook his head fondly. "You must not feel offended by Ebony Black's mistrust of you," he said. "He trusts no one where my well-being is concerned. He thinks he owes his life to me and he is determined to pay the fancied debt as best he can. He was on the verge of blindness from old batterings and raw booze, like that other great fighter, Sam Langford, when I picked him up and gave him a job as my retainer."

Tommy Twotoes poured brandy into our glasses.

"We are behind closed doors in a soundproof room," he said. "The time has arrived for true confessions."

He took a sip of the brandy and the shrewd little slits of his eyes regarded me. "I don't believe in police methods," he continued. "I have found that the surest way to invite the truth from another is to tell the whole truth yourself. Drink, Soldier. Fortify yourself. Prepare to listen to an old man's maunderings."

Tommy Twotoes cradled the bulge-bellied brandy inhaler in his pudgy palm, heating the fluid and sniffing sensuously at the fragrance of distilled grape.

"Danise Dalian, whose real name was Dottie Dorfman, was—shall we say?—a protégée of mine back in the days when I owned the Three Ring Circus," he said.

"I thought Vince Parada had the Three Ring Circus," I interrupted.

"He did, in a sense," replied the old man. "He was my front man. I always found front men most convenient in my enterprises. I don't suppose you remember the night clubs of the speakeasy era. No. You were too young. Some were rather extraordinary places.

The Merry-Go-Round on the East Side had a slowly revolving bar and the customers straddled gaily painted horses, lions and tigers instead of stools. The Park Avenue Club was operated by mobsters but had a decor of dark blue glass and spiral stairways that was designed by Joseph Urban. I designed the Circus myself. The main drawback of most such clubs was the dime-sized dance floor on which the entertainers also worked. I acquired a vast amount of space and had three circular dance floors—hence the name of the club. The tables were arranged about the dance floors in tiers, like the bleachers of a circus. An enormous tentlike canvas structure covered the walls and ceiling. My master of ceremonies wore the high silk hat and carried the whip of a ringmaster. My orchestra was heavy on the brass and was clad in the red and gold uniforms of circus bandsmen. My waiters were dressed like circus clowns and my hat check and cigarette girls wore the spangled tights of bareback riders. I even had a cage of monkeys for a while, but their fragrance was too overpowering and they had to be dispensed with."

I drained my glass at a swallow, violating all the niceties of polite brandy drinking. Tommy Twotoes refilled my glass, sniffed and sipped at his own.

"I booked the services of old-time vaudeville and circus acts," he continued. "Acrobats, jugglers, animal trainers, even a snake charmer. During the floor show, acts were performed simultaneously in the three rings—except for one act, the star spot. That was the Lady Godiva number. She rode into the center ring alone on a white horse, clad only in blue light and talcum powder. I can assure you that, unlike the original lady of Coventry, *my* Lady Godiva attracted more than one Peeping Tom. Danise Darlan appeared as Lady Godiva."

The memory of Danise sitting her white horse, clad only in blue light and talcum powder, was something he wished to relish. He paused and sipped his brandy silently. Then he said, "Danise came to me after Prohibition, when the Circus went legal. She was in her twenties then, but she was already in the full bloom of mature womanhood. She was close to forty when she met her untimely end. That must seem old to you, but it is not. A woman like Danise does not age. She merely ripens."

"She looked all right to me," I blurted out. I realized that I'd led with my chin again. Up to then he'd had no way of knowing that I had seen the corpse. He regarded me quizzically.

"So you saw her?" he said.

Yeah, I'd seen her, all right. I'd seen one hell of a lot of her. I merely nodded in reply.

"I was her lover once," said Tommy Twotoes softly. It was grotesque, almost obscene to think of this bald old man, this mountain of flabby flesh who hobbled about painfully on crippled legs, as the lover of the full-blown, rose-tinted siren who had flaunted her glorious nudity from the back of a white stallion.

He must have read my thoughts.

He said, "Don't look at me, Soldier. Look at the pictures on the wall. Danise admired lithe young men. Successful men. Men with money. I was not young, even then, before the stroke laid me low. But I was still vigorous. I was successful. I had money. My waistline was a trim thirty-four. Our affair was neither as preposterous nor as one-sided as you might think. I was more than twice her age, but still this was no sordid mating of Beauty and the Beast. I was very happy, although I did not delude myself. Only a self-deluded fool can lay exclusive claim to the possession of such a lush creature as Danise. She was prodigal of her favors. There was a middleweight boxer. A band leader. A newspaper columnist. And a cop. But she always returned to me in the end."

"Was the cop Romano?" I asked.

"Yes," said Tommy Twotoes. "But of course all this was long ago."

"What about Parada?" I inquired. "I've heard he knew her pretty well."

"Vince came later in the life of my none-too-chaste Danise," said Tommy, "while I was helpless in the hospital, almost convinced that my sins had found me out at last. It was a stormy episode, I understand. It ended when Vince was named co-respondent in the divorce suit of some society woman."

"I think Vince Parada killed her," I said, realizing that I should keep my mouth shut. "She had a ticket to Miami. He was in Miami. But he came back in time to kill her."

My words seemed to shock the old man.

"So she was going to have a last fling with Parada!" He said it softly, but he put an exclamation point after the words. Suddenly he looked very old and tired. "She was going to amuse herself with Parada while she was awaiting her divorce. I wondered why she insisted upon Florida instead of Nevada. The residence requirements of Florida law are longer than those of Nevada, and handsome cowboys make their living hiring out as gigolos in Reno."

He drank what remained of the brandy in his glass. Then he refilled the glass and drank deeply.

He said, "It is quite possible that Vince did murder her, I suppose. He was on the sixth floor of the hotel that day."

"What?" I fairly bellowed the question.

Tommy Twotoes had regained his composure.

"I would warn you to keep your voice down, Soldier," he said, "but fortunately the room is soundproof. As I say, Vince was on the sixth floor of the hotel that day. About an hour or so after I saw you. I had had Room 617 under intermittent observation. I had just knocked on the door of the room. There was no answer. There was a 'Don't Disturb' sign on the door, but I knocked anyway. As I turned a corner of the corridor on the way to my own suite, I glanced back. Vince was examining the room numbers. I concealed my elephantine form as well as possible, peering around a corner, and doubtless looking slightly ridiculous. Vince also knocked on the door of 617. He knocked several times. It was not opened, and so he left."

He gazed into the balloon inhaler as if it were a crystal ball, seeking to adjust his thoughts. He said, "But we should take things in their proper chronological order, or we will become lost in a hopeless maze. After Danise broke with Parada, while I was still recuperating in a wheel chair, she wed Malcolm Little. He is a few years younger than I. He had suffered no debilitating illness. And his youthful indiscretions had not caused him to go suddenly to fat. Also he was successful. He had a great deal of money. Oddly enough he had met Danise through me. He was a silent partner at one time in a few of my enterprises. It is not generally known how many men of Groton and Harvard and Social Register backgrounds invest their money in such promotions as sports and night clubs. Sometimes they are even the partners of out-and-out mobsters. That was particularly true during the Prohibition era. The impeccable Mr. Little was one of those men."

Tommy Twotoes leaned forward and tapped me on the knee. I had the feeling that he was attempting to justify himself in my eyes.

He said, "On the occasions when Danise left me temporarily for younger and handsomer men I did not fret too much over my cuckoldry. She was a magnificent, healthy animal, with a healthy animal's natural instincts. That, perhaps, was her greatest attraction. Certainly I did not welcome the attentions she accepted as her due from other men, but I could understand and even respect the impulse that prompted her acceptance of them. I did not resent the boxer or the band leader or the newspaperman or even the cop too much. But I did bitterly resent Malcolm Little, the man who became her husband. He was only a few years younger than I. He had nothing to offer her but wealth and social position, and when she accepted him solely for these advantages I felt that she had failed me and befouled my conception of her, that she was bartering her charms more sordidly than the cheapest prostitute. I did not consider Malcolm Little a fit mate for such a woman. I looked upon him as a prim, anaemic caricature of a man. Even though I myself had become little more than a fleshy carcass in which old lusts and half-forgotten dreams stirred faintly, by the bulging biceps of virile Vulcan, I had lived in my day, and I deemed myself a better man than Malcolm Little ever thought of being."

Again he sipped the fragrant grape.

"You see," he said, "I had idealized Danise in a strange sort of way. I looked upon her as warm-fleshed, eternal Woman, generous of her abundant favors, a proud pagan who could enslave a man in the soft tyranny of temptation or break him on the grinding rack of passion. When she accepted the standards of her sterile sisters and married Malcolm Little I was both hurt and appalled. I determined to make her recant her apostasy and realize the dream I had of her. I built this house to be near her. I saw her on occasions when chance or social intercourse permitted. The reclamation of Danise from the unfamiliar paths of homely virtue became an obsession with me. I even insinuated an agent of my own into Malcolm Little's house as a private secretary. His name was Heath and he was a former financial writer who had been fired from every paper in New York, Boston and Philadelphia for drunkenness. With the help of my recommendation, he obtained the post. And with the help of Alcoholics Anonymous, he retained it.

"I soon learned from Heath that matters were not so distressing as they first had seemed. After a few months, Danise was no longer true to her marriage vows. She was, in fact, almost flagrantly contemptuous of them. There were, I infer, numerous lovers. One was a chauffeur, whom Malcolm Little fired. Another was a cop, perhaps Romano again. She may possibly have renewed her affair with Vince Parada. But there was one man in whom she was particularly interested. He might have been any of the men I have mentioned. Or he might have been someone else entirely. I think he was the man she went to the Sheridan Towers to meet. Perhaps he was the man who murdered her. I do not know his identity. Was that man you, Soldier? Danise always fancied young men of your build and impulsiveness."

"No," I told him. "I never saw her until after she was dead."

He shook his head.

"In any event," he said, "even the obtuse Mr. Little grew suspicious. He fired the chauffeur. Heath informed me that the outraged husband had the private phone in his wife's bedroom suite tapped and that part of his duties as private secretary was to record her conversations. I saw the transcripts. Many were revealing, but none was conclusive. They cheered me greatly, however, for they indicated that Danise had become Danise again."

He paused to refill our glasses from the blue crock.

"Mr. Little is well named," he continued. "He is a small man. Becoming suspicious, he became vengeful. He told his wife that he would not divorce her but that he was arranging a will through which most of his money would go to the furtherance of disgusting cultural projects. He informed her that he had filed with his attorneys proof of her infidelities in case she attempted to break the will. It was, perhaps, an idle gesture since the widow's mite is assured her in this state. But Danise was not too well versed in legal niceties. They ceased to live as man and wife. His sole pleasure in the possession of her seemed to be the sadistic one of enchaining a noble, pagan spirit, although Danise never allowed her fetters to become too binding. I suppose, in a way, it was poetic justice for Danise, her penance for having strayed just once from the primrose path."

He chuckled at the irony.

"Danise came to me for advice. I urged her to take advantage of the liberal divorce laws of the sovereign State of Nevada and to rid herself of her inconvenient spouse without asking alimony. I offered her my support and protection after she had done so. She agreed, but she decided upon Florida instead of Nevada as the locale in which she would obtain her legal freedom. The plane ticket you mentioned was purchased by me, or rather by Ebony Black in my behalf. I was to join her in Miami after the divorce. Friend Malcolm, of course, was not privy to our deep-laid plans. I did not think he would contest the divorce. To have done so would have been to brand himself a cuckold. He was willing enough to sully his name with his wife's indiscretions after his death, if that could possibly prevent her from inheriting. But it would have been beneath his dignity to do so while he lived. Danise was to spend a few days in New York on a shopping tour, obtain the necessary wardrobe for Miami, then suddenly depart without informing her husband. But something happened."

He again turned his attention to the drink, caressing the glowing bowl of the glass, inhaling the fragrance of the brandy, sipping slowly.

At length he said, "Danise had a telephone call from New York. It was duly reported to me by Heath. He stated that the voice was that of the man in whom Danise had appeared most seriously interested. Danise, apparently, had written him saying that she was going away to start a new life and that their affair was finished. She asked him to return certain of her more foolish letters. He seemed overwrought. He told her that the only possible way she could obtain the letters was to meet him in Room 617 of the Sheridan Towers. He said he was registered there as J. K. Provost. Danise agreed to the rendezvous. Ordinarily I would have been indulgent about such an assignation. But I thought that this man might be demanding money of Danise and that if he were a blackmailer he might prove a nuisance later. I determined I would discover his identity. That is why I went to the Sheridan Towers and engaged a sixth-floor suite. That is how I happened to see Vince Parada knocking at the door of Room 617 and to observe you enter the room across the hall. I recognized your face at once. But I could not put it in its proper setting. Not until I read the newspapers last night."

He finished his brandy as a token that he had also finished his long dissertation. He dabbed at his mouth with an embroidered handkerchief. He said, "Talking makes me hungry as well as thirsty. Will you join me in a snack, my friend?"

"I couldn't eat a mouthful after that feed at Grogan's," I replied.

"You will excuse me then," he said. The young davenport that served him as a chair was mounted on rollers. He shoved it along the edge of the massive desk with his hands until he reached a wall cabinet. He slid back a panel of the cabinet, revealing a small, built-in electric refrigerator. He opened the door of the refrigerator and took stock of his provender.

"Liederkranz, limburger and goat's milk cheese," he said, like a train conductor calling out way stations. "Norwegian anchovies, pickled walnuts, spiced cherries, herring, brockwurst, pâté de foie gras, cold borscht, red caviar, and something without a label on it. Can't I tempt you, Soldier?"

"Emphatically, no," I said. "I'll just pour myself another shot."

"Help yourself, by all means," he invited. "I think the anchovies will do very nicely for me."

He took the jar of the snaky little fish from the ice box and propelled his chair back to the desk. He reached into his pocket and produced an old-fashioned, many-bladed knife.

He cut around the lid of the jar with a knife blade, then flipped the top of with a hook. He pressed a button and a small, skewer-like device sprang from the knife. On this he impaled a little worm shape and drew it from the jar.

I felt suddenly sick watching the old man devour the curled-up little fish. It occurred to me that the small, sharp spike he was using to convey the salty morsels to his mouth would have made just as pretty a hole in the heart of Danise Darlan as the ice pick I had tossed into a Bowery garbage can.

"I thought you ate those things on crackers," I said.

"I abhor crackers," he replied, his mouth full of the anchovies that he'd taken straight. "Crackers and milk are among the pap that my physicians recommended as a steady diet for me. I am on the road to complete recovery largely because I have persisted in consuming large quantities of most of the things they forbid me, among them anchovies—without crackers—and alcoholic beverages."

He polished off the anchovies and poured a slug of brandy for a chaser. He said, "I have bared my soul, or what's left of it, to you. It's your turn, Soldier. If you will permit me an expressive vulgarism—*give!*"

I gave. Maybe it was the brandy or maybe it was just desperation. I kept on talking. I couldn't stop talking, although I knew all the time that I was being a fool, leading with my chin again. I told him about the war and the wound and the spells and the hospital and the drunkenness that only made things worse. I told him about Chet Lassiter and Ginny and Vince Parada and the naked woman with the hole in her heart. I even told him about finding the little blood-crusted ice pick in my pocket, and about the telegram and the attempt to murder me in Ginny's apartment.

He listened intently. He even took notes. From time to time he interrupted me to ask a question or to have me repeat certain details that seemed utterly unimportant.

He was especially interested in getting the timetable of the twentieth straight.

When my true confession was ended, he advised me against making a phone call to Chet as I had agreed to do. He said I should write him a letter to explain the situation instead. He pointed out that Romano might already have the house under observation and the wires tapped. He said that since the publication of the picture

I was a marked man and should not be seen in any place in Tarry-town where I might find a public phone booth. I agreed to write a letter and he shoved the gold-plated portable typewriter and paper to my side of the desk.

I wrote Chet a brief note, telling him where I was and asking him to call and ask for Mr. Jones and speak cryptically if he had to contact me. I noticed that the letters of the typewriter were caps and small caps, a type face that some writers prefer and that is found on only one out of several hundred machines.

While I was typing the letter, Tommy Twotoes produced an enormous and oddly wrought pipe. The bowl was made in the shape of a naked woman. He packed the insides of the naked woman with an odorous Turkish tobacco and sat puffing aromatic smoke and peering intently at the notes he had taken. This, I thought, was a new eccentricity. He was giving me his whole rou-tine, I guessed.

When I had finished the letter and marked it "Special Deliv-ery," he asked me to help him to his feet. He stood for a moment, leaning against the desk, billows of smoke curling about the naked lady's sculptured head and torso. He stood looking at the window, with his back to me. He couldn't see out the window. The Vene-tian blinds were closed.

He said, "Your recital was most interesting, Soldier. Most in-formative. I am now quite certain of the identity of the murderer."

"What!" I exclaimed. And again my tone of voice verged on a bellow.

"It is quite obvious," he stated calmly. "Only one person could possibly have committed the crime."

I stood for a moment, looking at his back, my mouth hanging open.

At last I said, "Meaning me?"

He scrutinized me in silence for a long while.

Then he said, "Examine the evidence, Soldier. Turn it over in your mind. Then draw your own conclusions."

We found Ebony Black waiting for us in the hallway. He was sitting in a stiff-backed Jacobean chair beside the totem pole. On a modernistic Swedish table there was a little salver filled with letters that had gone unmailed in the hurried departure for the city of the Twotoes ménage. Tommy told me to place my letter with the others.

Ebony Black relieved me of the old man. The big Negro pressed a button of the escalator and the great dinosaur neck began to undulate upward. The journey on the escalator was a perilous one, with Ebony Black holding his boss in a death grip and Mr. Twotoes clutching the rail tenaciously, like a kid on a roller coaster.

When we had finally ridden the dinosaur's neck to the second floor, Tommy pointed to a door and told me that was my room.

"We may know more by this time tomorrow," he said in parting. "The boys are coming up. I was not quite clear as to what use I might make of them, but now I know. I am going to use them as private operatives and have them shadow a certain person in the city. Polvo and Ebony Black can assist them if necessary."

I exploded with hysterical laughter. I couldn't help myself. The thought of someone being tailed by a rum-dumb nuclear-fission expert, a bearded jockey, a punch-drunk baby sitter, a tattered Shakespearean scholar, a dwarf with a monocle, an organ grinder with George Washington's false teeth, and a one-eyed black man as big as a house was too much for me.

"I told you I work in unconventional ways," Tommy Twotoes said. "But there is always method behind my actions. No man would believe that such startlingly noticeable individuals as those I will employ would be set to spy upon him."

"I'm afraid Shakey won't relish playing copper," I said.

"I feel sure he'll be delighted with the assignment," replied Tommy Twotoes. "You see, I'm going to have him tail a cop."

8

Tommy Twotoes' guest chambers were furnished richly and comfortably enough, but unlike the rest of the house, they didn't resemble Dickens' Old Curiosity Shop. About the only furniture I noticed at the moment in the room was the very large and very soft-looking bed. I stripped off my clothes rapidly. Somebody had left a gaudy pair of silk pajamas on the bed for me, but I disregarded them as I was accustomed to sleeping raw. I was mentally exhausted and brandy-doped and I thought I would fall asleep immediately, but I was wrong. As soon as I closed my eyes the tom-toms started beating in my head.

I was convinced that Tommy Twotoes thought I was the murderer, and I could not be absolutely sure that he was wrong. After my ill-advised confidences, he had stated that there was only one person who could possibly have committed the crime. Well, I had been telling him about my own actions, so obviously I was his prime suspect. But someone had tried to murder me. That must mean something. It almost certainly was Parada who tried to murder me, and Tommy Twotoes had said that Parada was on the sixth floor of the hotel that day and might well have killed the woman. Also he had said that he was going to employ Shakey and the others to tail a cop. And Romano had previously had relations with the dead Danise. But maybe his putting a tail on Romano was what we called a diversion in the Army, or what is termed misdirection by

147

a magician. Maybe the sly old conniver was just trying to lull me into a false sense of security. And what about Mr. Malcolm Little, of Groton, Harvard and the Social Register? In my book, he still had the most compelling motive of any of the men connected with Danise because he'd been the only one who'd married her. And his alibi of just having wandered around the streets during the crucial period was hardly a story to hold up under police investigation.

For that matter, what about the fantastic Mr. Twotoes himself? There were enough nasty sex crimes on record to prove that an old man's passion can drive him to queer and brutal perversions. He had worshipped Danise in his own peculiar fashion. There was no doubt about that. He had known of her assignation with another man after she had consented to accept his support again. He had been on the sixth floor of the hotel and had had her room under observation. He could not move about too well under his own power, but he could probably manage spasmodic movements under stress, and both Ebony Black and Polvo would have killed for him without question. And he had the little sharp-pointed skewer on his knife. I could hardly picture a man eating wormlike little fishes with the same weapon that he had used to puncture his sweetheart's breast, but Mr. Twotoes had uttered a masterpiece of understatement when he had declared that he was somewhat unconventional.

At last I lapsed into coma if not into sleep. I awakened suddenly and found that I was out of bed, wandering around the room. I wondered if I had been out of the room. Sleepwalking was another symptom that the doctors had warned me against. The cold light of early morning shone palely through the Venetian blinds and made a latticed pattern on the floor. I fell back into bed and finally I slept the dreamless sleep of sheer exhaustion.

When I awakened the sun was riding high. I felt awful. Somebody was twirling an egg beater in my stomach and the taste of stewed rubber tires was in my mouth. The little green men in puce top hats were laughing shrilly while they tossed their small javelins through my skull. Then I realized that the little green men weren't really laughing, that the discordant chorus wasn't sounding inside my head at all, but came from somewhere outside the room. It was an ark-ing noise, so I figured it must be the penguins. I struggled to a sitting posture and was surprised to discover that my head didn't fall off. Ebony Black must have been waiting outside the door to hear the first creak of the bedsprings, for he knocked immediately and entered, carrying a glass of dark amber fluid in his hand.

"Good morning, sir," he said politely. "How do you feel?"

"I feel like I had a mouthful of molting penguin," I told him.

He handed me the glass. "Drink this," he said. "Mr. Twotoes recommends it for first thing in the morning."

I took the glass in a shaking hand, held it for a minute, then managed to get it to my mouth by grasping it with both hands. I swallowed the stuff at a gulp. My tonsils burst into flame, my larynx became a glowing ember, my eyes swam with acid tears and for about thirty seconds I sat there gasping and hawking while somebody stuck a talon hand inside my skull and tugged at the roots of my hair. Then all of a sudden I quit shaking and sweating and hawking and gasping and felt just fine.

"Wh-what the hell do you call *that?*" I asked the big Negro.

"We used to call it a brandy-whisky on account of they ain't nothin' in it except brandy and whisky," Ebony Black replied. "I tried adding a few drops of lemon juice once, but the boss said that spoiled the taste. But since we got the penguins we call it a penguin cocktail on account of you drink it and it makes you feel as chesty as them birds look."

"What the hell's the matter with those damned birds?" I asked. "Do they always make that kind of racket?"

"No, sir," answered Ebony. "Usually they act like right well-behaved little ladies and gentlemen. It's the Killer's fault. Polvo and I drove to town today and fetched him and the other boys up, only the boss sent the Professor back to town to do a job for him. Polvo told that Killer not to sing to the penguins, but he got hisself a couple slugs of the boss's brandy and he slipped off and started singing anyway. We made him stop, but them penguins is still expressing their disapproval of his voice. Them penguins is very funny birds once you get to know them. Polvo, he's got a special phonograph for them down to the rookeries. He plays them records of Mr. Bing Crosby singing and they just love it. But let him put on a record of that Mr. Frankie Sinatra singing the same song and they'll holler even worse than they did at the Killer. Them penguins is most particular about some things."

I took a bath in a fancy stall shower and when I returned to the room I found that Ebony had laid out a fresh wardrobe for me. It fit pretty well, too. Tommy Twotoes evidently kept clothing of assorted sizes on hand for his guests, since most of his visitors didn't carry week-end cases. I went down to breakfast, taking the ramp instead of the escalator. Polvo prepared me some delicious-looking eggs Benedict. I didn't think I could possibly eat them, but after another one of Ebony Black's penguin cocktails, I found I was hungry.

While he was serving my breakfast, Polvo suddenly slapped his hand to his mouth and flushed with embarrassment. It seemed that he wore his false teeth whenever he was performing any function as a retainer of Mr. Twotoes and that he had forgotten to insert the unwieldy dentures. He searched frantically in his pocket for the replicas of George Washington's teeth and failed to find them.

"I must've left them down to the rookeries," he apologized. He poured my coffee and hurried off in search of his teeth.

I could see the man-made cliffs and refrigerated glaciers of Mr. Twotoes' miniature Antarctic through the windows of the breakfast room. Ebony Black explained to me that during the warmer months the rookeries were kept at a constant temperature of 52 degrees, which appeared to be the most agreeable temperature for penguins. Basserty and Knotty and the Killer and Shakey were standing around looking at the penguins, which had finally quieted down, and the penguins were standing around looking at them. The penguins appeared to find the boys an even stranger sight than the boys found the penguins.

Ebony Black told me that Tommy Twotoes wished to see me in the study after I had eaten. I found him reading a fat volume of Clausewitz, with a blue crock of brandy near to hand. The naked lady was suspended from his mouth, with smoke billowing out of the top of her head.

"Good morning, Soldier," he greeted me cheerfully. "I trust you spent a restful night. Still troubled by guilt complexes?"

"Good morning," I said. "As far as I'm concerned, the jury's still out. But I suspect you're prejudiced against the defendant. You think I'm guilty as hell, don't you?"

"You should read Clausewitz, Soldier," he replied. "There's a lesson for you in his disquisitions upon strategy and tactics."

"I take it that all I have to do to solve my problems is become a student of Clausewitz and penguin lore," I said.

"Both subjects would help you, at least, to understand your peculiar problems," replied Tommy Twotoes somewhat abstrusely. He indicated a chair, the bottle and an empty glass. I sat down and poured a drink.

Tommy caused more smoke to belch from the naked lady's cerebellum. "Take Clausewitz," he said. "He enunciated the principles of the war of attrition, the slow, insistent pressure that in time wears down the resistance of an adversary."

The old man looked like an inscrutable Buddha. He was trying to tell me something, but he spoke in parables and I could not understand him.

"Open the window, will you, Soldier?" said Tommy Twotoes. "The room is becoming stuffy. I do not wish to overwhelm you with the aromatic fumes of Turkish weed."

I opened a window. The room was no longer soundproof. There was one hell of a racket. The penguins, it seemed, were acting up again. Tommy Twotoes rang for Ebony Black. When the one-eyed servitor appeared, Tommy asked, "What has roused this raucousness in our aviaries, Ebony? Has the Killer burst into song again?"

"No, sir," said the Negro. "It ain't the Killer's fault this time. Cleo's acting up again."

"Cleo," explained Tommy, "is a frustrated penguin."

"Yes, sir," said Ebony Black. "Cleo's a lovin' kind of a girl-penguin and the boy-penguins won't do what she wants 'em to do. That Polvo, he left his false teeth down to the rookeries. Cleo, she thought them teeth was a egg and she's a-settin' on 'em now. She's trying to hatch 'em, I guess. Polvo's doing his best to chase her off, but she won't move. Just keeps a-screamin' and a-peckin' at him."

"This is a serious matter that calls for action," declared Tommy. "Those are no ordinary dentures. They are reasonably exact replicas of the ones worn by George Washington himself. When I rescued Polvo from a life of virtue, he was toothless. I offered to supply him with an artificial means of mastication. He had read somewhere that his idol, Washington, wore false teeth and was greatly troubled by them. He insisted upon duplicates of those ancient dentures, evidently wishing to suffer the same discomforts as his hero. He went to the library of the New York Academy of Medicine and consulted the excellent historical work of Dr. Bernhard Wolf Weinberger, the nation's leading orthodontist, which I now have on my shelves."*

The erudite Mr. Twotoes went on to say that Charles Willson Peale, the artist, had made one cumbersome set of dentures for the long-suffering George, using the teeth of an elk; that Gilbert Stuart had stuffed Washington's sunken jaws with cotton when he

---

* *An Introduction to the History of Dentistry,* by Dr. Bernhard Wolf Weinberger. C. V. Mosby Co.: St. Louis, 1948.

painted the famous portraits, and that John Greenwood, Washington's favorite dentist, had the last tooth he pulled from the mouth of his distinguished patient mounted in gold and wore it as a charm on his watch chain the rest of his life.

"And now," said Tommy Twotoes, "we face a grave emergency. The replicas of George Washington's teeth must be recovered from the maternal Cleo by some means. Gentlemen, assist me to my feet."

With Ebony Black and I acting as derricks, Tommy Twotoes arose from his reinforced chair. We assisted him to the rookeries. Ebony unlatched a gate and we went inside. Polvo was pleading with the nesting Cleo to give him back his teeth. There were tears in his eyes, but the penguin wasn't moved by them. Knotty, Basserty, the Killer, Shakey and a flock of penguins were standing around watching the scene and making comments. It was hard to distinguish Knotty, the dwarf, from the penguins. He was similar in physique, though slightly taller; he had the same pigeon-proud look and he was wearing the monocle, which heightened the resemblance in profile, since penguins have a little white ring around their eyes.

Tommy looked the situation over. "I suggest that we try strategy," he said. "Soldier, I insist that you must have a good baritone. Cleo is an impressionable female. Try singing to her. Something sentimental, I think."

Ebony Black's brandy-whisky penguin cocktails plus a couple of straight slugs from the blue crock had overcome my inhibitions as far as vocalizing was concerned. I burst into "The Dream Girl of Pi K A," my fraternity song. When I sang about turning down the light, Cleo regarded me coquettishly and the other penguins quit chattering among themselves to give me their rapt attention. When I came to the part about my dream girl's sweet little smile making all life seem worthwhile, Cleo positively began to drool. Finally, when I reached the climax and was searching everywhere and finding none so fair as the Dream Girl of Pi K A, Cleo quit hatching George Washington's false teeth, left her nest and came over to my side. She rubbed herself caressingly against my leg.

"The eternal, fickle female," said Tommy Twotoes, shaking his head sadly. "She reminds me of a certain lady."

Polvo dashed to the deserted nest and retrieved his half-hatched dentures. We left the penguin compound and Polvo latched the gate after us, but a few moments later, as we neared the house, I felt Cleo rubbing herself against me again. And when I glanced down, she was gazing up at me with the foolish, adoring eyes of a moonstruck calf.

"How the hell did *she* get out?" I asked.

"That Cleo's a smart cookie," said Polvo proudly. "She's learned how to unlatch the gate with her beak."

Polvo attached something that looked like a dog's leash to Cleo's neck. "I got to carry this around especially for Cleo," he explained. "She's always goofing off somewhere or another."

He dragged Cleo, who was squawking, spluttering and arking her protests, back to the penguin corral. The other penguins rushed around her and began chattering at her reprovingly. One penguin, who appeared larger and older than the others, was especially vociferous, even taking a couple of vicious pecks at the errant lady.

"That's Cotton Mather," said Tommy Twotoes. "He's an evangelist and reformer. A hard-shelled puritan. I suspect that his preachments have had a great deal to do with the sterility of the flock."

Poor Cleo hung her head and seemed crestfallen because of the rebukes Cotton Mather was heaping upon her.

Polvo propped a piece of lumber against the gate to the rookeries to prevent Cleo from escaping again, then he went into the house to cook lunch for the master and his guests. I declined the meal, except for liquid refreshment, since I had just finished breakfast. I sat in the Chinese throne chair in the living room while they were eating, gazing at Delacroix's turbaned Moslems and ample-bosomed houri and Dali's weird dream world of ladies with snakes for eyebrows and gentlemen with alarm clocks for stomachs. I was thinking that Tommy Twotoes' parlor was even more fantastic than Mme. Tussaud's waxworks and that it would be one hell of a place for a man to come down with a hard case of delirium tremens.

I looked at the reproduction of Leonardo DaVinci's "Mona Lisa" and wondered why that smile had always been considered so enigmatic. Maybe it was just stupid. Maybe Mona was just a dumb dame who was a pushover for the first tall, dark and handsome guy who came along, like a certain babe I knew. Or maybe the smile was sort of mocking—the kind of smile a chick might wear just after she's two-timed her boy friend.

After the others had had their lunch, Mr. Twotoes escorted us to the soundproof study and proceeded to deliver a learned lecture on the sex life of the penguin.

"I regret that I cannot demonstrate to you the most interesting phase of life among the penguins," he said, "because of the lack of amativeness on the part of all my birds excepting Cleo. The courtship of penguins is, I feel sure, something worth seeing. The males woo the females by proffering them penguin jewels, just as swains in our own society might tempt the objects of their desire with trinkets from Tiffany's. These 'jewels' are lava pebbles with almond-shaped crystals imbedded in them. They are about the size of pigeon eggs. You can see a large number of them in my rookeries. I had them imported from the Antarctic at considerable expense and trouble in the hope of encouraging the mating instincts of my birds. If the female penguin accepts a jewel from her suitor, she automatically accepts the suitor himself, and they begin to build a nest of penguin jewels."

"'And I as rich in having such a jewel as twenty seas, if all their sand were pearl,'" Shakey quoted from *Two Gentlemen of Verona*.

Tommy Twotoes nodded toward me. "You may remember my remarks about Malcolm Little and his bride, Soldier," he said.

At this point Shakey felt called upon to quote the Bard again. "'Stol'n the impression of her fantasy,'" he declaimed, "'with bracelets of thy hair, rings, gawds, conceits, knacks, trifles, nosegays . . .'"

"The *spheniscidae* employ only penguin jewels," interrupted Tommy. "Shakespeare's Lysander resorted to many other tokens of esteem in his suit of Hermia."

"I feel sorry for that Cleo," said Basserty, the bearded jockey. "It ain't no good for animals—or birds, either—to be inhibited, makes 'em nervous."

Shakey switched from *A Midsummer Night's Dream* and *Two Gentlemen of Verona* to *Romeo and Juliet* to find an apt quotation. "Love is 'a madness most discreet—a choking gall and a preserving sweet,'" he said.

"Sometimes," said Tommy, "the madness of love is not too discreet. Murder has been done because of it."

The discussion and drinking continued while I sat there, partly anaesthetized by brandy, wondering if I were a murderer. I kept repeating to myself that most men don't kill, but I found little comfort in the phrase. I felt certain that Tommy Twotoes was convinced I *had* killed, and I wondered why he was prolonging the comedy. I wondered why he didn't turn me over to Romano, the cop with the classic profile, who was hot on the trail of the elusive George Spelvin. I also wondered why the hell I just sat there listlessly, allowing the old man to amuse himself with me like a fat, sleek cat teasing a helpless mouse. I should take off. I didn't quite know where I might take off to, but anywhere would be less dangerous than here. Seemingly, however, I had lost all initiative. I was apathetically content just to sit still and drink Tommy Twotoes' fine brandy and wait for the inevitable. When I became conscious of my surroundings again, Tommy had changed the topic of conversation from penguins to pugilists.

"John Jackson," he was telling the Killer, "was champion of England from 1795 to 1800. He was the most famous boxing instructor of his day and was known as Gentleman John. He taught Lord Byron to box, and despite his club foot, the poet was an apt pupil. Byron shocked his friends by making a boon companion of Jackson. When he was criticized for consorting with a low character, Byron said, 'I find Jackson's manners infinitely superior to those of the fellows of the college whom I meet at the high table.'"

The telephone rang. Tommy answered it. He muttered a few "yeses" and "is-that-sos" and "uhms," and then he said, "I'll be sending Shakey into town in an hour or so to relieve you, Professor. He'll try to find you in the place you mention, but if there's a change let me know by phone."

He hung up and said, "Ebony, you will drive Shakey into town directly. The Professor has our subject under observation. He thinks he may remain at his headquarters for a while. But if there is a change, he will call me, and when you arrive in the city, you can check back. In the meantime, don't fail to pick up the other party who is going to visit us."

"We're having more visitors?" I inquired.

"Yes," said Tommy Twotoes. "A surprise for you, Soldier. Someone you will want to see."

"Lieutenant Romano, no doubt," I said bitterly.

"The lieutenant would doubtless like to see you, Soldier, but I don't imagine the desire is mutual. This is someone you should welcome."

"Chet!" I exclaimed. Tommy was giving me a break after all, I figured. He wasn't throwing me to the lions without giving me the benefit of counsel. Chet, I thought, could tell me what I should do.

As Ebony Black and Shakey prepared to leave for town, I said to Tommy Twotoes, "What's the idea of putting on the act of having Shakey go to town to shadow Romano? You're not fooling anybody. You're already satisfied in your own mind as to the identity of the murderer. You said so last night. Why don't you go ahead with the Great Exposé and get it over with?"

Tommy Twotoes packed odoriferous Turkish tobacco into his pipe and set fire to the naked lady's head.

"Let's say for the moment that it is a process of substantiation rather than a process of elimination," he said. "As you point out, I am convinced of the murderer's identity. But I also wish you to be convinced beyond the shadow of a doubt. When all the evidence that my operatives have to offer is in, you will be convinced, Soldier."

I suppose it was his idea of fair play, or perhaps of giving a man enough rope with which to hang himself. But I doubted I would be convinced that I had killed the delectable Danise even if he produced an eye witness to the murder.

Polvo said that it was feeding time for the penguins. Knotty, Basserty, Killer Carney and I helped him carry bushel baskets of shrimp to the penguin pens. Then we assisted Tommy Twotoes to the same place. The penguins set up a great and clamorous ark-ing as we showered them with crustaceans. Suddenly Polvo froze and looked worried. He began to count heads. He counted over the individual members of the flock twice and then he cried, "We're one short! Cleo's got loose again!"

"How the hell do you know it's Cleo?" I asked. "How can you tell one penguin from another? I can spot Cotton Mather because he's bigger and noisier and mangier looking than the others, but the rest all look alike."

"I can tell Cleo, all right," asserted Polvo. "She's got a certain look in her eyes." He dashed over to the rear gate of the rookeries and found it open.

"Well," he said, partly worried and partly boastful, "that's the first time she ever thought of using that gate. I gotta get padlocks if I'm gonna keep Cleo home."

We escorted Tommy back to his study, seated him in his reinforced chair, and formed a search party. We searched the house.

We searched the estate. We beat the surrounding woods. But we failed to find Cleo. Poor Polvo was inconsolable.

"Maybe it's a kidnapping," he said. "Maybe we should oughta call the FBI."

"I wouldn't worry too much, Polvo," Tommy Twotoes consoled him. "I knew another lady who had a habit of wandering off. But she always returned. Until the last time."

"Them damn boy-penguins," said Polvo. "If they just had taken proper care of Cleo this would've never happened."

"Try to forget your worries, Polvo," Tommy advised. "Go to the kitchen and start preparations for dinner. We will have your incomparable shish-kebab in honor of our guests."

Polvo took himself off, muttering through the false teeth he had inserted when he was called upon to act in the official capacity of penguin-feeder. The brandy I'd absorbed in the study and the fresh air I'd absorbed in chasing the run-away penguin had made me sleepy. I took a nap in my chair. I was awakened quite a while later by the ringing of the phone.

Tommy answered the phone and again emitted a few noncommittal "uhms," "yeses," and "is-that-sos." When he hung up, he said, "It is a good thing I provided Shakey with an adequate expense account. Soon after he relieved the Professor, our subject took to an automobile and headed out of the city. Shakey was able to follow by cab. The subject is pointed in this general direction. He has paused at a wayside tavern for refreshment and Shakey took advantage of the break to call me."

"Well," I said, "you expected that Romano would put this place under observation. That he'd even tap the wires."

"So I did, Soldier, so I did," Tommy Twotoes replied.

The guy who wanted me for murder was headed in my direction, but I no longer seemed to care. I fell asleep again.

A window of the study that overlooked the rookeries had been left open as an outlet for the smoke that belched from the cranium of the naked lady. I was awakened from my troubled nap by the ark-ing of the penguin flock. The station wagon that Ebony Black had driven to town was turning in the drive. It was growing quite dark by then.

We assisted Tommy into the curio-littered living room to greet the newcomers. Only Ebony Black and the Professor entered.

"Where is our guest?" Tommy inquired.

"There was a second party which wouldn't let the first party come unless'n he come along, too," said Ebony Black. "So the second party is driving the first party up here hisself. They was right behind us most of the way. They should be here in a minute or two."

"This may make for complications," said Tommy Twotoes.

I heard another car coming into the driveway and I looked out a window. In the light that spilled from the house I saw a sporty convertible being parked. A man and a woman were in the convertible. I knew them both. The red haze clouded my eyes. I ran into the hallway. I opened the front door.

Ginny came in. She looked very surprised when she saw me. When Vince Parada followed her into the hallway, I swung with everything I had and landed right on the button. Mr. Parada sat down on the floor, a glassy look in his eyes. Then he closed his eyes and lay down at full length.

Ebony Black had assisted Tommy Twotoes into the hallway. Behind them the Professor, the Killer, Knotty and Basserty stood, their mouths agape at my unexpected show of violence. Ebony looked at the boss questioningly, waiting for instructions.

Ginny screamed, "You crazy, jealous jerk! What are you doing up here?"

Tommy Twotoes shook his head sadly. "I find you guilty of a serious breach of hospitality, Soldier," he said, "but I am forced to compliment you upon your left hook. It reminds me of Ebony Black in his prime. One of you look in the drawer of the table by the totem pole. You will find smelling salts, a relic of the chef who died from overindulgence in cooking sherry. He suffered from fainting spells."

Killer Carney found the smelling salts and began to work over the prone Mr. Parada, holding the little bottle to his nostrils and slapping his face lightly. Eventually Vince began to come around. He blinked a few times, then he saw me and glared.

"So it was you!" he said. "You're a lucky bastard that I'm not packing a rod."

"Why don't you use the little pick?" I asked. "You killed Danise with it, didn't you? Or maybe you'd prefer to slug me with the blackjack again."

"This bastard's crazy," said Vince, getting to his feet with the assistance of the Killer. "Romano's looking for him. I'll make a point of telling the lieutenant where he can find George Spelvin as soon as I get out of here. Maybe the screwball can cop an insanity plea."

"You will do no informing," said Tommy Twotoes. "You are not leaving here, Vincento, now that you have come. The Soldier has sought sanctuary with me and he will receive it until I am ready to summon the authorities in my own good time. You are not unwelcome, Vincento, although your arrival is somewhat inopportune. I would have had to interview you, anyway. But having arrived unheralded, you must remain until I deem it meet for you to leave."

"I can't stay," said Vince. "I've got to be in town tonight."

"You will remain," repeated Tommy Twotoes. "See to it, Ebony."

"He'll stay," the gigantic Negro said.

"It's all my fault," sobbed Ginny. "I didn't know you had Terry up here. When Vince said you wanted me to come up, I thought you were after a girl to do a striptease at a stag, or something worse. I wouldn't come alone. So Vince agreed to drive me."

"I didn't think it best to mention that the Soldier was in my custody," said Tommy Twotoes. "Up to now that fact has been top secret. It must not be disclosed for a while longer. I thought the presence of his charming lady friend would soothe the Soldier's nerves and make him more content. Besides, I wished to talk to you myself. Fortunately, no real harm is done, except for temporarily inconveniencing friend Vincento. My house has many chambers and my larders are well filled."

"You!" said Ginny, meaning me, and when she uttered that one-syllable pronoun I felt that a drunken longshoreman had assailed me with every curse word that he knew.

Tommy went through the formality of introducing his ill-assorted guests. Then we went into the living room. There was some attempt at desultory conversation as Ebony Black passed the drinks, but Ginny and Parada just sat and glared at me. As for me, I just sat in the Chinese throne chair and kept filling my glass and emptying it again.

So Shakey hadn't been assigned to tail a cop, after all, I thought. He must have been tailing Parada, since he'd called to say the man he was following was headed in our direction and Vince had arrived a short while later. While the Professor was launched upon a discussion of the latest developments in the nuclear fission field, which didn't seem to interest either Vince or Ginny very much, Tommy took Parada into the soundproof study and closed the door. So I had only Ginny to glare at me. After a while Vince returned and glared at me while Ginny went into the study. Finally Polvo came into the room, inserted George Washington's false teeth, and announced that dinner was served.

Polvo's shish-kebab was delicious, but I couldn't enjoy it as much as I should have. That was because each diner was served the dripping, succulent chunks of lamb on a little individual skewer.

Vince saw me regarding my skewer doubtfully and said, "Is that the kind of shiv you used to kill her with, Rooke?"

I started to lunge across the table, but Ebony Black, who was serving the meal, was standing right behind me and he put two heavy, restraining hands that were more like hams on my shoulders.

After dinner, Tommy Twotoes did his best to play the perfect, charming host, and his best was pretty good. He had an inexhaustible fund of entertaining tales about his checkered career. The boys were enjoying themselves immensely, but Ginny, Vince and I remained silent. Ginny pouted. Vince glowered. I just drank.

It was well after midnight when we retired to our rooms. Copious quantities of brandy had mellowed me some and made me hopeful. Ginny's room was just down the hall. I thought she would come and tap at my door, fall into my arms, explain everything and beg forgiveness. I was prepared to forgive her, too, even though I was convinced any explanation she might make would be as phony as hell. That's what a doll like Ginny can do to a guy, I guess. I even left the door slightly open so she wouldn't miss my room. I didn't bother about the fact that the man who had tried to kill me was in the same house.

I donned the fancy pajamas that Ebony Black had laid out for me. I hadn't examined them the night before, when I had disdained them in favor of sleeping raw, but I had noted they were gaudy. Now I saw that they were scarlet silk with a design of black, white-ruffed penguins rampant upon the vivid field.

I sat waiting for Ginny to come to the door. A long time passed. Somebody had thoughtfully left a blue crock in my room as an antidote against insomnia, and I kept sipping at it, not even bothering to pour the stuff in a glass. I had consumed about half the bottle before I heard the light slap-slapping of footsteps in the carpeted hall. Ginny, I knew, wore frivolously feathered mules for house slippers. The footsteps paused uncertainly at my door and I bounded across the room to open it.

It wasn't Ginny.

Cleo, the frustrated penguin, stood in the doorway, gazing up at me with foolish, adoring eyes.

She must have hidden herself in the house somewhere before the doors were locked for the night and found her way to me by instinct. She came into the room, ark-ed softly a couple of times, and stood rubbing herself against my leg.

I hastily closed the door and locked it. I had to get Cleo out of there. If Ginny *should* come to the room and find me pitching woo with an amorous penguin, she'd be sure I was nuts. Besides, I had no way of knowing if Cleo was house-broken, and I didn't want her ruining Mr. Twotoes' pretty rug.

I put on my shoes and threw the trench coat over my penguin-studded pajamas, with Cleo rubbing herself lovingly against me all the time. I reached down and stroked her head, and maybe I was a little drunk, but I could have sworn she quit ark-ing like a penguin and began cooing like a dove. I didn't have any leash, but I didn't need any, because Cleo stuck to me like a wet elastic bathing suit sticks to a Hollywood starlet. I opened the door and cased the hall. No one was in sight, so I left the room, with Cleo paddling along beside me, still making soft turtle-dove sounds.

We went downstairs, taking the ramp instead of the escalator. I unlocked a back door and we left the house. As we neared the rookeries, a great commotion arose. I didn't think we had made enough noise to disturb the penguin colony, but strident ark-ing filled the darkness. Then I heard another sound. A gate to the rookeries banged and there were running footsteps. They were too heavy to be the footsteps of a paddle-footed penguin. They were the footsteps of a man. I hurried to the rookeries, almost falling over Cleo, but the man was lost in the shadows by the time I arrived. The lights of the house began to go on. Then the floodlights of the rookeries, which were controlled by a switch in the house, blazed. The penguins were standing in a great circle about something that lay on the ground. They were chattering hysterically about the thing they saw.

People began to come out of the house. I shoved penguins aside to right and left of me, and I was standing looking at the thing on the ground when Tommy Twotoes, supported by Ebony

Black, and the others arrived on the scene. There was a penguin lying on the ground. It was the only penguin I could identify from the others—Cotton Mather.

He was quite dead, his white-ringed eyes staring up foolishly at the chattering circle. There was a little red hole pierced through his white ruff.

"Why you want to kill a poor ole harmless penguin, Mr. Soljer?" asked Ebony Black. He spoke softly, but I didn't like what he said.

I started to protest, but Tommy Twotoes interrupted me.

"Just like poor Danise," he said. "It would have been more fitting if Cleo had been stabbed."

Cleo ducked suddenly and picked up something off the ground. She paddled off to her nest with it. Cleo was the only penguin in the flock who had bothered to build a nest of the lava pebbles that Tommy Twotoes had imported from the Antarctic. Cleo placed the thing she had picked up in her nest and squatted down upon it.

"Cleo's hatchin' something again," said Polvo.

"We have to get her off that nest," said Tommy Twotoes. "You had better sing, Soldier."

I couldn't think of anything to sing except a touching ballad my dad had taught me when I was a child.

My rendition of "Snagtooth Sal" had the anticipated effect. Cleo left her nest to rub herself against my leg. We all looked down at the thing she had been hatching. It was a little ice pick, crusted with blood.

On the wooden handle was printed "Inter-City Ice Co."

It was exactly the same kind of ice pick that was missing from Ginny's kitchen.

It was the same kind of ice pick I had found in the lining of my coat and had thrown into a garbage can on the Lower East Side.

9

The next day it rained—and I received a letter.

When I awakened the weeping veil of rain obscured my windows. I lay for a while and listened to the soft, insistent splash of the steady downpour. The sound and sight of the sobbing, sorrowing world was depressing enough in itself. And I was shaking and sweating and gripped by terror. It wasn't just the hangover. As I fought my way falteringly from the fog of alcohol and sleep, I came suddenly face to face with an ugly reality.

They thought that I was a murderer and they thought that I was mad.

I had tried to tell them the night before about the penguin, Cleo, hiding in the house and finding her way to my room, about returning her to the rookeries and hearing the excited clamor of the flock. I had tried to tell them of the shadow that banged the gate and then pounded its way into the dark woods. But all of them, including Ginny, had looked at me with incredulous eyes. I could hardly blame them. I could scarcely believe the story myself.

They thought that I was a crazed murderer whose mad lust to kill had led him to stab a ludicrous-looking, harmless bird to death, merely because life had pulsed warm in the creature.

I tried to convince myself that Vince Parada had murdered the woman and had killed the penguin. He had had the opportunity, perhaps, on both occasions, because he had been on the scene of the killings. He might well have had a motive for slaying the woman. But the killing of the penguin was a weird and senseless business that could only be put down as the act of a madman.

Besides, I felt sure that Ebony Black must have kept close watch over Parada's room the night before. And the running footsteps I had heard had been carrying the shadow into the woods. Vince Parada had reached the rookeries from the house, with the others.

The killing of the penguin was a madman's act, and they thought that I was mad.

I felt that I was being held a prisoner. My jail was a fantastic one where fine brandy and rich food were served and where the beds were soft. But I thought that the eccentric old man who was my jailer would grow tired of the farce he was enacting and end it very soon.

Then the police would lay heavy hands on me.

And after that there would be the little room in which there was a grim, wooden chair with straps dangling from it, and a pale man standing before a board of blinking lights, waiting to throw a switch.

Or, worse, there would be a little room with padded walls and stout bars on the windows, and burly men who wore white coats, and other men who screamed out the torment of their lunacy.

But the extraordinary household of Tommy Twotoes functioned quite as usual, even though the master must have believed there was a maniac beneath his roof. Ebony Black appeared with my morning medicine, the brandy-whisky penguin cocktail, and I took it gratefully. Polvo prepared my breakfast, but I was unable to eat. After I had picked at the food awhile, I went to find Tommy Twotoes and the others, excepting Knotty who had gone to the city presumably to relieve Shakey at the senseless task of shadowing Romano, assembled in the living room. Ginny regarded me coldly and did not speak. Vince Parada strode up and down the littered room, darting venomous glances in my direction. The boys, including Shakey, who was back from town, were already well on the way to becoming mellow. They made a show of welcoming me, but I disliked the look in their eyes. Tommy Twotoes greeted me in a casual, friendly way.

"Good morning, Soldier," he said. "A letter came for you. It was sent special delivery, but I had no wish to disturb your slumbers after the excitement of last night."

He handed me the letter. It was in a long, white envelope, similar to those that Tommy Twotoes kept in the study. It was addressed "Soldier, Care Thos. Twotoes, Hudson Bluff Road, Tarrytown, N. Y." There was no return address. It had been postmarked the night before in Tarrytown.

The letter had been addressed on a typewriter. The type face of the typewriter was caps and small caps, the same as that on Tommy Twotoes' gold-plated portable.

I ripped open the envelope.

The letter was typed on ordinary bond paper, the same kind of paper I had found on Tommy Twotoes' desk. It was undated, but there was a salutation.

It read:

> Dear Soldier:
> Why don't you confess what you know to be true and throw yourself upon the mercy of the authorities? Unless you are restrained, you know that you will keep on killing. Ginny, the girl you love, may be the next to die. Do you want that, Soldier?
>
> Act now, and avoid further tragedy. They will never execute you. You will be sent away to an asylum if you confess. After all you have a record of insanity. Perhaps you can even be cured by the proper treatment. Such things have happened before, you know.

Think it over, Soldier. There is nothing else for
you to do. You have only one hope.

This is your conscience speaking.

The letter was not signed by hand. The signature was typewritten.
The signature read TERRY BOB ROOKE—my own name, of course.

I stood looking at the letter. Tommy Twotoes said softly, "May
I see it, Soldier?"

"Haven't you seen it already?" I asked.

"What do you mean, Soldier?"

"It seems to have been written on your typewriter. It's the same
kind of envelope and paper you keep in your study," I replied.

Tommy Twotoes said, "I didn't write it, Soldier."

I handed him the letter.

Before he even read it, he held the paper up to the light. He
said, "It is the same watermark as the bond paper that I use."

He read the letter very carefully. He read it over twice. When
he finished reading it, he did not give it back to me. He handed it
to Ebony Black. "Lock this in the study safe," he said.

He turned to me. "That is all we needed," he said. "The evidence is in. The case is solved. There are only the formalities to
dispense with."

"You think *I* wrote the letter?" I asked.

"I can only give you the same advice that your correspondent
gave you," Tommy Twotoes replied. "Think it over, Soldier."

Shakey quoted *Macbeth:* "'And when we have our naked frail-
ties hid, that suffer in exposure, let us meet and question this most
bloody piece of work.'"

Tommy shook his head. "There will be no questioning now,"
he said. "We will reserve that for a more opportune time when
all involved are present and due process of law can be invoked. I
advise you to relax, Soldier. Have a drink of brandy. The denoue-
ment is near. It is a matter of hours at most, if all goes well."

Polvo came in, water dripping from the yellow slicker and rain hat that he wore. He said that he had dug the grave and completed preparations for the funeral of Cotton Mather, the puritanical penguin.

"I will not attend the obsequies," said Tommy Twotoes. "I dislike funerals. They are a sanctimonious excuse for the living to weep ostensibly over the dead, but in reality to exult in their own good fortune in still nurturing a spark of life. Besides, it is raining and I am subject to head colds. But Polvo would appreciate it, I'm sure, if you others would join the penguins in paying last respects at Cotton Mather's grave. There are numerous umbrellas and raincoats in the house."

Polvo, who had inserted his false teeth for the important occasion of the funeral, bustled out to obtain umbrellas and slickers.

Shakey said, "I'm gonna deliver the eulogy. I got it all wrote out. They say nobody can improve on the Bard of Avon, but I've just changed a few words of Mark Antony's speech over Caesar's corpse to make it fit the circumstances."

He took a piece of paper from his pocket. "Since you ain't attending the funeral, I'll read you some excerpts," he said to Tommy.

Shakey read from the paper:

> Friends, penguins, countrymen, lend me your ears:
> I come to bury Cotton, not to praise him.
> The evil penguins do lives after them;
> The good is oft interred with their bones;
> So let it be with Cotton. The noble Twotoes
> Hath told you that Cotton was a puritan;
> If it were so, it was a grievous fault;
> And grievously hath Cotton answered it . . .
> My heart is in the coffin there with Cotton,
> And I must pause till it come back to me.

Shakey paused dramatically, and then continued, pointing an accusing finger as if he were gesturing toward the penguin's blood-stained ruff:

> Look! in this place there ran an ice pick through:
> See what a rent the envious murd'rer made:
> And as he pluck'd his cursed steel away,
> Mark how the blood of Cotton followed it . . .
> This was the most unkindest cut of all . . .
> Then burst his mighty heart . . .
> . . . Great Cotton fell.
> Oh, what a fall was there, my countrymen!
> Then I and you and all of us fell down,
> Whilst bloody treason flourish'd over us . . .
> Here was a penguin! When comes such another?

"Excellent!" Tommy Twotoes complimented the eulogist. "I'm sure the penguin mourners will appreciate your funeral oration. It should move the lava pebbles of my rookeries to rise and mutiny."

Polvo returned and passed out raincoats and umbrellas. He offered me a slicker, but I shook my head.

"I'm going upstairs and think things over, like you said," I told Tommy.

"What's the matter?" asked Vince Parada. "Can't you stand to watch them bury your dead?"

I started for him, but Ebony Black again intervened.

Ginny glared at me and addressed me for the first time. "I guess you're hopeless," she said. And there was more despair than anger in her words.

The others trooped out into the driving rain to bury the penguin. I went upstairs to my room. I could see the burial party from my window. Polvo had dug the grave on the edge of the woods, just inside the rookeries. The penguins stood around solemnly and listened to Shakey deliver his funeral oration over the coffin, which was made of a large brandy case.

I wanted a drink. I had drunk all that was left of the brandy in the crock in my room the night before, after I'd found the murdered penguin. I went downstairs to get one of the bottles that were placed conveniently on all fourteen of the large and small tables in the living room. The living room was deserted, but I could hear Tommy Twotoes' voice in the study. The door to the study was half open. Tommy was talking on the telephone.

I heard him say, "Yes, this is Tommy Twotoes, Lieutenant Romano. I think you had best come up tonight at the time I mentioned. . . . No, it won't be exactly a social call. It's about the murder of Danise I will turn the murderer over to you."

There was a pause, then Tommy said, "Yes, he is here. We know him as 'Soldier.' He is the George Spelvin you are seeking. His real name is Terence Robert Rooke. I will arrange that you meet him, Lieutenant. Be here shortly after six, then."

I grabbed a blue crock and went back upstairs. I took a stiff drink. One thing was very clear indeed. Tommy wasn't wasting any time now in turning me over to the cops. I had to get out of there. It was a dreary day and darkness would come early, fortunately. I would make a break as soon as it was dark. That should give me at least an hour's start on Romano. I still had several hours to kill. I decided to remain in my room. I drank sparingly of the brandy. I did not want to get too drunk I needed a clear head, and I was addled enough to begin with.

Besides Tommy Twotoes' ancient Rolls-Royce and the station wagon, there was Vince Parada's sporty convertible job on the grounds. But I feared that all of them would be locked. And any journey down a highway in a stolen, easily identifiable automobile would be extra perilous. I decided that I would take to the woods that grew thickly on the bluff above the Hudson and rely on luck to come out at some place where I could find transportation.

At some time during the afternoon I heard the catlike tread of Ebony Black in the hall. An idea occurred to me. I hated to waste the stuff, but I went into the bathroom and poured the brandy down the toilet. Then I returned, slumped down in a chair, ran a hand through my hair to rumple it, and cried out drunkenly. Ebony Black came in and asked politely what he could do for me. I held the bottle upside down to indicate it was empty and demanded more brandy. He looked at me doubtfully, but he said he would get it. If they thought I was blotto drunk, they wouldn't expect me to try to escape. Ebony returned with the brandy and I put on an act of gulping at the bottle as soon as it was uncorked.

"You best not hit that stuff too hard, Mr. Soljer," Ebony warned. "We got important guests arriving in a little while."

"T'hell with 'em," I said, and collapsed in a chair. Ebony shook his head and left the room.

Finally it was dark. The black skies spilled rain in a splashing torrent. I donned the trench coat and peaked cap. I thrust the brandy bottle in the slash pocket of the trench coat. It was going to be cold and wet in the dripping woods and a little interior warmth would be welcome. I left the room, closing the door softly.

There was no one in the hallway. I could hear voices and the tinkle of glasses coming from the living room downstairs. I tiptoed down the ramp, hid behind the totem pole for a minute, then crept to the back of the house. I could hear Polvo clattering pots and pans in the kitchen. I slipped out the back door without attracting attention. I made toward the rookeries. In sixty seconds I was soaking wet. As I skirted the rookeries, a lone penguin gave voice. I figured it must be Cleo.

I slipped into the woods at about the same point as the heavy-footed shadow had disappeared the night before. It was rough going at first. And then it became a nightmare. I slipped in the viscous mud, stumbled over snaky roots, catapulted into trees, fell into deep puddles. But I kept floundering on into the black, wet void. I sank to my ankles in soggy leaf-mold.

The bare trees wept for their lost foliage. The gusty wind breathed fitfully, like a hurt and hunted animal. After a while I moved very slowly. I knew that somewhere ahead there was a precipice and a sheer drop to the rocky banks of the river. Once I stepped forward and found nothing beneath my foot. I expected to plummet headlong to the rocks below, but I fell into a shallow gully. I twisted my ankle painfully. There was blood on my face. My body was bruised. But I went on.

I paused from time to time and drank liquid warmth into me from the bottle. Sometimes I sat down in slimy mud to catch my breath and massage my injured ankle. In combat there had been nothing but the present, a world of flaming hell and rending sound. Now there was no world except one of rain and mud and utter darkness. There never had been any other world. But I kept going. Panting, groaning and cursing, I kept going. And at last I saw a light. It was dim and far away. I made for it. I no longer feared that I would pitch into a bottomless abyss. I plunged and slithered and stumbled on toward the light. Where there was a light, there must be a road, I thought.

Then suddenly I stopped dead in my tracks. I heard voices. I froze against a tree. The voices were familiar.

I had made a complete circle in my floundering. In the light that shone from Tommy Twotoes' house I could see the rookeries and the fresh-dug grave of Cotton Mather, the murdered penguin, hardly ten yards away. The boys were clustered about the rookeries, discussing my disappearance.

"His footprints lead into the woods, all right," said the Professor, who was bending down with a flashlight and making like Kit Carson or Buffalo Bill Cody. "He can't have got far in those woods on a night like this."

"The boss say bring him back wherever he got," said Ebony Black.

"Maybe we oughta have a bloodhound," suggested Basserty.

"Maybe we got one!" exclaimed Polvo. "That Cleo tracked him right to his room last night, he said. Let's get Cleo and give her a whiff of them tracks."

While the boys went in search of Cleo, I slithered back into the deeper shadows of the woods. I dropped on my hands and knees and tried to remember my Army training in creeping and crawling. After I had crept and crawled for a while I got to my feet and began to run. Presently I heard the patter of little penguin feet in the squishy mud behind me, accompanied by a happy arking. Cleo was overtaking me rapidly, paddling along in my direction with the unerring instinct of a homing pigeon. I could hear the boys lunging along a considerable distance back of Cleo.

Eliza never had a bloodhound like Cleo pursuing her in her flight across the ice. No man had ever been hunted through dripping, ghostly woods by such a weird posse as this, even in his wildest nightmares. A squawking, lovesick penguin. A one-eyed colossus with a hide as black as the night itself. An undersized organ-grinder with ghastly false teeth. A jockey with a bushy beard. An overeducated wino who chattered of nuclear fission. A rum-dumb, punch-drunk baby sitter. And a Shakespearean student who had a psychopathic hatred of cops.

I slipped and fell, and Cleo was upon me. She nuzzled me with her beak, making the queer turtle-dove sounds I'd heard the night before when she had waddled into my room. I could hear the boys coming. I could even see their flashlights winking. I struggled to my feet and started to run.

I said, "Go 'way! Scat!" to Cleo, but she stuck right to me. In addition to tripping over roots and sinking into potholes, I kept stumbling over Cleo. She continued ark-ing shrilly. I told her to shut up and even tried to grab her by the beak, but it didn't help. I reflected that you could never trust a woman. I was about to conk her with the brandy bottle when the woods began to thin out suddenly and I saw a white ribbon that must be a road. I slowed down and approached as cautiously as I could with an ark-ing penguin at my side. A car was parked on the road. It was a taxi cab.

Despite my numerous falls, the brandy crock wasn't broken. I took it from my pocket. I knew no heap jockey would willingly take a blood-stained, limping mad-man as a fare. I was going to brain the driver with the bottle, leave him by the roadside, and steal his cab.

I saw that I had come out of the woods to the highway at a point near Tommy Twotoes' house. An embankment led down to the road. I made my way carefully down the embankment, the crock grasped tightly in my fist. But I had reckoned without Cleo. Tommy Twotoes had told me how playful penguins disported themselves by coasting down ice banks on their bellies. Lacking an ice bank, Cleo coasted down a mud bank. She landed at my feet. I took a header over Cleo and I fell flat on my face in the middle of the road. The brandy bottle smashed.

I got to my knees, cursing.

The back door of the cab opened and a penguin walked out. I knelt there staring at the penguin. The penguin stared right back at me.

The penguin said, "What the bloody hell is this, naow?"

Then I saw it wasn't a penguin. It was Knotty, the dwarf who wore a monocle. He walked over and examined me.

"Gorblimey!" he exclaimed. "It's the Soldier bloke! Yer must 'ave been wallowin' in a bloody bucket of muck, yer must."

"Ark," said Cleo happily.

The boys came thundering out of the woods, led by Ebony Black. The colossus pulled me gently to my feet.

"You gotta come along, Mr. Soljer," he said. "Tommy Twotoes wants you should meet certain folks."

"You all right, Cleo?" Polvo inquired solicitiously.

"Ark," replied Cleo.

"Muddiest damn course I ever went over," Jockey Basserty declared.

"We sure 'chased these pagans in those holy fields,'" said Shakey. "That's from *King Henry IV,* Act one, Scene one."

"What are you doing here, my Lilliputian Anglophile?" the Professor asked Knotty.

"I had to hail a hansom to pursue our subject," Knotty said. "He led me all the way back here. A merry chase and all that sort of thing, y'know. He's up to the house now. We parked here so as not to alarm the quarry. Scotland Yard methods, and all that."

Shakey spat and snarled. "Goddam cop! You don't suppose he'll hurt Tommy, do you?"

"The boss all right," said Ebony Black. "Mr. Parada's with him. And he done oiled up and loaded that ole six-gun of his'n, too."

One way or another, everybody, including Cleo, piled into the cab. The driver groaned. "Damnedest fare *I* ever hacked," he said. "From now on I ain't a-going off Manhattan Island. You go off Manhattan Island and you meet up with a lot of screwballs every time."

Just as he started the cab, a cry rang out.

"Hey! Wait up!"

It was Killer Carney, the punch-drunk baby sitter. "I got losted in them woods," he explained as he climbed into the cab.

It was a short trip to the house. That was fortunate, because eight mud-caked men, plus a driver and a penguin, make quite a load in a New York cab, especially when two of the men are as big as Killer Carney and Ebony Black. Ebony Black managed to keep a tight hold on me all the way. In fact, I was sitting in his lap. Cleo sat in Polvo's lap right next to me and made cooing sounds.

When we arrived, Polvo put the dog leash on Cleo and led her back to the rookeries. Ebony conducted me into the living room immediately. I didn't see Romano around anywhere.

Ginny got one look at the mud and the blood that formed most of my outer layer and came running forward. "Terry!" she cried. "You're hurt!"

That made me feel good all over, like Little Annie Rooney, despite the fact that Ginny had lured me into a murder trap and was on hand to gloat when Tommy Twotoes delivered me over to the police.

Suddenly I saw that Chet Lassiter was also in the room. "Terry!" said Chet, coming toward me. "What the hell have these goons been doing to you?"

"I got losted in them woods," I told him.

Polvo returned from the rookeries. He conducted another person into the room. The stranger was a small, gray, meek-looking man, who wore eyeglasses. I figured him for a high-ranking police official. A lot of high-ranking police officials are small, gray, meek-looking men.

"I believe you are acquainted with this gentleman," Tommy Twotoes said to Chet, nodding toward the newcomer.

Chet looked blank. The small, gray man looked blank.

Tommy Twotoes said, "No? Mr. Chet Lassiter, meet Mr. Malcolm Little. I was under the impression that Mr. Little was a client of yours, Lassiter."

Chet said, "Oh, Mr. Malcolm Little. No, we never met. His secretary made the arrangements."

"Neither my secretary nor any other employee of mine ever made any arrangements of any sort with you on my behalf, Mr. Lassiter," Malcolm Little said icily.

"It was a delicate matter, of course," said Chet smoothly. "Perhaps I shouldn't have spoken out like that."

"No," said Tommy Twotoes. "You shouldn't have. That was one of your mistakes. You did not foresee, of course, that you might be brought face to face with Malcolm Little. You made other mistakes, Lassiter. Such as warning Frayne and his employees to deny that the Soldier was in their place that evening. They thought it was merely because he had had a spat with his girl friend, Ginny, here. When they discovered he was involved in a murder case, it was a different matter. They talked quite freely to my friend, Lieutenant Romano, then."

"Just what the hell is this?" demanded Chet. "You called me to come up here because you said my pal Terry was in trouble and needed help. I came up to help him. What the hell is this you're driving at?"

"You very nearly helped your friend into the electric chair. Or at best into a cell for the dangerously insane," said Tommy Twotoes calmly. "It was a clever scheme. Devilishly clever. Elaborate. And it almost worked. The Soldier himself was half convinced of his guilt, I think. But you did not reckon upon my having met the Soldier once. What is this, you ask, Lassiter? I'll tell you what it is. The word is murder. The murder of Danise Darlan, Mrs. Malcolm Little. Once I had the facts, it was obvious you were the only person who *could* be guilty."

"Why, God damn you . . ." Chet moved menacingly toward the fat old man. Ebony Black moved faster. He locked his arms about Chet. Chet was a big man, and he was strong. But he was helpless in the grip of the giant Negro.

"Search him, Ebony," said Tommy Twotoes. "If he is carrying a gun, remove it from his person."

Ebony Black relieved Chet of a Police Positive revolver.

Tommy Twotoes took an oversized pistol from a drawer and laid it on the table beside him. It was a big, shiny-barreled Colt six-gun with an elaborately carved ivory butt—the kind the bad men of the Old West once used.

"You may as well sit down," said Tommy Twotoes. "I have much to say. Polvo, pass the drinks."

Ebony Black shoved Chet into a chair and stood guard behind him, arms crossed over his chest. He needed only a turban and a scimitar to resemble a eunuch at the harem portal. Polvo passed the drinks and even Chet accepted one.

"Some of this is conjecture," said Tommy Twotoes, "but most of it is demonstrable fact. I believe that your affair with Danise must have begun about the time that she and Vincent here broke off their relations. You were once a Broadway cop and had ample opportunity of meeting her. Then you joined the Army and were sent overseas. While you were away, she married."

The meek-looking Mr. Little winced.

"You will pardon me, Malcolm," Tommy Twotoes said, "but by the time that Lassiter returned to this country, Danise was chafing at her marital ties. She renewed her affair with this man."

Tommy Twotoes sipped his drink. Again he addressed Chet directly. "Malcolm Little knew of your existence," he said, "through intercepted phone calls, but he did not know your identity. I knew of the phone calls, too. But I did not know your name. Danise had a habit of addressing all her male acquaintances as 'Honey.' Since your bass voice is easily recognizable, it was not necessary for you to identify yourself when you called her."

Tommy Twotoes turned to Malcolm Little. "I am sorry," he said, "but your trusted private secretary was in my pay."

After asking Ginny's permission, he set the naked lady's head afire. Then he said to Chet, "In time Danise grew tired of you, too, Lassiter. She planned to divorce her husband and to accept my support. She had written you foolish letters, through boredom, perhaps. As she grew older, she grew more careful. She thought these letters might prevent her divorce if you peddled them to Malcolm Little, or that I might withdraw my offer if they were shown to me. She wrote you, saying that she was going away, that she was breaking off with you. She asked you to return the letters. You refused. I doubt you were after money. You knew instinctively that the letters were the only hold you had left over the woman you loved."

Tommy Twotoes shook his bald head.

"I could almost sympathize with you, Lassiter. Danise was a woman who might well drive any man to madness and to murder. You planned to kill her rather than to lose her to another man. I think you planned the crime for a long while. But when you decided to involve our innocent friend, Soldier, you went too far. Your attempt to make him the victim, to drive him insane, even, was beyond understanding or forgiveness. Soldier was an ideal man for your purpose. He was dissatisfied with his job. He had been shell-shocked and wounded and bitterly disillusioned. He had been treated for nervous instability. He had tendencies toward alcoholism. He had a violent temper, which he exhibited publicly upon occasion. And with it all, he was still a naïve fellow. You employed his services, not because you needed him in your failing business, but with this murder specifically in mind."

Chet sneered. "I hope you think you can prove these absurd and outrageous statements in a court of law," he said. "I am not acquainted with most of the strange characters you have here, but when I sue you, they will be called as witnesses."

Tommy Twotoes puffed at his pipe, sipped his brandy and paid no attention to the interruption.

He continued, "After you had completed your arrangements for the crime, you called Danise on her private wire. You had no way of knowing that the phone was tapped, of course, and so you made another grave mistake. You told her that the only way she could obtain the letters was to meet you in Room 617 of the Sheridan Towers Hotel on the morning of the twentieth. I saw the transcript of that phone call, but the secretary, Heath, did not show it to Malcolm Little. Therefore Mr. Little could not possibly have engaged your services, as you claim he did, because he had no knowledge of the assignation. Then you told your employee, the Soldier here, that the woman he was to report upon would not arrive at the hotel before the twenty-first. That in itself is evidence of your guilt. Even the name you assumed at the hotel is indicative. You had served as a military policeman. You served under the provost marshal. You engaged the room as early as the thirteenth under the name of J. K. Provost. You occupied it for brief periods to lull any possible suspicions on the part of the management.

"You engaged Room 616 under the name of George Spelvin for occupancy on the twentieth. On the morning of that day Danise met you in Room 617, as she had agreed to do. You did not give her the letters at once. You acted very strangely. Danise became badly frightened. Toward noon, you left the room; otherwise she would not have been able to make the calls she did, calls that Lieutenant Romano informs me were duly recorded by the hotel operator. You probably told her you were going to get the letters. Actually, you went to your office, to make sure that Soldier had left for the hotel and to await a call from him.

"As I say, Danise was confused and terrified by the way you acted. When a man is on the verge of murder, it may show in his face. As soon as you left her, she put through a call to me here in Tarrytown. But there was no answer, for the very simple reason that I was on the same floor of the hotel as she was at the time. Danise was a woman who could not stand to be alone, and she did not enjoy female society. In her state of nerves, she instinctively sought a man she regarded as dependable. She had learned that Vince Parada had business interests in Florida, that he was already down there, and that he would spend much of his time in Miami during the winter. The prospect of a protracted residence in Nevada alone was unattractive. She decided upon a final fling with Parada instead. That is why she changed the venue of her divorce action from Nevada to Florida at the last minute.

"When she could not reach me, she must have thought of fleeing the hotel, but she wanted those letters and there was no way of getting them except to wait. However, she wanted desperately to talk to someone. Illogically enough, she put through a long-distance call to Parada in Miami Beach. That call, too, is a matter of record. Parada was alarmed. It was not like Danise to become hysterical. He had to return to New York soon, anyway, he has told me, so he took a plane at once, not even checking out of the hotel. He arrived in New York a few hours later and went directly to the Sheridan Towers. But it was too late. He knocked upon the door of Room 617, despite the 'Don't Disturb' sign, just as I had done a few minutes previously, but he received no answer, because Danise lay dead, and you, Lassiter, had no desire to entertain guests at the moment. Parada called the room repeatedly during the late afternoon and evening, but he received no answer. Those phone calls, coming at a time when you were locked in with the corpse of the woman you had murdered, must have upset your nerves no end."

Tommy Twotoes motioned for Polvo to refill the glasses.

"We will return to your own actions, Lassiter. You received a phone call from the Soldier at your office. You advised him to leave the hotel and see his girl. After Soldier left the hotel, you returned to Room 617. You had no letters, but you did carry a small ice pick, one of those which Frayne's gave away to customers who asked for them. You had previously obtained it with a very specific purpose in mind, since you have no call to crack ice in a non-housekeeping hotel suite. At some time during the afternoon, probably between the hours of three and five o'clock, you killed Danise. Then there was a long and nerve-racking period of waiting.

"I knocked on the door. A moment later Parada knocked on the door. The telephone rang several times. People kept passing back and forth in the halls. About six o'clock—the exact time is on the hotel records—you called Room 616 to make sure the coast was clear. But to your surprise, Soldier answered the telephone. Your call was the only one made to Room 616 that day. Soldier talked to you, so you had to be the man who made the call from Room 617, where the murdered woman lay. You told Soldier to have his dinner and get a few drinks. A short while later you called the room again and there was no answer. So you crossed the hall. You were a private detective and you carried several types of passkeys. Doubtless you had tested the lock previously. You entered 616. You left the door slightly ajar when you left again. You returned to the room across the hall."

"I am forced to admire your iron nerve, Lassiter," Tommy Two-toes continued, knocking out the cremated contents of the naked lady's head. "It was no more than five steps from Room 617 to Room 616, but it was a dangerous journey for a man who supported a corpse. You made it without detection. Then you began to put your plan for driving the Soldier insane into operation. You stripped Danise down to the last thread. You sat her in a chair. You took her clothing back to Room 617. There was nothing now for you to do but go home and wait. You were morally certain that the Soldier would call you as soon as he discovered the corpse. You set the stage to pretend you were expecting a guest, to lull any possible suspicion on the Soldier's part. A man who has just murdered one woman is unlikely to entertain another at an intimate supper in his rooms. The Soldier phoned you. He visited your rooms. He told his story. You found the opportunity to slip the little ice pick into the pocket of his coat, which he had thrown upon a chair. You could not foresee that it would slip down into the lining through a hole. The fact that Soldier did not report the discovery of the ice pick to you at once must have bothered you, but you had devised other means of making him doubt his own sanity."

Tommy Twotoes motioned for more brandy and refilled his pipe.

"Now began the most vicious part of your plan," he said. "You told the Soldier to disappear. You returned to the Sheridan Towers, obtained Danise's clothes and dressed the corpse in them. You moved the body from the chair to the bed, so that when it was found, the Soldier would begin to question what might really have occurred, despite the evidence of his senses. You put Danise's luggage in Room 616. You made off with your own, a comparatively simple feat in a crowded hotel. You went to Frayne's, told them of a lovers' quarrel and asked that they deny the Soldier had been there. Since Soldier had attempted to become friendly with several strange women that evening (Ginny glared at me when he said this) they readily agreed. To convince Soldier that they could keep his secret, they denied his presence there even to his face on the following night.

"That same night you called Ginny and arranged to meet her at her apartment at an ungodly hour of the morning, after her last show was finished, telling her that her sweetheart was in dire trouble. You implored her to urge Soldier to go to the medics and confess that he might have killed a woman during one of his blackouts. Ginny refused, but she did agree not to tell her boy friend of your visit. You went to the kitchen and made a highball and found another of Frayne's ice picks. Perhaps you already knew it was there. You took it, since its disappearance might confuse the Soldier even more."

Tommy Twotoes paused, but no one said anything. We were under the spell of the old man, it seemed.

Chet's lips were curled, but he wasn't smiling his nice, grinny smile. He looked contemptuous—and dangerous. The big Negro still stood guard over him.

"You were by no means at the end of your resources, however," Tommy went on. "You knew a reporter. The reporter knew you as a responsible private detective who had once been on the cops. Under a pledge to keep the source of his information secret, he learned the identity of 'George Spelvin' from you. You visited Ginny again to urge her to advise the Soldier to surrender himself, and again she refused. But your visit was not entirely fruitless. You found the picture and turned it over to the newspaper.

"When Ginny discovered the loss of the photograph, she phoned you. She was already slightly suspicious of your actions because you had had the opportunity of appropriating the picture and because you insisted so stubbornly upon the guilt of her sweetheart. But she had to call you. It was the only way she had of getting in touch with Soldier. At first you put her off. Then an idea occurred to you. Perhaps you had planned right along to eliminate Soldier and make it appear a suicide if the opportunity offered. You gave Ginny the number of Grogan's saloon, but told her Soldier would not appear there until the next day. Then you told her there were important new developments and that you had to discuss them with her and Parada. You urged that they meet you at your hotel immediately after the dinner show. You told them you were going to see Romano but that they should wait if you were not there when they arrived. That would assure Ginny's absence from her apartment when you had need of it, and if your plan went wrong, Ginny's absence from the club might appear suspicious. Then you sent the telegram. You used one of your trick keys to enter Ginny's apartment. You typed a suicide note on her portable machine. You unscrewed the bulb from the ceiling light and waited in the darkness. When Soldier arrived, you struck him down.

"You took the telegram from his pocket and replaced it with the note you had typed. You attempted to throw the unconscious man out of the window. If the fall had not killed him, it would have made little difference. The suicide note in his pocket, coupled with his hospital record, would have been evidence enough for the police who found him. But the Soldier came to before you could heave him from the window. He resisted you. You were afraid he might land a lucky blow and stun you long enough to make a light. You were terrified of being recognized, and so you fled. You called Grogan's at once, probably from a pay booth. You must have called from other pay booths on the way uptown, and left messages so that the Soldier would believe you had been phoning him during the time he was attacked. Ginny and Parada were waiting for you in the hotel lobby. You told them some cock-and-bull story of Soldier planning to turn evidence against Parada over

to the police and again you begged Ginny to urge that her sweetheart surrender himself to the medical authorities instead. Soon
after Parada and Ginny left you, Soldier called. By seeing Ginny
and Parada in the lobby, you avoided any chance of receiving the
Soldier's call within their hearing. You were perplexed by the fact
that Soldier did not tell you of the attack. You were afraid that he
was growing suspicious and you determined that he must be eliminated either by being arrested or by being murdered.

"Then you learned by letter that your intended victim was
up here. My men had you under observation by then. You visited agencies that rented typewriters. You visited three before you
found a machine with a type face like that of my portable. You
bought stationery with a watermark like that I use. You wrote a
letter to the Soldier and signed his own name to it. Or rather you
typed his name. I am not accusing you of forgery—only murder.
You rented a car and drove to Tarrytown. You were followed by
my man in a cab. You mailed the letter special delivery from the
Tarrytown post office. Late at night you came up here. Probably
you meant to kill the Soldier and make it seem a suicide, which
might have been confirmed by the strange letter he was to receive.
But you could not reach the Soldier. So you committed an act that
was meant to convince me that my guest was mad. You entered the
rookeries and stabbed a penguin to death, just as you had killed
Danise. You purposely left the weapon, the ice pick you had taken
from Ginny's apartment. No doubt it was free of fingerprints."

Tommy Twotoes took an extra large sip from his glass.

"And then," he said, "I called you and told you the Soldier was
in trouble and that you should come up here. That is all, I think.
Ebony, assist me to my feet."

Shakey had to quote from one of Shakespeare's least-known
plays, *King Henry VI,* to make a fitting speech, but he was equal
to the occasion.

"'In sight of God and us, your guilt is great,'" he said. "'Receive the sentence of the law for sins such as by God's book are adjudg'd to death.'" On his own he added, "Dirty, stinking cop."

I saw it coming, but Chet was closer than I was. While Ebony Black was helping his master to rise from the chair, Chet dashed over to the table and grabbed the antique six-gun.

He pointed it at Tommy Twotoes.

Tommy Twotoes said, "If I were inclined to be melodramatic, I would tell you it isn't loaded. Unfortunately, it is."

"Toss me back the gun you took from me, bud," Chet said to Ebony Black. Ebony looked at Tommy Twotoes, who nodded. The big Negro tossed over the gun.

"Who owns that convertible outside?" Chet asked.

Vince Parada admitted it was his.

"It looks like a hyped-up job and I may need more speed than I've got in the rented heap," said Chet quite calmly. "Throw me the keys."

Parada threw him the keys.

"I've got twelve shots in these two guns without reloading," Chet said conversationally. "There are just twelve of you here and I don't waste bullets. I might kill you all and make it look as if Terry were an insane mass murderer who'd got his blood lust up and then killed himself. But that would be too noisy and troublesome. I'll just take the fast car and a hostage instead. If nobody tries to stop me within the next two hours, the hostage will not be harmed. If they do, the hostage will be killed."

He nodded toward Ginny.

"You'll be the hostage, darling," he said.

I started to leap forward. The gun swung toward me.

"No!" I said. "You're not taking her."

I set myself for a flying tackle. The gun didn't waver. Then I saw something.

The secret door to the study had been left partly open. Chet had his back to it. Someone was standing in the opening.

"Drop the artillery, honey boy," said Lieutenant Romano, the cop with the classic profile. "I could always outshoot you on the range when we were rookies and I've got a great big heater pointed right at your back."

Chet dropped the guns. Two more cops from the local force came out of the study. For once, Shakey didn't snarl at cops. The cops put handcuffs on Chet. They took him away without ceremony or further conversation.

Ginny slumped down in a chair. I went over to her.

"You all right, Butch?" I asked.

Vince Parada shoved me aside. "She don't want to talk to you, even if you're not a murderer," he declared. "Come on, honey, I'll take you back to town."

I made a lunge and this time Ebony Black didn't stop me. I landed right on the button again. Mr. Parada sat down on the floor.

Ebony Black chuckled and apologized to Tommy Twotoes. "I thought the Soljer had jes one comin'," he said. "That man sure do have a nice left."

Tommy Twotoes shook his head and sighed. "Someone get the smelling salts," he said.

When Vince was revived he left in what the fancy writers term high dudgeon. After the boys and I had scraped the mud off us, we all sat down and ate a late dinner and did a lot of drinking. The boys agreed to stay on as Tommy's guests for a few days. Tommy sent Ginny and me back to town in the ancient Rolls-Royce, and insisted that both Ebony Black and Polvo accompany us as chauffeur and footman respectively. Polvo, of course, inserted George Washington's false teeth for the occasion.

Ebony Black drove no faster than thirty miles an hour, but I wouldn't have minded if he'd traveled even slower, because I had

Ginny in my arms all the way and she was the cooing, oil-bathed baby again.

We told the gigantic, one-eyed black man and the little organ grinder with sea-horse teeth good night in front of Ginny's apartment house. I asked Ginny if she wanted to go somewhere for a drink.

"It's getting late," she said. "It's time for bed."

"I don't feel sleepy," I told her.

"I won't tuck you in on the couch right away," Ginny said. "You can kiss me good night a few times first. It will be wonderful to be alone at last."

I was inserting the key in the front door when Ebony Black shouted at us.

"Hey, Mr. Soljer!" he called. "Wait up. We forgot to give you the present from Mr. Tommy."

Ebony Black and Polvo took a big case out of the trunk of the car.

"Well, now," I said. "That's mighty nice. Tommy Twotoes is giving us a case of his special brandy."

They set the big case at our feet on the sidewalk.

There wasn't any brandy in the case.

In the case was Cleo, the amorous penguin.

MURDER IN BLACK AND WHITE

The author is indebted to Dr. Frederick M. Remer, noted pathologist, toxicologist and criminologist of Greenwich, Conn., for his invaluable help with technical portions of this book.

1

The funeral parlor had an imitation bronze front. Tufted oyster-colored curtains were draped back from the window to reveal a rubbery-looking plant that had been stuck into an enormous urn. The mortuary was on the corner of Father Demo Square in Greenwich Village, where the Avenue of the Americas and Bleecker Street come together to form a triangle that is one of the major traffic hazards of Greater New York. Any time you tried to cross the square, even when you had the green light, trucks and cars bent upon your destruction roared at you from at least half a dozen different directions, it seemed.

I thought the undertaking parlor was located in a fine spot for attracting business. I knew that at least one of the mortician's present customers had got his from a hit-run driver right in front of the establishment.

I stood for a moment recovering from the nervous strain of crossing the square while I pretended to admire the funereal flora. Then I opened the door and entered a tiled lobby that had more funeral urns and plants as its decorative motif. There was also a large gumwood desk with mahogany veneer. A short, fat man who seemed to be in mourning all over sat behind the desk.

His thinning hair, which hung down in a Hitler-like forelock, was jet black. He hadn't shaved for several days and the stubble on his jowls was black. His shirt might have been white when it first came back from the laundry, but it had come back from the laundry quite a while ago. He wore one of the old Army-issue black ties and a black mohair suit. I noted that even his fingernails were in mourning. You might have expected such a character to be reading a comic book. He was reading Franz Kafka's *Diary*. He looked up at me and said one word in a questioning, high-soprano voice.

He said, "Yes?"

I told him I'd come to pay my last respects to the mortal remains of Fighting Phil Caselli.

He gestured toward a narrow, dimly lighted hallway with a dirty thumb, hitchhiker fashion. He said, "Parlor C. Third door on the left." Then his eyelids flew up and his black-stubbled moon-face took on a ludicrously startled expression. He was looking at something over my shoulder. After all, it was my shoulder, so I looked over it, too. I saw at once why the little undertaker was startled.

Another little man was standing there. But he was a very thin little man, thin almost to the point of emaciation. He might have tipped the scales at slightly over one hundred pounds if he were wearing a set of deep-sea diver's boots, but somehow or other *menace* was written all over him. This little man was completely white.

He was an albino. He wore no hat. His pate was covered with a down of silvery spun-silk and melting snowflakes. His face was fish-belly white. His most remarkable feature was his eyes, which were greatly magnified by thick, rimless glasses. His eyes were pink. I had never seen a man with pink eyeballs before, and it gave me a start. Despite the fact that it was February and the cold air was blowing snow flurries, the little man had accentuated his natural whiteness by his clothing. He wore a white shirt that had just been laundered and a white string tie of the type William Jennings Bryan used to affect. He wore no overcoat. He was clad in a white linen suit. He also wore canvas sneakers, which accounted for his silent entrance over the tiled lobby.

He was white as snow and he seemed cold as ice.

The little man who was white all over didn't say a word. He slid by us silently and took off up the narrow hallway like a ball of fire. Or, more properly, a ball of snow. I exchanged glances with the fat man who was in mourning all over. He shrugged and returned to his reading.

I turned into the dimly lighted hallway myself. Suddenly there was a resounding crash. Then there were a lot more resounding crashes. I pinned myself against the wall and began to shake. The war was a long time over, but I hadn't recovered from my allergy to loud and sudden noises. Women began to scream. Men and women streamed out into the hallway from half a dozen little parlors where death lay quiet. The man in mourning appeared from the lobby, still clutching his volume of Kafka.

Then the snow-white, ice-cold man reappeared. He came out of Parlor C. This time he had something gripped tightly in his small fist. His fist was full of a big, fat heater, a .45. He waved the heater at the screaming women and the muttering men and immediately a hush befitting a house of the dead prevailed. The albino didn't say a word. The gun did his talking. He gestured with it, and everybody, including the slack-jawed fat man, lined up against the wall. I'd counted the shots and I figured his gat must be empty. For a minute I thought of risking a flying tackle. But he'd had time to reload and the pink eyeballs that bulged as big as Malaga grapes through the thick lenses were very menacing indeed. He passed down the line of terrified innocent bystanders like an inspecting officer. When he was at the end of the line, he about-faced, his back to the door, his gun still covering us. He walked backward to the open door. I heard him bolt it from the outside.

I dashed to the door and tried it. It wouldn't budge. Those who had come to mourn their dead again set up a shrill commotion. I ran into Parlor C. A tall, stooped, very old woman with a seamed face was standing against the wall, her hand pressed to her mouth. She wore old-fashioned widow's weeds that seemed rusty from age.

The other mourners gawked from the doorway of the room, but only the undertaker's assistant entered.

The only dead body in the room was in the casket that rested on two black-draped trestles. I looked into the casket. The corpse of Fighting Phil Caselli no longer had a face. The albino had fired a whole clip of .45-caliber bullets directly into the corpse's face at very close range. There wasn't any blood, of course. The undertakers had seen to that. There were fragments of bone and rouged flesh. Fighting Phil Caselli's face resembled a shattered, smoke-singed paraffin mask.

When the undertaker's assistant saw what had happened, he squealed, "Oh, no, no! Oh, what a shame! Mr. Dinwiddie, our embalmer, did such a beautiful job on him! And now it's ruined. All ruined!"

"Let's not have hysterics about this, chum," I advised him.

"Such a shame," the fat little man repeated. Disregarding the presence of the old woman who still had her hand pressed to her mouth, he confided, "He looked like a bulldog when they brought him in, but Mr. Dinwiddie made him look human in death. And now we'll have to have a closed casket. So much work for nothing."

I put my hand lightly on the shoulder of the old woman in black and said, "Tell us what happened, Mama."

The old woman was still suffering from a severe case of shock. She took her hand from her mouth and said in a quavering voice, "The ice-cream man . . . The ice-cream man came in. . . ."

That would be the albino dressed like a Good Humor peddler, I figured.

"You knew him?" I asked.

The old woman spoke with a heavy Italian accent. She said, "No, no. I no know this man, this ice-cream man."

"He came in here," I prompted. "What did he do?"

"He walk to coffin. I think he will cross himself and kneel, make prayer for Phillip's soul. He does not. He takes out gun and shoots at Phillip. Then he leaves. Why he shoot my poor dead Phillip?"

"I don't know, Mama," I said. "Phillip was your son?"

"No, no. What you call the nephew. I am the aunt."

"What is your name, Mama?" I asked, taking out a pad and pencil.

"Theresa," she replied. "I am Theresa Caselli, the aunt."

"Where do you live, Theresa?" I inquired.

She gave me a number on Bleecker, not far from the funeral parlor.

The mortician's aide suddenly realized that his authority was being usurped. He blustered up and demanded to know who I was.

"The name is Rooke," I told him. "Terry Bob Rooke. My friends call me Soldier." I produced a brand-new private detective's license. The State of New York hasn't issued badges to private richards for a number of years.

The little man who was in mourning to his fingernails seemed impressed. He said, "Police?"

"Not exactly," I replied. "Private operative. My client had an interest in the deceased."

I unscrewed a dark shade from a table lamp and told the fat man to hold the lamp so the light would shine directly on the mutilated corpse in the coffin. He obeyed without protest. But when he saw me taking a small Leica from my pocket, he started squawking.

"You mustn't take a picture!" he cried in a shrill voice. "Mr. Dinwiddie would be outraged. Nothing like this has ever happened here before."

"Got to," I said. I used an army term to impress him. "It's S.O.P.—Standard Operating Procedure."

I snapped a close-up of the smashed head. Then I took a picture of the upper torso, with the hands folded across the chest. The lower part of the casket was closed, of course. I wasn't much of a photographer, and I hoped there'd be something on the film when it was developed. I'd synchronized the f.-stop of the camera for a slow shutter speed. There was no need for hair-trigger timing, because Fighting Phil Caselli wasn't likely to make any sudden movement.

I turned to the crowd of persons who were craning their necks through the door of Parlor C and asked them if anybody had seen anything that I hadn't. Nobody had. They'd only heard the shots and seen the little man in white emerge with the big, fat .45 in his fist.

I said to the fat little man, "How do we get out of here?"

He told me there was a window at the back of the hallway which gave upon an alley.

I said, "I'll go through the window, come around and open the door. As soon as you get back to your desk, call the police."

The mourning man wrung his hands. "So disgraceful," he squeaked. "It will give the firm a bad name. Poor Mr. Dinwiddie!"

I walked down the hall and raised the window. I crawled through it to the alley, took a wrong turn in the snow-spangled darkness and came up against a brick wall. I about-faced and came out in Father Demo Square. I asked a couple of rumdumb bums who were standing in the snow and appeared to have been standing there for quite a while if they had seen an albino in a white linen suit. They looked at me as if I were crazy, then shook their heads and tried to brace me for coffee money. I went through the front door of the undertaking establishment, breezed past the rubbery-looking potted plants and unbolted the door to the hallway. The fat little man led the procession of mourners into the lobby. There was an audible sigh of relief as they scurried out. They must have developed a hard case of claustrophobia, locked in like that with their dead.

I told the mortician's assistant I had to go out and question people and maybe look for the extraordinary all-white man.

"You're not waiting for the police?" he asked suspiciously.

I shook my head, indicated the telephone, and went out to the street. As I crossed the square the juggernaut of traffic bore down on me with murderous intent and I was pinpointed in the glare of a dozen baleful headlights. I managed to cross the no man's land without accident. I went into the San Remo Restaurant at the corner of Bleecker and MacDougal. The place was bursting at the seams with a lot of young guys and dolls. The guys wore stocking caps and berets and lumberjackets. The dolls wore levis and mackinaws and had scarfs tied around their hair. There was a bubble of talk about social consciousness, Jean-Paul Sartre, and, of course, Sex, with a capital S. I dug a tunnel through the budding bohemians to reach the bar. I slapped a five-dollar bill on the bar.

I didn't like to ask such a busy bartender to make change unless I bought something from him, so I ordered a double rye. I figured I needed it anyway after seeing a corpse with its face shot off. I asked the bartender to give me my change in silver. I gulped the rye, blazed a trail through the closely clustered young intellectuals, and went into a telephone booth. I asked for Western Union.

When a professionally dulcet voice answered I said I'd like to send a telegram to Tommy Twotoes, Beverly Gardens Hotel, Beverly Hills, California. I had to repeat the name several times. Nobody is willing to believe right off that any living person actually goes under such a name as Twotoes.

When she finally spelled the name back to me correctly, if doubtfully, I dictated a message:

AN ALBINO IN A WHITE LINEN SUIT JUST
BLEW THE FACE OFF YOUR EMBALMED PAL
FIGHTING PHIL CASELLI WITH A BIG FOR-
TY-FIVE STOP ALBINO DISAPPEARED STOP
WHAT DO I DO NOW QUESTION MARK
WILL WAIT YOUR CALL IN OFFICE
                                                SOLDIER

The operator came on and asked for some money. I dropped it in the slot. The telegram came under the heading of expenses, so I didn't mind throwing in extra words and spelled-out punctuation marks.

I figured it would be at least a couple of hours before I heard from Mr. Twotoes. The three-hour difference in time meant it would be only five o'clock in Beverly Hills, so he probably hadn't returned from the races at Santa Anita Park. I made like a bull-dozer again and burrowed myself a path through the socially conscious characters. At the bar I ordered a double shot. I wanted to think things over and I always think better with a shot in my hand—or in my stomach.

First, I wondered what charge could be brought against a man who shot the face off an embalmed corpse. Disturbing the peace, probably, I decided. The peace of the dead. Then I wondered just what the hell I had to do with the corpse with the shattered face and the little white gunman. I didn't really know. After Tommy Twotoes had solved the murder of the former Broadway butterfly, Danise Darlan, he had begun to fancy himself in the role of a criminologist. Certainly, he'd played almost every other part in his lifetime of some seventy years. The three-hundred-pound millionaire, who suffered so severely from alcoholic neuritis that he could hardly walk without assistance, was the only man I ever knew who was big enough to get a hard case of claustrophobia in the Pentagon Building. He had been a bum on Skid Row in his youth. He had been a prospector in the Klondike, had managed the best fighters of his day, owned a motion-picture studio, headed a rum-running syndicate during Prohibition, operated a racetrack in Mexico and had "angeled" numerous Broadway shows and night clubs. After he became involved in the murder of Danise Darlan, he decided he was the greatest sleuth since Sherlock and I'd been expecting him to break out with a fore-and-aft cap, an off-key fiddle and a cocaine needle at any moment.

Instead, he had given me the financial backing to open a private-detective agency. The fact that I was issued a license was a tribute to Mr. Twotoes' influence in the right places. You are supposed to have three years' investigative experience before the Secretary of State gives you a private richard's card in New York. Besides working briefly as an operative, I'd been a crime reporter once. After I'd been blown out of an M-4 tank in the war, I'd been assigned to an easy job in G-2—Intelligence—where my duties consisted mainly in getting naturalization papers for alien GI's. And after the war, I'd tramped around asking questions for opinion polls. Thanks to Mr. Twotoes' persuasive ways with politicians, all this had counted as "investigative experience." The idea was that Tommy Twotoes was to be the silent partner and the brains of the agency and that I was to be the cluck who acted as leg-man and answered the telephone calls, if any. I'd only had the license for a few weeks and in that time I'd had exactly one job. A show-girl had hired me to tail her wealthy benefactor. She'd thought he was spending too much time with his wife. Naturally, that job hadn't even paid the rent on my none too luxurious office, but that fact didn't worry me too much. I had a generous drawing account and plenty of time on my hands. I'd even had the leisure to skip through two books I'd always intended to read but hadn't got around to before—*War and Peace* and *Les Misérables*.

A few weeks before, Tommy Twotoes had felt the urge to attend the races at Santa Anita Park. His faithful retainer, Ebony Black, an ageing, one-eyed Negro who had once been a heavyweight contender, had driven him to California in his quarter-century-old Rolls Royce town car. Tommy had led a fast life and he didn't want too much speed to catch up with him in his old age. The governor of the car was set so that it could go no faster than thirty-five miles an hour. Anticipating a long and thirsty journey, Mr. Twotoes had had a portable bar, complete to refrigeration, installed in the ancient vehicle.

Then, a couple of days before my visit to the mortuary, Fighting Phil Caselli had made the papers for the first time in twenty years by the simple expedient of dying under the wheels of a hit-run driver. Fighting Phil had once been a great middleweight in Tommy's stable. The papers had resurrected yellowed clippings from their morgues and had given the forgotten man a good send-off. Tommy had read the story in California and had wired me to make sure the old pug wasn't buried in a pauper's grave. For some unaccountable reason he had also instructed me to take a photograph of Fighting Phil Caselli's corpse. I'd traced what remained of Phil to the funeral parlor on Father Demo Square. Then the little man in white had made his impressive appearance and his even more theatrical exit. I had wondered what the eccentric old millionaire had in mind when he instructed me to take pictures of the corpse. It didn't seem likely he had anticipated that Caselli's face would suddenly become decidedly unphotogenic.

An hour had passed and several more doubles plus a few singles had slipped down my throat. I felt warm inside, and it was a nice sensation. I'm a fairly tall guy and I could see over the heads of most of the young devotees of Sartre, Stein and surrealism. I looked out the window and saw that the snow flurries had mounted to a real storm. There wasn't any use looking for an all-white little man in an all-white world like that. He'd be camouflaged as effectively as a chameleon. It was nine o'clock in New York and six o'clock in California. Tommy should have been able to make the trip from the racetrack in Arcadia to his hotel in Beverly Hills, even in the slow-moving Rolls.

I again emulated a sandhog and burrowed my way through the bunched bohemians. By the time I reached the subway on Third Street the fleecy, wind-whipped snowflakes had made me as white as the gun-toting albino. I went down into the bowels of Manhattan, hopped a Sixth Avenue train and got off at Forty-second. My office was in one of those old buildings in the forties, the kind with ornate facades that have needed a face-lifting for forty years. I suspected that the other occupants of the building were slightly shady characters, like shysters, loan sharks, and racetrack tipsters. I knew for certain that one of the offices in this cave of sad-faced men was used occasionally for New York's floating crap game. My office hadn't been done by an interior decorator. There was a grass rug on the floor, a second-hand desk, a few second-hand straight chairs and a big leather chair. The leather was cracking, but the chair was nice and soothing to the *derrière*. There were a couple of green filing cabinets with empty files inside them. The walls were tastefully decorated with a Petty Girl calendar and a framed copy of my private operative's license. The only ornament on my desk, besides an ancient portable typewriter, a bottle of gummy ink and a few sawed-off pencils, was a photograph of my fiancée, Ginny. Ginny didn't look at all like the girl whose pictures were displayed outside Vince Parada's Village sucker trap, where she performed as a strip-tease artiste. The photo on my desk showed a young woman in adequate and demure dress, with saucer eyes that made her look like a kid on Christmas morning.

The filing cabinets were a fine place to keep booze. I had two fifths stored there. One was the office bottle of cheap rye. The other was the company bottle of good Scotch. Only the blonde who hired me to tail her benefactor had thus far sipped from the company bottle. I took out the office bottle and poured a shot into a tumbler that needed washing. Then I got the first volume of Gibbon's *Decline and Fall of the Roman Empire*, another book I'd never had time to read before, out of the desk drawer, dropped into the leather chair, and relaxed. I was working on page two of the book and shot two of the whisky when the phone rang.

After the operator had ascertained my name and other pertinent facts, Tommy Twotoes' voice boomed over the wire.

"Soldier!" he said. "What nonsense is this? I lose at the races and return to find your wire. Such things spoil a man's appetite for dinner. They may even drive him to drink."

"No nonsense," I replied. "I went to the funeral parlor about seven-thirty, Eastern Standard Time. I inquired for your friend Phil, and was directed to Parlor C. A little albino wearing a white linen suit despite the snowstorm here was right behind me."

I gave him a detailed account of the melodramatic occurrences of the past two hours.

"I photographed the corpse, interviewed the chief and only mourner, the late Phil's aunt," I added.

"Aunt?" boomed Tommy. "Impossible."

"Aunt," I repeated. "People have them, you know. This was a very old aunt. Very poor looking. Italian. No spik so good. I've got her address. Then I went out a window, released the others, and wired you from a gin mill on the corner."

Tommy said, "You spend too much time in gin mills. Drug stores also have telephones, you know. The albino you describe is doubtless Snowy Sylvester. He was one of Phil's closest friends, a kind of mascot in Phil's fighting days."

"Oh," I said. "Then shooting Phil's face off was just a touching tribute to his old pal. We can forget the, whole thing."

"On the contrary," replied Tommy. "This may be most serious. There is a plane tomorrow that arrives in New York at eight in the evening. I will take it. It may be difficult to make reservations for five at this late hour, but I have influence and will use it."

"Five?" I exclaimed. "Who's coming with you besides Ebony Black?"

"Ebony will proceed back at his leisure, since he will have to drive the car," Tommy Twotoes replied calmly. "But I have picked up a few old friends during my stay in the Golden West, and they have consented to visit me back East. It may be a bit inconvenient for them to leave on such short notice, but they will do so. You will meet the plane. You will also instruct Polvo to meet the plane with the station wagon."

Polvo was Tommy Twotoes' chef. He had been an organ grinder on the lower East Side before he became a retainer of the fat old millionaire. He also took care of the penguin flock which Tommy Twotoes had housed in a miniature Antarctic on his place at Tarrytown. Among other things, Mr. Twotoes was a penguin-fancier.

"Now get this carefully," Tommy Twotoes said. "You will proceed at once to the Suffield Hotel on Murray Hill. Go to Suite 411. It is occupied by Dr. Thaddeus Mulholland. It has been occupied by him for nearly half a century, in fact. You will ask Dr. Mulholland when he last saw Phil Caselli. You will also query him concerning the whereabouts of our albino, Snowy Sylvester. He will know. He is an extraordinary old man, over ninety and eccentric, but remarkable. I fear for his safety. If the door is not opened, force it. You have a variety of keys."

"What the hell is all this?" I inquired. "How does the old doc figure in this jackpot?"

"Don't ask questions. Merely proceed as instructed. Wire me immediately the state of Dr. Mulholland's health and any other pertinent information. If you find him well, let the albino rest until my return. But be sure to wire me this evening."

"Yes, sir," I said, with exaggerated courtesy. "Any further instructions, sir?"

"Yes," replied the fat man. "You will make sure to determine the result of the third race at Santa Anita tomorrow. I am interested in a certain horse and it will be difficult for me to obtain race results while traveling through the skyways."

"Who's the horse?" I asked.

"I never give tips," replied Tommy. "If they win, people annoy you for more information. If they lose, people are resentful of the tipster rather than the horse. Now you will give me a report on the penguins, please."

"I called Polvo this morning as usual and sent you a report air mail," I answered. "The flock is in good health. They are eating their shrimp with relish. They show no signs of breeding in captivity, but you hardly expected them to, after all these years. Cleo, your house pet, has taken to sleeping in the master's bed during his absence."

Tommy Twotoes chuckled. "Cleo is a warm-hearted female," he said.

I knew that. Tommy had once made me a present of Cleo, the affectionate penguin, but I'd had no proper accommodations for her in my cold-water flat, so I had returned her to the rookeries in Tarrytown.

Tommy said, "Call on Dr. Mulholland. Wire me. Call Polvo. Get the result of the third race at Santa Anita tomorrow. Meet my plane. In that order. Everything clear?"

"Yes, *sir,*" I replied. "Anything else?"

"Stay sober," instructed Tommy. "But not *too* sober, of course. Good night, Soldier." He hung up.

I knew something about the Suffield Hotel and Dr. Mulholland from my newspaper days, but I couldn't figure how either could be connected with the recently deceased Mr. Caselli or the albino with a .45 in his mitt. The Suffield was an ancient pile of brick and stone. General Grant had been an honored guest of the hostelry before he became President and Edward VII had stayed there when he was Prince of Wales: Very old characters sat around the enormous, marble lobby from breakfast to bedtime, playing euchre, working jigsaw puzzles and listening to their arteries harden.

Dr. Mulholland had once been dean of the law school at Empire State University. He was the author of numerous weighty tomes, dealing mainly with the niceties of international law. He had broken into the news again only recently when United Nations delegates had consulted him concerning the legal standing of Formosa and Korea. The old man's mind was still remarkably keen regarding involved legal questions, but for many years he had devoted himself almost entirely to a strange, senile hobby. He left his hotel suite early each morning, regardless of the weather, and spent most of the day filling a burlap sack with choice tidbits from trash cans and garbage pails. If he hadn't been a prominent old duffer with a fat pension they'd have put him away in a county nut factory years before.

It was going on ten o'clock and I figured the old boy would be in bed. He must have had an arduous day of rag-picking and I hated to wake him up. But orders were orders. I took a cab through the snowstorm to the ancient hotel on Murray Hill.

The occupants of the enormous marble halls had retired to bed. A bald clerk was working a crossword puzzle at the desk. I skirted by him and entered a big cage with a fretwork front. The elevator operator was a very fat and very black Negro who wore horn-rimmed glasses. There was a funny smell in the elevator and when I saw the queer look in the Negro's eyes, I recognized the odor. Reefers. The muggles smoker conveyed me to the fourth floor.

I wandered around cavernous corridors for quite a while before I found a sturdy door marked 411. Hanging to the doorknob was one of those little cards that old-fashioned family doctors once used. At the top was printed "Doctor Is Out." Below that was printed "Will Return At." And below that was a little clock with the hands set at three o'clock. I thought three A.M. was pretty late for an old guy over ninety to be coming home. Doc Mulholland was an LLD. and a Ph.D. but he wasn't an M.D., so the little card seemed out of place. Despite the card, I rapped on the door. No answer. I rapped again. I kept on rapping until my knuckles smarted. Then I tried my keys. The fourth key I tried opened the lock.

I entered a foyer, used a pencil flash to find the light switch. I'd half-expected something as weird as the interior of the Castle of Otranto, but what I saw made me start. The foyer was piled from floor to ceiling with assorted junk, old newspapers, old rags, old boxes, old metal, cracked statuary, books with broken bindings, fragments of furniture. I thought of the junk-littered mansion where the fantastic Collyer brothers had been found dead, and I hoped the old doc hadn't booby-trapped this place against intruders.

I picked my way through the debris and entered a door to the right. More of the same. There was barely room for a bed, a dresser and a straight chair in the huge chamber. Junk took up all the other space. I crossed a narrow path through the litter of the foyer and entered the living room. There was more junk and some large, unwieldy, dark furniture. The light switch lit bulbs in a great brass chandelier that was suspended from the high ceiling. A big buzzard seemed to be flapping slowly beneath the chandelier.

Only it wasn't a buzzard. It was a very old man, dressed in baggy black clothes.

One end of a rope was attached to the chandelier. The other end was looped around the scrawny neck of the very old man.

The old man's feet weren't touching the floor.

2

A man nearing the century mark isn't too pretty to look at when he's alive. In broken-necked death he can afford a very revolting spectacle indeed to a guy of my delicate sensitivity. The old doc's body swayed slightly at the end of the rope. The baggy black tail-coat was ruffled by the breeze from a half-opened window, giving the illusion of a gorged buzzard lazily flapping its wings. The skinny neck, the hawk beak of the parchment-crinkled face, and the knotty, long-nailed, talonlike hands all added to the vulturine appearance of the hanging corpse. The head jutted forward from the broken neck and long, snow-white hair partially covered the face that had been made hideous by strangulation. The tongue protruded from the mouth and the eyes bulged obscenely.

At first glance, I realized that the old man hadn't killed himself. I took mental measurements. I judged the ceiling to be at least fourteen feet high. The brass chandelier swung from heavy metal links about two feet below the ceiling. The rope hung another two feet below the chandelier. The old man was stooped, but he was tall, nearly six feet, I judged. From just beneath his chin, where the rope was looped to his feet, he would measure around five feet, four inches. That all added up to a few inches over nine feet, leaving a space of over four feet between the old man and the floor.

Two of the walls of the room were taken up by ceiling-high junk. Another wall framed two large windows. The fourth wall had built-in bookshelves which reached to the ceiling. In front of the bookshelves was one of those library ladders, about six feet high, with a flat top. It was half the length of the room away from the swaying corpse, but I figured it could have made a nice taking-off place for a hanging, so I went over and examined it. I mounted a few rungs and looked at the flat top. There was a film of dust over it, as there was over most of the furniture in the room. There were footprints in the dust. The shoes that had made the footprints had very sharp toes and new heels, because a triangular design on the heel and a brand name were well enough defined. I crossed over and looked at the old man's shoes. They were sharp-pointed. They were old and cracked but they had just been re-soled and re-heeled and the rubber heels had the triangle and the brand name stamped in them. The old doc had evidently stood on the ladder, stepped off it and broken his neck. How the ladder had got back in front of the bookcase was another question entirely.

I jotted all these observations down in the notebook that contained the address of Theresa Caselli and a complicated list of figures that recorded my daily play in the ten-cent numbers pool. I thought I was being a very scientific detective, even though I was new at the business.

I also congratulated myself upon the fact that I hadn't removed the pigskin gloves that Ginny had given me for my birthday. Ginny was always giving me gloves, ties, mufflers and other articles of clothing for such special occasions as birthdays and Christmas, maybe because she was a strip-tease artiste and had a kind of reverse psychological fixation on clothes. Once I'd left my fingerprints around and about in another murder room when Danise Dalian was killed and the results hadn't been pleasant.

My mellow mood of self-admiration was interrupted rudely by a wild, screeching scream. I jumped several feet, as I am a very nervous guy when noises rend the night. I stumbled over a set of rusty andirons that were among the old doc's treasured junk, and fell flat on my face. I got up cursing and the unearthly noise continued. Whatever was making the noise spoke English. It screamed, "Stop, thief! Stop, thief!"

In a dark space between the snow-dusted windows, I saw a big bird cage. As I moved nearer to it, I saw that there was an oversized, malevolent-looking green parrot inside the cage. The parrot was squawking its fool head off. I judged from its heavy-lidded eyes that it had just awakened from a nap and didn't welcome the presence of a stranger in the room. I went over to the cage and tried to soothe the bird, which was whipping itself into a feathered frenzy.

I said, "Polly wanna cracker? Polly wanna cracker?" I figured that was the conventional approach.

The parrot said, "Goddam right. Goddam right." Then it let out a few hideous squawks to emphasize its statement.

The only trouble was, I didn't have a cracker. I tried offering the parrot one of the mints I chew to disguise the liquor on my breath. The parrot nearly bit my finger off. It spat out the mint and shrieked, "Stop, thief! Stop, thief!"

I was thankful for the thick walls and heavy doors of the old hotel. I had noticed an alcove at the end of the littered foyer. I went out to the foyer, parted the curtain that hung from the alcove and snapped on another light. As I had expected, there was a kitchenette. There were a few cracked, dirty dishes in the sink. There was a fishy smell from an open can that had contained sardines. On a soiled plate by the can were the remnants of crackers. I took the cracker crumbs into the living room and offered them to the squawking parrot. The green bird gobbled them down, cocked one basilisk eye at me and said, "Goddam right! Goddam right!"

"Sure," I said. "You be nice and quiet and I'll get you a filet mignon."

I saw a piece of black cloth near the cage. I hooded the cage with it and the parrot became quiet after making a few grumbling sounds.

I tried to think things over. I decided that the old recluse who was flapping from the ceiling must have been chilled for money. It is in the classic tradition for old recluses and rag-pickers to have bundles of grand notes stashed away somewhere. In such a wild litter, however, I wouldn't have known how to begin looking for the treasure trove, and besides I figured the murderer had probably beaten me to the cache. I had already remained in the old doc's suite too long. The elevator boy was half-grogged with the weed, but he might become suspicious and remember the time that had elapsed since he had brought me up. I turned out all the lights except those in the foyer. As I was about to turn off the foyer light, I noticed a telephone sitting on a crate that was filled with junk. Beside the telephone was a pad. On the pad there was one notation. The name, address and telephone number of my patron, Tommy Twotoes, were written on the pad. I tore the sheet with the address off the pad and stuffed it in my pocket. After all, I had to protect the interest of my patron, who in this case was also my client.

I switched off the light and left Suite 411, making sure that the lock of the door snapped behind me.

I felt like a lone archaeologist exploring an ancient ruin as I wandered through the vast, dim corridors, trying to take an azimuth on the elevator. The Suffield had more waste space than that decorative but nonfunctional pile on Forty-second and Fifth, the New York Public Library.

Once I found the elevator, it took a long time for the fat, marijuana-doped operator to lift the cage up four floors. When the elevator finally shuddered to a stop it was so far below the floor that I nearly broke my ankle stepping into it. The cage smelled more strongly of the weed now and the operator had reached the somnolent stage. His eyes were as heavy-lidded as the parrot's.

I said, "You know old Dr. Mulholland?"

"Sure, sure," he answered drowsily. "Ole doc, he here when I first come, ten-twelve years ago. He been here fawty-fifty years, they say. Ole doc got big brain, but ack like little child sometimes. Most ev'ry day ole doc go out and pick up things other people th'ow away. Once awhile he take things out and th'ow 'em away hisself, so he make room for more things. Been doing that for years and years."

"He usually out this late?" I asked.

The fat Negro shook his head emphatically. "Never," he said. "Ole doc go out early morning. Ole doc come back late afternoon. I mostly has to take him up on freight elevator. They won't let him ride on this elevator when he's gotta sack of junk. Sometime junk smell bad."

"He must be out now," I said. "I knocked. There's a sign on the door says he won't be back till three o'clock."

The Negro chuckled. "That's ole doc's clock," he said. "Ole doc ain't out. He been in two-three days now. Sometime he don't want company. He take up grub, put sign on door and sets around using his big brain to figure out big things."

We had reached the ground floor, but the Negro left the door closed.

I said, "Does he have much company?"

"Not much. Two fellows, they come to see him once awhile."

"Who are they?" I asked.

"One a little fellow. Real little. Whitest white man I ever see. Mr. Jenks, the room clerk, he laugh out loud when he see little man standing by me in elevator, 'cause he's so white and I'm so black. Little white man all right. Give me smokes."

"What kind of smokes?" I asked.

The Negro chuckled and winked. "*Right* kind of smokes," he said.

"Does the little guy smoke the same brand you do?" I asked.

"Guess he do," said the Negro. "Guess you do, too, mister."

"Why do you guess that?" I asked.

"Take a teahound to smell tea, mister," he replied.

I didn't tell him that marijuana was one of the few vices I hadn't yet cultivated. Instead I said, "Who's the doc's other visitor?"

"Big, rough man," he answered. "Big, ugly man. Look like bulldog."

"Either of them been up to see the doc recently?"

"Little white man was. 'Bout two days ago. Give me extra lot of smokes, so maybe he didn't want me to say he been here. You wanna contribute a donation to my church, mister?"

The question took me by surprise. It was a new way of chiseling a tip. "What church?" I asked.

"Church of the Sanctified Soul, up to Harlem. I preach there my night off," said the Negro.

I handed him a buck. "If you can remember some more things, I might make another donation to such a worthy cause," I told him.

He opened the elevator door. "Remember things best when I got the right kind of smokes," he said, winking at me.

The bald room clerk was still working the crossword puzzle. I said, "Did you happen to notice Dr. Mulholland going out this evening?"

He bit his lips and looked up at me, perplexed. "What's a four-letter word meaning horse's sidewalk?" he asked.

"Path, maybe," I hazarded. "Bridle path."

He shook his bald head. "Begins with an H and ends with a T," he said. "Just the reverse of path."

"Halt, then," I said. "String-halt. A string-halt horse throws his leg out sideways. Horse's side-walk, get it?"

"That's *exactly* it," said the delighted clerk, filling in the squares. "Now what did you want?"

"Dr. Mulholland," I repeated. "I knocked at his door. He didn't answer. He hardly ever goes out at night, I understand. I'm afraid he may be ill."

The room clerk, Jenks, gave me a superior little smirk. "Was the clock on his door?" he asked.

"Yeah," I said. "According to it, he'll return at three A.M. Don't tell me a guy that old plays the gin mills."

"The doctor never allows anyone in his rooms when the clock is on the door," explained the clerk. "The maids haven't been able to get in for the past two days. He's afraid they'll throw out his junk or steal something if he isn't there when they clean. But sometimes, when he doesn't want to be disturbed, he puts the sign out when he's *in* his rooms. It's very annoying. That junk of his is a real health hazard. Fire hazard, too. But what can we do? He's our oldest tenant. Been here half a century. No one else would take him. And he's a nice old man, except for his peculiarities."

"I'm afraid he's sick," I persisted. "I want you to go up there with me and open the door with a house key."

"Quite impossible," the clerk declared. "It's ten-thirty. That's a very late hour for the guests in this hotel. Nearly all of them are elderly persons. Dr. Mulholland will be in bed. I couldn't disturb him. You shouldn't have gone up and hammered on the door, you know."

I produced the private richard's license. The room clerk was impressed. "Police?" he asked. "But why would the police wish to see a harmless old man at this hour?"

"Private detective," I told him. "My client is interested in the doctor. He thinks the old man may be sick. If you don't open the door, I'll call the city cops and have it opened."

"This is very irregular," complained the clerk. "I couldn't think of having the police here. This is a quiet, orderly hotel, full of older people. The police would shock them, scare them to death."

"You've been criminally negligent in not seeing whether a tenant over ninety is dead or alive for the past two days," I said threateningly. "Either you open the door now or I call the cops."

"I suppose I'll have to," said the clerk, "but I warn you the doctor will be most put out."

He took a huge ring with a single key suspended from it off a rack. Despite the fact that he was in the drowsy stage of a marijuana binge, the fat elevator operator regarded us with interest. We went to 411. Jenks knocked lightly on the door. Then he knocked more loudly and called the doctor's name. Finally he used the key.

I let him lead the way. He switched on the light in the corridor and timidly called, "Dr. Mulholland? Dr. Mulholland?"

He was answered by a muffled squawk from the parrot's hooded cage.

"Stop, thief! Stop, thief! Goddam right!"

Jenks started violently. Then he gained control of himself and said, "It's only Quasimodo, the doctor's parrot." He switched on the light in the bedroom.

"Why, he's not in his bed," he said. This fact seemed to perplex him even more than the crossword puzzle had. He crossed to the living room, turned on the light.

When he saw what was swaying beneath the chandelier, he staggered, supported himself against the doorjamb. It took long moments for him to regain the power of speech. When he did, he cried out in anguish.

"Oh, no. Oh, no. He couldn't have!"

"He didn't, chum," I informed him. "Somebody else did."

"What—what do you mean?" he asked.

"Look around," I advised him: "If the old man had hanged himself, he'd have had to step off something, or kick it from under him. He's several feet off the floor. And there's not a piece of furniture within kicking distance of him."

"Cut him down!" cried the clerk. "Maybe he isn't' dead yet."

I went through the motions of feeling the old man's heart, his pulse.

"He's dead," I said. "We can't disturb things. Now *you* will have to call the cops."

"This is awful! Awful!" said Jenks, wringing his hands.

"It's worse," I told him. "It's murder."

The parrot confirmed my statement from its hooded cage.

"Goddam right! Goddam right!" the parrot said.

"What on earth will I do?" asked the clerk. "This is awful. Awful." He was wringing his hands again.

"Polly wanna cracker. Polly wanna cracker. Goddam right," said the parrot.

"You have to call the cops," I said patiently. "Ask for Homicide. Tell 'em just what happened."

"But I don't *know* what happened," Jenks protested.

The door to the foyer had been left open. Someone tapped at it. The hopped-up elevator operator entered the foyer. The clerk said petulantly, "Eddie! What are *you* doing here?"

"It's the switchboard, Mist' Jenks," said the Negro apologetically. "It's been a-buzzin' like a beehive."

"I'll have to go down," said the clerk. "I'll call the police from the office."

"The *po*-lice?" said Eddie. "Why, Mist' Jenks? Why?"

He moved forward in the foyer and looked through the living-room door. He saw what was hanging from the chandelier and let out a yelp. The yelp started the parrot squawking again.

"Shut up, both of you," cried Jenks to Eddie and the parrot. In the presence of a hired hand, he had become brisk, efficient.

Eddie clasped his hands beneath his chin, tilted his head heavenward. "Lawd have mercy on the soul of poor ole doc," he prayed. "Why he do it, Mist' Jenks? Why?"

"Quiet!" admonished the suddenly authoritative Jenks. "Out of here, now. All of us."

As we left the suite, the parrot screamed, "Stop, thief! Stop, thief!"

The switchboard was still buzzing monotonously when we reached the lobby. Jenks ran to it, hooked the passkey to a nearby rack and plugged in. He said, "Hotel Suffield, good evening," and then he seemed startled.

"Who?" he asked incredulously. "Dr. Mulholland?"

I shoved Jenks aside. "Let me take it," I said, close to his free ear. I stuck the receiver to my own ear, spoke into the mouthpiece. I said, "Yes, hello?"

"This 411?" a very deep bass voice asked. "I want the doc."

"Who's calling?" I inquired.

"Who's this? Snowy?" asked the voice.

"No," I said, stalling. "You want Snowy? Who's this calling?"

"Put the doc on, please," said the voice. "If he's gone to bed, wake him up. Tell him it's important. Tell him it's Phil."

"Who?"

"Phil. Phil Caselli," the voice answered.

That stopped me flat. It was the first time I'd ever talked over the phone to a corpse without a face. Finally I said weakly, "Where are you?"

"Hey, what the hell is this?" inquired the voice from outer space. "You gonna call the doc or ain't you, bud?"

"Dr. Mulholland's had an accident," I said. "You'd better get down here right away."

"What kind of accident?" asked the ghost of Fighting Phil Caselli. "Who's this talking?"

"A serious accident," I ad-libbed. "This is Dr. Mulholland's physician. You'd better hurry down here if you're a friend of his."

There was a short silence. Then the voice from the grave said, "It'll take me about half an hour." The, receiver clicked.

Well, I thought, it's a short trip back from eternity. Maybe this modern age has produced jet-propelled zombies.

"What's this all about?" demanded Jenks, the clerk. "What do you mean shoving me like that? And pretending you're a doctor?"

"Nothing to worry over, chum," I assured him. "Just one dead man calling another dead man on the telephone."

"I demand to know who you were talking to," flared Jenks.

"Guy name of Phil Caselli," I said. "Friend of the old doc's."

"Caselli?" exclaimed the clerk. "But he's dead! I read it in the papers. They ran his obituary right next to the crossword puzzle."

"Just like I said," I replied. "Now call the cops, like a good little boy."

Jenks glanced disapprovingly at the open-mouthed Eddie, who was standing by, taking it all in. The clerk nodded toward an office marked "Manager."

"We'll call from inside," he said.

We went into the office, which was decorated with ancient photographs of General Grant, Edward VII, John L. Sullivan, Berry Wall, Tod Sloan, Minnie Maddern Fiske, a few assorted duchesses and other celebrities that the Suffield had entertained in its heyday. Jenks picked up the phone nervously and finally got connected with Homicide. After a lot of hemming and hawing he convinced the person on the other end of the line that an old man was hanging by the neck from a chandelier in Suite 411.

After that there was nothing to do but wait, and Jenks rose to the occasion in a gallant manner I hadn't expected from a slightly timorous crossword-puzzle addict. He produced a bottle of good bourbon whisky. We had time for two drinks apiece before the Homicide Squad arrived, headed by my old friend, Lieutenant Romano, the cop with the classic profile.

Jenks glanced toward the closed cage of the only elevator that was in operation and looked annoyed. The semicircular indicator above the elevator showed that the car was in the basement.

"That Eddie," complained the room clerk. "I think he sneaks down to the basement to drink, but I never smell it on his breath."

I figured an innocent guy like Jenks wouldn't be able to identify the heavy odor of marijuana which clung about the fat elevator operator.

Romano looked at me suspiciously. "Hello, honeyboy," he said. "You hanging around corpses again? Haven't seen you since they chilled poor Danise."

I gave him my winning smile, but didn't answer. Jenks was leaning against the elevator buzzer and cursing under his breath.

"Funny thing," continued the Lieutenant. "I wasn't on the call myself, but I heard about a case earlier tonight. Seems a corpse got its face shot off in an undertaking parlor. Seems a tall, lean private eye with a zigzag scar on his face was hanging around the joint, but dusted before the cops arrived."

I'd got that scar in the war and once it had identified me as a murder suspect. The subject wasn't pleasant. I said, "Strictly in the line of duty, Lieutenant. It might interest you to know that the corpse you mentioned just called Dr. Mulholland on the telephone. I talked to him."

Eddie finally arrived. I explained further details of the call while we rode to the fourth floor. I told the Lieutenant that Fighting Phil had promised to put in an appearance in half an hour or so.

"It'll be interesting to see what he looks like when he's wearing his face," Romano commented.

Soon after we entered the murder room I had a queer sense that something was wrong, something was missing from the picture, but there was so much activity around me that I was distracted and couldn't place the source of my faint uneasiness at once. They didn't question Jenks or me until after they'd gone through the usual procedure of dusting for fingerprints and photographing the hanging corpse and the living room from numerous angles. Then an assistant medical examiner arrived and they took the body down.

The medical examiner was a neat little man with a bushy mustache. He made a cursory examination of the corpse, said, "Cause of death strangulation, probably. Neck's broken, too. Knob on the back of the head. Hit with usual blunt instrument before he was hanged. Probably been dead about thirty-six to forty-eight hours. It's hard to be too accurate about these old codgers. Can tell more after we get him down to the morgue. Might come closer when we examine the stomach contents."

"He ate sardines," I said helpfully. "There's an empty can in the kitchen."

I instantly regretted that statement. I hadn't gone into the kitchen while Jenks was with me. But Jenks didn't pick me up, and I gave silent thanks.

The medical examiner said, "Sardines are damned indigestible for an old codger like him. Maybe he died from acute indigestion after all."

Romano took Jenks into the bedroom and questioned him. Detectives continued to putter around the littered mess in the living room. Then Eddie was brought up for questioning and Jenks took the elevator down to await the promised call of Mr. Caselli, the walking-talking cadaver without a face. Eddie must have lit up another stick of tea. His eyes were enlarged and were shining with an abnormal brightness. I hoped he wouldn't remember how long I'd been on the fourth floor the first time I went up.

When the Negro left the bedroom, Romano summoned me. I told a straight and factual story except for omitting the fact that I had entered the suite before Jenks had opened it with a house key.

Romano said, "Hmm," and didn't seem too convinced.

"Just why did you call on the Caselli corpse?" he inquired. "Social visit, no doubt? And what interest do you have in the old doctor? You don't mind answering those questions, do you, honeyboy?"

"I was acting in both instances in the interest of a client," I said stiffly.

"Client's name, please, honeyboy?" asked Romano.

"You know it wouldn't be ethical for me to give you that information," I protested. "I'm a private investigator."

"Fancy name you eyes are giving yourselves nowadays," mused the Lieutenant. "Me, I just call myself a cop. I could be a nasty man, honeyboy. This is murder, kind of a serious offense. I could hold you as a material witness if I wasn't such a good-hearted slob. But I know my old pal Tommy Twotoes put up the dough for your business. I can put two and two together. Used to know Tommy right well during Prohibition when he was operating Broadway sucker traps and I was pounding a beat. Cadged a lot of drinks off him. A few birthday presents, too. One year when the horses weren't running to form on Long Island, I had four birthdays."

The Lieutenant scratched his classic Roman nose.

"Tommy used to be a fight promoter," he continued. "Phil was an old-time pug. The poor old character in the next room was one of Tommy's friends. Seems to me I heard Tommy was out of town. When'll he be back, honeyboy?"

"I may be in touch with my *client* tomorrow evening," I said, putting the chill in my voice.

"Uh-huh. What time, honeyboy?"

"Around eight."

"Yeah. Seem to remember Tommy went to California. Stratoliner from the Coast gets in at La Guardia at eight. I'll be there to meet it. Haven't seen old Tommy for a long time."

To change the subject I told him that I'd found footprints similar to the old man's shoes on top of the library ladder.

"You're getting to be quite a sleuth, honeyboy," said Romano. "I saw those footprints. They're kind of screwy. Judging from the knob on the back of his noggin, the old man must have been knocked out when he was trussed up. Figure it's a hard job to drag even an undernourished old man like him up a ladder, stand him upright so he'll make a *perfect* footprint like that. Seems the dust would have been messed around a little bit, huh, honeyboy?"

I hadn't thought of that angle. "Well, maybe he just stood on the ladder to reach a book *before* he was hanged," I said.

"Would've been pretty hard for him to do that *after* he was hanged," replied Romano. "But after all, we already got one corpse which come to life. By the way, where *is* your pal, the guy without a face?"

I looked at my watch and shook my head. Over an hour had passed since my weird telephone conversation.

There was a knock at the door. Romano yelled, "Come in." A detective entered.

"We found something, Lieutenant," he said.

"You're good finding anything in that owl's nest," replied the Lieutenant. "What'd you find, honeyboy?"

"A will. It's in the old man's handwriting. At least it's in some-body's handwriting. It's witnessed by this fellow Eddie, the eleva-tor boy. And by some woman. Understand the woman's a cham-bermaid here. Also we found this card in the old man's pocket."

Romano looked at the card and grinned widely. He handed the card to me, said, "Ever see one of these before, honeyboy?"

The card read "Terry Bob Rooke, Private Investigator"—my own business card. My mouth gaped open. I said, "I don't know where in hell he got this."

"Maybe he found it in a garbage can," Romano offered. He looked at the will. "What they call a holograph," he said. "Might have stood up in court, even without witnesses." They were carrying the corpse out in a basket. Romano left the room, crossed the foyer, entered the living room, reading the will. The detective and I followed him.

The Lieutenant said, "Tommy Twotoes is executor of the old man's estate, it says here. He left most of it to a character named Sylvester and to Phil Caselli, the corpse that talks like a man. That Sylvester's name is given as Stanley, but it's probably Snowy. Used to be a kind of second to Phil in the fight game. In the minor rack-ets now. Funny-looking guy. Albino. Old man left Snowy one key to a safe-deposit box and Phil a key to another safe-deposit box. Snowy's key is marked Merchants' Bank. Phil's is marked Manu-facturers' Bank. It says here Tommy Twotoes will know where to find the keys. Funny kind of will."

He read further and suddenly began to chuckle. "Hey, honey-boy," he said to me, "your client's a beneficiary, too. The old man left Tommy Twotoes a goddam parrot name of Quasimodo."

Suddenly I knew why I had experienced the vague feeling that something was missing from the room. There hadn't been a sound out of the usually vociferous parrot.

I looked toward the wall where the parrot's cage had been. The brass standard still stood there between the window. But the cage that had hung from it was gone, parrot and all.

3

It was after midnight when Romano and his cohorts finally finished their business at the Suffield, leaving a detective behind in the lobby to welcome the man who claimed to be Fighting Phil Caselli in case he made a belated appearance. The snowfall of early evening had turned into a howling blizzard and icy pellets stung into my face as I stood uncertainly for a moment on the windswept sidewalk outside the hotel. Romano asked if he could drop me anywhere, but I refused the ride.

I headed in the general direction of the subway, spitting snow and fighting for my breath against the snarling wind. When I was sure the police car had driven off, I about-faced and walked back toward the hotel. I ducked into an alleyway and found a huge door marked "Service Entrance." I looked at the old-fashioned lock and doubted that any keys I had inherited from Chet Lassiter, who had once owned the agency that now bore my name, would open it. On an impulse I tried the heavy door. It opened with a creak that could be heard above the storm. Inside there was utter darkness. I stabbed my pencil flash into the black curtain.

The vast, vaulted cellar was piled high with baggage. Some of it must have been left in lieu of payment by guests who were AWOL from McClellan's Union Army. There were Saratoga trunks and straw suitcases and, probably, a few carpetbags.

I sought a light switch and couldn't find one at once. As I stumbled about the place, playing my flash upon the rotting personal effects of a long dead generation of travelers, I kept calling foolishly, "Nice Polly, nice Polly. Polly wanna cracker?"

There wasn't any answer.

I heard a sound. Or, rather, I *sensed* a movement, not far behind me. If it were actually a sound it was very soft indeed. It might have been the ruffling of a parrot's feathers. It might have been the scuffing of rubber-soled sneakers. It might have been the padded scurrying of a rat. I wheeled suddenly and flashed the feeble light in the direction from which I thought the faint sound or the movement had come. I saw a flash of white dart behind a small mountain of piled-up, ancient luggage. I switched off the pencil flash. I moved on tiptoe through the darkness, trying to feel my way around the pile of luggage. Then I did hear a sound, an ominous sound. The darkest part of the darkness was teetering toward me. The pile of luggage was falling. I leaped aside. The avalanche of old trunks and suitcases missed me by inches. Something hit my leg. I stumbled over it, fell flat, cursing. Something white fled past me on silent feet. Still prone, I heaved the piece of luggage at the fleeing white figure. The legs of the figure became entangled with the piece of luggage, and the figure sprawled. There was a metallic clattering. I got up, groped for my flash, found it.

The white figure had risen. It was going through the big, creaking door as the sliver of my flash shot into the darkness.

By the time I got to the, alley, the white figure was lost in the white snow. The door was creaking to. Behind the door I heard wild, screaming oaths.

"God damn it. God damn it to hell!"

I shoved the heavy door and re-entered the black basement. The thin stream of my flash found an object on the floor. It was a big bird cage, turned on its side. Inside the cage, the parrot,

Quasimodo, was cursing shrilly, flapping madly, seeking to gain an upright position.

I barged out the door into the alley, ran slipping and sliding on the crusted snow of the alley to the street. The wind-whipped, snow-screened street was entirely deserted. The neon lights of a bar glowed through the icy curtain, like firelight through frosted glass. I crossed the street and entered the bar. A few characters were exercising their elbows at the bar and tables. The only person in the bar who wore white on such a night was the bartender. I went into the men's room. It was empty. I glanced in the phone booth. Also empty. I went back to the bar, downed a double shot and returned to the hotel's service entrance. The big door creaked open.

I finally found the light switch. Beside the bird cage lay an old-fashioned piece of telescope luggage. That was what I'd stumbled over, what I'd hurled at the little man in white. I set the bird cage upright.

Quasimodo said, "Goddam right! Goddam right!"

I said, "Take it easy, chum. You don't want to have a nervous breakdown."

The ceiling bulbs made a wan light in the hotel basement. At the far end of the room I saw the doors to a freight elevator and a passenger elevator. I threaded a circuitous route through the piles of luggage and leaned on the buzzer of the passenger elevator. It took a long time for the reefer-smoking parson to bring the cage down.

I stood aside as the door of the elevator opened. Eddie peered out.

"Mist' Sylvester," he whispered, "that you?"

I stepped in front of the Negro.

I said, "Hello, Reverend. Let's you and I talk about parrots."

Eddie was surprised. He said, "You ain't got no business down here."

I said, "Your pal Snowy, he's got business down here, though?"

Eddie clammed up. "Don't know nothing," he said.

"Your cloth won't protect you, Reverend," I assured him. "Not when Romano and the boys get hold of you. They'll take your tea away and let you suffer for a while. Then they'll put a big bright light on you. They'll tickle you with a foot or so of rubber hose. You ever been tickled with rubber hose, Reverend? It doesn't leave a mark, but it hurts like hell. And you won't have any weed to ease the pain."

For all I knew, Romano might be a kindly guy who spent his off-hours feeding bread crumbs to pigeons in the park. But the Reverend looked scared.

"Ain't done nothing," he declared.

"You must've seen your friend Snowy while the room clerk and I were upstairs looking at the old doc's remains," I went on. "While we were in the office calling the cops, you snatched the house key off the rack. You went upstairs and took the parrot out of 411. You planted it in the basement, unlocked the alley door so Snowy could get to it."

I guess the marijuana hadn't worn off entirely. Eddie became suddenly bold. "All that's to be proved, mister," he said. "Condemn not, lest ye be condemned. But maybe I might remember something if somebody should make a little contribution to the Church of the Sanctified Soul."

"How big a contribution?" I asked.

"Make it light on yourself, mister," he said. "But not too light."

I fingered a fin. Eddie eyed it.

"Church of the Sanctified Soul owes a electric bill," he said. "Old Man Edison about to turn off the lights. Bill comes to a sawbuck, even."

I added a five to the bill in my hand.

"Seem to remember Mr. Sylvester right fond of birds," said Eddie. "'Specially fond of that ole parrot of the doc's. Told me anything happen to ole doc, I was to get parrot and keep it for him. Tonight he come in and I tell him you-all up there. He give me one hundred of the *right* kind of cigarettes, say get that parrot. Say put it down in basement, leave the door open and he come for it later. So I took key and got parrot. Ain't no harm in giving poor ole parrot a good home."

"Where does the little albino get so many right kind of cigarettes?" I asked.

"He's in business," replied Eddie. "He sells 'em. He sells what he don't smoke hisself, that is."

"You haven't told me anything I couldn't have guessed," I said. "You haven't earned the sawbuck, Reverend."

"I told you what I know. You an Injun-giver, mister?"

"Where does the albino hang out?" I asked. "Where does he live?"

"Don't know that. Only see him here. Live lots of different places, I hear. Always moving around. You gonna make that donation to the Church of the Sanctified Soul, mister?"

I handed him the ten bucks. "If you don't mention me to the cops, I won't mention you," I said.

"They ain't got nothing on me," he repeated.

"You've got a nice rap coming for possession if they find those hundred *right* kind of cigarettes," I told him. "They could turn you over to the Feds. They could send you down to Lexington, Kentucky, for the cure. There's a big place there for guys like you, with bars on the windows."

"Can't be making no trip like that," he said. "They'd miss my preaching up to Harlem."

"I'm taking off the way I came," I told him. "Through the alley. Tell your pal Sylvester if he really wants the parrot to drop around and see me. I'm taking Quasimodo with me." I handed Eddie one of my business cards.

I picked up Quasimodo's cage, called over my shoulder, "Maybe you'd better lock that alley door."

As soon as the cold blast in the alley hit Quasimodo, he emitted a shriek that would have drowned out a battalion of banshees. Parrots, it seems, dislike cold as much as Tommy Twotoes' penguins dislike heat. I stuck the parrot's cage under my overcoat and crossed the street to the bar with the rosily glowing neon sign. I set the parrot's cage on the bar and a couple of drunks almost went into leaping DT's when I ordered a double and the parrot squawked, "Goddam right! Goddam right!" Since I'd been exposed to the parrot I figured I needed the drink. For all I knew, liquor was a specific against psittacosis as well as snakebite.

I got a fistful of change from the bartender and took the parrot to the phone booth. I sent another wire to Mr. Twotoes. When the operator spelled the name back, the parrot shrieked, "Goddam right! Goddam right!" The operator warned me against using profanity. The message I dictated read:

FOUND YOUR FRIEND THE DOC STRUNG UP BY THE NECK AND QUITE DEAD STOP APPARENTLY MURDER STOP HE WILLED YOU A PARROT NAMED QUASIMODO STOP PARROT DISAPPEARED BUT I RECOVERED IT FROM ALBINO IN HOTEL BASEMENT STOP THEN ALBINO DISAPPEARED STOP VOICE SAYING IT WAS FIGHTING PHIL CASELLI PHONED HOTEL STOP I TALKED WITH IT STOP PROMISED TO SHOW UP AT HOTEL BUT HASN'T APPEARED STOP YOUR PAL LIEUTENANT ROMANO PLANS TO MEET YOUR PLANE STOP WHAT KIND OF JACKPOT IS THIS QUESTION MARK LOVE AND KISSES

SOLDIER

I ordered another shot at the bar and did some thinking. I decided that the old woman, Theresa Caselli, might be the key to the whole puzzle. It was around one o'clock in the morning, a hell of a time for paying a call upon an old woman whose dead nephew had just had his face shot off, but I decided to make the trip to Bleecker Street anyway without further delay. There was a short delay, however. Quasimodo began to yelp, "Polly wanna cracker! Polly wanna cracker!" The bartender didn't have a cracker, so he gave the parrot a pretzel. While the parrot was eating the pretzel, I had another shot just to while away the time. Then Quasimodo and I took a cab to the Triangle Club on West Fourth Street, the place where my girl Ginny did her strip-teasing. I didn't expect to find Old Lady Caselli in the Triangle Club, but it was only a few blocks from the tenement where she lived and I had to park the parrot somewhere.

The parrot created quite a stir among the customers, but the Triangle is a Greenwich Village sucker trap and anything goes in the Village. I told the waiter, who knew me as Ginny's boyfriend, to bring me a shot from the boss's bottle instead of the watered stuff he served the patsies, and ordered a plate of crackers for Quasimodo. The floor show came on about the time our order arrived. When Ginny came out under a blue light to do her turn, she didn't notice us at once. She was fingering her zippers provocatively and looking at the customers with big, questioning eyes as if to ask, "Should I take it off?"

Right then Quasimodo sputtered cracker crumbs from his beak and squawked, "Goddam right! Goddam right!"

Ginny saw us and became so flustered she nearly peeled off her G-string by mistake.

When Ginny had stripped down as far as the Legion of Decency allows, the blue light flicked off and her act was over. So was the floor show. After she had put on the spangled gown that contrasted so ludicrously with her big-eyed, innocent, little-girl face, she barged over to the table that Quasimodo and I were occupying.

"What the hell do you mean by bringing that mangy bird in to squawk at me?" she asked.

"Used to be a gal named Rosita Royce did a strip-act with doves," I told her. "Very artistic. I thought maybe you'd like to be original and use a parrot."

"Goddam right! Goddam right!" shrilled Quasimodo.

"I wouldn't be caught dead with that feathered juke-box," declared Ginny.

"An old man was," I said, cryptically.

I told Ginny I was working on a very important case that maybe had international complications. I told her that the parrot might be the key figure in the mystery and that she had to guard it with her life while I went out and interviewed one of the parties involved.

She said, "You're drunk again. I can tell by the way your eyes are crinkled up."

"No," I told her. "I'm not drunk. I'm just in one of my ratiocinative moods."

Finally she agreed, although somewhat dubiously, to sit up with the parrot while I made the call. I rescued my hat and coat from the chick at the checkroom and took off through the snowstorm for nearby Bleecker Street.

The address Theresa had given me was one of those bleak, six-story brownstone walk-ups with a fretwork of fire escapes. The little lobby was littered with baby carriages and garbage cans. There were several rows of mailboxes with numbers and names on them, but no bells. The name "Caselli" was on Box 32. I lived in a cold-water flat myself and I knew the front door wouldn't be locked. I opened it and walked up two flights of dingy, uncarpeted stairs. In the low-watt light of a naked, dusty bulb, I found a door marked "32." I knocked. I knocked repeatedly. I stood there a long time knocking.

There wasn't any answer.

It was a hell of a time of night for an old gal like Theresa to be gallivanting around. Especially in a snowstorm.

I clattered down the stairs again. I almost fell over a young guy and a young doll who were necking on the staircase. I asked them to pardon me. They blushed. I asked them if they knew an old party by the name of Caselli. They shook their heads, still blushing. I asked them where I could find the super. They told me he lived in the basement.

I went out into the storm, slipped down an outside stairway and rang a bell on an iron-grated door. After I'd rung a long while, the door was opened by a dumpy, dark-faced man wearing red-flannel underwear. He was very angry. He carried a sawed-off pool cue in his hand.

"Wassamatta, you?" he demanded. "Wassamatta you wake up pipple middle a night, huh? You crazy, you dam' stew-bum?"

I flashed my ever-ready license.

"Policemans!" he said disgustedly. "Trouble. Always trouble. You come middle a night to tell me about garbage cans, maybe?"

He opened the door. I entered a combination living room and kitchen that was full of broken-down furniture.

"I'm looking for Theresa Caselli," I told him. "I went to her apartment. She doesn't answer."

"Dam' right she don't answer," he said. "She left, about hour ago. She go to Italy. Boat sail midnight, she say. She pay month's rent, only live in flat a week. She told me to take all her furniture, everything but what she take out in trunk and suitcase bag."

"Did she live alone?" I asked.

"Sure," he said. "All alone."

"Did she leave alone? She didn't cart a trunk and suitcase down two flights of steps herself, did she?"

"I help," the dumpy, dark-faced man in the red flannels replied. "Me and funny little fellow what come with her in taxi. They wake me up to help."

"Who was this fellow?"

"I should know? Funny man. Little. Dam' little. Big, pop eyes. Big, thick glasses. Dress all in white like summer. Dam' fool, funny man."

"I want you to let me in that flat," I said. "Maybe she left something behind her."

"What she left belongs to me," he replied. "What you want with old woman like that? Old woman like that hurt nobody."

"Do you open up or do I break it down?" I asked.

He kicked off the mules he was wearing, put his bare feet into a pair of galoshes. He threw an old army overcoat over his red flannels.

"Dam' job," he grumbled. "Dam' cops. Dam' trouble."

We went to the third floor, again interrupting love's young dream on the staircase. The dumpy, dark-faced man reprimanded the young doll. "Go home, Maria," he said. "For young girls hugging-kissing middle a night is no good."

Theresa's former residence was a typical railroad flat, with the entrance through the kitchen. The kitchen contained a stove, an old-fashioned ice box, a sink, a table and a combination washtub and bathtub. There were a few canned goods left on the shelf. The airless middle room had only one article of furniture, a cot with sagging springs and a soiled mattress. The tiny living room was furnished with another cot, two straight chairs and a battered table. There was a closet. I opened it and found an old pair of white sneakers. They were soaking wet. The albino had evidently got his feet wet in the snow and changed his shoes. That led me to believe that he must have kept clothes in the flat, that the old woman's place had been a base of operations for him. But the old woman had pretended he was a stranger when he shot her nephew's face off.

On the table was an empty gin bottle and a couple of dirty glasses. There was also an ash tray, with one cigarette stub. A familiar odor hung over the room. It smelled like the elevator cage in the Suffield. I picked up the cigarette stub and sniffed it. Marijuana.

The dumpy man sniffed disdainfully. "What she leave ain't worth for me three dollar in junk shop," he complained.

I slipped the super a couple of bucks for his trouble and left the place. Maria hadn't taken the dumpy man's advice. She was still clasped in her boyfriend's arms on the staircase. This time they didn't even bother to unclinch as we squeezed past.

By the time I reached the Triangle Club, the last floor show of the evening was on. Ginny was out of her clothes and Quasi-modo was out of his cage. Ginny, clad in a G-string and bra, was cavorting about under a blue light with the parrot perched on her shoulder. The hawk-beaked bird looked as smug as a kitten with a bellyful of milk. Every time Ginny broke into the bumps, the parrot squawked, "Whoopee! Some fun! Goddam right!" The customers seemed to love it.

When the show was over, Ginny came to the table. She'd washed off the war paint and had shed the spangled evening gown. She was wearing a strictly tailored street suit and she looked as young and innocent as the prettiest freshman in Miss Dalyrymple's Academy for Socially Acceptable Young Ladies. She was carrying Quasi-modo, who had been put back in his cage. I ordered a drink for myself, a glass of hot milk for Ginny and a plate of crackers for good old Quasi.

"We'll have to get Quasi's cage fixed," said Ginny. "The bottom drops out when you open the door. I had a hard time getting it back in again."

I picked up the cage and unhooked the door. The door worked on a spring. As it flew open, the weighted base of the cage dropped down an inch or two. Quasimodo stuck his head out of the door and cocked a rheumy eye at me.

"What the hell now, bud?" he asked.

I closed the door again. The base snapped back into its former position. I reopened the door and the base dropped down. Quasimodo walked out of the door and hopped down to the table.

"What the hell?" he said. "Polly wanna cracker." He began to munch at the plate of crackers, making satisfied sounds in his throat.

I turned the cage on its side and gave the round base a half-turn. It became completely detached from the floor of the cage. The detached base looked like one of those round tin candy boxes. It had a lid. I pried the lid off.

Inside the false bottom of the cage was a sealed envelope. It was addressed "Tommy Twotoes, Esq." in a copperplate hand. I was very curious and wondered if I might be justified in opening the envelope. The flap was plastered down with sealing wax. I decided I'd better leave it sealed until Tommy's arrival. There was something else inside the base of the cage. A key, wrapped in paper so it wouldn't rattle around, with a tag attached to it. The same copperplate hand had written on the tag "Stanley Sylvester, Key to Safe Deposit vault 97, Merchants' Bank."

I let out a yip. "I *told* you the parrot was the key to the whole puzzle," I said, holding up the key. "Well, here's the key, babyface."

Ginny wasn't interested in the key at the moment. "Hey, Quasi's got loose!" she exclaimed. While we had been concentrating on our discovery, Quasi had flown over to the next table. He was lapping up a stinger cocktail and squawking between drinks, "Whoopee! Some fun! Goddam right!"

The occupants of the table, a fat, bald man and a blondined babe with a full-blown facade, seemed vastly amused. The man offered to buy the parrot, but I refused to sell. I recovered Quasimodo and put him back in his cage. I put the lid on the false bottom and attached the base. When I closed the door, the base snapped back flush with the cage. The key and the envelope were still where I had found them.

The orchestra was playing a medley of such numbers as "Good Night, Ladies," "Home, Sweet Home" and "Auld Lang Syne" as a gentle reminder of the fact that closing hour was near. Patrons were adding up their checks and overtipping waiters.

I didn't relish the idea of going home to the cold-water flat I still occupied despite the fact that I was a full-fledged private investigator. I figured the oil stove had probably gone out.

I said tentatively, "It's probably cold as hell in my place. I wouldn't want old Quasi to catch pneumonia. Parrots are used to tropic climes, you know."

"I'll take Quasi home with me, if you like," Ginny replied.

"Well," I said doubtfully, "Quasi's a very important witness in this investigation. I wouldn't like to be separated from him."

"So you're hinting to come up and sleep on the couch again," said Ginny. "Why the hell don't you swallow your pride and marry me so you can move in legally?"

"You know I won't have a wife who makes her living strip-teasing," I said haughtily.

"And *you* know damned well you're not making enough to support the two of us," she replied. "So long as I can make a hundred and a quarter a week just pulling zippers, I don't intend to go on home relief."

That argument always ended right there.

Old Quasi squawked protests as we were trying to flag down a cab, even though I had his cage bundled under my overcoat. Ginny's apartment was a brownstone walk-up on West Twenty-third. It was a cozy little place. Quasi glanced around and seemed content with his surroundings. Ginny hooded his cage with a black nylon slip. The parrot continued to make soft sounds after his cage was hooded. I decided he must be snoring. It was probably the first time he'd ever been night-clubbing and he was tired out.

I poured a healthy drink from a bottle of rye I had cached in the kitchen. Ginny heated herself some warm milk for a nightcap.

When she had finished the hot milk, she spread sheets and blankets on the couch and plopped a pillow on top of them. "Be sure to hang up your clothes," she said. "They're wet and they'll be a mess in the morning if you don't."

She kissed me good night. It was a nice, long kiss.

I stood for a while looking at the closed door of the bedroom, like a hungry guy looks into the window of a bakeshop.

4

When I awakened, snow was still coming down outside the windows. I wondered if Tommy Twotoes' plane would be able to make it through the blizzard. I'd only slept four or five hours. The door to the bedroom was still closed. I expected that. Noon was an early hour for Ginny. I dressed and went to the kitchen and made some breakfast. My breakfast consisted of a raw egg dunked into a glass of tomato juice, and some black coffee. Being a hair-of-the-dog man, I chased this with half a tumbler of rye. I found a box of Rye-crisp crackers in the kitchen and took a couple in to Quasi. When I took the black nylon cover off his cage, he squawked unintelligibly and regarded me with sleepy red eyes. He had no appetite for the crackers. I concluded that the stinger cocktail had given him a hangover. Quasi wasn't used to night life.

Before I left the apartment, I made use of Ginny's telephone. I called Tom Broderick, a friend of mine who operated a travel agency. I asked him what ships had sailed for Italy the night before. He took time out to consult some schedules and then informed me there hadn't been any ships sailing for Italy the night before and that there wouldn't be any sailing for a couple of days.

It was after nine o'clock. I took a chance on catching Romano, the Homicide cop, in his office. I got him on the phone after a couple of sergeants had asked me questions. I needed an excuse for calling him, so I said, "The old Caselli dame, the aunt of the walking corpse, has lammed. She's supposed to be on her way to Italy, according to the super at her flat. Only she must be swimming, because there won't be any boats for Italy for a couple of days."

"Honeyboy," replied Romano, "I don't know what the Department ever did without you. Before she left she gave orders to have her ever-loving nephew's remains shoved into a great, big oven. He was cremated out on Long Island last night. The cops who investigated the corpse-shooting last night didn't see any reason to put a hold on an embalmed body, but this morning I thought we might like to look the cadaver over. Mr. Dinwiddie, the undertaker, said it had already gone to the crematorium, and the boys on the Island said it was done to a turn before I called them."

"Did the guy who told me he was Fighting Phil ever show up at the hotel?" I inquired.

"Nope. Nary a hair nor hide of him."

"Did your boys uncover any clues among the old doc's junk collection?"

"They uncovered something kinda funny. Lots of boxes, each labeled "One Dozen Men's Socks," with the sizes marked on 'em in pencil. Snowy Sylvester used to peddle socks, seconds they were, around barrooms and such places. Only there weren't any socks in these boxes. They were filled with ready-made cigarettes. Marijuana cigarettes. Around three thousand of 'em."

"You think the old doc was a dope peddler?" I asked.

"I doubt it. Snowy probably cached the reefers in his apartment. Old Doc probably thought they were just socks, like the labels said."

"Are you picking up the albino?" I asked.

"Yeah. If we can find him in a snowstorm. He hasn't shown up at any of his usual haunts. Maybe he's swimming to Italy, too. Haven't got too much on him so far as the murder goes, of course.

We can hold him for illegal possession of firearms on the testimony of witnesses in the funeral parlor, and make some kind of charge stick about his shooting off the stiff's face. Or maybe we'll catch him with tea on him. Anyway, we can hold him long enough to ask some questions."

I had decided I wouldn't tell Romano about the parrot. I wanted to prove to Tommy that I was like one of those private ops in the mystery stories—a couple of jumps ahead of the cops at all times. I found out immediately I wasn't quite so far ahead as I thought.

"Funny thing you stayed upstairs so long the first time you went to the old doc's suite, honeyboy," said Romano. "What was the matter? Have a hard time finding a key that fit?"

"Who said I was up there a long time?" I asked feebly.

"The elevator boy. He's a preacher on the side, so he must be truthful."

"Also he smokes the weed. That makes you lose your sense of time, I understand," I answered.

"Maybe so. Give my regards to that parrot if you happen to run into him. But be careful you don't come down with parrot-fever."

"You shouldn't pay attention to what a teahound says," I told him, thinking Eddie had been talking.

"Maybe not. Anyway I'll be seeing you. Want to talk to you about that parrot and a few other items. But I want to see your boss, Mr. Twotoes, first. Maybe we'll meet at LaGuardia tonight if that plane's not forced down."

"You're jumping to conclusions, Lieutenant."

"So long, honeyboy," replied the Lieutenant calmly. "Tell that parrot not to take any wooden crackers." He hung up.

I put in a long-distance call to Tarrytown and got Polvo on the phone. He was sputtering so that I couldn't understand a word he said.

"Take out your false teeth," I told him. Polvo was a harmless character. He was an excellent chef and a devoted attendant of Tommy Twotoes' penguins. But he rather fancied himself as a reincarnation of George Washington. When he'd been an organ grinder on the lower East Side he had had a monkey named General Lafayette. At Polvo's insistence, Tommy had had a set of dentures that were exact replicas of George Washington's cumbersome false teeth made for him. He. couldn't eat with them or talk plainly when they were in his mouth, but he wore them proudly just the same.

When he had taken out the teeth, I told him to check with the airways and if the plane was coming in as scheduled to meet it with the station wagon. I also told him his boss was bringing guests with him from California. Then I asked him for the daily report on the penguins.

"They like this snow," he said. "Eating hearty. Playing around like little kids. Coasting down snow banks on their stummicks. Having a fine time. All except Cleo. She's been staying up in the boss's room. Had to turn off the heat and keep the window open for her. Guess I'll have to send her back to the rookeries now, turn on the heat and close the window, if the boss is coming home."

"I guess you will," I said. "Give Cleo my regards."

"She misses you, Soldier," said Polvo. "I think she's right sweet on you."

I wondered how Cleo and Quasimodo, the parrot Tommy had inherited, would get along when they were formally introduced.

I put on my hat and coat, waved good-bye to the dozing Quasimodo and left Ginny's apartment. By the time I arrived at the office I was snow-powdered and blue with cold. I opened a drawer of the filing cabinet and drank the last of the office bottle, making a mental note to replenish it. I opened another drawer of the cabinet and took out a clean shirt. It was a very fancy shirt. Bright red, with white polka dots. The shirt was a present from Ginny. It didn't match the mauve tie with green flowers I was wearing, but it was freshly laundered. Ginny had also given me the tie.

I got the negatives of the pictures I had taken the night before and made my way up Broadway to a photographic agency run by a guy who had once worked on a paper with me. He said he'd put them through special and have them developed inside of two hours.

I stopped at a liquor store on the way back to the office and bought a fifth of cheap rye. I took the bottle up to the office, sat down in the easy chair and drank to celebrate the fact that it was Wednesday and Wednesday only comes once a week. I looked over the Morning papers I'd purchased on my way uptown. The peculiar story of a corpse getting its face shot off was given more play than the murder of the old doc. None of the papers connected up the two happenings. After I'd read the papers and had a few more shots, I fell asleep in the leather chair. When I awakened, it was past noon and it had stopped snowing. I looked out the window. A bright winter sun was shining and the towers of the town were sparkling with diamond dust.

I called the airport. They said the storm had been local and that unless there was more snow the eight o'clock flight from the Coast would arrive on time. I left the office and walked back to the photographic agency. My photographs were ready. They had come out fine, too, both the close-up of the blasted head and the view of the upper torso with the hands folded across the breast. The hands looked very pale and soft against the black coat the corpse was wearing.

"Gory subjects you go in for," said the guy who had developed the negatives.

"They're stills for a Karloff film," I told him.

I walked over to Charley Frayne's place in the upper forties and had lunch. My lunch consisted of four ryes and two pretzels. I had another rye on the house for dessert.

When I finally returned to the office the phone was ringing. That was a very unusual event in the office of Rooke, Private Investigator. I hurried and answered the phone. Oddly enough, it wasn't a wrong number this time. A resonant bass voice asked, "Is this the Rooke Agency?"

I was too flabbergasted to reply at once. It was the same bass voice I had talked to over the phone at the Suffield switchboard. It was the voice that was supposed to belong to the corpse of Phil Caselli.

I finally managed to tell him that I was Rooke in person.

"Your agency was recommended to me by Doctor Mulholland," the voice said. "I would like to discuss your handling a little matter for me."

I said, "Who is this talking, please?"

The voice said, "Never mind that right now. I wish to talk to you privately. May I come up?"

I said, "Well, I'm pretty well tied up, but if you come right away, I could give you a few minutes."

The voice said, "It won't take more than ten minutes to get there."

After I cradled the phone, I sat tapping my fingers on the desk. I was considering whether I should call Romano and tell him that I had talked to the ghost of Phil Caselli again and that the rejuvenated corpse was due in my office in ten minutes. I decided against calling the Lieutenant. It was just possible that two persons who knew the old doc might have deep bass voices. Also, Romano's smugness had annoyed me. I was still anxious to get a jump on him in this case if possible. I could see the headlines: PRIVATE OP SOLVES CRIME THAT BAFFLES COPS.

I took a drink from the office bottle and set the company bottle on the desk. I rinsed out a glass to go with the company bottle. When eight minutes had passed, I began to get nervous, so I took another drink out of the office bottle. Just as the liquor hit my throat, there was a knock and the door opened.

I almost spewed out the whisky that was burning my tonsils.

Snowy Sylvester stood in the doorway.

He glanced behind him cautiously and closed the door.

He was still dressed all in white, but because of the frigid weather and the snow he had donned a white rain hat and a white raincoat. I guess they don't make white raincoats for men, not in his small size, anyway. It was a woman's coat. The buttons were at the left. Even in my astonishment I noted that. I complimented myself upon such a keen observation. I must really be a Great Detective.

The little albino stood regarding me curiously, saying nothing. I remembered the .45. I nudged the desk drawer open with my knee, so the Police Positive I owned would be handy. I hoped it was loaded.

The bass voice was all the more startling because it came out of such a shriveled little man.

It said, "Mr. Rooke? So you were the scar-faced man in the funeral parlor yesterday."

I nodded, inching my hand toward the drawer.

The albino noted my action. His pallid lips twisted into an ugly grin. He said, "You needn't be alarmed. I won't pull a gun on you."

The patronizing tone made me sore. A big guy like me shouldn't be afraid of something about five feet tall, should he?

I gave the albino my best sneer. "I take it you only shoot corpses," I said.

"I'm afraid I lost my head last evening," Snowy apologized.

"So did Fighting Phil Caselli," I replied.

The albino made a rumbling bass sound that might have been a chuckle. Then he said, "May I sit down, Mr. Rooke?"

"Sure," I answered. "But I don't guarantee your feet will touch the floor."

I didn't like the look in his grotesquely enlarged pink eyes when I said that. My hand inched toward the gun again. Snowy unbuttoned his raincoat, removed the rubber hat from his fuzzy pate and sat down on the edge of a straight chair.

He regarded me with the unblinking rabbit eyes. "I may need your help," he said at length. "I seem to be in something of a jam."

"My rates are forty bucks a day, with a two-hundred-dollar retainer," I told him.

"That might be arranged," he said. "I believe I have quite a sum of money coming to me."

"You use better grammar than you did last night," I remarked.

"I don't understand."

"I talked to you on the phone last night," I informed him. "You said you were Phil Caselli."

The rumble that might have been a chuckle again. "So that was you, too!" he said.

"What kind of help do you think I might give you?" I led him on.

"I can't go too far into that without incriminating myself to a certain degree," he replied. "Before I speak frankly, I should like to have your word that you will act in my behalf."

I shook my head. "I've got a license to think of," I said. "I couldn't make you any guarantees until I know what this is all about."

"Let us say for the moment that I wish you to recover a certain parrot which has disappeared," he answered.

"You want the S.P.C.A., not a private detective," I told him. "And how do you know the parrot disappeared?"

"I arranged for the disappearance. I had the parrot in my possession. Some person I could not identify in the darkness tripped me up. I dropped the parrot and fled."

"And all you want me to do is recover this twice-stolen parrot?"

"I also require that you recover the cage. And there are other important functions you must perform for me."

"Such as?"

"Such as convincing the police of the truth. You must convince them that Phil Caselli murdered old Doctor Mulholland in cold blood before he himself was ironically killed by a hit-run driver."

"Maybe the old doc killed himself," I stalled.

He shook his head. "According to the evidence that the police saw, he could not possibly have killed himself."

"You can't always go by newspaper accounts," I said.

"No," he replied calmly. "I have better proof. I arranged the evidence."

"What?" I exploded.

Snowy said, "The killer, Caselli, set the scene so that the murder would appear to be a suicide. The doctor considered him and me to be his best friends. We both had keys to his apartment. Two days ago I went to the Suffield and knocked on the doctor's door despite the little sign which said he was out. I received no answer. I was worried. I opened the door and found the old man hanging from the chandelier. Beneath his feet was an overturned library ladder. I knew what had happened, for I had long been suspicious of Caselli. I reset the scene to make it appear to be what it actually was—murder. I righted the ladder. I climbed it and struck the corpse a hard blow on the back of the head with my .45 revolver. Then I returned the ladder to its proper place by the bookcase. The natural inference, of course, was that the doctor had been knocked unconscious and then hanged."

"Why did you shoot the face off the Caselli corpse?" I inquired.

"I have already incriminated myself," he said, "without first getting your promise that you would act in my behalf. I may as well go all the way now. I once considered Phil my friend. Later I became convinced he was a sadist. As long as he was in the ring, he had a natural outlet for his sadism. When he grew too old for fighting, his abnormality made itself manifest in many small ways. He tormented me. I need not go into detail. I am one of nature's unfortunates, cast in an unusual mold. Like persons who are deformed and misshapen, I have been forced to endure many cruel taunts. I was once one of Doctor Mulholland's best students in law school. But my appearance was against me. No one wanted a counselor of my unusual appearance to represent him. Tommy Twotoes was a friend of the doctor's. He managed to procure some small cases for me among boxers, promoters, fight managers. That is how I met Phil. He considered me a kind of mascot, just as some persons consider it lucky to rub the hump of a hunchback. Sometimes I acted as his second. I loved the sport of boxing. So did the doctor, with whom I remained very close.

"Phil and Tommy Twotoes retired from the boxing field at about the same time. I lost most of the small accounts that had provided me with a livelihood. Phil had money then, and I handled some legal matters for him. He was often in scrapes with women, for instance. He retained me mainly as a court jester, however. He delighted in making remarks in public about my size, my appearance. He often had coarse women pretend to make love to me to afford a spectacle in cabarets and other public places. Once he presented me with a white, pink-eyed rabbit for Christmas. I began to hate the man. But Dr. Mulholland continued to admire and trust him. The doctor was growing old, senile, childish, but he was still brilliant at times—harmless and lovable.

"He informed us that he had made us his heirs, that a considerable sum of money was coming to each of us when he died. He said we should cultivate the friendship of the parrot, because the parrot would be the actual executor of his estate. As I say, he grew queer in many ways, but he had inherited a small fortune and he spent very little.

"Phil grew desperately broke. I myself was reduced to menial and even illegal undertakings in order to live. I sold socks in barrooms and on the street. I was a runner for the numbers racket. I took bets for a bookmaker."

"You peddled a little marijuana on the side, too, didn't you?" I asked.

"I don't admit to that!" he said sharply. "There is no proof to sustain such a statement. I may have resorted to marijuana myself. Also to more potent opiates. My health is not good. I have not led a pleasant life."

"We'll skip that for a moment," I said. "Also the fact that you pack a gat."

"I bought the gun because I became convinced that Phil was planning to kill the old doctor. He as much as told me so in a sly, insinuating way. He enjoyed torturing me. His actions were most suspicious. When I found the doctor dead, I knew the murderer. I set the scene so that the police would know it was murder. I believed that their investigation would lead them to the right man. I planned to come forward otherwise. Then I lost my head. I heard of the sudden, easy death that Phil had had. The afflicted are, perhaps, more perverse than normal people. I decided to view the body of the man who had killed my friend. I went to the funeral parlor. The undertaker had eliminated all the brutal lines of his face, had removed the sagging bulldog jowls. When I saw that smug, placid, painted face, I gave way to emotion, a luxury I do not normally permit myself. I blazed away at it with my gun. Then, as you know, I fled in panic."

"And now you want the parrot," I said. "Also the parrot's cage."

"I do. I am desperately in need of money. I know the old doctor would not have made a cruel joke. I am an heir of his, as Phil was. And the will, or the key to the estate, is somehow tied up with that parrot, or concealed in its cage."

I slopped Scotch into the clean tumbler and pushed it toward him. I poured myself a stiff rye in the dirty tumbler. He drank the Scotch. I drank the rye.

I said, "I almost believe your story. It's too fantastic not to be true. I was in a bad jam once myself, and nothing made any sense, it seemed. But there's one thing that spoils the whole business. I was down at the tenement where Theresa Caselli lives last night."

"Who is she?" he asked. "A relative of Phil's?"

"Don't you know?" I asked. "His aunt. The old lady who was standing in the undertaker's when you made boom-boom with the gat."

"I had never seen her before last night."

"No?" I said. "You accompanied her in a taxi to her house from some point, I don't know where. You and the superintendent helped her downstairs with her baggage. He described you accurately. You left a pair of wet sneakers behind in her closet. You got back into the taxi with her, presumably headed for a boat bound for Italy."

The little man's watery, absurdly magnified pink eyes regarded me steadily, almost pathetically.

"I have told you the truth," he said. "I know nothing of the woman. I never knew Phil had an aunt. I did not ride in a taxi with her, visit her home, help her with baggage. I am rather a rare specimen. It would not be too difficult to imitate my superficial appearance. A small man wearing a white linen suit in a snow-storm is noticeable. Thick glasses are noticeable. Other men might wear such clothes and such glasses for purposes of deception."

He paused. I said nothing.

"I can't guess accurately just why such an impersonation was made," he said at last. "But the family of a convicted murderer could hardly inherit the estate of the murdered man. It would be advantageous for them to cast suspicion upon me, since the murderer and I were the doctor's closest companions and his heirs."

I didn't know whether to believe him or not. But I had to admit that his story made some sense. I had wondered why a murderer would resort to such an awkward method of killing as hanging unless he was trying to make his crime appear to be a suicide. I tried to punch holes in the story, however.

"Why didn't you take the parrot the day you found the old doc strung up, the day you moved the ladder and hit the corpse on the head?" I asked.

"I can think of several reasons for not doing so," he replied. "Perhaps I was too upset by the death of Dr. Mulholland to think of other matters. In any event, it would have been most awkward to walk out of that hotel carrying the parrot that both the elevator operator and the clerk knew belonged to the doctor. And perhaps I realized it would be best to let nature take its course, have the police discover the secret of the parrot's cage. Then things happened. Phil was killed. I saw a scar-faced man in the funeral parlor asking where he was laid out. I assumed you were a relative or friend, perhaps a confederate in the crime. Later I risked visiting the hotel to see the elevator operator, Eddie. You and the clerk, Jenks, were upstairs at the time. Eddie informed me a scar-faced man with a policeman's license had demanded the room clerk open the doctor's suite. Eddie is naive. A badge out of a popcorn package would impress him. I concluded you were probably after whatever was concealed in the cage.

"I told Eddie he must get the cage. I was afraid you and Jenks might remain upstairs, call the police from there. So I went out and called the switchboard from a drug store. Eddie could not operate the board. He would have to call Jenks back downstairs. That might give him a chance to get into the doctor's suite, procure the parrot. I kept the line open a long while until I was answered. I had given Eddie my key to the suite."

So the Negro hadn't had to use the passkey after all, I thought.

"When you answered the phone I assumed you were the scar-faced man of the funeral parlor and could not resist a jest at your expense. I told you I was Caselli and I would see you soon. I even asked if I were there. I had instructed Eddie to leave the parrot in the basement, unlock the door. I planned to pick it up late that night when the coast was certain to be clear. I had just picked up the parrot when someone entered the basement. I hid, but he pursued me. I threw something at him. He fell. But he threw something at me. I stumbled, dropped the cage and fled in panic."

"How did you get my name?" I asked.

"The doctor had one of your cards. He had told me he feared for his life. He would not say why. He showed me the card once, said he might hire you to protect him from the forces of evil he felt were pursuing him. I put it down to an old man's idiosyncrasies at the time, although I was even then suspicious of Phil's intentions. The doctor said that you had been recommended by his friend, Tommy Twotoes."

That explained the card in the corpse's pocket. Tommy had given it to the old man.

The albino continued, "I remembered the name of Rooke. This morning I got to thinking. I recalled Eddie's mention of the policeman's license. I took a chance, looked you up in the book, and called."

"Tell me," I said, "if you're sensitive about your—er—appearance, why do you make yourself more noticeable by wearing white clothes in winter?"

"It is, I suppose, a form of defiance," he replied. "As I have said, afflicted people are more perverse in some respects than others. I am like a beggar who flaunts his sores. If people are going to stare at me, I give them something to stare at. Once I even owned a white fur coat. It was a present from Phil. One of his little jokes."

"Why were you suspicious of Caselli?" I asked.

"He was broke, and he could never get used to not spending large sums of money, playing the big shot. He made veiled threats, jests in poor taste, about how we might advantage mutually if we murdered our friend. I think he was more than half-serious, was playing with the idea, that he even thought I might be a party to the crime. He was addicted to drugs. I suppose you think that statement sounds funny, coming from me, since you seem to know my weakness. But Phil was much worse than I have ever been. Emotionally unstable to begin with. A drunkard even in his fighting days. Then liquor didn't give him the kick he required. Drugs made him dangerous. I really grew suspicious when he disappeared completely."

"He disappeared?"

"Off the face of the earth. About two months ago. Without a word to anyone. The doctor said he received a letter saying Phil had committed himself to a sanitarium for a cure. I don't believe he had. It was not like him to do a thing like that."

"You never saw him after he disappeared? Not until he was dead?"

"Oh, yes. I saw him the day before the murder. He had the monkey on his back. He was wild, mean."

Monkey on the back is a junkie term, meaning under the influence of narcotics.

"He came to see me at a little hotel downtown where I was living. Not much more than a flophouse, really. He demanded money. I gave him a dollar or two. He wasn't satisfied. He asked for more, said he'd be a rich man because a certain party was about to die. He said I might be a rich man, too, if I wasn't dead myself by then, or doing time for murder. He beat me up because I had no more money to give him. He wouldn't say where he had been. I was worried about the doctor, of course. That is why I went to the hotel that day, let myself in despite the sign on the door."

He paused. I poured him a drink. I didn't forget to pour myself one, too.

He said, "Have a cigarette?" He thrust a pack toward me.

I said, "I don't think I smoke your brand. And maybe I'd better open the window if you're lighting up."

The throaty chuckle again.

"There's no stick in these," he assured me.

I took a cigarette. It turned out to be plain tobacco.

He said, "I can't give you a retainer now. But I loved the old doctor. He and Tommy Twotoes were among the few men who never laughed at me, who accepted me as an ordinary human being. I want to see the police put the blame for this murder in the right place. And I want that parrot. Tommy Twotoes will vouch for me. I used to know him a long time ago."

I said, "Mr. Twotoes gets back to town tonight. I'll discuss the matter with him then."

"And you won't take any action before then? You won't put the police on me as soon as I walk out of here?"

I said, "You give me your address, phone number to show good faith, and I won't."

He shook his head. "I don't have an address now," he replied. "I will call you tomorrow. You can let me know your decision then."

I had to settle for that.

I said, "But the cops are after a guy who looks just like you. It'll be easier to find you now it's quit snowing. Don't blame me if they pick you up, Snowy. What time will you call?"

"I will be busy. I can't call until late afternoon. About five, let us say."

"Okay, Snowy."

"Would—would you mind calling me Stanley?" he asked. I could have sworn his pink eyes were swimming with tears.

"Okay, Stanley," I replied.

"Good-bye, Mr. Rooke," he said, "and thank you." His rubber-soled sneakers made no sound as he walked to the door. I occupied one of the cheaper offices in the building. The elevator was directly opposite my door. There were two elevators in the old building, but the management was economical. Only one was in operation. I waited for exactly thirty seconds before I crossed to the door. No elevator had arrived. I would have heard it, for it made an unholy clatter. I opened the door a crack. No one was waiting for the elevator. I opened the door wide. No one at all was in the hall. The indicator of the elevator showed that the car was on the top floor, the tenth. My office was on the fifth floor. I grabbed my coat and hat. I ran to the stairs. I ran down the stairs, pausing only to glance around me at each landing. I saw no one.

I reached the street floor and glanced at the elevator indicator again. The cage had progressed only to the eighth floor in its slow descent. The operator had a habit of making long pauses at each floor, just in case he might pick up a belated customer. I asked the bosomy girl at the cigar stand if she had seen the little man in the white rain clothes come down. She had seen him go up. She hadn't seen him come down. Anyone coming down the stairs or getting off the elevator had to pass the cigar stand. I rang the elevator bell frantically hoping to hurry the slow-moving cage. It finally arrived. Two passengers got out. One was a plump, swarthy man smoking a cigar. The other was a very large character. He must have been from the wide-open spaces because he wore a ten-gallon hat.

I questioned the elevator man. He had taken Snowy up all right. He hadn't brought him down. I slipped the elevator man a buck. I told him I was going to search for the little albino and if he got on the elevator to stall, pretend mechanical difficulty, anything to delay him until I rang for the elevator from the top floor. I mounted nine flights of steps and looked around on each landing. No albino. Sweating and panting, I finally reached the top floor. I rang for the elevator. Snowy hadn't been seen, the operator said. I descended to the ground floor. The cigar stand girl said Snowy hadn't come down the stairs.

It was all right to lose the all-white little man in a snowstorm. That was just camouflage. But this disappearance into thin air was sheer magic. Black magic performed by a white sorcerer.

I returned to my office. For weeks the phone had hardly rung at all. Today it seemed to ring every time I opened the door. I answered it. It was Ginny. She said her boss had called her. The water pipes at the Triangle had burst. The club would be closed for several days. She asked if her harried Hawkshaw could spare a little time for her that evening. I said I thought it could be arranged, that I'd pick her up for dinner and she could drive out with me to meet Tommy. I asked about the parrot. She said he was fine and very talkative, but that most of his conversation was shockingly profane. She had gone to a pet store and bought him a box of sunflower seed. She said Quasimodo had consumed this exotic food with relish.

After Ginny rang off, I tried to think what further work an efficient private operative like myself should accomplish that afternoon. I decided to do a little further work on the bottle I'd bought. I worked on the bottle off and on until about five-thirty, filling up the intervals between drinks with Gibbon's *Decline and Fall.*

I walked uptown to the garage where we kept the jeepster, a second-hand job that Tommy had bought in case an emergency arose and the office required a car. Thus far the heap had been used only by Ginny and me for Sunday driving. I drove to Ginny's apartment house. A taxi stuck close to my tail all the way to Twenty-third Street. I kept glancing in the rear-view mirror, but it was dark and I couldn't see the occupant of the cab. When I parked, the cab drove by me—fast.

As I entered the flat Quasimodo greeted me with, "What the hell! Stop, thief!" He seemed in high spirits.

Ginny had provided for my needs as well as Quasimodo's. In addition to buying the parrot a package of sunflower seeds she had bought me a bottle of rye. I took a drink to celebrate the fact that I had been on the wagon almost half an hour.

I said, "I'd take old Quasi along to meet his new owner except there's no heater in the jalopy and he might catch cold."

"You ought to buy a heater," Ginny said.

"I like it better having you snuggle up to keep warm," I told her.

Ginny gave Quasi his supper of sunflower seeds with a cracker for dessert. Then she covered his cage with the black nylon slip so he would be nice and cozy. We drove uptown to Charley Frayne's place. I figured a big, healthy kid like me couldn't do his best sleuthing on a raw egg and a couple of pretzels, so Ginny and I split a planked steak. Ginny stalled around with a crème de menthe and I stalled around with a few shots of rye until it was seven-thirty. Then we drove over the ice-crusted Queensboro Bridge to La Guardia Field. We found Polvo waiting at the gate where the flight from California was due. He was wearing a coonskin coat, a felt hat with a turned-up brim and large gold earrings. He was also wearing George Washington's false teeth for this special occasion, so we couldn't understand a word he said.

I looked at a big blackboard and saw that Tommy's plane was seven minutes late. I made some rapid calculations and figured I wouldn't have quite enough time for a quick one in the bar.

A voice behind me said, "Hello, honeyboy. You're right on time."

"Well, if it's not my friend Inspector Lestrade of Scotland Yard," I greeted Romano.

Ginny and the Lieutenant had met before. They exchanged courtesies. Romano was old enough to be her father, but I didn't like the admiring glances Ginny cast at his classic profile.

"You locate the little guy in the white suit?" I asked Romano.

"No, honeyboy," he replied. "Did you, by any chance?"

I didn't know just how to take that. I thought of the taxi that had seemed to be following me earlier that evening. I wondered if Romano had had one of his boys tail me all day, if he knew of Snowy's visit to my office.

A silver bird flashed out of the night sky into the brilliant beams of La Guardia's searchlights.

Tommy Twotoes had arrived.

The arrival of Tommy and his party created a small sensation at the field. Airport attendants had great difficulty in disembarking the enormous bulk of the crippled old man over the plane's gangway. That wasn't the only thing that attracted attention. Tommy usually dressed in baggy clothes of somber black. But he had gone Hollywood during his stay in California. He wore an overcoat of green and purple tartan plaid that must have been cut from the blanket of the original Trojan horse. A fuzzy, pearl-gray fedora with a length of red rope for a hatband covered his bald head. His necktie blossomed with the colorful flora of tropic jungles. He supported himself with a heavy ebony stick that was capped by an ivory owl's head. To complete the picture, he lit his pipe as soon as his feet touched terra firma. The queerly wrought bowl of his pipe was fashioned in the shape of a naked woman.

Other members of the Twotoes entourage were attracting notice in their own right. Three of them were insistent upon obtaining certain articles of luggage immediately without trusting them to the mercies of airport porters. These articles consisted of a large, live gander, an even larger and equally live Great Dane and a crate full of guinea pigs.

After considerable argument, an old girl dripping mink and wafting musk walked off triumphantly with the gander on a rhinestone-studded leash. The old girl's hair was dyed a light purple and her face was painted the flaming colors of a Grand Canyon sunset.

The stallion-sized dog was claimed by a three-foot midget wearing a velvet collared Chesterfield, a gray bowler and an ascot tie. The dog was taller than the midget who led him off the airfield.

A tall, wild-eyed man with fierce mustachios waxed to spear points hoisted the crate of guinea pigs upon his shoulder.

The other member of the party was a lean, cadaverous, ferret-eyed character who was helping the airport men support Mr. Two-toes' bulk. He was carrying a funny-looking, cased musical instrument under the arm that wasn't hooked to the Twotoes' avoirdupois.

When the entire group was assembled, Tommy made the necessary introductions. I learned that all the members of the slightly daffy entourage had ambitions to appear on television, which explained a lot. The lady with the gander was Eve Eden, who had been a cliff-hanger in the days of Pearl White and the silent screen. Her pet gander was named Montmorency, and he was an arrogant and ill-tempered bird. The tiny character called himself Colonel Thomas Finger. He'd been a stand-in for Shirley Temple when she was a child star and had become a midget wrestler when she out-grew him. His Great Dane, a painfully bashful hulk that stood in mortal dread of Montmorency, was called Ivan the Terrible. The gent with the waxed mustachios was Mephisto the Magnificent, a magician who pulled guinea pigs instead of rabbits out of hats. The cadaverous citizen supporting Tommy was Wisey, a racetrack tout who played the zither.

After introductions had been made, Tommy turned to Romano and said, "Well, Lieutenant, what brings you out in the cold?"

"Murder," said Romano. "It's a crime, they tell me. I'd like to ask you a few questions, if you don't mind."

"I mind very much," replied Mr. Twotoes loftily. "This is neither the time nor the place. If you wish to drive to my home in Tarrytown, I will oblige you at my leisure and offer you excellent brandy as a bonus. Otherwise you will have to put me under arrest before I will place myself at your disposal."

"Don't be that way, Tommy," said Romano. "It's a long drive up there. The roads are icy."

"The station wagon is conveying my guests. You may ride with them, or you may follow in your own car. I will arrive later this evening. Soldier and I have business in the city first," Tommy replied.

"You still got that brandy you import from France? The special kind in the blue crocks?" Romano asked.

"I have. A plentiful supply."

"How long will you be in the city?"

"I can't say how long the business at hand may take. You may comfort yourself with the brandy in the meantime."

Romano agreed to drive to Tarrytown.

Tommy turned to me. "Your report, Soldier," he demanded, like a field marshal interviewing a subaltern.

"Well," I said, "I wired you about the old doc getting knocked off . . ."

Tommy raised his hand. "I am not interested in that at the moment, Soldier. What was the result of the third at Santa Anita?"

My mouth fell open. I had forgotten to check the race result. I hurried to a newsstand and bought a racing paper. I came back and informed Tommy that Angel's Sin had won the race.

"The price?" he demanded.

"Fourteen bucks. Six to one, even."

"Excellent," he said. "I invested heavily on his chances. My winnings should pay the initial costs of the television program I plan to sponsor."

I shouldn't have been surprised at his angeling a television show. He'd subsidized nearly everything else in his day, including me.

"I can't allow such talented people as my friends here to go unemployed," he said. "We will advertise our detective agency on the program if we can think of nothing better to publicize."

The baggage was loaded into the station wagon, and Polvo took off for Tarrytown with the car full of Tommy's guest stars.

Romano followed them in a police car. I assisted the old man into the back seat of the jeepster. He took up nearly all of it. I started to climb in front beside Ginny, but he shook his head.

"Let Ginny drive," he said. "Come back here with me."

By assuming a slightly oblique position I managed to squeeze in beside him. Ginny stalled the motor but finally the car skidded away on the icy pavement.

"First," said Tommy, "the photographs you took of the Caselli corpse. Then you will inform me in detail of everything I need to know."

I took the photographs out of my inside pocket and handed them to him. I also handed him the pencil flash. He examined the pictures intently for a long while.

Then he said, "Hmmff."

"Is that all you've got to comment?" I asked. "Those are the greatest photographs since Brady's Civil War pictures."

Tommy produced a blue crock of brandy from the interior of the plaid coat. He took two metal cups from another pocket. He handed one cup to me. He filled the cups with brandy, replaced the bottle.

He said, "Your photographs arc revelatory, at least, Soldier."

He drank the brandy.

He said, "They prove the body is not that of Fighting Phil Caselli."

5

I started to say something.

I said, "How the hell . . . ?"

Then the car skidded and swerved on a ramp to the bridge.

I cried, "Ginny! Watch out!"

Ginny righted the car, said, "Don't worry about the chauffeur. But you might tell me where you want to go."

Tommy said, "In view of recent developments, take us to the undertaking parlor where the alleged Caselli was laid out."

"Father Demo Square," I said.

"And," added Tommy, "I dislike traveling at more than thirty miles an hour. Thirty-five at the absolute maximum."

I turned to Tommy again and completed the question that had been so rudely interrupted.

"How the hell can you tell that's not Phil from the picture?" I asked. "There's nothing left of the face but bone dust."

Tommy approached the question in a circuitous manner that was peculiar to him. "There was once a painter named Andrea Del Sarto," he replied. "He painted models with wooden, expressionless faces, but he has lived through the ages because he painted beautiful, eloquently expressive hands. Dürer was a great artist in every respect. He made hundreds of studies of hands. They are among his most famous works."

"You mean Phil's hands were easily identified? They had some sort of peculiarity, like a scar or a birth. mark?"

Tommy shook his head. "They were the hands of a fighter. Large hands. Big-knuckled hands. Hands that were out of shape from battering against heavy punching bags and hard heads. If memory serves, the record books will show that Phil had sixty-eight professional fights against the best men of his time. You don't come out of such a career with small, soft, brittle-looking hands." He handed the torso photo to me. "Observe this man's hands," he said. "They are almost womanish.

"Now," said Tommy, "tell me everything I need to know."

As Ginny drove over the icy streets to the funeral parlor, I gave him the details of the last twenty-four hours as briefly as I could. I mentioned the albino's call at my office, of course.

He said, "Hmmff."

Then he added, "It seems peculiar that Snowy, who saw the corpse's face, should not have known that the man in the coffin wasn't Phil. However, Snowy's action in blowing the face to atom dust is entirely understandable and typical. Snowy is a thwarted and pathetic character. His whole life has been a series of frustrations. His strange attachment to Phil must have been based upon his admiration of the animal qualities of abundant health and strength which he himself lacked and envied."

Tommy nearly had heart failure as Ginny negotiated the complex traffic of Father Demo Square over the gelid surface of the street. At last she found a parking place that wasn't too close to a fire-plug. Tommy took a drink to quiet his nerves. Then I helped him out of the car and into the funeral parlor. It was quite a job on the icy pavement. The fat little man who was in mourning all over greeted us. He hadn't changed his shirt or removed the mourning from his fingernails.

"Soldier," said Tommy in a lordly manner, "fetch me one of those high-backed monstrosities that should grace a Renaissance banquet chamber instead of a house of the dead." He indicated one of the plush-upholstered, claw-footed chairs that were ranged against the wall. I moved it over and helped lower the huge man into it. It supported his bulk, but the joints groaned in protest.

"Now, my man," said Tommy to the fat little mortician's assistant, "I wish to ask you some questions regarding the late Phillip Caselli."

"Police again?" asked the man in mourning. "I'll call Mr. Dinwiddie. He's the boss."

"Call him, my man," commanded Tommy. "At once, please."

Mr. Dinwiddie was summoned. He had evidently been hard at work prettifying a corpse. He wore a fulvous yellow smock. His luxuriant dark hair was allowed to grow far down on his neck, like a ham actor's. He looked as if he'd just given himself a Toni. A stray ringlet curled fetchingly over his high, white brow. He had very long eyelashes and I could have sworn there was a touch of rouge on his high cheekbones. He smelled of lilac cologne and embalming fluid. He spoke in a high-pitched voice.

He raised a manicured hand to brush back the stray curl, said, "I really can't spare you much time. We are very busy. It's the weather. Pneumonia, traffic accidents, people slipping on the ice. This is almost always our very busiest season."

"So death also has its seasons," said Tommy. "Do you ever offer bargain rates in your off-months, Mr. Dinwiddie? But that is beside the question at hand. I wish to inquire about the late Caselli. How did he come here?"

"Why," said the shrill Mr. Dinwiddie, "the poor fellow was killed just outside the door. Eustace here," he indicated the fat little man, "happened to be looking out at the time. An auto, a black car, came very fast. It struck Mr. Caselli and raced away. He landed right in front of our door."

"Convenient," Tommy commented.

"Quite," agreed Mr. Dinwiddie. "The police came and brought him inside. He was killed instantly, apparently. Right after the police arrived, an old lady came screaming through the door. She was speaking Italian. Finally we calmed her down and found she was the aunt. She lives near here and had been informed of the accident. The police found identification cards on the body. There was no need for an autopsy. The cause of death was quite evident, and there were witnesses, including Eustace. They turned the body over to the lady. She asked that we take over the arrangements. Frankly, I doubted she could afford the price we ask. We rather pride ourself on our work, you know. But she didn't cavil at the sum mentioned. Many of the neighborhood Italians, even the poorest, save for years in order to assure their dear departed proper rites."

"What did Caselli look like?" queried Tommy.

Mr. Dinwiddie pushed back the wayward curl again, smoothed his fulvous yellow smock. "I hesitate to say this, but he was a very difficult subject," he replied. "He looked like a bulldog. I had quite a problem smoothing out the flabby jowls, covering the scars, building up the smashed nose. One of the ears was mangled, too."

"It does sound like Phil so far," said Tommy.

"Oh," said Mr. Dinwiddie airily, "the identification was quite positive, of course. The hands were rather remarkable. Out of keeping with the rest of him. Delicate hands. The hands of an artist or musician."

"Did many persons pay their respects?" asked Tommy.

Mr. Dinwiddie made a moue "That was the provoking part," he said. "I considered the job one of my real masterpieces. I eliminated all the brutality, the bulldoggishness, the malformation of features. He was actually *handsome* in death. But nobody at all came to see the body. Except the horrible little man who ruined all my painstaking work."

"Maybe Snowy took the undertaker's art into consideration when he accepted the body as that of Phil," said Tommy.

Eustace spoke up for the first time. "Mr. Dinwiddie is a real artist, too," he said admiringly.

Mr. Dinwiddie smoothed his smock. "Thank you, Eustace," he said, accepting the compliment as his due. "After the *horrible* thing happened, I thought perhaps it was some jealous competitor who wished to spoil my work. There was nothing to do but to advise the poor old lady to cremate her nephew. She agreed, and when we received a release from the police, I shipped the remains to the crematorium on Long Island that very same night."

"Did you see the old lady after that?" asked Tommy.

"I did not."

Tommy said, "There is nothing more to be done here, Soldier. Next on the agenda, you will introduce me to the parrot that bears the name of Hugo's tragic hero."

Mr. Dinwiddie was eyeing Tommy's huge bulk speculatively. "If you'll pardon my saying so," he said, "you would make a *most* interesting subject. Yes, indeed, you would pose a problem that a true artist would rejoice in solving."

"I'm afraid I can't oblige you, sir," replied Tommy gruffly. "I have willed my body to the National Foundation for Research on Alcoholism."

"Such a pity," said Mr. Dinwiddie ruefully. As I helped Tommy to his feet, he waved a languorous hand at us. "Good night, all," he trilled. "I'll be seeing you soon. Unpleasant reminder, isn't it?"

We drove uptown to Ginny's house on Twenty-third. I told Tommy to wait in the car while we got the parrot.

"No," he said. "I am frozen to the bone. We must purchase a heater for the car if I am to ride in it in winter." He took a drink. "Interior warmth is not sufficient on such a night," he added. "I will go inside and warm myself."

"But, Tommy," I protested, "this isn't an elevator apartment, and Ginny doesn't have an escalator like you have in your Tarrytown house. I could never get you up two steep flights of stairs."

"He can wait in the hall," said Ginny. "There's a chair outside the superintendent's door."

I had trouble enough getting the old man up the stoop, but finally managed it. At last I got him established in the chair outside the super's flat. Ginny and I started up the stairs. We were halfway up the first flight, when a sudden exclamation from Tommy stopped us.

"Wait!" he commanded. "Silence!"

We listened and heard a low groan coming from somewhere. Tommy leaned over in the chair, pressed his ear to the door of the super's flat. "Someone inside is in distress," he said. "Come down at once."

We clattered down the stairs. I knocked at the door. I was answered by a groan, louder this time. I tried the knob. The door opened.

The room was in darkness. Something in the darkness moaned like a wounded animal. I switched on the light. A man wearing a red sweater was lying on the floor. There was blood on his head.

"It's the super!" I said.

Tommy was wriggling around in the big chair, attempting to rise, craning his neck to look into the room. He looked like an up-ended seal.

"Assist me to my feet, damn it!" he ordered.

I helped him into the room. Ginny had run over to the super's side. She was wiping the blood from his head with a wispy handkerchief that was soon dyed red. I parked Tommy against a library table and bent over the mumbling man. I handed Ginny another handkerchief, a bigger one. The man was regaining consciousness.

"Who hit you? What happened?" I asked urgently.

"Don't know," he mumbled. "Couldn't see."

"When? How long ago?"

"Supper time. Six, about. Little later, maybe. What time now?"

Tommy said, "His watch is on the floor there."

"No watch," said the super. "Got no watch."

I helped the super to the couch. He sat holding his bloody head in his hands, my handkerchief against the wound. Ginny picked up the watch. There was a small charm at the other end of the chain, a pair of boxing gloves, I saw, as Ginny handed the watch to me. It was a thin model with a gold case. The super was right. It wasn't his watch. On the back of the case was engraved:

'FIGHTING PHIL' CASELLI
From An Ardent Admirer
Thaddeus Mulholland
1925

I handed the watch to Tommy. He said, "I remember when the old man presented this to Phil. It was after the Kid Kenneally fight. The old doctor was a great devotee of the manly art of maul and murder."

Ginny had gone to the bathroom. She came back with first-aid materials, bandaged the super's head. When she had finished, she said, "We'd better call the cops."

"Not just yet," said Tommy. "Call a doctor."

Ginny called a doctor she knew. I assisted Tommy to a chair beside the couch.

"How do you feel?" Tommy asked the super. "Do you think you can talk?"

"My head aches," said the super, looking at Tommy with dazed eyes. "But I guess I'm all right."

Ginny said the doctor would be right over. He had offices in nearby London Terrace. She went to the bathroom again, came back with aspirin. Tommy produced the blue crock, poured a stiff drink. The super chased the aspirin with the brandy, wiped his lips.

He said, "Little after six. Doorbell rang. I clicked to let them in. I opened my door. No one there. I stuck my head out to look. Something hit me. That's all I know."

"See if you are missing anything," Tommy instructed.

The super fumbled for his wallet, found it. He counted the money in it, shook his head.

"Your keys," said Tommy.

The super fumbled at his belt. "They're gone," he said.

"Soldier!" said Tommy peremptorily. "Upstairs! Check the parrot!"

I climbed the stairs two at a time. Before I unlocked Ginny's door, I knew Quasi was okay. I heard him squawking, "Goddam! Goddam right! Stop, thief!"

I opened the door with my key. I carried keys to Ginny's apartment as well as my own. I even had my name on her mailbox, because they were very careless about mail at my cold-water building. The boxes were often rifled, and I had a fairly fat disability-compensation check arriving in a telltale brown Government envelope each month

Quasi was out of his cage. He was sitting on top of the marble mantelpiece. He was perched on a limp-legged rag doll. He was still squawking.

"Goddam it! Stop, thief!"

The parrot was there all right, but his cage was missing.

I examined the room hastily. So far as I could tell, nothing else had been disturbed. On the floor of the room, I found the super's passkeys.

I picked up the keys. I persuaded Quasi to perch on my shoulder. He was willing enough, but he pecked playfully at my ear a couple of times. On the way downstairs, he shouted, "Whoopee! Some fun! Goddam right!"

The doctor was attending the wounded man. He gave me a startled glance when I entered with the parrot perched on my shoulder.

"Don't mind me, Doc," I said. "I'm just an old bird-fancier."

"Goddam right! Goddam right!" confirmed Quasi.

The doctor looked even more surprised at that, but he continued to sew up the super's skull with a little trick needle and thread
he had brought along. Tommy put his finger to his mouth while
the doctor wasn't looking, so I said nothing about the missing cage.
Ginny, however, asked, "Why did you take Quasi out of the cage?"

"He wanted to ride piggy-back," I told her. "Even a parrot's got
to get a little fun out of life, you know."

After the doctor had patched up the super's skull, he said,
"There doesn't seem to be a fracture, but we'd better make an
X-ray at the office tomorrow. I'll give you some pills to relieve the
pain. I suppose you have called the police?"

"That will be attended to," Tommy assured him.

The doctor left. Tommy told the superintendent that we were
leaving, too, as we had to catch a train, and advised him to call the
cops. I gave him back his passkeys. When we were out in the hall
again, Tommy said, "Well, Soldier? What about the cage with the
false bottom?"

"Gone," I told him.

"You are quite sure you didn't read the letter addressed to me?"

"No," I said. "I didn't think that would be ethical. Besides, the
flap was stuck down with sealing-wax."

"That is most unfortunate," said Tommy. "The loss of the cage
is a major setback at this stage of the game. Without it, the murder
of the old doctor may well go unpunished."

"I didn't like that old cage much anyway," said Ginny. "I was
planning to get Quasi a nice red one to match his eyes."

"I'm afraid your cage won't have the same contents as the one
that has been purloined," said Tommy.

"It will if we put Quasi inside it," declared Ginny.

"Goddam right," said Quasi. He hopped from my shoulder
to Ginny's. He seemed to think she was his champion. "Goddam
right!" he repeated.

"I wasn't thinking of the parrot," said Tommy. "His worth is decidedly dubious, like the worth of my persistently sterile penguins. His vocabulary is even limited, though it seems profane enough. But Soldier tells me the secret compartment in the base of the cage had some interesting articles in it."

"Oh," said Ginny contemptuously. "That old stuff! Terry seemed to think it was so gosh-awful important, I decided not to leave it in the apartment. I've got it right here."

She pulled up her skirt, affording us a pleasant view of silk stocking, black garter and white flesh. She extracted the folded envelope and the tagged key from the top of her stocking. She handed them to Tommy.

"Soldier," Mr. Twotoes said, "I congratulate you. Not upon your perspicacity or intelligence, but upon your fortunate choice of a female companion. Let us depart. The Lieutenant will be champing at the bit. Lacking a bit, he will certainly be champing at the bottle."

I went through the physical exertion necessary to get the old man down the stoop and back into the car. This time I drove, and Ginny sat beside me. Tommy had the entire back seat to himself. It was no more room than he required for comfort.

"Tarrytown?" I asked.

"I think we will go to Murray Hill first," replied Tommy. "I wish to call at the Suffield. I will talk to the clerk, Jenks, and to your sanctimonious friend, Eddie."

As I turned the car east, I said, "Granting your theory that Caselli is alive, I can't see how he knew the bird was stashed in Ginny's flat. And I can't understand why he took the cage without the bird."

"You said you were followed by a taxi earlier this evening. The intruder did not want the bird. He wanted the cage and what was in it. He probably took the cage because he did not know the combination of the hidden compartment and wished to examine it at his leisure. It was awkward enough to carry the cage. It would have been more awkward had the cage contained a voluble parrot like Quasimodo."

Quasimodo made a short flight from the front seat to the back seat, from Ginny's shoulder to Tommy's capacious lap. "Goddam right!" he said. "Goddam right!"

"I thought it was one of Romano's men following me," I said.

"Obviously your supposition was erroneous," replied Tommy. "Now, if you will hand me the flashlight, I will read the letter. First I should tell you that several months ago I received a letter from the old doctor. He expressed vague fears, seemed to believe that his life was in danger. I put it down to his advancing age and his increasing eccentricity. He told me that he was willing me a parrot. He adjured me to see that the parrot had a good home for the rest of its life. He said that the key to his entire estate was contained in the secret compartment of the cage. He had deposited large amounts of cash and bonds in safe-deposit boxes which were held in the names of Phil and Snowy. I was to give them the keys, to advise them in the expending and the investment of their inheritance. He said that only three living things had comforted him in his old age. They were strange beings. An ancient parrot. A pink-eyed albino. And an old fighter with a bulldog's face."

Tommy paused for a moment. Then he said, "The key for Phil is missing. That may be highly significant."

I said, "It doesn't make sense. If Casein took the key the day he strung the old man up, he could have taken everything else if he'd wanted it. And if he took the key, he knew the combination, so there was no sense in him walking off from Ginny's with the whole cage. He would have simply opened the compartment and got what he wanted."

"Sound enough logic as far as it goes," replied Tommy. "But it is quite possible Phil did not take the key from the cage. The old man may have grown suspicious of him and hidden the key somewhere among the littered junk of his rooms. Or he may have even withdrawn the money from the safe-deposit box and placed it elsewhere for safekeeping."

We were nearing the Suffield by the time Tommy broke the seal and began to read the letter by the light of my flash. When I parked, he switched on the ceiling light of the car and handed the flash back to me. "Remain in the car for a moment and I will read you a queer and perhaps revealing document," he said. "The doctor's letter to me unfortunately is not dated."

He began to read:

> Dear old friend:
> I am presuming upon our friendship of twenty-five years ago and our mutual interest in the sport of pugilism in writing you this and asking you to act as executor of my will. I wrote you recently to tell you that I stand in fear of my life, though I am healthy enough, I suppose, for a man of my advanced years. I explained to you in that letter that two keys would be found in the secret compartment of the cage that belongs to my ancient friend and house pet, Quasimodo, the parrot. You have been informed how to open the secret compartment. It remains only for you to see that Stanley Sylvester and Phillip Caselli each receives the key bearing a tag with his name, and to counsel them in the expenditure of the money they inherit, if you will be so good.
>
> These two men have been my friends to the end. I have adopted this method of willing them what assets I possess in the hope that possible claimants of my estate will not hear of their inheritance and protest. So far as I know, I have no relatives living except a great-nephew whom I do not admire.

Stanley Sylvester has never had more than barely enough money to sustain life in his frail body and will need your advice. Phillip Caselli has had large sums of money at times, all of which he has spent foolishly upon fair-weather friends who have forgotten him now he is no longer either rich or a celebrity.

There have been several attempts upon my life. I have thought of going to the police for protection, but feel sure they would regard me as an old lunatic, because I take delight in collecting those things that others discard, since I am deeply interested in the theory that an entire new economic system might be based upon the daily waste of the world we live in.

On two occasions, automobiles have attempted to run me down. On one of these occasions, a driver whom I could not recognize came at me the wrong way of a one-way street. Only recently an intruder attempted to smother me in my bed. I awakened late at night to hear a soft noise in my room. Before I could make a light, a pillow was pressed down upon my face. I was left for dead, but recovered. I went to the night clerk of my hotel, one Jenks, and told him what had happened, but he did not believe me. He said no one had passed the desk during the late hours of the evening, that my apartment could not have been entered through a locked door, and suggested I was dreaming. He warned me that if I called the police, they would doubtless take my "queer" habits into account and commit me to an institution.

I feel the murderer is drawing closer and that soon he will be successful in his designs upon my poor old person, although I have no idea of his identity and cannot assign to him any motive for such a crime. Doubtless he will attempt to make his deed appear accidental or natural death, but I tell you now that if I am found dead, I will have been the victim of a cold-blooded killer.

Please believe that I am sane of mind as I write this, and that I do not fear to die, for I have lived far longer than my allotted span. I look forward to my approaching end with considerable interest and wonder in what manner the killer will strike next.

With deepest appreciation for carrying out my last wishes, I am, with respect and admiration,

Your humble and ob'd't serv't,

Thaddeus Mulholland

Tommy folded the letter and placed it in his pocket. He shook his head and said, "Anyone would have been fully justified in believing that such an odd old man was suffering from a persecution complex. Yet he called the turn exactly.

"Of course," he added, "the autos that bore down upon the doctor might have been driven by innocent motorists who were merely careless. But it is significant, I think, that the man who impersonated Fighting Phil was killed by a hit-run driver."

Tommy took a drink to steel himself before he entered the hotel. Ginny refused one. He wouldn't offer me a snort because I was now driving the car. We left Ginny in the jeepster to parrot-sit Quasimodo. I assisted the old man over the icy sidewalk and into the mildewed mausoleum that still did business as a hostelry. The clerk, Jenks, was the only person in sight. As usual, he was working a crossword puzzle.

Jenks looked up and inquired, "What's a six-letter word meaning a *zygodactyl bird of the psittaci order?*"

"Try *parrot*," I suggested. "And meet Mr. Tommy Twotoes. He was an old friend of Dr. Mulholland's."

"That's *exactly* it!" exclaimed Jenks, filling in the squares. "Glad to meet you Mr. —. I think I misunderstood the name."

"Twotoes," replied Tommy. "It derives from an ancestor of mine who was a brave of the Potawatomi nation. Despite my pallid face, I am one-thirty-second Indian. The family disowned the name for the more conventional Tuthill, but I revived it legally. Now, please. We would like to visit the doctor's suite. The scene of the crime."

Jenks looked dubious. "I'll be glad to run you up, of course," he said. "But I doubt the police will let you in. They're still up there, poking around in that awful mess, poor fellows. Looking for a clue, I suppose."

"Where's Eddie?" I inquired, glancing at the empty elevator cage.

"I don't know," said Jenks. "He didn't show up at all. I've had to run the elevator as well as attend the desk and the switchboard all evening. I'm at my wit's end. No wonder I'm not doing better on this crossword."

"Tell me," said Tommy. "Did Dr. Mulholland ever express to you any fears for his safety? Was he suspicious of anyone?"

Jenks said, "The old man was odd, of course. Spent a lot of his time collecting junk, for instance. Had queer friends. A little albino and a man who looked like a bulldog. He suffered from delusions, I'm sure. Once he came down in the middle of the night to tell me someone had just tried to murder him. Imagine that! In a conservative hotel like the Suffield! I calmed him down. He was just childish, had bad dreams."

"Yet it was no delusion, no bad dream that he was hanged by the neck," asserted Tommy.

"That was most distressing," said Jenks, primly. "Most puzzling, too. Who on earth could have wished the old man harm?

He had nothing, I'm sure. One of the chambermaids and Eddie witnessed a will for him once, just to humor him. I didn't see it, of course. But I understand from Lieutenant Romano he left a couple of keys to safe-deposit boxes to his friends, the albino and the bulldog. Probably there's nothing in the boxes except junk or old newspapers, if the boxes actually exist."

"Some years ago," said Tommy, "the doctor inherited a considerable estate, I believe."

"My goodness!" exclaimed Jenks. "Imagine that, now! I always thought he lived on his pension from the university. He was certainly tight enough with his money, if he had any. Never tipped. One Christmas he gave the colored boy, Eddie, a Gideon Bible he'd stolen from the hotel."

"He is supposed to have had a nephew," said Tommy. "Did the nephew ever visit him to your knowledge?"

Jenks shook his head. "Never knew of any relatives," he said. "His only visitors were the albino, the bulldog, and sometimes lawyers or professors who wanted his advice on some legal matter."

Tommy said, "If you will be good enough to pilot this decrepit conveyance upstairs . . ."

Jenks shoved aside the crossword. "Of course," he said, ushering us to the elevator.

A cop wearing a uniform opened the door. Other cops who weren't wearing uniforms were sorting out a hopeless maze of litter in the rooms and cursing quietly. The uniformed cop looked doubtful and called a beefy detective sergeant.

"I was a friend of Dr. Mulholland's," said Tommy. "I am the executor of his estate. Lieutenant Romano is waiting for me at my home now. I would like to look around."

The beefy cop looked at me and said, "I know *you*, all right."

"I'm getting notorious," I replied.

"Who're you?" he inquired of Tommy. "You must be Tommy Twotoes. The Lieutenant mentioned your name."

Without waiting for confirmation, he added, "Come on in if you want to. Nothing in here you couldn't see on the city garbage dump."

I supported Tommy as he gave the rooms a cursory examination. He looked at the chandelier from which the old doctor had been hanging. He showed especial interest in the ladder on which the footprints were still quite clear. He said to the beefy detective, "Any developments today, Sergeant?"

"Yeah," replied the Sergeant. "One. We come across something. Romano called from your place up in Tarrytown. We told him about it. He can tell you if he wants to. I won't."

"I shan't urge you to," said Tommy. "We will be seeing the Lieutenant shortly. I suggest we all have a drink before we leave. All except Soldier, here, that is. He is driving, the roads are icy, and I value my person."

Tommy produced the blue crock and the cluster of metal cups.

"Well," said the Sergeant, "we're on duty, but it's a mighty cold night."

Everybody had a drink. Everybody but me. I just licked my lips.

We descended in the shuddering elevator again. Jenks returned to his crossword puzzle. I expended the last of my waning strength in convoying the three-hundred-pound Mr. Twotoes to the waiting car. Quasimodo greeted us profanely and vociferously.

"I have a feeling," said Tommy, "that Quasimodo and my penguin, Cleo, will get along famously. Both are uninhibited souls."

The drive to Tarrytown was no pleasure trip for me. The car slipped and skidded over the icy roads and snowdrops as brittle as glass began to pelt against the windshield about the time we entered Westchester County. I had no desire to exceed the speed limit imposed by Mr. Twotoes.

As we climbed the bluff that led to Tommy's home, the old man said, "I trust Lieutenant Romano will not find me derelict in my duties as a host. I instructed Polvo to prepare his incomparable shish-kebab for our guests' supper and there is an ample supply of brandy about. The Lieutenant should not be bored, at least. The guests I brought from the Coast are all persons of rare talent. Madame Eden is a medium as well as an actress. She communes with spirits, both bottled and astral, and may be able to summon up the ghost of Dr. Mulholland for Romano."

The manufactured cliffs and glaciers of the miniature Antarctic that Tommy had fashioned for his penguins towered behind the house of modernistic design. The penguins were evidently sleeping in cold comfort, for no arking greeted our arrival. The interior of Tommy's home was by no means modernistic. The furnishings came from all countries and dated from all periods. We hung our hats and coats upon the totem pole that served as a hall-tree.

There was, to understate the situation, considerable activity in the house.

Tommy had installed an escalator, since his semi-paralysis made stairs difficult for him, and someone had set the device in motion. Cleo, the house penguin, was hopping up and down the moving steps, and arking stridently. Evidently she did not find the steam heat of the house uncomfortable, for she appeared supremely happy as she bounced down to greet her master. Seeing her, Quasimodo, who was perched on Ginny's shoulder, shrieked, "What the hell? What the goddam hell?"

Montmorency, the gander, was careening madly around the room in pursuit of Ivan the Terrible, the bashful Great Dane, which appeared to be on the verge of nervous prostration as he slunk about the enormous chamber, seeking a hiding place and frequently upsetting furniture. Quasimodo hopped off Ginny's shoulder and joined in the chase, muttering gay obscenities. Cleo, the penguin, came paddling in and attacked poor Ivan from a different flank.

The amazed Romano sprawled in a Cape Cod rocker, his eyes popping and his mouth agape. He held a balloon inhaler limply in his hand. Polvo, who wore a white coat and George Washington's teeth, refilled the balloon glass with brandy from a blue crock as soon as it was emptied.

With my assistance, Tommy made his way through the pandemonium to the Lieutenant. He apologized for our late arrival. Romano couldn't hear him above the honking of Montmorency, the shrieking of Quasimodo, the arking of Cleo, and the whining of Ivan.

The Lieutenant cupped a hand to his ear, said, "What? What say?"

Tommy's answer was lost, for at that moment, Madame Eden let out a scream: "Wallawoochee! Wallawoochee!"

"Wallawoochee," explained Tommy, his mouth close to my ear, "is the Madame's spirit control."

To add to the confusion three of the Magnificent Mephisto's guinea pigs had joined the pursuit of the unfortunate Great Dane.

Tommy gestured toward a tapestry-hung wall. The tapestry concealed one of his pet conceits—a secret panel that opened into his soundproof study. I pressed an ornamental knob and the panel slid open. I motioned to the befuddled Romano.

Before the panel slid shut to insulate us from the din, we heard Eve Eden scream, "Death! Death! Wallawoochee sees Death all around us!"

Once the three of us were isolated in the soundproof chamber, Tommy ensconced himself in a huge chair that had been specially constructed to bear his weight. He filled the pipe that was made in the form of a naked woman, lit it and puffed tranquilly at the aromatic tobacco. Romano wiped sweat from his brow.

"Christ!" he exclaimed. "I knew you were an unusual guy, Tommy, but where do you *find* people like that?"

"In Hollywood," replied Tommy, "these people are considered hide-bound conservatives. Amusing and talented, aren't they?"

"Nuts is what I'd call 'em," said the Lieutenant.

"Seat yourself, Lieutenant," invited Tommy. "Have a drink and calm down."

"Could I maybe have a drink now, too, please?" I inquired.

"Certainly," answered Tommy magnanimously. "You deserve one. You have driven me safely over icy roads. And you have assisted me in the solution of a puzzling murder mystery."

"What?" I asked. I didn't wait for an answer, though. I poured a drink. A stiff one.

Tommy turned to Romano.

"Some work on the part of the Soldier and his careful chronicling of facts have established an important fact, Lieutenant," he said. "Fighting Phil Caselli is alive."

"Yeah," said Romano complacently. "I kinda figured that after I heard something coupla hours ago."

"What did you hear?" Tommy asked.

"Called the Sergeant I left in charge at the Suffield," said Romano. "Boys found something after all in that mess. A receipted bill, addressed to the doctor. From a sanitarium for hopheads and drunks, over in Rockland County. Dated just five days ago. Seems the doc was paying a patient's bill. Patient name of Phil Caselli."

6

"This is a most interesting development," said Tommy. "I trust you have checked the sanitarium to see if our rather lively corpse is still a patient there?"

"Not much sense in doing that tonight," replied Romano. "If he's there, he's on ice and we can get to him when we want him. If he's not, we don't know where he is anyway. Those places, they have dumb nurses and orderlies in charge at night. Couldn't learn much from 'em. Probably have the files locked up, too. Better to go over in the morning and see the head man. It's just across the river. Not too far from here. You got a room I can sleep in to-night?"

"Of course," said Tommy, refilling our glasses from the blue crock. "As an honored guest you rate a private chamber. The others will share a bedroom. Soldier, I think I will put you up with the Magnificent Mephisto."

"Jeez," I said. "I'll have guinea pigs crawling over me all night."

"That should be more comfortable than sharing a bed with the Great Dane," replied Tommy. "Great Danes take up a lot of room."

"You got something to tell me I ought to know?" Romano asked the old man.

"I have," replied Tommy.

He reported our activities that evening. He gave the Lieutenant the gist of what I had related to him earlier. He omitted the part about Snowy Sylvester's visit to the Rooke Agency, however. The Lieutenant was sore enough at me for not telling him I had recovered the parrot in the basement of the Suffield. He indicated that he could book me for withholding important evidence and interfering with police officers in the discharge of their duties.

When he finished his discourse, Tommy said, "I should say that the identity of the murderer is fairly evident, *unless* we find that Phil Caselli has been under lock and key the whole time."

Romano said, "Yeah? Well, me, now, I'd kinda like to talk to that Snowy, if we can dig him out of his hole. First thing tomorrow, I'll check that junkie joint across the river. Then I'll have to get that key from you and see what's in the box it fits. Have to get an order to open it. The D.A. knows a judge who's obliging in such matters. As executor of the estate, you won't object, will you?"

"No," replied Tommy. "Not if I am fully informed of the contents of the box."

"Can do," said Romano. "If there really *is* a box." He finished off his brandy. "This fancy rat poison of yours makes me sleepy," he said. "Got to get up early. Busy day ahead. Think I'll turn in."

"I am interested in Caselli," said Tommy. "He used to fight for me. If you have no objections, the Soldier and I will accompany you to the sanitarium. So we had best retire ourselves, although I usually sit up to greet the dawn."

I assisted Tommy to his feet. Before I opened the secret panel into the living room, he turned to the Lieutenant and said, "Lieutenant, unless we can apprehend this killer very quickly, there are going to be more murders."

Romano grinned.

"Honeyboy," he said, "you talk just like a character in one of them mystery books."

When we entered the living room, our assorted breeds of birds had apparently tired of chasing Ivan, the bashful Great Dane.

Quasimodo, the parrot, and Montmorency, the gander, were in a fight. The air was hideous with angry squawkings and honkings and green and white feathers flew like confetti. The fight was evidently a duel over Cleo, the amorous penguin. That lady, long neglected by the ascetic males of the penguin flock, was in a seventh heaven of excitement.

Madame Eden was still passed out cold or in a trance, according to how you wanted to look at it. Tommy ordered Polvo to separate the brawling birds and to get the smelling salts for Madame Eden. When she showed signs of returning consciousness, we lifted her to her feet. She let out an unearthly scream.

"Wallawoochee! Wallawoochee sees a white ghost walking! The ghost means murder!"

"The little albino wears white," remarked Romano.

"And Phil Caselli is a walking ghost," Tommy reminded him.

At the door to his bedroom, Tommy turned to Romano and me and said, "I could wish that my stout and trustworthy friend Ebony Black were here instead of driving the Rolls back from the Coast. I always feel safe with such a reliable watchdog in the house."

"You don't feel safe?" asked Romano.

"I am convinced that someone will try to murder me," said Tommy cryptically.

"Who?" asked Romano.

"The same man who murdered Dr. Mulholland, of course," replied Tommy. "Sweet dreams, my friends."

The Magnificent Mephisto and I retired to our bedroom, the former carrying the crate of guinea pigs on his shoulder.

"Listen," I said. "You sure you've got 'em all? I don't want to wake up with a bed full of guinea pigs."

"Nothing to be alarmed about," he assured me. "Guinea pigs don't bite. They're friendly little creatures." He stroked a guinea pig named Osric. "See?" he said. "Soft and cuddly."

"I still don't want 'em for bedfellows," I replied. "Rooming with a magician has its disadvantages."

The Magnificent Mephisto tittered. "You should be thankful I'm not a snake-charmer," he said.

The magician, the guinea pigs and I finally corked off. I had fitful dreams of the guinea pigs dancing a gavotte to the tune of a zither strummed by a white-clad ghost. Sometime during the middle of the night the strings of the zither twanged a wild, discordant note that was like an explosion, and I was awakened rudely. All hell had broken loose, it seemed. Someone was screaming out in the hall. The penguins were arking back at the screamer from the rookeries. Doors slammed open. Feet scuffled. The gander honked. The Great Dane whined. I didn't hear any squawks from Quasi because Polvo, lacking a cage, had taken the parrot to the kitchen and placed him under a large wire wastebasket that was turned upside down.

The Magnificent Mephisto threw his silk-lined cape around him and ran out into the hall. I followed him. Madame Eden, clad in a flowing white negligée, was standing in the middle of the dimly lit hallway, screaming her lungs out. Ginny, Colonel Finger and Wisey were trying to calm her down. The Colonel's Great Dane was sitting on his haunches now and howling like dogs are supposed to do when there's been a death in the family. I started toward Madame and tripped over Montmorency, the arrogant gander. He honked a protest and took a peck at my bare ankle. Little Polvo came dashing up the ramp.

"Wallawoochee!" shrieked Eve Eden. "He saw the white ghost! He warned us! Death! Murder!"

At that moment Tommy Twotoes emerged from the master bedroom. He was clad in a gold-embroidered Mandarin robe that might have served as Barnum's big top. His fat-larded face, usually pallid, had taken on the sickly tinge of verdigris.

He spoke in a hollow voice. "Someone shot at me. Someone tried to murder me. I don't like it. I don't like it at all!"

"Wallawoochee warned us!" repeated Eve.

"Where's Romano?" Tommy demanded.

The Lieutenant came out of his bedroom, knuckling sleep-ooze from his liquid Italian eyes.

"What's the matter, honeyboy?" Romano asked Tommy. "Something wrong?"

"Lieutenant," said the old man sternly, "I respect you as an able police officer—when you are awake. Unfortunately you seem to sleep too soundly. Someone just attempted to murder me. He fired through the window of my bedroom. Such things upset me. I have only been fired upon once before in my life. That was when Pancho Villa raided the Juarez racetrack in 1916."

"Now, honeyboy," said Romano, "how could anybody take pots at you through a second-story window?"

"The obvious inference," stated Tommy acidly, "is that he climbed the elm tree outside my room. I suggest you search the grounds at once, although I suspect such a gesture will be futile at so late an hour. The assassin drove into the grounds in an automobile. He departed in the same manner. At least we may find footprints and tire tracks."

"How did the guy know which window was yours?" inquired Romano. "How did he know who he was shooting at in the dark?"

"I suffer from insomnia," replied Tommy. "I have a phobia about complete darkness. I keep a small night light burning in my room. He had only to look through the window to see me in my bed. My bulk affords a somewhat ample target. It is only a miracle that he could have missed."

"Did you see the guy who fired at you?" Romano asked.

"I was in no mood to stick my head out of the window into the barrel of a killer's gun," fumed the exasperated Mr. Twotoes. "I heard a car coming into the grounds. I heard the penguins, which appear more alert than certain police officers, set up a clamor at the disturbance. I heard the car stop and the icy branches of the tree creak and tinkle. I raised myself on an elbow. There was a blast and a flash at my window. I rolled out of the opposite side of the bed to the floor. The crash of my falling body alone was enough to awaken an ordinary sleeper. I crawled on my belly to my bathroom. I remained lying on my belly, out of the line of fire, until I heard a car start up and heard Madame Eden screaming. At least one of my guests had the courtesy to awaken while her host was being murdered."

"You ain't murdered, honeyboy," Romano assured the fat man. "You're just kinda green around the gills. I'll take a look in your bedroom."

"I suggest you search the grounds first, although it is unlikely the intruder has been obliging enough to linger about and await your awakening," said Tommy.

"We'll take a look later," replied the unperturbed Romano. "But there's not much use. It quit snowing long before we went to bed, and a deep freeze set in. Grounds were like a skating rink when I opened my window before I turned in. May be some evidence of tire tracks, but no good for footprints. Like glass."

The Lieutenant entered Tommy's bedroom. I followed him. Tommy Twotoes came in after peeking through the door first to make sure that the would-be murderer had departed.

There was a hole in the paneled wall above Tommy's enormous, specially reinforced bed. The Lieutenant took a penknife from his pocket and dug a shell from the hole. He held the misshapen bullet in the palm of his hand. It looked like a chewed-up Chiclet.

Romano said, "Seems almost like this guy was trying to miss. The bullet went at least five feet above the bed. I'd say at a rough guess it came out of a .32. Anyway, it couldn't have been fired from the .45 the little albino used for his face-lifting operation on the stiff in the funeral parlor."

The Lieutenant crossed to the opened window from which a frigid breeze was blowing. Upper branches of the tree almost touched the sill. One of the smaller branches was freshly broken. From the broken branch something white was hanging, and it wasn't snow. The Lieutenant reached out and plucked the white fragment from the branch. It was a small square of linen. It might have been ripped from a white linen suit.

The others, including Madame Eden, thronged into the bed-chamber. I noticed for the first time that Ginny was wearing a white satin dressing gown that must have belonged to Eve. It trailed on the floor behind her. She looked like a bride. A rather prettily disheveled, sleepy-eyed bride.

Romano held up the square of linen. "Snowy left his calling card behind," he said.

"Who is this Snowy person?" the Magnificent Mephisto inquired.

"A magician," said Romano. "He disappears into thin air."

"Pfaw," snorted Mephisto contemptuously. "An old trick. It's done with mirrors and trap doors."

"On the contrary," said Romano, "this little character does it with white linen suits and snowstorms."

Romano picked up the extension telephone near Tommy's bed. He called the local police and reported the fact that an intruder had climbed a tree and shot at Tommy.

"They'll be here shortly," he said. "They'll want to question you, but I doubt there's much anybody can tell 'em. I'll take a look outside when I get some clothes on." He was wearing a pair of the pajamas which Tommy kept in assorted sizes for unexpected guests and had a lilac-colored blanket draped around him.

The Magnificent Mephisto and I went to the room we shared and threw on our clothes. I glanced at the crate of guinea pigs and

it seemed to me to be very crowded. I wondered if there had been
any new arrivals during the night.

Tommy showed no disposition to change from the old-fashioned nightshirt and the gold-embroidered Mandarin robe he was
wearing. He didn't accompany us outdoors. Maybe that was because he believed he was subject to head colds. Maybe he was just
sulking at the Lieutenant because the latter hadn't become appro-
priately excited over the attempt upon the large and precious Twotoes person. Or maybe he suspected that the killer was still lurking
somewhere around the premises.

The tire treads of the jeepster, the station wagon and Romano's
car were frozen into the ice. There were faint traces of another
car having entered the driveway after the snow had frozen hard.
Near the tree on the lawn the crusted ice had been broken in a
few places. But there were just shallow holes, not clearly definable
footprints.

The local police arrived presently. They questioned everybody
at some length but they learned little more than what Tommy had
already related to us. They seemed to be confused by the necessity of interviewing a midget, a medium, a magician and a zither
player, not to mention a strip-teaser and the extraordinary Mr.
Twotoes himself. They seemed even more confused by the presence of the cocky gander, which honked around under everybody's
feet, the guinea pigs, and the ludicrously timid Great Dane. They
gave up entirely when Madame Eden attempted to tell them of the
revelations of her spirit control, Wallawoochee.

We finally got back to bed around five-thirty. It seemed only
a few minutes later when Polvo shook me to announce that it was
eight o'clock and that Mr. Twotoes desired me to arise, dress and
breakfast so that I could accompany him and the Lieutenant to
the sanitarium in Rockland County. I figured that the nut factory
which housed such comparatively sane characters as rummies,
junkies and teahounds would be a relief after the Twotoes manse.

Polvo brought me a penguin cocktail, a tonsil-blistering drink which Mr. Twotoes recommended as an eye-opener. A penguin cocktail consisted of equal parts of whisky and brandy. After the appetizer I went down and ate eggs Buckingham, which was one of Polvo's specialties—scrambled eggs and melted cheese poured over milk toast. Tommy, Romano and I were the only early risers.

We laced our coffee with brandy from one of the blue bottles to fortify us against the weather, then we got our wraps off the totem pole and set forth for the sanitarium. Romano planned to go directly to New York after our visit. He drove his own car. Tommy and I took the office jeepster. As I proceeded slowly over the plate-glass roads to the Bear Mountain Bridge, Tommy discussed Phil Caselli at some length.

"I have always defended the inalienable right of every human being to go to hell in his own peculiar fashion," he said. "I myself have experimented with alcohol in virtually all its forms for more than half a century. As a result I am corpulent and crippled. I have an enlarged liver and a fatty heart. My eyes have grown so permanently red that they are best described as white-shot. Yet I have never trifled with drugs, even the widely used and frequently prescribed barbiturates. There is a cold ball of fear inside me so far as drugs are concerned, for I have traveled the skid rows of the land and I know what drugs can do to a man. It is a well-established medical fact that an alcoholic may steal to obtain his grog, but that he will never murder for that reason alone. A dope addict will kill in order to procure his poison.

"It is sad indeed to think of a fine physical specimen like Fighting Phil wrecking himself with drugs. He was, in my book, one of the greatest middleweights of all time and only a series of flukes deprived him of the championship. He possessed Dempsey's ferocity, Johnson's cunning, Tunney's speed and Louis' reflexes. Those are abundant gifts for the gods to bestow upon one man.

"To all this I might add that he also had the fighting heart and the love of living that were attributes of immortal Harry Greb. He enjoyed good food and good drink, the cheers of the crowd, the adulation of women, the companionship of men. He spent his money in profligate fashion as soon as he had earned it. When bums asked him for a dime, he gave them a dollar. He was a soft touch. He made no secret of his drinking habits. He did not aspire to become a model for the youth of the land, but to live his own life as he saw fit. I was once his manager and later I promoted his fights, but I never objected to his drinking, for it seemed to hurt him no more than copious libations harmed Rabelais' Gargantua.

"Perhaps his indulgences caught up with him at last. I saw him five years ago, when he and Snowy, who had remained his companion through the years, visited me. I do not believe he was addicted to drugs then. But his drinking was beginning to show. His hand quivered slightly and there was an unaccustomed obesity about his middle. His eyes had grown cloudy and shifty. I did not fear too much for him, however. I was saddened when I learned that he had met an untimely and undistinguished end beneath the wheels of a hit-run driver. It saddens me even more, however, to think that he may be living on as a wreck that mocks the fine animal he once was, that he may even be suspect as the murderer of his friend."

Tommy paused, filled and lit the pipe that was fashioned in the shape of a naked woman.

"I am praying now," he said. "I am praying to whatever gods an immoral old man may have. I am praying we find that Fighting Phil has never left the sanitarium."

We crossed the Bear Mountain Bridge, drove through a section of Interstate Park into Rockland County. Romano's car was leading us. He seemed to know the way. At length he turned into the driveway of an imposing estate. The buildings might have belonged to an ivy-league college—except for the bars on the windows. The ice-glistening grounds had been beautifully land-scaped. There were tennis courts, a nine-hole golf course, even bridle paths.

"This," I commented, "is a lot fancier than any of the souse traps *I* ever made. If I ever go into the rams, I hope you'll send me here, Papa."

"I imagine," said Tommy, "that the old doctor paid a pretty penny for Phil's bed and board at this resort."

We parked and I assisted Tommy from the car. We followed Romano into the administration building. Romano interviewed a pretty nurse who might have stepped out of a "Young Dr. Kildare" film. She led us to a handsome doctor who could have been Young Dr. Kildare himself.

The young doctor looked at Mr. Twotoes with interest.

"So this is our new patient!" he said with enthusiasm. "Interesting case of alcoholic obesity and incipient paresis. Here, let me have a look."

Before anyone could stop him, he had pried back one of Tommy's lids and flashed a little light into his eye.

"Unhand me, sir!" roared the old man. "I am no patient of yours, prospective or otherwise. I detest all medicos! I particularly detest those who paw at me. I have the utmost contempt for those practitioners who pretend to probe the psyche with their snide analyses. Back to your Freud and your Krafft-Ebing, you fledgling spawn of Hippocrates!"

"Hmm," said the doctor, rubbing his hands and appearing to relish Tommy's outburst. "Typical alcoholic pattern. Inflated ego. Violent resentments."

"Damn it, sir . . ." Tommy began to sputter. Romano held up his hand. "Let's understand each other, honeyboy," he said. "Mr. Twotoes doubtless needs your treatment, but he isn't here as a patient. He's an unreconstructed rebel against all the established moral codes. I am a police officer from New York. Mr. Twotoes is an interested party in a certain case. We wish to inquire about one of your patients here."

"Oh," said the crestfallen young doctor, looking like a kid who has just been deprived of a live frog. "Let me see your credentials, please," he demanded testily of Romano.

Romano produced his leather-cased badge. "We're interested in a patient named Phillip Caselli," he said.

"Well," replied the doctor, "I'm afraid I can't give you much information about the present condition of *that* one. He escaped from here just a week ago today."

"He escaped?"

"Perhaps *escaped* is too strong a word. Let us say he left without notice. He had not really been under any sort of restraint for quite a while. He committed himself here, and he was free to leave at any time he wished. He was not a disturbed case by any means. He had only to go through certain formalities in the office here. Instead he went over the fence, and left clothing and other effects behind him. He was taking a hike with a guard and some other patients when it happened. He liked outdoor exercise. He'd been some kind of athlete, I think."

Tommy snorted. "Some kind of athlete!" he said. "The greatest damn middleweight boxer who ever lived!"

"I'm afraid I don't follow the sports pages," the doctor said. "In any case he must have been before my time. He was on this hike and another patient became somewhat violent. The guard was occupied. Caselli must have wandered off and scaled the fence at the time, although he wasn't missed until quite a while later. It was a senseless act, really."

"Did you try to recapture him?" Romano asked.

"We don't 'capture' our patients, sir," replied the doctor. "We did make inquiries in the village about three miles from here. A man of Caselli's description was seen boarding a bus for New York. We called the only person who appeared to be connected with the patient"—the doctor fingered rapidly through a file—"a Dr. Mulholland at the Suffield Hotel in New York. Possibly he was the patient's physician. He told us not to worry, that the patient would doubtless call on him. We dropped the matter. We are still holding some of the patient's personal effects."

Romano asked the doctor, "Did you read of Caselli being killed in an auto accident?"

"What?" exclaimed the doctor. "He was killed? Why, no. No one here read that. No indeed."

"Apparently," said Tommy, "the sports section isn't the only part of the paper you fail to read."

"You didn't read of Doctor Mulholland being murdered?" persisted Romano.

The doctor looked blank. "Why, no," he said. "Or if I did, I didn't connect it up. You see 'Dr. Mulholland' was just a name on a card to us."

"Also a name on a big, fat check," Tommy commented drily.

"Tell us about Caselli's stay here," said Romano. "What sort of condition was he in?"

The doctor shuffled through another file, brought out a sheaf of cards. "Generally speaking a very tractable patient," he said. "Suffering from vitamin deficiency and malnutrition. Highly nervous upon arrival. Addicted to both alcohol and narcotics. Smoked marijuana and took morphine upon occasion. No indication alcoholism had reached acute and incurable stage medically termed 'wet-brain.' Some motor disorder resulting in lack of muscular co-ordination. Drug addiction considerably advanced, but thought to be definitely arrested after first two weeks of treatment. Notable improvement in mental condition and relief of hypertension after first month."

The young doctor put the cards back in the file, said, "He was with us for about two months altogether. He never had a visitor. He did receive some mail. Just a few days before he left, his chart

shows that he exhibited some restlessness. Cause of the mild disturbance was not revealed. Could have been a letter he received,
perhaps. Anyway, his sedation was increased a bit during the last
days he was here."

"I'm interested in hearing more about his mental condition,"
said Romano. "Would you consider him dangerous?"

The young doctor drummed his fingers on his desk. He said,
"I think I'll let you talk to our staff psychiatrist and analyst about
that—*if* your prejudiced friend here promises not to assault him."

Tommy had been standing all the while, supporting himself
against the doctor's desk. He said, "If I am going to listen to a
dissertation upon complexes, compulsions and other pseudo-
scientific abracadabra, I insist that someone find a chair which
will support my weight without collapsing."

I got the largest chair in the room and helped lower him into
it. When he was seated, he shook his head, "Poor old Oedipus,"
he said. "We have resurrected that long-suffering king to bear the
brunt of all our modern woes."

The young doctor picked up the phone and asked that Dr.
Freylinghuysen be good enough to come to the administration
building. The psychoanalyst proved to be an ancient gnome who
might have been invented by Walt Disney. He had all the physical
attributes of one of Snow White's merry playfellows. He appeared
to be over seventy and about five feet tall. He had a cheerful grin
and twinkling eyes. A semi-circlet of silver hair ringed his pink,
bald dome. Foxy Grandpa seated himself in a large leather chair,
drew his feet up under him, tailor-fashion, and lit a king-size cigarette.

It was hard to believe that such a cheery little Santa Claus had
spent most of his life peering into the dark, depressing depths of
disordered human minds.

"Well, gentlemen," he said pleasantly, "tell me what this is all
about."

Romano and the young doctor explained the situation to him.

Dr. Freylinghuysen said, "I will try to use the simplest terms in giving you my estimate of the patient. The jargon of the psychiatrist seems to fascinate the layman. To me it is both boresome and confusing."

I saw that Tommy Twotoes was regarding the little gnome with a certain admiration.

The jolly little man continued, "The patient was essentially the victim of an abrupt emotional letdown. That can do some rather drastic things to the most normal of human beings. He had been nurtured upon the limelight. He had existed in a world of fast action and rapidly changing drama. Quite suddenly he was shut out from the world he knew. The same thing has happened with many combat soldiers. They resorted to drink or drugs or went insane at the end of the war. Not only did the patient cease to be a prominent actor in the world he knew, but he was deprived of the means of earning the money which would permit him to move in his accustomed circles, even as a spectator. He began to drink more heavily, attempting to substitute intoxication for old excitements. In time he became so tolerant of liquor that he experienced sickness and depression rather than stimulation when he used it. He tried marijuana. At first he regarded the drug as more stimulating but no more harmful than tobacco. Finally he went for more potent poison. Morphine.

"The inevitable physical, mental, moral and nervous collapse ensued. He was no longer able to control his own actions or to manage his own life. He came here as a last resort. I had high hopes that we could effect a complete recovery in his case. We might have done so, had he remained with us long enough."

"You say he could no longer control his actions," said Romano. "Tell me, Doctor, do you believe he was, capable of murder?"

"All men are *capable* of murder," replied the gnome-like little doctor, "and I fear that some men must kill. The behavior pattern of the addict is completely unpredictable because it is subject to sudden change. The drunkard who is gay and noisy usually remains that way throughout his alcoholic career, the one who is mean and ugly continues so. But not the narcotics addict. Marijuana alone has many different reactions. Sometimes it results in a sense of exaltation which the smoker describes as 'floating.' Sometimes it brings on deep spiritual depression. Often the effects are purely physical, aphrodisiac. At other times the smoker's mental aware-ness is so acute he feels that he has left his body entirely. There are also periods of complete blackout. The mildest-seeming man may become a killer if the slightest imbalance occurs. Mind you, one marijuana user may go through each and every one of these expe-riences. The pattern does not necessarily remain the same.

"Marijuana is nothing more than a fancy name for a hemp derivative which is known as hashish in the Far East. The mari-juana user is not an addict in the strictest sense of the word. He has no actual physical craving. His urge is strictly mental. An in-teresting experiment was conducted in Connecticut recently. A group of marijuana users were given cigarettes made of tea leaves. They were told the cigarettes contained an extra-powerful dose of marijuana. They smoked, and each exhibited a typical pattern of a subject administered drugs. The behavior pattern may vary widely, however, because the alkaloid content of different batches of the stuff is highly variable.

"The reaction depends mainly upon the psychic state of the subject at the time he uses the drug. If he is despondent, he is like-ly to become more morose. If he is happy, he may become hilari-ous. If he has been brooding over a criminal act, such as murder, the drug may cause him to commit the crime, because it serves to remove his inhibitions. The reaction is like that of post-hypnotic suggestion in hypnotism, which is now widely used in the treat-ment of alcoholism and drug addiction. If I hypnotize a subject and tell him to sock the cop on the corner in the nose at noon the next day, the result depends entirely upon the man's psychic state. If he is ill-disposed toward the policeman and has always harbored a wish to hit him, the subject will strike the blow as directed. If he likes and respects the policeman he will approach him at the stated time, but he will *not* hit him."

"I guess we have our answer," said Romano. He glanced at his watch. "It is after ten, and I have business in the city before the banks close."

Before I helped him to his feet, Tommy Twotoes addressed the little man who still sat cross-legged on his chair, puffing at his cigarette.

"I just expressed to your young colleague here my contempt for most practitioners of psychiatry," he said. "But your simplicity, Doctor, commands my highest admiration. You did not mention poor old Oedipus once. You did not use such words as *complex*, *compulsion*, or even *trauma*. I find the simplest men are the wisest. Perhaps you are wise because you are old, as old as I am, I judge. Even age may have its compensations, though I find it emphatically inconvenient for the most part."

The jolly little doctor chuckled. "Unfortunately," he said, "it is not only the young who are devious. Observe our elder statesmen."

When we left the sanitarium Romano bade us goodbye. He was heading down 9W for New York. We took the same road in the opposite direction.

Tommy said, "It is much too early for lunch. Drive slowly. We will eat at the Bear Mountain Inn. The Brooklyn Dodgers baseball team and the New York Giants football team have trained there. The fare must be solid and substantial. Furthermore, the chairs of the inn are fashioned out of great logs and are fairly certain to support my weight. But we will pay a visit first. When you reach Rockland Lake, turn off for Congers. I will direct you from that point on."

"Mind telling me where we're going?" I asked.

"We are going up a dirt road, perhaps on a wild-goose chase," he answered. "A few years ago Fighting Phil invested the last of his money in a small farm near Congers. I visited the farm once. He had hopes of attracting fighters there to train. A few third-raters worked out at his place and left owing a board bill. Then he decided to raise chickens, although the only chickens he had known ate lobster instead of corn and wore furs instead of feathers. I suggested to him that he might introduce whisky into his chickens' mash, since it is well known that all alcoholics develop enlarged livers. I reminded him that the burghers of Strasbourg had made a fortune peddling the *pâté de foie gras* made from the livers of especially fattened geese. Poor Phil also failed as a chicken rancher, however. I doubt he took my advice. He was no businessman."

"You think we'll find Phil at the farm?" I asked.

"I do not know what we may find there," he answered.

"Listen," I said, "I know you're getting your kicks out of playing the Great Detective. You want to be real mysterious and then produce the murderer like Mephisto produces his guinea pigs, when you've got the proper stage setting. But there's one thing I'd like to ask. Why did you want me to take a picture of the corpse that was supposed to be Caselli?"

Tommy said, "There were several reasons. First, when I asked you what equipment you would require for a private detective agency, you mentioned a gun, a car, a charge account at the liquor store—and a camera. It was my belief that you wanted the camera solely to take pictures of your girlfriend, Ginny, and I determined I would make you use it in the line of duty at the first opportunity. Secondly, when I read of Caselli's death, I was faintly suspicious, largely because of his association with Dr. Mulholland and the strange letter the old man had written me. Finally, I read that Phil was survived by an aunt. I knew he had been brought up in an orphan asylum. He had often told me he had no living relatives. He grew maudlin over his lack of kin when he was in his cups. Suddenly, when Phil is well on in years, when he is supposedly dead, in fact, an aunt appears and claims the body."

"Of course," I said, "that faceless body in the coffin *could* have been Phil's. He had plenty of time to escape from the sanitarium, kill the old doc and get himself knocked off. If Mr. Dinwiddie made his face so pretty, he might have done things with the hands, too."

Tommy shook his big head so emphatically that the naked-lady pipe seemed to be sending up smoke signals.

"No," he said. "Our besmocked and effeminate mortician remarked that his subject had the delicate hands of an artist. And Phil's hands had been broken, battered, bruised and malformed. The most artful embalmer could not repair such a knotty structure of bone and cartilage."

Rockland Lake slept the winter sleep of summer resorts. Most of its buildings were boarded up. A lonely seagull from the Hudson kept frozen vigil on a hot-dog sign beside the ice-sheathed lake. We drove through Congers and Tommy told me to turn up a dirt road outside the village. The rutted, slippery road would have posed a problem for the M-4 tank I had bounced around in during World War II. I could tell the old man beside me was very nervous, but he was also grimly determined. He directed me to stop beside a deserted farmhouse.

The frame and fieldstone house was very old and in miserable repair. No smoke came from its chimney. Icicles hung like frozen tears from its weathered wood. At the entrance gate a crudely painted sign read "For Sale."

"This place is eerie," Tommy said. "I need a drink."

He produced a blue crock and a metal cup from a capacious pocket of his coat. He drank. He said, "You may have none, since you are driving."

"I'll be damned glad when Ebony Black gets back from the West Coast to chauffeur you," I told him.

Once more I made like a tugboat hitched to the Queen Mary and piloted the enormous old man to the front door.

"I doubt any of your keys will fit this ancient lock," he said.

The door was slightly ajar, I saw. I pressed against it. It creaked open.

"We don't need a key," I said. I looked into the dim, cob-webbed interior. "This looks like a place where Madame Eden's Wallawoochee might shack up," I added.

A battered trunk and suitcase were piled in the hallway. I tried a light switch. As I expected, the current was turned off. The living room was furnished simply, man-style. A large, beamed kitchen led off the living room. Off that was a shedlike structure with a sloping roof that was apparently used as a storage room. Heavy iron hooks had been screwed into the beams of the roof. Hoes, rakes, shovels, other tools hung from the hooks. At the highest part of the sloped ceiling a rope dangled from one of the iron hooks.

Something was attached to the rope.

For the second time in two days I saw a big, black buzzard flapping beneath the ceiling of a room.

Only this was a female buzzard.

The old woman who had called herself Theresa Caselli still wore rusty widow's weeds.

"You recognize her?" asked Tommy Twotoes.

"It's the old dame who said she was Phil's aunt," I answered.

"Make sure she is dead," Tommy ordered. It was useless, but I went through the motions of touching the pulse, the heart.

"Dead as the other one," I said.

Tommy was pointing downward.

"There is something on the floor. Examine it," he said.

It was a broken pair of rimless glasses.

The lenses were very thick, like the glasses the albino wore over his pale pink eyes.

"What do we do now?" I asked. "Call the cops?"

"No," said Tommy calmly. "Not just yet. In the first place there is no phone here. We will look around a bit. Then we will drive to the Inn for lunch. I have been interviewed by the police enough for one day. When you call them, you will remain anonymous. We can find a pay phone at the Inn."

It was a hell of a time to be thinking about lunch, but I didn't argue. I was still kneeling down beside the broken spectacles. "You want to take these with us?" I asked.

Tommy shook his head. "We will leave everything just as we found it. After you call the Rockland County police I will phone Lieutenant Romano and tell him the truth. Do you know what's the trouble with this case, Soldier? There are too many clues."

"Yeah," I said. "Up to now, though, Snowy's two up on Phil. Phil only left his watch at Ginny's place. Snowy left his sneakers at the Bleecker Street flat, a piece of his suit in your tree and his glasses here."

"A murderer might be expected to make one mistake," said Tommy. "But it is unthinkable that he would leave *three* highly damaging pieces of evidence behind him."

"Yeah," I said. "It looks like the little albino is being framed by somebody, all right. I've been reading a lot of mystery stories lately. Figured I ought to, since I'm kind of new at the private-op business. The guy that all the evidence points to is never the guilty party."

"Not in fiction, at least," agreed Tommy. "And don't forget that there are confederates involved. Most of them seem to come to a bad end. A man impersonated Phil—at least he carried Phil's identification cards on his person. He was killed. The old woman who is hanging here in front of us impersonated Phil's aunt. I hardly need to mention that she is also dead. Snowy maintains that a small man impersonated him at the Bleecker Street address. We have yet to find the small man's body."

"It'll probably turn up in some dank old cellar," I assured him cheerily. "By the way," I added, "that little guy who impersonated Snowy wore thick glasses, the super said. These could be his."

"That is quite possible, of course," Tommy replied.

"Assuming you're right and that Phil is alive, I still can't see the purpose of someone impersonating him, or at least carrying Phil's identification cards and old clippings around in his pocket," I remarked.

"Perhaps the impersonator was hired, and later disposed of by a prearranged 'accident,'" Tommy replied. "If you have committed a murder, it would be most convenient to have yourself declared legally dead and to assume a new identity."

"There doesn't seem to be much else we can do in this chamber of horrors," I said. "And it might be inconvenient if anyone happened along and found us here. I suggest we take a look at that luggage in the hall and then scram."

Tommy said, "First see if this corpse has been slugged as well as hanged."

I dragged a kitchen chair into the shedlike storeroom where the female buzzard was flapping from the rope. I stood on the chair and examined the old woman's head through the sparse gray hair. I could find no mark.

We returned to the hall. The old-fashioned, battered luggage was held together with straps and ropes. I opened the trunk and suitcase. The suitcase contained the kind of clothing that old women wear, dresses and coats of cheap, dark stuff that smelled of laundry soap. There was more clothing, a couple of plaster images of saints, a few ancient hats, a couple of pairs of low-heeled old-lady shoes and four shoe boxes in the trunk. I opened the shoe boxes. They were packed full of cigarettes—cigarettes that had "sticks" of marijuana in them. One of the boxes was heavier than the others. I took a handful of cigarettes out of it. In the bottom of the box was a gun. I looked into the chamber of the gun. One bullet had been fired. I smelled the barrel of the gun. The bullet had been fired recently.

I said to Tommy, "The gun's a .32. It was fired not so long ago. It may be the gun that was fired in your general direction last night."

Tommy waggled his big, bald head. "Marijuana cigarettes and a .32-caliber gun," he said. "More clues pointing to Snowy. This is growing decidedly monotonous."

I replaced the gun and the cigarettes and strapped and tied the luggage together. The dark old house, the musty smell, the obscenely swaying corpse of the aged woman had made me shaky. There was a queasy sensation in the pit of my stomach. I wanted a drink. I wanted fresh air, too. But Tommy seemed calm enough.

"Our morning's exertions have made me ravenous," he said. "Let us repair to the Bear Mountain Inn for lunch. It isn't far from here."

A short while later we entered the lobby of the Inn. The barked wood, the red leather upholstery, the crackling log fire in the enormous stone fireplace, the young people in brightly figured ski clothes made this seem a cheerful place indeed in contrast to the cold house of death that stood beside the rutted country road.

It still lacked quite a while of being noon, but the clerk told us the dining room would open in ten minutes. I seated Tommy in a chair fashioned from a great tree trunk, and on the pretense of visiting the men's room, slipped into the bar and sneaked two double ryes.

When I returned to the lobby, Tommy said sternly, "I am quite aware that you did not leave me to perform an operation that is euphemistically termed washing your hands, Soldier. You have had a drink, perhaps two. I hardly think you have had time for more than that. I warn you that if you have any further libations I will phone for Polvo to bring the station wagon and pick me up. I will not trust myself to a drunken driver on icy roads."

"Relax," I said. "I've been chauffeuring you over the slickest terrain this side of the Aleutians all morning. You've dragged me into a nut factory and into a haunted house where an old hag is hanging by her neck. You've had eight or ten belts out of that blue crock of yours since we left Tarrytown. I deserve at least one shot."

"What you may deserve is entirely beside the point," said Tommy. "The pertinent fact is that I hold you entirely responsible for the safety of my person."

"You want me to call the cops now?" I asked.

"No," the old man answered. "On second thought, we will not call the local police at all. By the time we have finished our lunch, Romano should be back at Headquarters. I will call him there. I will be frank with him about what we found this morning. I will suggest that he have county police investigate the house solely because it is the property of the missing Phil Caselli, who may possibly be involved in a murder case. There will be no need to drag us into the matter. I do not wish to be interviewed by rural constables this afternoon. I have promised Wisey that I will take him to New York. He wishes to buy a serpent."

"A what?" I exploded. "Listen, boss, you've got a house full of penguins, Great Danes, parrots, guinea pigs and ganders already, not to mention an assortment of the damnedest characters this side of a sideshow. At least none of them is poisonous. Just what in hell do you need with a serpent, if the question doesn't offend you?"

"A serpent," Tommy explained patiently, "is an ancient musical instrument, so called because its undulating shape makes it resemble a reptile. A more modern adaptation was called the ophicleide, which means 'snake.' The serpent was used extensively in church choirs centuries ago. It was a forerunner of the Russian bassoon, invented by Frichot in 1790. Wisey needs one for the orchestra of ancient instruments he is forming to play the background music of my television variety show. Romeo Bosanetti, who runs a queer little shop dealing in esoteric musical instruments on East Seventh Street, is offering a serpent for sale."

I chuckled. Mr. Twotoes had pretended to be an authority on many subjects. Once he had fancied himself a military expert and had read all ten volumes of Clausewitz's treatise on strategy and tactics. When he imported the penguins he had perused all the available material regarding the flightless birds, even having an obscure Russian work translated at his own expense. When Polvo had expressed a desire for a set of false teeth like those of his hero, Washington, Tommy had made a deep study of the various dentures worn by the Father of His Country. Now, apparently, he was delving into ancient musical lore.

Despite his crippled condition, Mr. Twotoes, with some assistance from me, managed to beat all the rosily healthy young skiers into the dining room when the doors were thrown open. We established ourselves at a table by a window that overlooked ice-gleaming playing fields and snow-soft hills. The warm coziness of the Inn, the serene panorama of ranging snowscapes, plus the two double slugs I had sneaked had composed me considerably. I found I had an appetite and did full justice to the venison steak that Tommy ordered. After Mr. Twotoes had topped off his light

repast by two portions of deep-dish apple pie under small moun-
tains of ice cream, he paid the check, and, despite the frowns of
the waitress, poured a water glass half-full of brandy from the blue
crock that he had transferred from his overcoat to the Tartan sport
jacket he was wearing. Having downed this, he demanded that I
conduct him to a phone booth.

Esconcing Mr. Twotoes' 300 pounds in the narrow, confines
of a phone booth was a major engineering feat, but I managed
to accomplish it. He talked to Romano for about five minutes.
When he opened the door to the booth and called for me, the
young skiers in the lobby looked toward us with astonished faces.
Tommy had lit his naked-lady pipe while he was phoning and the
booth exuded smoke that might have billowed from a three-alarm
conflagration. Mr. Twotoes failed to notice the startled attention
he had attracted, even though the room clerk had begun to detach
a fire-extinguisher from the wall.

"After some persuasion, Lieutenant Romano has agreed not to
involve us in the matter of the murdered woman," the old man
told me. "He will call the police himself, as I suggested. He is to
visit the banks where Dr. Mulholland kept safe-deposit boxes in
the names of Snowy and Phil this afternoon. I will consult with
him later concerning the results of his investigation."

We drove back over the bridge and down the east side of the
river to Tarrytown. Tommy's house was fairly quiet considering the
temperament of its two-footed, four-footed, web-footed, furred
and feathered occupants. Ginny had been shopping and had purchased a red enamel cage for the parrot. It stood in the very center
of the large, crowded living room, and old Quasi perched content-
edly inside it, chuckling to himself as he observed the others with
a cynical eye.

Polvo had brought Cleo, the penguin, in from the rookeries.
She sat beneath Quasi's cage, looking up at him with foolish, adoring eyes. Ivan the Terrible, the Great Dane, had hidden himself

behind a sofa, out of the range of Montmorency, the arrogant gander, who was strutting around the room in search of the big dog. The Magnificent Mephisto sat in the Chinese throne chair, idly stroking a lapful of cuddly guinea pigs. Wisey was practicing on his zither, making queer noises. Madame Eden was stalking around the room in a flowing gown, her hand held out in front of her and her lips moving. I thought she was in another trance, but I discovered that she was rehearsing the sleepwalking scene from Macbeth, which she planned to perform on Tommy's television show. Colonel Finger, the midget, was giving the ottoman hell, trying out wrestling holds.

"I gotta good one," he informed me, hurling the ottoman in the general direction of Mephisto and his guinea pigs. "It's a special adaptation of the Flying Mare that the big fellows use. It's for midget wrestlers, so I'm calling it the Flying Filly. Maybe I can even whip Buzzbomb Nussbaum with it. Buzzbomb's the world champion of television midget wrestlers. He's got a special hold called the Guided Missile. Idea is to hit the television cameraman with his opponent. Never fails to stop the show when he does."

There was the usual array of blue crocks on the tables of the living room. I sampled several of them. Their contents all tasted the same, and they all tasted fine. Tommy eyed me disapprovingly. So did Ginny.

"Wisey," said Tommy, "you drive a car, don't you? It will be necessary for you to take me to town in the station wagon. The Soldier is drinking again and is no fit chauffeur."

Wisey twanged a particularly weird note on the zither. "Sure I drive," he declared. "Out in California I used to practice steering the car with my knees and playing the zither with my hands."

"Even a man who steers with his knees is preferable to a drunken driver," said Tommy, tossing off a healthy slug of brandy.

It was finally decided that the entire company would go to town with Tommy and Wisey to purchase the serpent. Only Polvo remained behind to feed the penguins and other pets their evening meal. Ginny rode with me and the others accompanied Tommy in the station wagon. That was all right with me. I figured if Wisey could steer with his knees I could steer with one arm, so I kept the other arm around Ginny. We stopped off at a roadside gin mill where I had two double shots of rye and Ginny had a cup of coffee. We stopped off at another roadside gin mill where I had three double shots of rye and Ginny had a glass of milk. Ginny looked worried when I ordered the third shot at the second tavern. I assured her it was all right.

"This is February 15," I said, "and I always have to celebrate that date, because on February 15, 1912, Yuan Shi Kai became the first president of the Chinese Republic."

Ginny didn't seem to share my reverence for historical occasions, so we made no more stops on the way to New York. Despite the fact that we had paused en route for refreshment, we reached East Seventh Street before the station wagon. Maybe Wisey had found it hard to negotiate the icy roads while steering with his knees. I found a place to park near Romeo Bosanetti's little shop and a short while later the station wagon that was bursting at the seams with odd characters pulled up.

Bosanetti's was right out of Dickens. The show window, which was almost obscured with layers of grime, was loaded down with a fantastic array of ancient instruments that varied from something resembling a piano in the shape of a crossbow to a Chinese banjo that appeared to have been manufactured from a cigar box and a broom handle. Inside the shop was as cluttered as Mr. Twotoes' extraordinary living room.

Romeo Bosanetti was a little pappy-guy who had a hair-do down to his shoulders in the manner of Franz Lizst and Veronica Lake. He seemed utterly overcome by the sudden surge of customers varying in size from the three-foot Colonel Finger to the three-hundred-pound Tommy Twotoes.

"Sir!" boomed Tommy Twotoes. "We have come to purchase a serpent from you!"

The bewildered Mr. Bosanetti beamed and rubbed his thin hands together. "Ah!" he exclaimed. "The serpent! A treasure. A real treasure. There are few of them left in the world."

"Maybe St. Patrick's been muscling in on the music racket," I suggested.

Romeo Bosanetti paid no attention to me.

He went into the back room and returned struggling under the weight of something that resembled a boa constrictor doing a belly dance to the accompaniment of a snake-charmer's flute. The serpent was almost as tall as Bosanetti, and if the wooden tube had been straightened out, it would have measured at least eight feet. Mr. Bosanetti lowered the instrument so that he could place his lips to the mouthpiece. The serpent let out a booming bass blast that nearly blew little Colonel Finger through the windowpane.

"Ah!" said Mr. Bosanetti rapturously. "What tone! What timbre!"

"Roland might well have used it for his trumpet," commented Tommy. "Or even Gabriel, although I doubt an angel would perform upon an instrument whose shape is symbolic of original sin."

"If you are interested in trumpets," said Mr. Bosanetti, "I have a genuine busine, the trumpet's medieval ancestor."

Wisey picked up a stringed instrument that might have been a bastard offspring of a guitar and a frying pan and said, "This here's a rotta, ain't it?"

"Ah, sir, you are discerning," replied Mr. Bosanetti. It is a Welsh adaptation of the rotta called a *crwth*. Spelt c-r-w-t-h and pronounced *kithe*, with the *th* sound hissingly sibilant. All such instruments, of course, descend from the lute and kithara families."

We spent most of the afternoon in the music shop. Tommy had been studying up on ancient instruments and was determined to discuss with an expert such hoary music-making apparatus as the

Greek epigonion and simmikon, the seventeenth-century theorbo, the eleventh-century syrinx and the eighth-century tamboura.

In the end, Wisey, our touting Toscanini, departed with the nucleus of an ancient symphony orchestra, except for the musicians. He even bought a bottle of liquid called Digidura, which zither players apply to their fingertips after playing to prevent blisters. Tommy not only purchased the serpent. He bought the crwth, a posthorn, which Bosanetti assured him was a precursor of the cornet, and a virginal. Tommy did not buy the latter because it was the earliest form of keyed instrument with plucked strings, but because he was fascinated with its name and because ancient barbershops kept virginals as standard equipment. Customers twanged the instrument while awaiting their turns in the chair.

I staggered out of the music shop with Mr. Twotoes on one arm and the equally unwieldy serpent on the other. Once we had stored the Twotoes musical acquisitions into the station wagon, there was hardly room for Tommy and his guests. We managed to squeeze 'em all, including Ginny, into the car, although Colonel Finger had to sit on the Magnificent Mephisto's lap and hold the serpent on *his* lap. Tommy said that he wished to show his guests the great city of New York and that the best way to do so was to take them to the tower of the Empire State Building and let 'em look. I didn't accompany them. I had to be at the office a little later on to await Snowy's call. Besides, I suffer from a malady called acrophobia, which means I'm allergic to heights, and the Empire State tower is very high indeed.

I agreed to meet Tommy for dinner at the 42 Club.

I had a little time to spare, so I walked down the street to McSorley's Old Ale House. I still liked the ancient place, despite the fact that it had lately become something of a tourist attraction. The sawdust on the floor, the photographs on the wall that dated to Civil War days and the fact that women were barred appealed to me. Also, I thought a few noggins of ale would make an excellent chaser for the brandy and whisky I'd had earlier.

After the third ale I belched, and the noise reminded me of the sound made by Wisey's serpent. I had to get back to the office to receive the albino's promised call. I left the place. As I was walking toward my car I saw a familiar figure some distance down the street. I couldn't be mistaken. It was Eddie, the missing elevator operator from the Suffield. I broke into a dogtrot and as I neared the fat colored man I called his name. He gave a startled lurch, then broke into a run. He could travel very fast for a man of his weight. I kept yelling at him as I ran, but just as I was beginning to wear him down, a cop put a heavy hand on me and wanted to know hey, bud, wassa matta.

By the time I had explained myself, produced my identification, and persuaded the cop that I knew Lieutenant Romano, Eddie's fleeing figure had disappeared.

I drove uptown and parked the car, cursing myself for missing the opportunity of questioning Eddie about his sudden departure from the hotel. I still had a little time on my hands, so I made use of it by getting a quick double in Charley Frayne's place, since it was still the fifteenth and I was still celebrating the inauguration of the first president of China in 1912.

When the rickety elevator of my office building deposited me at my floor I saw a fat black man wearing a clerical collar fumbling with the knob of my office door. It was Eddie, of course.

"Hello, Parson," I said. "What were you doing down on Seventh Street a few minutes ago?"

"I been further downtown than that," he replied. "I been 'way downtown looking at a corpse. I been trying to see you. Six-seven times I been up here today."

"Why'd you run from me when I called you?" I asked.

"Didn't know it was you. Thought it was man what wants to kill me."

"Why does the man want to kill you, Eddie?"

"'Cause I know who killed ole Doc."

"Who? Who killed him?"

"Same man what wants to kill me. Same man what killed the corpse downtown."

"Who, Eddie, who?"

"Mist' Jenks," said Eddie. "Mist' Jenks, the night clerk at the Suffield."

8

I unlocked the door and motioned Eddie into the office.

The man was frightened, thoroughly frightened. There could be no doubt about that. I poured him a shot. Since he wasn't a client, I poured it from the office bottle. He reached for the glass with a trembling hand, downed the liquor.

"Now," I said, "tell me all about it. Why do you think Jenks chilled the old man?"

"Because he was ole Doc's relative. Nephew, I think. He wanted the money what the ole man left."

"What makes you think that?"

"Heard him talking over the phone when he didn't know I was listening. Think he was talking to a lawyer-man. Said he was legal heir to ole Doc's money, but ole Doc was crazy in the head and had left it all to couple of guys what weren't no relation of his. Said he didn't want to come right out and claim the money just yet, account of it would be better to wait till the police pinned the ole Doc's murder on one of the guys he left the money to. Said ole Doc never liked him. Wouldn't give him no money when he was dead broke but helped him get job in hotel where he lived. But ole Doc told him not to tell anybody he was his kinfolks. Some kind of family trouble, long time ago."

"All that doesn't prove Jenks killed the old doctor," I said.

"I seen Mist' Jenks right after he kill somebody else. I seen the corpse he kill, too. Figure he kill one, he kill two."

"Who did Jenks kill? What corpse?" I demanded.

"Downtown corpse I see. See it yesterday. See it again today. Heard another phone talk of Mist' Jenks. Figure I might make a little money for the Church of the Sanctified Soul if I find out enough. Mist' Jenks say on phone, 'So that's where he's hanging out, huh? I'll go down there.' So yesterday morning when he goes off duty I follow him. Follow him down to little ole beat-up street underneath Brooklyn Bridge. Goes into ole, beat-up house. I see a light go on upstairs, second floor front, so I sneak in. They's a window in the hall onto fire escape. I crawl out that window. Blind pulled down in room where Mist' Jenks go, but it's all cracked and torn. I can see through it. There's a dead man on the bed. Mist' Jenks is standing over body with bottle in his hand. Guess he beat man to death with bottle. I start to move away. Stumble over flower pot, make a big noise. Mist' Jenks pull up blind, look out the window. He must of seen me. I run like hell. Don't go back to work. Scared he'll kill me, too, if he find me."

"Did you recognize the man on the bed? The man you thought was dead?" I asked.

He shook his head. "Uh-uh. Lying on his stummick. Just took me a quick look. Didn't even see corpse's blood."

"How do you know he was a corpse? Live men can lie on their stomachs, too," I told him.

He shook his head emphatically again. "This man wasn't live. I thought about that. Went back today, climbed out on fire escape and had another look. Pretty dark inside, but I could see enough. Man still lying there. Same position. Must be dead to do that."

"What was the address of this place?" I asked him.

He gave me a number of a dead-end street under the approach to the bridge Steve Brodie made famous. I jotted it down.

"I'll take a look when I get time," I said, "but I just can't imagine a mild little guy like Jenks doing anything more drastic than working a crossword puzzle."

"You goin' down right away?" asked Eddie eagerly.

"No," I said. "I'm waiting for an important telephone call. It may come in any minute. And after that I've got a date for dinner. I never like to find corpses on an empty stomach. I'll go down some time later this evening."

I poured a drink for both of us. Eddie licked his lips, said, "Mighty mellow liquor." He looked at me speculatively. "I ain't working," he said. "Scared to go back there even to collect what's owed me. Sure could use a little contribution to the Church of the Sanctified Soul."

"You've still got your preaching sideline, haven't you?" I asked.

"Preaching business ain't so profitable nowadays," said Eddie. "Especially in Harlem. Too much competition. Since Father Divine lit out for Philadelphia, everybody trying to succeed him."

I had a sudden inspiration. I said, "You don't happen to play a musical instrument, do you?"

"Only the ukulele," replied Eddie, "and that don't hardly count. Church of the Sanctified Soul took up a collection for an organ once, but one of the backsliding brethren lost the money in a crap game. So I accompany the choir on the ukulele."

"That's fine!" I said. "I know a man who's just bought a crwth. He needs somebody to play it. It's kind of like a ukulele. You go up and see him tomorrow, and maybe he'll give you a job." I scribbled down the address of Tommy Twotoes' home in Tarrytown. "Ask for a man named Wisey," I said. "Maybe you'll get a job playing in a television orchestra."

Eddie looked doubtful. "What you call that whatchumallit I'm supposed to play?" he asked.

"A crwth," I said. I wrote down the name for him. He looked at the paper, said, "I can't even pronounce it. Much less play it."

"Wisey'll teach you," I assured him. "He's the best zither player in the country."

I had an idea that the case was rapidly reaching a climax. I was damned tired of hauling something as big as Mr. Twotoes around from place to place. The exertion made me feel weaker than the ladies who resort to Vegetable Compound. I decided that I'd try to corral all the persons involved in the matter into one place. That would save a great deal of wear and tear on both my muscles and my nervous system.

"Take money to get 'way up to Tarrytown," said Eddie tentatively. He wound up by chiseling a fin off me and promising to appear at Tommy's house the next day for his audition on the crwth.

It was five minutes to five when Eddie left the office. I toasted Yuan Shi Kai again and waited for the phone to ring. It rang at exactly thirty seconds after five o'clock, Eastern Standard Time.

I said, "Hello," and the resonant bass voice answered, "You wanted me to call. Are you alone?"

I said, "All alone by the telephone. Tommy Twotoes got in. He wants to see you very much. There've been some developments since yesterday. I think they're in your favor, so far as Tommy is concerned, at least. Why don't you come over here and talk things over?"

"I can't," he replied. "I've got some important matters to attend to."

"I want to talk to you, Snowy—I mean Stanley," I told him. "Where can I see you. When?"

He hesitated. "Maybe about ten. If you come alone. I don't want to see Tommy before I talk to you. And no cops, now."

"No Tommy," I agreed. "No cops. Where?"

He thought it over. "You know a place called the C-Note Club?" he asked.

I knew the joint. It was a jazz musicians' hangout midtown. It was just a saloon where the boys had jam sessions over their drinks, but it had a club license and customers were scrutinized through a peephole before they were admitted, speakeasy-style. I wondered how the albino had ever become a habitué of such a place. Then I recalled that a great many "hot" musicians sent themselves with the weed before they tuned up for a jam session. Such a resort might be a profitable source of revenue for a guy in Snowy's business.

I said, "I know the place, but I've never been there."

"Use my name," said Snowy as if he were giving me a visitor's card to the Union League Club. "They'll let you in. You'll be there at ten—alone?"

"I'll be there all by my little self," I assured him.

Snowy rang off.

I thought of going down to the street beneath the bridge at once. But I wanted to discuss the matter with Tommy first. It was his show, and I didn't intend to chase him up to the top of the Empire State Building. I figured that if the man on the bed was a corpse, he wouldn't be likely to wander off, although one corpse had already come to life in the case. If he were just a sick relative of Jenks, it would be a wild-goose chase anyway. I paid a little more homage to the memory of Yuan Shi Kai until the bottle gave out. By that time I was due to meet Tommy and his party.

The 42 Club didn't get its name just because that was the number of the premises it occupied on a very swank street. The upper-class lunch-counter was twice as exclusive as the famous 21 Club. Movie actors, with or without stuffed panda dolls, were barred as a matter of course. Even college boys who made the All-America, wore Phi Beta Kappa keys and ate bowls full of live goldfish were not admitted. The only newspaperman who ever got into the place was a Boston character named Cabot Lowell Lodge who conducted an Advice to the Lovelorn column and was annually voted one of the Ten Best-Dressed Men in America. I figured if a Grade B private detective like myself ever walked into the hallowed premises, the vichysoisse would curdle and every souffle in the kitchen would fall with a resounding thud.

Nearly all of the ultra-exclusive, ultra-expensive resorts frequented by the upper crust of café society in New York are operated by ex-muggs and ex-mobsters who date back to Prohibition and who have deserted the mayhem rackets because the delicate art of insulting Social-Register customers at outrageous prices is far more profitable. And most of the muggs and mobsters were beholden to Tommy Twotoes because he had been one of their main supplies of liquor during the Great Drought and had employed many of them in his night clubs.

A thug who dressed his hair with salad oil presided at the silken rope of the 42 Club. I doubted he was entitled to wear the Stuart plaid dinner jacket he affected, for he had been born Giulio Vascelucci in a Tenth Avenue tenement. Since becoming one of the high priests of café society, he had changed his name to Jules Vannever and packed a three-dollar Irish linen handkerchief in his hip pocket instead of a blackjack. His carefully massaged olive complexion paled when he saw Mr. Twotoes and his incredible guests, and his glossily manicured fine Italian hand trembled on the silken rope. He tried to force a smile of welcome at the same time his shifty eyes were seeking frantically to attract the attention of his boss, a gentleman who had once borne a Sing Sing Social Security number but who was now striding arrogantly about the premises, sneering contemptuously at members of New York's First Families. The elegant Sicilian with the Dutch name and the Scottish dinner clothes was in a quandary. He had once been a busboy in one of Tommy's Prohibition sucker traps.

"Hello, Giulio," Tommy boomed in a voice that caused every lorgnette in the joint to be raised in our direction. "I haven't seen you since that time you hid in the ice box and nearly froze to death when Federal agents raided the old Chi-Chi Club. A table for seven, please. The best in the house."

The miserable Mr. Vannever made incoherent sounds with his mouth and finally managed to stammer, "I—I'll call Mr. Cholomondeley. He—he'll want to welcome you in person, I'm sure."

"Mr. Cholomondeley?" Tommy's voice rattled the fine china service on the tables. "You mean Polack Pete Czernowski? I'll never forget the coming-out party he gave when they sprung him from up the river back in '27."

Polack Pete Czernowski, now known as Peter Gibson Cholomondeley, was striding across the floor of the restaurant toward the cause of the undue disturbance. He saw Tommy and a sickly attempt at a grin spread over his face. Mr. Twotoes had bankrolled the first speakeasy operated by Mr. Cholomondeley, né Czernowski.

Tommy's fire-siren voice greeted the host of the exclusive 42 Club. "Well, if it's not the Polack! What's become of the cauliflower ear and the broken nose Brass Knucks Brannigan gave you for hijacking one of his trucks? Plastic surgery? You look almost human."

Mr. Cholomondeley, who was elegantly turned out in a maroon dinner jacket, matching tie and boiled shirt, held out a hairy paw. "It's good to see you again, Tommy, dear old boy," he said, affecting an accent that went with tweeds, beagles and shooting preserves. He took a horrified gander at the rest of us and asked, "Are all these—these *people*—with you?"

"All six of them," Tommy replied.

Mr. Cholomondeley counted rapidly. "Six?" he said. Suddenly he discovered Colonel Finger. "Oh, I couldn't see the little one there behind the rubber plant."

"Show us to a table, Polack," Tommy demanded.

"At once, please. I have undergone unusual exertion today, and I am tired and hungry."

"Well," said Mr. Cholomondeley doubtfully, "we usually demand that our guests dress for dinner, but in your case, of course . . ."

"Dress?" boomed Tommy. "Are you implying that I am guilty of indecent exposure of my person? That I am growing so absentminded in my old age I have forgotten to don my pants?"

Mr. Cholomondeley essayed an unconvincing chuckle. "Never change, do you, dear old boy?" he said. "Always joking." He snapped his fingers, and a goon in dinner clothes who seemed to be the head waiter appeared. We divested ourselves of coats and hats and I noted that even the chick in the checkroom wore *haute couture* and kept a five-dollar bill instead of a prop quarter on her little silver platter. She nearly swooned when she was handed the Magnificent Mephisto's silk-lined cape, and Wisey's battered black felt, and Colonel Finger's tiny gray bowler. She sniffed disdainfully at the label in my hat, a brand widely advertised at $6.95. Mr. Cholomondeley was further upset by the fact that Wisey refused to leave either his zither or the serpent, posthorn, crwth and virginal he had purchased in the checkroom.

There were audible gasps as the strange procession, bearing ancient musical instruments of outlandish shapes, was led to a table with the mountainous Mr. Twotoes, puffing at his naked-lady pipe, in the van. When we were finally seated, two waiters confronted us with an enormous blackboard on which the menu was written in French, and the wine steward hovered near, a chain jingling about his neck. The blackboard caused Wisey to strum a bar or two of "School Days" on his zither. Madame Eden said she would have only a hearts of palm salad since she was dieting in order to accentuate her psychic perception. After some persuasion from Tommy, she also ordered side-dishes of caviar canapés, oyster bisque, mushroom omelet, white African guinea hen under glass, pommes noisettes, broccoli hollandaise, bombe glacé, Edam cheese and toasted crackers and demi-tasse, together with the appropriate apéritifs, wines and liqueurs.

Mr. Cholomondeley lurked near our table throughout the meal, as if he were afraid we might make off with the silverware. Ginny suggested to him that his joint was dead and that he could liven it up considerably by employing the services of a strip-tease girl. When a string orchestra broke into subdued chamber music, Wisey insisted upon accompanying the musicians on his zither.

Comparative peace prevailed through several courses, except for the fact that Colonel Finger blew an earthshaking blast on the serpent every time he wished his wine glass refilled, which was frequently. Between tumpy-tump-tumps of the serpent, I managed to tell Tommy of Eddie's visit to my office, of the parson's suspicions of Jenks, and of the body that lay in a tenement beneath the Brooklyn Bridge. I also told him of my appointment with Snowy.

Tommy said, "If the body belongs to the person I suspect it does, the case is solved. I expect to reveal the murderer no later than tomorrow unless I myself become one of his victims before then. You will meet Snowy as arranged. Tell him that I offer him sanctuary in my home until the killer is unmasked. Tell him that if the police apprehend him the experience will be most unpleasant. Try to see him on the eleven o'clock train for Tarrytown. I will have Polvo meet him at the station. After that you will go to the address under the bridge and ascertain what awaits you there."

Tommy also told me that he had called Romano and had been given a report on the safe-deposit boxes in the two banks. The one in Snowy's name held $50,000 in cash and negotiable securities. The one in Phil's name held nothing whatsoever. A bank employee remembered that it had been emptied recently by a man with a face like a bulldog. Because of his rough appearance, they had been leery about giving him access to the box, but he bore identification that established him unquestionably as the man in whose name the box was held. The man with the bulldog face had been accompanied to the bank by an old woman with a foreign accent.

Tommy said, "Lieutenant Romano also had local police investigate the house near Congers, in the company of one of his detectives. He informs me that the nice old lady we found hanging by the neck is an underworld character named Marie Seducci. She

has operated candy stores on the East Side. The candy stores had
back rooms where illegal booze was sold after hours and at times
when licensed bars were closed. Her shops were also hangouts for
bookmakers and numbers salesmen. And the police have reason to
believe they might well have been 'drops' for dope peddlers, too."

After Tommy had paid a bill large enough to activate a full ar-
mored division, complete to Pershing tanks, we left the place, carrying our weird musical instruments. Wisey strummed a few bars
of Sousa's "Stars and Stripes Forever" on his zither as we marched
out. The Triangle Club was still suffering from frozen pipes, so
Ginny climbed into the station wagon to accompany the others
back to Tarrytown. I set forth to keep my appointment with the
little man in white.

A panel in the door of the C-Note Club slid back and a wizened monkey-face regarded me through the aperture. I said that
I had come to meet Mr. Sylvester and the door was opened. The
character who admitted me appeared to be an ancient Japanese.
He went behind the bar and began to spoon clabbery stuff out of
a china bowl on which pagodas were painted. I regarded the curds
without whey he was consuming with curiosity. It didn't seem to
me that the wizened Oriental resembled Little Miss Muffet very
closely. The Jap bartender pointed to the stuff in the bowl with
his spoon.

"Yogurt," he informed me. "Fine health food. Not like this
stuff that poisons your stomach." He pointed a contemptuous
thumb toward the liquor he was paid to sell and returned to his
yogurt with relish.

I was a little early and Snowy Sylvester had not appeared. Since
there seemed to be no chance of my getting a drink before the
ancient Japanese had consumed his yogurt to the last delicious
curd, I looked around me. A framed hundred-dollar bill, which
evidently gave the C-Note Club its name, hung over the bar. A few
disconsolate-looking characters were sitting on a small platform

in the rear, drinking and smoking and occasionally playing a sad note or two on their instruments. My only companion at the bar was a very tall, skinny guy, with a neck like a corkscrew. He held a banjo on his lap.

He said, "You're new here, aren't you? Old Suki-Yaki's quite a character. I wrote a song about him." He plunked his banjo and began to sing in a nasal tenor:

> "I'm Yokohama's yogurt-eating yogi;
> I never smoke a cigarette or stogie.
> I can't become a souse or
> I will anger Gayelord Hauser,
> For I'm Yokohama's yogurt-eating yogi."

"Very silly song," commented the ancient Japanese, wiping a stray curd from his lips with the sleeve of his white coat. He washed his yogurt bowl carefully. "You want something?" he inquired.

"Double rye," I told him. "And see what my friend here will have."

The banjo player ordered straight gin. Pressed, he made it a double. He said, "This place is like a morgue nowadays. Most of the boys were be-bop musicians and be-bop's deader'n Kelsey's unmentionables. They just sit around and mourn all the time."

"You know a character named Snowy Sylvester?" I asked.

"The albino? Sure. In here a lot."

"He doesn't play an instrument, does he?" I asked.

"He's just an amateur, but he's pretty good," replied the banjo player with the corkscrew neck. "Plays a funny kind of horn. The bassoon. Used to sit in jam sessions to put the old umpty-ump in be-bop."

"The bassoon!" I exclaimed. The erudite Mr. Twotoes had told me that the serpent was the granddaddy of the bassoon. I figured

I was recruiting musicians for Wisey's orchestra very fast, with no aid at all from Petrillo.

The buzzer buzzed. Suki-Yaki seemed to be arguing through the panel. Finally, he said, "Oh, it's you!" and opened the door. A very small man dressed in black from head to foot entered. He even wore dark glasses.

Snowy Sylvester seemed amused by the fact that I did not recognize him at once. "You see, my friend, how simple it is for a person of my unusual appearance to disguise himself," he said. "Everyone expects to see me clad in white. So I dress in black and I become incognito with a mere change of wardrobe. I have a confession to make. When I visited you the other day, I was afraid you might follow me. The long raincoat and the rain hat I was wearing were of the kind that fold up and fit into the pocket. I also had a black raincoat and hat in my pocket. When I left your office, I ran down to the next landing, changed my outer covering from white to black, descended to the first floor and walked out of the building. I daresay if you had asked about me, you would have discovered that many people saw me come in, but no one saw me leave."

That, at least, explained one of the minor mysteries of the case. I was chiefly concerned with Snowy's dark glasses at the moment. I said, thinking of the smashed glasses we had found beside the hanging corpse of the old woman, "I see you broke your glasses."

"Why, no," he said. He detached the dark lenses that fitted over his regular thick spectacles. "An albino's eyes are very weak. Bright sun and the reflection from snow are blinding. My oculist prescribed these lenses to fit over my regular pair. They go so well with my new costume I continued to wear them even after sunset."

I made excuses to the banjo player. Snowy and I went to a table in a remote part of the room.

"Here's the score," I said to the albino. "Since I saw you last there's been another killing, also an attempted killing. I can't tell you about them. Tommy Twotoes will, though. Anyway, you're plenty hot with the cops. They've got reason to think you were present both times. Tommy Twotoes says he will offer you sanctuary. He thinks he knows the killer and that he can produce him no later than tomorrow. You'll be safe enough in his house in the meantime. He wants to talk to you. And there's a real excuse for you going up there."

I told him about Tommy's proposed television variety show and how he needed a serpent player for his orchestra of ancient instruments. "Maybe if you get a job on television you'll be able to quit peddling socks and marijuana," I added.

Snowy said, "You have no proof I have ever sold marijuana. I deny the accusation categorically!"

The force of this last remark was somewhat diminished by the fact that one of the musicians from the platform sidled up to Snowy and said hoarsely, "Hey, Snowy, I didn't know you when you first come in. My credit good for a coupla sticks?"

Snowy's pallid face assumed a savage expression. He cursed the musician and dismissed him.

"Tommy Twotoes wants me to put you on the eleven o'clock to Tarrytown," I told the little albino. "My car's outside. Tommy will have you met at the station. How about it?"

He finally agreed. There was plenty of time, so we had a few drinks to seal the bargain.

I drove Snowy to Grand Central. I accompanied him through acres of marble halls, bought him a ticket to Tarrytown, went right through Gate 16 with him. I didn't leave him there, even. I put him on the train and waited until the train pulled out before I left. Snowy was in a smoking car. I hoped the conductor didn't have a sensitive nose in case the albino decided to light up a reefer.

I went to a pay booth in the station and called Polvo at Tommy's house in Tarrytown. I told him that when Tommy arrived he should be told his little friend was en route on a milk train and must be met at the station. The liquor store where the agency had a charge account was open until midnight. I stopped by and bought an office bottle to replenish the one I'd finished that afternoon. I went back to the office and since it still lacked midnight and was therefore still the fifteenth, I drank a final toast to the first president of the Chinese Republic. Then I took the Police Positive out of my drawer and made sure it was loaded. I put the gun in my pocket. If the body under the Brooklyn Bridge wasn't dead, I figured I might need the gun.

I drove downtown. Even the snow on the dead-end street beneath the bridge wasn't white. It was the sick gray of a dead man's hide. The piled snow was pocked in places by garbage that festered like open sores. The dark street was a place where cats with evil eyes tread softly, where furtive phantom figures lurked in the deeper shadows. It stank of the sluggish river, of fetid refuse and foul flesh. I parked the car and locked it. It took me some time to find the old-law tenement at the address Eddie had given me. Street numbers in this forgotten corner of the city were rusted with age and weather. The building should have been condemned years before. It tilted at a perilous angle. The fire escapes were covered with a leper's skin of scaly, ancient paint. The blind-staring windows gazed with glassy idiot's eyes upon the putrescence of the street. Many of the panes were broken and stuffed with heavy butcher's paper. The front door was not locked. Tiny chunks of rotten wood spattered from the jamb as I pushed the door.

The dimly lit hallway was filled with breathing corpses, zombie-drunk vagrants who had floundered in from the frigid, icy streets where their wretched lives were lived. Only one of the bodies stirred as I stepped over it. The body belonged to an old man with a nightmare face that seemed horribly burned by acid. He stared at me with baleful, rheumy eyes. Even the eyelids were raw and scabby. He clawed at his body with filthy, broken nails that were crinkled like clam shells, then produced a bottle of rubbing alcohol from his rags. He uncorked the bottle, cackling like an insane chicken. He drank and made a strangled, bloodcurdling sound in his throat before he collapsed again, the uncorked bottle spilling its contents over the burlap bags with which he had swathed himself against the cold.

I mounted a flight of groaning stairs with broken banisters. I went to a door at the front of the house. I felt for my gun, seeking reassurance. I knocked on the door. The echo of my knocking trembled in the graveyard silence. "The dead don't answer," I told myself.

I tried the knob. The door was locked. I studied the latch. It was an inexpensive standard brand and fairly new. The first key that I tried opened it. I squeezed a thin ribbon of light from my pencil flash. I found a dangling cord and turned on a naked ceiling bulb.

Eddie had not been entirely right in saying I would find a body here.

There were two bodies in the room.

9

Neither of the bodies, however, was quite dead.

The body on the bed lay on its stomach. It breathed stertorously. It was the body of a heavy man. On a wooden chair, beside the bed, there was a half-filled bottle of whisky and a glass. I turned the body over. The heavy-breathing body had the face of a bulldog. The hands were the hands of a fighter—hard, misshapen, great-knuckled hands. I knew at once that this was Phil Caselli. I wondered who they had burned in a crematory furnace under the name of the man on the bed.

The man on the bed was more than drunk. He was heavily drugged. But he was alive.

The other body was on the floor. It was the body of a slight man. It breathed fitfully, painfully. There was blood on the head of the body on the floor. There was a thin cord looped tightly around the neck, garrote-fashion. The body was clad in a white linen suit. There was a large three-cornered tear in the crumpled white coat of the suit. The fragment of cloth we had found dangling on the limb of a tree at Tommy Twotoes' might just have fitted the tear. The body wore no thick spectacles. But a broken pair of thick spectacles had been found beside the old woman who had been hanged by the neck. The body's eyes weren't pink. The bloodied bald pate was not covered with down a silkworm might have spun.

This was not the body of Snowy Sylvester.

This was the body of Jenks, the room clerk at the Suffield Hotel.

A foolish thought ran through my head. "What is an eight-letter word meaning a room clerk who works crossword puzzles?" I asked myself.

"M-u-r-d-e-r-e-r," I answered myself.

Jenks was not as ludicrously small as the albino, but he was still a small man. If he dressed in white clothes and wore thick-lensed glasses he would be described as—a small man dressed in white and wearing thick-lensed glasses. That was the way the superintendent at the Bleecker Street flat had described the man who led the old woman away to her death. Jenks was obviously in disguise now, but an important part of his disguise was missing. He was not wearing the thick-lensed glasses. And a pair of thick-lensed glasses had been found beside a murdered woman. As room clerk at the Suffield he would have had an opportunity to enter Dr. Mulholland's suite with a passkey, kill him at his leisure. It was Jenks who had persuaded the old man not to call the police when someone had attempted his life in the still of the night. Jenks was the old man's nephew. The old man had refused to recognize the relationship. That must mean that there was bad blood, enmity between the nephew and the uncle. As the old man's only kin, Jenks might inherit a considerable fortune if the murder could be charged to one of the friends named in Dr. Mulholland's strange will.

As these thoughts raced through my brain, I was fumbling with the strangling cord at Jenks's neck, loosening it. Jenks gasped painfully and sucked at air. He was returning to groggy consciousness, it seemed. The eyes of strangled men don't close; they bulge. The eyelids fluttered. Color receded in the purple-flushed face.

Jenks attempted to speak, but only a rasping sound came from his bruised throat. I put my mouth close to his ear. "Who hit you?" I asked. "Who strangled you?"

Jenks made a feeble attempt to rise. I lifted him to a sitting posture. He saw the body on the bed. The rasping sound came from his throat again. He raised a leaden arm, pointed a trembling finger toward the body on the bed. Then he passed out.

I attempted to revive him. I massaged the cords of his neck gently. I pulled a pillow from the bed and put it under his head. I wasn't sure if I should try to force the raw whisky down his strangled throat. I picked up the bottle, uncorked it, started to pour the whisky into the glass. Then I hesitated. I smelled the bottle. I thought it had a queer odor. I put a drop on the tip of my tongue. There was a queer taste, too.

Now I thought I saw the pattern. Fighting Phil had been on a drunk. While he slept in a drunken stupor, someone had doped his whisky. Each time he returned to consciousness, his head swollen, his tongue too large for his mouth, the bottle would be there at hand. He would grope for it, seeking the drunkard's antidote for the poison in his system, the hair of the dog. He would drink and be doped again. This might have gone on for days. Jenks had visited the unconscious man, had raised the bottle to finish him with a blow on the head. But there had been a noise on the fire escape. Eddie had kicked over a flower pot. Jenks had run to the window, seen Eddie. That had interrupted his murderous plan. He had decided to leave the doped Caselli on the bed, to see Eddie at the hotel that evening, find out how much he knew. But Eddie had not shown up for work.

So Jenks had returned to the room where the drunk and doped old fighter lay. He had worn white clothes, like Snowy's, in case he was observed entering the building.

This time, however, the dazed Caselli had returned to consciousness briefly. He had struck his assailant down, probably with the bottle. In his crazed, doped delirium, he had grabbed a piece of cord and twisted it about the little man's neck. But he himself had collapsed again before Jenks strangled to death.

And so I had come along and found them both unconscious. It reminded me of the time that there had been a double knockout between Sammy Secrete and Pat Carroll back in 1941.

Since the whisky was undrinkable I sought another restorative. I pushed aside a curtain that screened a dingy little room. This was the kitchen. I found a coffee pot, remnants of food, a can of coffee. I brewed the coffee strong. While I was waiting for it to boil, I prowled around the little room. There was a pile of soiled laundry in one corner. I poked into it. Soiled shirts and underwear fell to the floor.

Beneath the laundry was a bird cage.

It was unquestionably Quasimodo's cage, the cage that had been stolen from Ginny's apartment. To make sure, I opened the little door of the cage. The bottom dropped down. I gave the lower part of the cage a half-turn and it detached itself. I pried off the lid of the base. I emitted a long-drawn whistle when I saw what was inside.

Inside was a long manila envelope with Phil Caselli's name on it. The envelope contained nearly $50,000 worth of large-denomination bills and negotiable bonds.

This discovery knocked my nice little theory about Jenks into the left-field bleachers of the Yankee Stadium. If Jenks had been instrumental in obtaining the legacy from the safe-deposit box and in stealing the parrot's cage, he would hardly have left such articles in a flat occupied by Phil Caselli. Caselli must have obtained the bonds and money *after* the death of the old doctor. So it wasn't the unidentified man disguised as Phil who had gone to the bank and presented false identification to obtain the contents of the safe deposit box. It was Phil himself. The key with Caselli's name on it had been missing from the parrot's cage at the time the body was discovered. That must mean that Phil had taken the key, that he knew the old man was dead. And if he knew the old man was dead, he had probably strung him up. Evidently the watch we had found in Ginny's house was no false clue.

I tucked the manila envelope in my inside pocket.

The coffee began to boil and bubble like the witches' cauldron in *Macbeth*. My aching head was boiling and bubbling, too. I had two murder suspects on my hands, one completely unconscious, the other semi-comatose and speechless. I didn't know just what the hell you did with murder suspects in such a condition, especially at that time of night. I'd read Emily Post and *What Every Young Boy Should Know*, but neither of those valuable works contained a chapter that covered my present situation. I could save myself a lot of grief by simply calling Romano and letting him take it from there. But I was afraid this might displease Mr. Two-toes, the gentleman who subsidized the private detective business operated by Terry Bob Rooke, alias Soldier.

I found two cracked cups and a jelly glass and poured black coffee into them. I drank down the glass of black, scalding liquid before ministering to my patients.

I wasn't sure if the coffee would kill or cure a man with a throat as tender as Jenks's. But I managed to get some down him. He gasped and choked and as the dark liquid drooled from his mouth I was reminded of the unpleasant symptoms of the Black Plague I had read about in historical novels. He must have been suffering the torments of hell from his crushed vocal chords, and he couldn't make an intelligible sound, but the coffee revived him some. I helped him to his feet and tried to guide him to a chair near the bed, but he resisted me with a sudden show of strength and indicated through gestures that he wished to be placed in the farthest corner of the little room. He seemed genuinely frightened of the man on the bed and did not wish to be too close to him, even though the old fighter with the bulldog's face was out like a light. I dragged the chair as far from the bed as possible and placed Jenks in it.

I went to work on Phil.

That was where I made a big mistake.

I slapped his face until he began to fight his way feebly out of the fog. I put the coffee to his mouth. He swallowed, but he didn't like the taste. He shoved me off and reached for the bottle, but I beat him to it. I put the bottle aside and poured more coffee down him. He looked at me dumbly, his eyes glazed. Suddenly he saw the little man who was sprawled in the chair across the room from him. The bulldog face became hideous with rage. The lips curled back from the teeth. He snarled like an animal.

He said one word: "White."

Then he said another word: "Bastard."

Then he leaped, and almost knocked me off my feet. He hurled himself drunkenly across the room and clutched wildly for Jenks's throat.

A strangled scream came out of Jenks's mangled throat. He fell from the chair. The crazed old fighter crashed into the wall. With a supreme effort, he pushed himself away from the wall, as a boxer bounces off the ropes, and tried again to assault the figure on the floor. I grabbed the wild bulldog. I had just revived him, but under the circumstances I could think of nothing better to do than to knock him out again. I clipped him on the chin and he thudded to the floor like a bag of cement. I didn't deserve too much credit for a K.O. over the once great middleweight. He was already punch-drunk, out on his feet.

I turned my attention to Jenks. I don't know whether he had hit his head when he fell or whether he had fainted again from sheer fright. But he was also out like Lottie's eye. I'd just wasted my time making all that coffee.

I tried to take stock of the situation. It seemed that my most urgent need was a drink, but I didn't want it badly enough to sample the booze that was loaded with a Mickey Finn. Thinking of a drink made me think of a saloon. Thinking of a saloon made me remember that most gin mills have telephones. I decided to seek advice from my sponsor. After all it was Tommy Twotoes' show and he should have been back in Tarrytown quite a while by now, even allowing for the slow rate at which his car proceeded. My charges were peaceful enough at the moment, but I had to assure they remained that way. I lifted Phil and dragged him back to the bed. I'd given him my Sunday punch, the kind of blow Bob Fitzsimmons referred to as "the old Mary-Ann." That combined with the dope and booze kept Phil quiescent. But I feared his powers of recovery. He had roused sufficiently twice to make a murderous attempt on Jenks. I picked up the length of cord with which Jenks had been strangled. I sliced it in two with my pocket knife. I tied Phil's ankles together with one half of the cord. I tied his hands behind his back with the other half.

I considered my other patient. He might rouse enough to stagger out of the flat. I went back to the kitchen and found clothesline. I cut the rope into desired lengths and trussed up the little man in white. Being a considerate soul, I put the pillow back under his head.

I left the flat. In the lower hall the zombies still snored and muttered at the creatures of their dreams. The old man with the acid-singed face was crawling around on his hands and knees in pursuit of the bottle from which all his rubbing alcohol had leaked. The bottle kept rolling away from him as he lurched for it, making terrifying, obscene sounds in his throat. The old man reminded me of something out of a Lon Chaney silent film. I hurried out of the ancient house with the blind-staring windows, the rickety house that leaned in the wind.

The night air of even this filth-fragrant street was tonic. I breathed it in, shook my head, and stood uncertainly for a moment. Only alley cats and wharf rats moved in the garbage-crusted snow. Lights from the span of the bridge sent pale fingers to probe the unwholesome darkness. I turned away from the river, made my way down a broader street. I reflected there was one good thing about New York. At any time between the hours of eight A.M. and four A.M. you could find a saloon open. They even had saloons in subways and penthouses to accommodate the descending and ascending members of the thirsty population.

It took me only a few moments to discover nervously quivering neon tubes that spelled out the word "Bar." The place I entered was depressing even to me, and I had wandered the Bowery in my hectic, uninhibited youth. The half-dozen customers at the bar had faces that were pallid beneath the grime. They gazed into their beer and wine and whisky like men who stare at their reflections in the waters of Lethe. Even the bartender was a figure out of a waxworks. I had to call him twice before he condescended to serve me. The bottles on the shelves belonged in a paint factory instead of a barroom, but two double shots of a dubious brand of neutral spirits with rye flavoring restored my rapidly flagging energy. I got change from the automaton in the white coat, and went to a phone booth in the rear.

When I finally got Tommy on the phone, he said, "Wait until I pick up the extension in the soundproof study. My guests are playing an insane symphony on the medieval musical instruments we purchased this afternoon."

Judging by the background sound effects, Donald Duck, Andrei Vishinsky, and the ghosts of Billy Sunday and Adolf Hitler were harmonizing in a barbershop quartet to the accompaniment of a threshing machine.

When Mr. Twotoes came on the wire again, he said that Snowy had arrived, had been met at the station and was presently blowing lusty notes out of the serpent. I then informed him that I was saddled with two unconscious bodies, that one of the bodies seemed intent upon strangling the life out of the other body each time it regained consciousness, and inquired what I could do about the matter, other than packing both of them neatly in cement and dropping them in the nearby river.

"Bring them up here, Soldier!" said Tommy peremptorily. "Bring both of them to me! At once!"

"Dear old boy," I said, assuming the tweeds-and-beagle accent of Mr. Cholomondeley, "did it ever occur to you that packing two unconscious bodies all the way from the Brooklyn Bridge to Tarry-town in the middle of the night might prove a somewhat difficult undertaking?"

"A scout is resourceful," replied the old man. "You were a Boy Scout once, weren't you, Soldier?"

"At the age of fourteen I was all broke out with Merit Badges," I informed him.

"Then the problem should be simple," he said complacently. "Both men need a doctor. The only doctor who has ever inspired my admiration is the fey little fellow, Freylinghuysen, we met this morning. Despite the lateness of the hour, I will summon him. He is familiar with Phil's case. I think he will come."

"What if one of 'em should die on me en route?" I inquired. "What then, dear old boy?"

"Resuscitate him," barked Tommy. "You should have learned the rudiments of first aid in the Boy Scouts."

"Just like that," I said. "Old Miracle Man Rooke."

"Soldier," he said, "this is of utmost importance. Your discovery of Fighting Phil virtually solves the case. The tangled skein is beginning to fall into a recognizable pattern. If all goes well, I will present the police with a murderer tomorrow."

"Dear old boy," I replied, "you're beginning to talk more like Sherlock Holmes every day. Please don't expect me to shout 'Incredible!' and 'Amazing!' every time you open your mouth, though. My name's Rooke, not Watson, and I'm not a straight man."

"Cease your flippancy," he ordered. "I assume you are calling me from a gin mill. You are evidently not aware that other places are equipped with telephones. I urge you not to overindulge. You will need your wits about you for the next hour or so."

"I'll take it easy," I told him. "Scout's honor," I added.

I thanked the Dan Beard of Tarrytown for his excellent advice and told him I'd take a refresher course by rereading the Boy Scout Handbook. Then I hung up.

When I again hurdled the zombies in the hallway I felt like a jockey going over the Grand National course at Aintree, second time around. The toughest hazard, the Becher's Brook jump of the steeplechase, proved to be the old man with the burned face. He was halfway on the stairs and halfway on the floor by this time, but I cleared him without coming a cropper.

I found that my two boyfriends were still bound neatly as Prometheus and was thankful that my Scoutmaster had taught me to tie good knots. Fighting Phil was still unconscious, which made me wonder if I shouldn't have adopted the career of a light-heavyweight instead of that of private eye. Old One-Punch Rooke. I was gratified to note that Phil was breathing evenly and showed no immediate signs of dying on me.

Jenks had recovered from his fainting spell. He regarded me with wide, frightened eyes. He tried to say something but only a sound like a peanut whistle came out of him.

After a cursory examination of the man on the bed, I knelt down beside the little guy on the floor. I had a plan. If Jenks were able to walk to the car, I could drag the old fighter down the stairs and across the street. The neighborhood had seemed almost entirely deserted at this hour. But even if anyone saw me, they would pay slight attention. Helpless drunks were no rarity in this section of the city. If I encountered a cops I could explain that Phil was my long-lost brother and that I had found him drunk and freezing in the gutter.

"Listen to me carefully," I said to Jenks in a low voice. "I want to see if you can walk. I'm going to take you for a ride."

It was the wrong phrase to use. Jenks's eyes bulged with terror and the peanut whistle sound came out of him again.

"Don't be silly," I added hastily. "Not *that* kind of ride. You know me from the hotel. I want to help you. I'm going to take you to a nice, quiet place in the country."

I thought of Tommy's guests and the musical instruments and wondered if *quiet* was an accurate description. "Well, a *nice* place, anyway," I said. "There'll be a doctor there to give you medical attention. I'll untie you, patch you up a little, then we'll see if you can walk."

I loosened the ropes, rubbed his wrists and ankles. I helped him to sit up. I always carried a couple of Band-Aids in my pocket just in case I bumped into something. I brought these out. I didn't think they'd do much good, but remembering my Boy Scout training, I stuck them over the dent in Jenks's bald dome. I assisted the little man to his feet. I walked him back and forth across the room a couple of times. He was wobbly, but he could move. I let go of him, and he didn't fall down. I told him to keep walking to get his sealegs. He had to support himself against furniture, but he managed. I turned my attention to Phil. I hoped he wouldn't choose this moment to come to. He didn't. I untied him. He groaned a little.

I said to Jenks, "We're going to take off. Where's your coat and hat?"

He shook his head. I searched the apartment. I found a coat and hat, a burberry that had seen better days and a brown felt with the initials P.C. in the band. They obviously belonged to Phil, so I put them on him. If Jenks had a coat and hat, I couldn't find them.

I took a tattered army blanket off the bed and wrapped it around Jenks's shoulders. He resembled the puniest of the ten little Indians. I lifted Phil off the bed with a fireman's hold. I told Jenks to go downstairs and to be sure he didn't stumble over the drunks in the hallway. I should have taken my own advice. As soon as I reached the bottom steps I tripped over the old man with the scarred face. Poor old Phil hurtled through the air and landed on top of a sleeping vagrant. The man with the burned face let out a horrible yell as I thudded down on top of him. Jenks stood in the doorway, weaving back and forth, supporting himself against the jamb. I scrambled to my feet and examined Phil. He was a hard guy to kill. He was still breathing. I picked him up again and motioned Jenks out the door.

As soon as he hit the street Jenks glanced back at me. He seemed to be setting himself for something. "The car," I said, "across the street."

Jenks floundered on his feet for a minute, then broke into a run. He started to run away from me. He was so weak he could hardly stand. He slipped on the ice and fell. I started to put Phil down and go to him. But a big guy was standing beside him now. The big guy helped him up and began dragging him back in my direction. When he had dragged Jenks back, he said, "Now just what the hell is this, fellow?"

I said, "Put him in that car across the street, will you? I've got all I can handle. Wait a minute." I fumbled in my pocket. "Here's the keys."

He took the keys, but he said, "Just a minute now. What's the big hurry? Where are you going with these men?"

I ad-libbed. "I'm a member of Alcoholics Anonymous," I told him. "These are a couple of backsliding brothers I'm rescuing from a life of sin. I'm taking them to a place where they can sober up."

The big man beamed. "Really?" he said. "I'm an A.A., too. I come down here often late at night to see if I can help any of the boys."

He took Jenks across the street to the car, unlocked it, thrust him in the back seat. I crossed the street and tossed Phil in beside Jenks.

"Thanks a lot, bub," I said to the big guy.

The big guy sniffed suspiciously. "Are you sure you haven't been drinking yourself?" he asked. "I could swear I smell liquor on your breath. Maybe I should drive you."

"It's cough medicine you smell," I assured him. I put my hand over my mouth and gave him a sample cough. "If you're looking for customers, though, there are plenty more where these came from. Just open the door of that house across the street. The hallway's crawling with stewbums."

"Really?" he asked, his eyes lighting up. He took off like a bird dog on a red-hot scent. I got in the front seat and started the car. I made a U-turn and headed away from the river. I said over my shoulder to Jenks, "Listen, jerk. You make one try to get out of this heap, and I lower the boom on you. I'd just as soon take you to an undertaker as a doctor."

I was answered by the peanut whistle. I hoped Jenks was trying to tell me he would be a good boy. It was long after midnight and there was little traffic over the icy streets. It seemed ages, though, before I reached the Henry Hudson Parkway. And my nerves were really frayed by the time I turned off on the Sawmill River road. Once we reached this highway, it seemed that no one else on earth was alive. I didn't see a single car. No lights showed in the windows of houses.

If you want a rare experience, try driving over an ice-slick, deserted country road in the dead of night, with almost fifty thousand dollars in your breast pocket and two murder suspects, one dope-crazed and the other voiceless, and both hating the other's guts, in the back seat of the car.

A horrible thought suddenly went through my mind. Suppose I had dropped the envelope containing the fifty gees when I stumbled over the old bum? I could imagine the scene in that hallway if the drunken derelicts awakened to find fifty thousand dollars strewn on the floor beside them. I guess I must be a masochist. I

moved my hand very slowly toward my breast pocket, prolonging
the agony. I could remember doing the same thing during my days
on the Bowery, when I had awakened in some strange place after
a blackout. I would move my hand slowly, very slowly toward my
pocket to see if I had any money at all left to buy that drink I
needed if I was going to stay alive. I was doing that now. It seemed
I just couldn't make my hand move faster, no matter how hard I
willed it to do so. I unbuttoned my overcoat, my jacket. Finally
my hand reached the inside pocket. The hefty manila envelope was
still there. I heaved a pent-up sigh of relief that sounded like steam
escaping from a valve.

I drove on for miles, the beam of the headlights thrusting the
darkness aside like billowing black curtains, no sounds but the
swish of tires on ice, the guttural snores of the unconscious Phil,
the rasping breathing of Jenks.

For a brief instant a startled deer was frozen in the glare of
the car lights. I swerved to avoid the unexpected apparition and
almost wrecked the car. Deer didn't belong in this thickly populat-
ed section of Westchester, but for that matter neither did Tommy
Twotoes' penguins, and I was sure that a temperate guy like me
wasn't seeing things. I figured I'd only had twenty or thirty shots
all days, even counting the doubles as two, and that was extreme
moderation for a guy who was celebrating the inauguration of
Yuan Shi Kai.

The dark miles fled behind us. A winter moon came out from a
sheltering snow-cloud and the road and fields were palely silvered.
I turned off on a narrower road that would lead me to the bluff
where Tommy Twotoes' house and penguin rookeries stood. There
was a bloodcurdling croak from the back seat, followed by a sound
like a death rattle. I turned my head and almost wrecked the car
again. Phil Caselli had his hands on Jenks's throat. In the dim light
from the dashboard his face was the face of a maddened murderer. I put on the brakes, but the car skidded as I steered it to the

shoulder of the road. The jeepster came to a jarring, rocking stop. I climbed over into the back seat, crooked an arm under Phil's chin, pressed a knee into the small of his back. I exerted enough force to break the neck of an ordinary man, but he had a maniac's strength. His grip on poor Jenks's throat did not relax. Jenks had ceased to make any sound at all. I made a supreme effort that nearly dislocated my shoulder, and broke Phil's grip. Jenks collapsed on the floor at my feet. The old boxer, half-strangled, his tongue lolling out of his mouth, still clawed for the little man. I managed to get the car door open and to haul Phil out into the snow. We floundered on the ice-crusted ground for a moment, then he was still, unconscious again.

I knelt beside him, panting painfully, exhaling smoky clouds of breath. I examined Phil. I waggled his head. His neck did not appear to be broken, although I had exerted all the strength I had in pressing back his head, and I am a big guy who fancies himself as being very tough. I knelt beside Phil for a moment longer, feeling his heartbeat, his pulse, listening to his labored breathing. The door on the other side of the car flew open. Jenks staggered out. He started across the snowy fields at a wobbling run. He fell flat on his face, rose, teetered for a moment, then set off again into the moon-silvered darkness.

I left Phil lying in the snow and ran around the car. I called, "Wait, Jenks, wait!" But he floundered on in the snow piles, driven by the desperation of terror. I ran after him, calling his name, wasting my breath. He disappeared over a small hillock. I churned through the snow in pursuit, slipping to my knees as I mounted the small rise, scrambling up it on all fours. When I reached the crest I got to my feet. Jenks lay still on the ground, a few yards from me, the blanket that was still around his shoulders a dark splotch in the white snow and silver moonlight. I slipped down the hill as if I wore skis, balanced myself when I hit bottom, ploughed toward the fallen man. I bent over him, lifting his head. He was barely breathing. He seemed more dead than alive. I wished for one of Tommy Twotoes' blue crocks of brandy, or for the smelling salts he always kept on hand. I picked Jenks's small body up in my arms. He was gasping horribly. I started to trudge back toward the hillock and the road, and then I heard a sound that froze me in my tracks.

The motor of an automobile was coughing stridently as a heavy foot pressed the starter.

The motor caught, roared into the still night like a mad bull, and tires shrieked as they skidded in the crusted snow.

The roar grew nearer, louder. Suddenly light blazed into the sky and my jeepster stood teetering on top of the small hill, the beam of the headlights swerving wildly as the car spun on the ice, like a searchlight seeking enemy planes. An ordinary car could hardly have made the rise over the sheeted snow, but this was an auto mounted on the chassis of the old army jeep, the incredible vehicle that had done so many incredible things on obstacle courses and pitted battlefields.

Suddenly we were pinpointed, zeroed in, by the blinding lights of the car. The jeepster was hurtling down the hill, thundering at us in its mad, careening course. My knees shook as I stood there with the small body of Jenks in my arms. I turned and attempted to run away from the light. The tires screeched as the car turned sharply, bearing down mercilessly upon us.

In that panic-stricken moment I thought of the cars that had roared down upon the murdered doctor, of the car that had crushed the unidentified man in front of the funeral parlor in Father Demo Square. Despite the burden in my arms and the slippery under-footing, I turned sharply on my heel, like a quarterback running a broken field, but the acrobatic jeepster's kill-crazed eyes still followed me. I fell, crashing heavily on top of Jenks, and I knew that this was it, that my luck had run out. In a matter of seconds

I would be smashed and broken as a dope-mad driver crushed me under his wheels again and again. I could almost hear his insane laughter as his modern juggernaut pressed down upon my body.

Then I did hear the mad, screaming laughter. But it wasn't laughter.

It was the screech of spinning tires on ice, a shrill sound that tore at the roots of the nerves. There followed a heavy crash and the splintery sound of broken glass and a hurt, animal sound from a human throat.

The jeepster had skidded when it was almost upon us and had swerved into a tree.

I rolled off poor little Jenks. I lay still for a minute, then I felt for Jenks to see if he was breathing. He was.

I took the Police Positive out of my pocket. I threw it off safety. One headlight of the car still burned. I skirted the light, moving slowly toward the jeepster. I called, "Phil! I've got a gun on you. Try anything and I blow your head off!"

There was no answer.

I reached the car. Fighting Phil Caselli was sprawled over the steering wheel. The dash lights still glowed feebly. I pressed the button of the pencil flash with the hand that wasn't gripping the gun. I played the light full on the old boxer's face. Blood dripped slowly from his fist-mangled nose.

The door of the car had been jarred open by the collision. I put away the pencil flash, reached inside, grabbed Phil by his hair, forced his head back. Fresh blood poured from his nose. He was slack-jawed. His breath snorted through his open mouth.

I went back, pocketed the gun. I wrapped the blanket around Jenks and lifted him in my arms again. I carried him to the back seat of the car. I looked the car over. The hood was crushed in, one headlight askew, a fender bent. I grabbed Phil by the collar of his coat, dragged him away from the wheel. I got into the driver's seat and pressed the starter.

The starter hawked asthmatically a time or two. Then the motor turned over. Imperishable chariot of modern armies, I thought. I wondered if even a hydrogen bomb could stop a jeep. I backed the car up. I skirted the hill, found level ground, bounced over the rutted, snow-covered field to the road. The jeepster was limping, swaying, but it was answering the rudder like a battered, gallant ship of the line. We were only a few miles from Tommy's house. I breathed a prayer of thanks for that.

I drove very slowly, the gun on my lap, one eye on the road, one eye on the unconscious man beside me. I knew him for a killer now. If he moved, I would blast him.

He didn't move. He sprawled grotesquely in the corner of the seat, blood dripping slowly, thickly from the misshapen nose that had been broken again.

At last I turned into the driveway of Tommy's weird estate. The night was hideous with the calls of angry penguins. When I entered the house, I knew what had disturbed their sleep. The practice session on the ancient instruments was still in progress. Even the gnome, old Dr. Freylinghuysen, was curled up on a big chair, plucking at the virginal. Wisey strummed his zither and Colonel Finger blew ear-shattering blasts from the posthorn. The Magnificent Mephisto was experimenting with the crwth, while Snowy made noises like the belchings of a drunken Rabelaisian giant issue from the serpent. Quasimodo awked, Cleo arked, Montmorency honked, Ivan the Terrible whined and the guinea pigs were apparently frightened into complete silence.

I was staggering from sheer exhaustion. I leaned against the high back of a Jacobean chair. At my appearance, the music ceased and even the birds and animals were quiet. Ginny rushed to me solicitously.

"Terry!" she cried. "What happened? What have they done to you?"

"What unkempt wraith is this the night has spawned?" demanded Tommy Twotoes, who sat at regal ease in his specially reinforced chair.

"We've got guests," I replied. "They're outside. They can't walk and I'm too pooped to carry 'em any further. Wisey, you and Mephisto look like big, strong boys. Go out and drag our visitors in from the car."

"What visitors?" Wisey asked. "Who?"

"Coupla musicians I shanghaied for your orchestra," I told him. I turned to the gnome who had been plucking at the virginal. "Doc," I said, "you'd better get your little black bag. These two guys are in bad shape. Psychoanalysis isn't going to help 'em any."

Wisey and Mephisto carried the blood-dripping Phil in first. They took him up the escalator, and, at Tommy's direction, placed him in the room I had shared with the magician the night before. Doc Freylinghuysen fairly scampered up the ramp. The escalator moved too slowly for the lively little medic. The next litter case to appear was Jenks. He was parked in the room that Romano had had the night before to wait the little doctor's ministrations.

I sank down on a sofa and put my head in Ginny's lap. It was a very soothing lap for a head that ached like mine.

The timid Great Dane slunk to my side and attempted to comfort me by glopping me with his king-size tongue. Cleo planted herself at my feet and made turtle-dove sounds. I figured it was a fitting reception for a returning hero, and no more than my due. I drank two large slugs of brandy. Then I told Tommy of my adventures en route.

"If I'd had my scout axe along, I'd have buried it in both their heads," I added.

Doc Freylinghuysen was with his patients for more than an hour. It was nearly four o'clock in the morning when he came hopping down the ramp to report that both would live. Phil, he said, had been given incredibly large doses of morphine, but had the constitution of an ox and would come around after a short rest and medication. It might be days before Jenks could speak properly, but by tomorrow he would be strong enough to write out any story he had to tell.

Before he left, the gnomelike doctor and Tommy consulted in the hall. I overheard the doctor say, "No, he would never be given the electric chair. No jury on earth could find him sane."

Mephisto and his guinea pigs were banished from their bed-chamber and forced to sleep on the living-room couch. I was assigned to the other bed in the room with Phil Caselli, since Tommy feared the latter might awaken in the night and cause further trouble. The fact that I had had quite enough of Mr. Caselli for one evening did not influence Mr. Twotoes in the least.

"You are young," he told me. "You are strong and healthy. You have been a soldier. You have even endured the rigors of the Bowery. Certainly you can bear up under this."

Finally we all went up to bed.

After Tommy had been hoisted up the escalator, he paused dramatically on the second floor and made an announcement that was doubtless meant to assure his visitors reposeful slumber.

"A murderer sleeps beneath this roof tonight," he declaimed in pipe-organ tones.

"Pleasant dreams, all," he added as an afterthought.

10

The fact that a man who might well be a homicidal maniac was lying within a few feet of me didn't keep me from falling asleep immediately. I hadn't lied, when I said I was pooped. The rugged Rooke constitution had had about all it could stand during the past twenty hours. It was bad enough having to haul the three hundred pounds of Mr. Twotoes around the countryside and through the city streets all day. Contending with two murder suspects, one of whom was crazed and mostly unconscious from dope, the other strangled voiceless and frightened out of his wits, had been too much, especially since one of the pair was bent upon murder and the other intent upon escape.

I was too tired even to don pajamas. I flopped down in my underwear. But I did take a couple of precautionary measures in case Phil should rouse again and try some of his tricks. I put the gat under my pillow. And I left a shaded lamp burning in the room.

I slept dreamlessly for more than two hours. The pale, timid winter dawn shone faintly at the windowpanes when something awakened me. I felt as if someone were pressing my aching eyelids down with heavy thumbs. I tried feebly to thrust my eyes open, and I couldn't. I must have moved in the bed, thrown my arm toward my head, seeking to shut out whatever thing it was that disturbed my slumber. My hand touched the cold steel of the gun beside my pillow. That awakened me to a sense of danger. With a great effort I forced my eyes to open. I grasped the gun so tightly the trigger guard cut into my palm. I heaved a sigh and raised myself to a sitting position on the bed, knuckled sleep from my burning, aching eyes.

My breath caught in my throat.

Directly across from me, so near that I could almost feel the animal heat of his body, a man was sitting on the edge of the other bed. Wide eyes stared at me from a grizzled, idiot face. Phil Caselli was tensed, and it seemed he was about to spring. I pointed the gun at him.

I said, "Relax, bub. I'm wide awake now. And I've got a gun. You're a second too late."

The idiot face licked its lips. The eyes bored into me unblinkingly. The mouth moved, said, "Wh-who are you? Where am I?"

I said, "You're in a safe place, Phil. They call me Soldier. And I shoot straight. Especially at this distance."

The broad bulldog face was made more hideous by the bandages that swathed the swollen, broken nose. A great misshapen paw touched the bandages curiously.

The old fighter said, "The doc? Where's the doc?"

"Doc Mulholland?" I asked. "You killed him didn't you?"

The big head moved slightly in negation. "I—I don't think so," he said. "Doc Freylinghuysen. He was here, I thought. Am I in the sanitarium again?"

"No," I told him. "The doc will see you again soon. You're all right. You're with friends now. You're safe."

The gun seemed to mean nothing to him. He tried to rise. I said sharply, "Careful, Phil. It's loaded, and I'll shoot."

He said, "The little guy. I almost had him. We've got to find him."

I said, "Sit still, Phil. The little guy's not here. You've done enough to him already."

"He'll kill again," the dazed man said. "He'll kill again," he repeated.

He looked around him helplessly, like a sick, caged animal. He said, "I almost had him. I think I did. I thought there was a car. I almost had him with the car, I thought. Then something happened."

"You almost had Doc Mulholland with a car a couple of times, didn't you?" I asked. "You killed the man in Greenwich Village with a car, too, didn't you? You drove the old woman up to Rockland County in a car."

He shook his head. "I—I don't know. Dreams. You dream a lot. I live in Rockland County. The sanitarium's in Rockland County."

His staring eyes were glazed, as heedless as the reflection of the pallid winter dawn on the windowpanes.

"The little guy," he said. "Got to find the little guy."

"Not now," I told him. "Do you want a drink of brandy?"

"A drink?" he said. "Yes, I need a drink, that's it. But Doc Freylinghuysen said I shouldn't drink. Drink or use the other stuff."

"The doc said it would be all right to have a drink of brandy if you woke up," I assured him. "To ease the pain of your broken nose."

The vacant eyes wandered. "Broken nose?" he said. "Bat Skelley broke my nose that time. In the ninth round, it was. But I knocked him out. In the eleventh, I think. But he wasn't the little guy."

I got up off the bed, keeping a tight grip on the gun, keeping an eye on the old fighter. I had put the blue crock on the chest of drawers, out of Phil's reach. I poured brandy in a glass, handed it to Phil.

He regarded the glass stupidly. Then he drank. He sputtered and choked. I was afraid his nose might hemorrhage again, despite the dressing. But I didn't move too close to him. I didn't know what effect the drink might have on him in that condition.

"Liquor," he said. "The doc said I shouldn't . . ."

"Lie down, Phil," I urged. "Go back to sleep. The doc will see you soon again."

"Yeah," he replied. "The doc. That's it. The doc'll know what to do."

He sprawled on the bed, shut his eyes. Minutes later he was breathing heavily. I sat in a chair and watched him. He didn't move. If it was an act, it was a good one. The pale sunlight washed slowly over the carpet. I switched off the lamp. At last I went back to bed. I fell asleep with the gun still grasped tightly in my right hand.

When I awakened again, Polvo was shaking me. Phil slept on. My wristwatch showed it was nearly ten o'clock.

"That little doctor's here," said Polvo. "He wants to look at Mr. Phil, see him alone. You'd best get up, Soldier."

When I awakened I was shaking and sweating and my mouth was full of owl's feathers. I felt sure that a little thing like mixing brandy, rye, ale and the assorted cocktails, wines and cordials I'd had at the 42 Club couldn't have left me with a hangover. I was just under too much nervous tension. I needed a vacation in the Adirondacks or on the beach at Waikiki. I was a little over thirty, and after you pass that thirty-mark, you slow up, I told myself.

Polvo handed me a brandy-whisky penguin cocktail, the standard eye-opener at Twotoes Manor, and I felt better after I gulped it down. I asked the combination chef and penguin-tender if he could find underwear, socks and a shirt in my sizes among the clothing Tommy kept for his unexpected guests. I took a cold shower and revived some. My clothes were laid out for me. The shirt was a dilly. A shocking-pink job with burgundy pin stripes and a Bold Look collar. It made a real pretty background for my mauve tie with the green flowers.

I found Tommy in the breakfast room with the little doctor. He had eaten long ago, he said, but he was still sitting at the table, blowing billows of smoke from his naked-lady pipe and sipping coffee royal. The little gnome from the Rockland County souse trap seemed none the worse for wear despite having been called out in the middle of the night. He looked as bright as a boss mobster's two-dollar manicure. He hurried upstairs to attend his patient.

"You sure a little guy like that will be safe alone with Phil?" I asked Tommy. "That punch-drunk goon of yours is a killer and he's plenty violent."

"That little guy," replied Tommy confidently, "could take care of himself in the midst of two battalions of North Koreans equipped with Russian weapons and full of Russian vodka."

I'd had almost six hours in the sack, not counting interruptions, but I was still drowsy. I yawned.

"I find your oscitancy offensive," said Tommy.

"My what?" I asked.

"Your oscitancy," repeated Tommy "Wonderful word, isn't it? I only came across it this morning. After Dr. Freylinghuysen had attended Jenks, the little man seemed vastly improved. He still cannot talk, but he was able to write out answers to questions I asked him. My pockets are stuffed with notes of the conversation which I will refer to presently when the murderer is revealed., Jenks then wished to pass the time with a crossword puzzle, so I procured the morning paper. One of the words in it was *oscitancy*. It means the act of gaping or yawning."

"So now you're a philologist," I said.

"I am a man of many accomplishments," replied Tommy modestly, pouring more brandy into his coffee. "And I have a nose for murder, as you can attest."

As Polvo served me eggs and kippers I asked, "So I'll ask the classic question: Who done it? As if I didn't know, after my adventures of last evening."

Tommy shook his head. "There is a time for everything," he said. "Even a time for unmasking murderers. That time has not quite arrived. I don't know whom you suspect, of course. But I am willing to wager you are wide of the mark as usual. As a muscular specimen, you measure up to the requirements of a detective. But I shudder to think what follies you might commit if the agile Twotoes brain were not directing you."

"You're a smug bastard, aren't you, dear old boy?" I said.

"*Confident* is a better adjective," he replied. "And I was born in conventional wedlock. However, if it's any comfort to you, it was your exertions, observations and reports to me which have solved three murders and prevented at least one other killing. The seeds planted by your efforts have reached fruition in the fertile Twotoes brain."

I reached for the blue jug and slopped brandy into my coffee.

"Go easy on that stuff," warned Tommy. "My trusty bodyguard, Ebony Black, may have reached the East with the Rolls Royce, but he can hardly arrive here today. I will need protection. This murderer is very dangerous. A psychopath, with complications. He may attempt to kill me when he is exposed."

Tommy's trick doorbell, which played the opening bars of "How Dry I Am" when it was pressed, sounded. Polvo answered it. The newcomer was Eddie, impeccably attired in clerical garb and a black homburg. He had come up for his audition on the crwth. He was ushered to the living room where twanging, tootling, tinkling and tumping noises indicated that Wisey and his orchestra of amateur musicians were already hard at their rehearsing.

I was still eating, so Tommy called for Polvo to assist him to rise and join his guests. As a preventive measure, he tucked the blue crock under his arm. As soon as he left, I went to the sideboard, opened a little swinging door and procured another blue crock. I made myself a second coffee royal that was very regal indeed.

I dawdled over my breakfast for a while, then tucked the blue crock in my pocket and went out in the hall and got my zip-lined trench coat off the totem pole. The noises that the ancient instruments were making didn't exactly act as a soporific for the squirrels that were scurrying around inside my skull, so I went out the back door and made my way to the rookeries. Polvo hadn't yet let Cleo, who enjoyed special privileges among the penguin colony, inside the house. She came paddling up to meet me and pecked at the fence with her beak to let me know she wanted out.

I unlocked the gate and the amorous penguin rubbed herself against my leg lovingly. Cleo and I set off for a walk about the estate. The cold air helped to clear my head. The squirrels were still scurrying around some but they were slowing down a little. I drank in the crisp fresh air and from time to time I also drank in a bit of the brandy. The air was cold and the brandy was warm, so I figured they'd balance each other nicely.

"You know," I said to Cleo, "everything that Tommy Twotoes gets himself involved in turns out to be screwy. Maybe that's because he's a screwball himself, even if he has got a million bucks or so. I think maybe he's leading with his chin by staging this Great Exposé. All the physical evidence points to Snowy, and when Romano sees the little albino he's pretty likely to get handcuff-happy and not listen to all Tommy's fancy deductions, I'm afraid."

Cleo said "ark" and nodded her sleek, feathered head in hearty agreement.

"Tommy said there are too many clues in this case," I continued. "Also there are too many corpses. The old doc. The unidentified corpse. The old lady. We don't even know for sure if the same guy chilled 'em all, do we?"

"Ark," said Cleo. It was the only word she knew, but she could give it different shades of meaning by her inflections.

"You can make out a very good case indeed against Fighting Phil," I went on. "He tried to strangle Jenks to death three times. He tried to make mincemeat out of me. There must be a slight touch of murder in him somewhere. But on the other hand, there's a good case against Jenks, too, especially from the standpoint of motive. Eddie said Jenks was about to slug Phil with a bottle when he peeked in the window and kicked over a flowerpot. Maybe he was about to do the same thing when Phil attacked him. As the old man's great-nephew, Jenks would come into a hundred grand if Phil was dead and Snowy was up for a murder rap. That would be a simple way of disposing of both the heirs the old man named in his will."

"Ark," said Cleo enthusiastically. Cleo was a very fine stooge for a guy who was thinking out loud.

"Likewise," I said, "there are too many detectives. To begin with there's Romano and his little playmates. Then there's Tommy and I. And there are a couple of self-appointed sleuths. Jenks, who ferreted out the flat where Phil was hiding. And Eddie, the elevator operator, who made like a bloodhound and shadowed Jenks to the Brooklyn Bridge. It's all very confusing and I need a drink."

While I was gulping from the bottle Cleo said "ark." Then she said "ark" in a different tone of voice. Something had attracted her attention. Two cars were turning into the driveway. Romano and one of his assistants got out of the first car. The other was a police heap containing uniformed cops from Tarrytown. I suppose they were present to make it official if Romano put the bracelets on somebody outside his own bailiwick.

"Well," I said. "This is it, I guess. For better or worse. We may as well go into the house and watch Mr. Twotoes stage the last act of his little melodrama."

Cleo paddled along beside me like a plumber's helper as I re-entered the back door of the house. I hung up my coat and Cleo and I went into the living room. Evidently the majesty of the law had had a sobering effect. The strange instruments the musicians held were stilled. Quasimodo perched on the swinging bar of his cage, his head cocked, regarding the musicians suspiciously. Montmorency quit chasing Ivan the Terrible, who slunk behind the couch. The Magnificent Mephisto sat in the Chinese throne chair, guinea pigs piled high in his lap.

"Soldier!" Tommy greeted me. "Where have you been hiding yourself? Phoning someone from a gin mill, no doubt? Go upstairs at once. I have sent Polvo up to see if Dr. Freylinghuysen will allow his patients to attend us for a moment. You may be needed if Phil still exhibits a hostile attitude toward Jenks."

I mounted the ramp. The sympathetic Cleo accompanied me to give me moral support. When I reached the second floor Dr. Freylinghuysen and Jenks were just starting down the escalator. From his chin to his shoulders, Jenks was swathed like an Egyptian mummy. Polvo was leading Phil out of the room we had shared the previous night.

I took over from there. I grasped the wobbly, weaving old fighter by the elbow and said, "Listen, bub. One false move and I break your ugly nose all over again."

He replied, "It's all right now. The doc's going to take care of me, he says."

His trusting nature was touching, but I would have wanted something more formidable than the little doctor between me and the electric chair.

When we were all finally assembled in the living room, Tommy Twotoes struck a pose in his specially reinforced chair like the enthroned King Canute defying the sea.

"I have invited you here for a grim ceremony—the unveiling of a murderer," he said. He paused to sip brandy and to light his naked-lady pipe.

"Three persons have been killed," he continued. "Dr. Mulholland was the first. A man who must remain unidentified unless, like the Phoenix, he arises from his ashes to proclaim his name, was next. And finally, the old woman, Marie Seducci, who assumed the name of Theresa Caselli for reasons that will soon appear, was found violently dead. The same man murdered all three. That is obvious. The motive for the first murder is simple and tawdry enough. Money. One hundred thousand dollars, to be exact. The murder of the old doctor was the direct cause of the other killings. Thus murder itself became a motive for murder."

Madame Eden interrupted Tommy's recital. "Pour me brandy, Polvo!" she demanded. "There is an evil aura in this room!"

"There is an evil *presence*," Tommy corrected her. "The presence of one whose mind has become deranged through drugs, frustrations, and the bitter gall of the life he led."

He turned to Romano., "I must apologize to you, Lieutenant," he said. "You might have solved the crime yourself had you been in possession of all the facts. I thought it unwise to tell you of a visit that Snowy here paid the Soldier and of the important revelations that he made. You might have made a premature arrest when pieces were still missing from the puzzle. I took it upon myself to conceal the facts until the proper moment. You see, this whole case hinges upon a simple medical fact. The great body of *circumstantial* evidence, and of actual physical clues in the case point to one man—Snowy Sylvester. We discovered shoes of the type he wore in one place, a piece of cloth similar to the suits he wore in another, broken glasses of the kind he wore near a hanging corpse. Only at Ginny's residence, where the comparatively minor crime of purloining a parrot's cage was committed, did we find evidence leading to another person. That was the watch inscribed with Phil Caselli's name.

"I point out to you that any murderer who would leave three pieces of damning evidence behind him must be incredibly stupid. Snowy Sylvester, to my certain knowledge, is not stupid. He is well educated. He is shrewd. He is versed in the law. In recent years he has led a life and has engaged in certain enterprises that required extreme cunning. It would have been sheer folly for him to have visited the house of the old woman dressed in the white clothes which were his hallmark. A man dressed in white during a snowstorm would have been conspicuous anywhere. Snowy proved conclusively that he could elude the police and elude the Soldier by the simple expedient of changing from his accustomed white clothes to dark clothes. Those who were seeking him were preconditioned to notice only a man in white. Yet we are asked to believe that he conducted a woman to her death, exposed himself openly to the superintendent of her building, while dressed in telltale white!

"The obvious conclusion, then, is that the evidence against Snowy was planted. I pause here to remind you that it is quite credible that a half-drugged man might drop his watch while assaulting the superintendent at Ginny's apartment house."

The albino's bloodless lips were smiling. The old fighter darted a frightened glance at Dr. Freylinghuysen. I touched the gun in my pocket.

Tommy motioned to Polvo to refill his glass. I figured he was so engrossed in his story that I could sneak one myself. I did, and he didn't bother to reprove me.

"There were three previous attempts upon the life of Dr. Mulholland, all of them crude and all of them unsuccessful," Tommy continued. "Twice the murderer tried to run him down with a car. Once he attempted to smother the old doctor in his bed. He left him for dead. But despite his ninety years, Dr. Mulholland was made of leathery-tough fiber. He survived. Then the murderer evolved a more elaborate scheme. Two other killings resulted. When I appeared upon the scene, the plot grew even more involved. The killer has a strange and devious mind. He thought he could follow the pattern of my thinking. However, my mind is more devious than his. *I* followed the pattern of *his* thinking. I checkmated his every move. Too late to prevent the murders. But in time to reveal his identity."

He turned to me. "On your guard, please, Soldier," he said. He drank deeply. He was enjoying the hushed attention. He looked deliberately at each of us in turn. At Snowy. At Jenks. At the Negro, Eddie. There was pity in his glance when it rested upon the cowering Phil.

To Romano, Tommy said, "You did not know that Snowy made a visit to the office of Rooke, Private Investigator, Lieutenant. At that time he made statements which have led to the solution of the case. He confessed to Soldier that he had visited Dr. Mulholland's suite shortly after the murder, that he had found the old man hanging by the neck, that the stage had been set to make his death appear a suicide. He said that he was convinced the death was the result of a murderer's work and that in order to convince the police of this, he rearranged the props. He put the ladder, which was overturned on the floor under the corpse, into a far corner of the room. And he struck the dead doctor a hard blow on the back of the head, to indicate that the murderer had knocked the old man unconscious before hanging him. The mark of this blow would, he thought, convince the police that the death could not be laid to suicide.

"Now we cease to deal with clues and circumstantial evidence and turn to incontrovertible medical fact. Had such an intelligent police officer as Lieutenant Romano been in possession of Snowy's statement to Soldier, he might have realized its implications at once, but I doubt it. Most of us have forgotten the elementary physiology we studied in school. Had the medical examiner known of the statement, he most certainly would have reached the proper conclusion.

"If I remember correctly, this is how Soldier quoted the remarks of the assistant medical examiner to me: 'Knob on the back of the head. Hit with the usual blunt instrument before he was hanged.'

"The medical examiner naturally assumed the old man had been struck on the head before he was hanged. That was the only possible assumption he *could* make. A blow after death might have broken the scalp. There might even have been some slight bleeding due to the tremendous intercranial pressure caused by strangling. But the blood would have been very light in color. There would have been no clot. And there could not possibly have been any discoloration, swelling or 'knob' had the blow been delivered after death. Such a swelling would have been caused by the accumulation of lymph and intercellular fluid, and this could occur only during life. You could no more raise a swelling on a corpse by hitting it with a blunt instrument than you could raise a bump on a side of beef by smashing it with a hammer.

"And so Snowy Sylvester lied. And Snowy Sylvester is our murderer. Watch him, Soldier. He is still dangerous."

I had been all set to leap at Phil. I changed course quickly and went to the side of the albino who was still holding the absurd-looking serpent in his arms. I put my hand on his shoulder, frisked him. No gun. No fight. The policemen moved close to us. The little man was limp, dazed.

The fat old man relit his curious pipe. He drank brandy. He said, "Dr. Freylinghuysen has assured me that Snowy will be found insane and confined in a proper institution. I am glad. There is little reason for society to seek vengeance upon one of its unfortunates. Snowy's mind is as warped as his poor, frail body.

"Snowy first planned to kill his old friend when he learned that he was his heir. The trusting old doctor also confided to him the secret of the parrot's cage. Snowy decided to kill him for the obvious reason. He thought that a large sum of money might buy him pleasures that had always been denied him—women, the admiration of his fellows. He made three crude attempts to take the old doctor's life and failed each time. Twice he used a rented car.

Once he tried to smother the old man in his sleep. He had a key to the apartment, of course. Then he learned that the doctor suspected Phil of the attempts upon his life. Dr. Mulholland had seen Phil under the influence of liquor and drugs and knew he could grow violent. He persuaded Phil to go to a sanitarium in Rockland County. While Phil was away, Snowy developed what to him was a much more satisfactory plan. By framing Phil for the murder, he might come into Caselli's share of the legacy as well as his own. By framing him, he would protect himself, of course. But there was, to Snowy's twisted mind, an even more urgent motive. Although Phil had befriended him for years, Snowy hated him. Phil was everything he was not. Big, strong, healthy. Although Fighting Phil Caselli has never been handsome, like many prize fighters he exerted an animal attraction for women. That, perhaps, was what hurt Snowy most.

"Snowy had already wreaked vengeance on Phil for imagined wrongs. He had encouraged him to become an addict of marijuana, morphine and other drugs he peddled. But now Sylvester's crazed mind conceived the ultimate revenge for all the misfortunes life had dealt to one of nature's unusual creatures. He would make a big, strong, physically robust man die in the electric chair for a crime he himself had committed. And he would enrich himself in doing so.

"Snowy had a wide acquaintance among the vagrants of the city who seek oblivion in marijuana and narcotics. He sold them their poison. He found one man who bore a superficial resemblance to Phil. Men of approximately Phil's size who have prognathous jaws and battered features are not unusual among the wanderers of the slums. Snowy supplied this man with whatever narcotics he used free of charge. He kept in touch with him day and night. Because he had a plan.

"Snowy was also acquainted with the Seducci woman, who had operated dope drops. She was, I fear, a foul hag of the underworld who grew more repulsive with age. Perhaps she has met her just deserts. This woman agreed to act a part for him, for a monetary consideration, of course. She assumed the identity of Phil Caselli's aunt.

"Snowy's next move was to write a letter to Phil at the sanitarium. He told him that the doctor's life was in danger, that he himself was not physically capable of protecting the old man. He urged Phil to return to New York. So Phil escaped from the sanitarium. He met Snowy in New York. Dr. Freylinghuysen says that the cure had by no means been effected when Phil left the hospital so unceremoniously. Snowy plied Phil with liquor and marijuana and morphine in the rat's nest he had rented beneath the Brooklyn Bridge. He told him he would need all his nerve to protect the old man's life, that the stuff he was giving him would sharpen his wits. An addict is easily persuaded to take the poison he craves. Snowy even doped Phil's liquor to make assurance doubly suit. For days Phil lay there in a stupor, unable to distinguish between his nightmares and reality. I talked to Phil briefly this morning, with Dr. Freylinghuysen's permission. He believes Snowy must have told him Dr. Mulholland was dead, that the police were looking for him as the murderer. This is highly possible. Snowy might have considered it a refined sort of torture to inform the helpless man of such news."

Tommy paused. I stood by the albino, tense, ready. Snowy said, "Even you're against me, Tommy. All of them, they've always been against me."

"I might remind you that totalitarian governments have kept political prisoners under opiates for weeks and months before their mock trials," said Tommy. "Phil had enough dope in him to kill an ordinary man. But he is a fine physical specimen, and he had developed a tolerance for drugs through usage. Snowy administered more morphine to him whenever he visited the flat under the bridge. Phil unwittingly took copious doses himself every time he awakened and reached for the bottle by his side.

"While Phil lay helpless, Snowy went to the hotel and murdered the old doctor. He struck his unsuspecting victim on the back of the head, probably with the .45 revolver he carried. I rather imagine he may have garroted the old man to death before he strung him up, to make sure that he would not come alive this time. In any event, he finally hanged him, probably with a piece of rope he found among the doctor's collection of junk. He took his time. At least enough moments elapsed between the blow and the doctor's death for a swelling to rise on the old man's head.

"Snowy knew the combination of the parrot's cage. He removed the key to the safe-deposit box from it—*Phil's* key. He left the key tagged with his own name inside, replaced the false bottom. It amused him to confuse the police with a false clue. He removed the hanging man's shoes, pressed them down on top of the ladder in the far corner of the room to make perfect footprints. The footprints and the position of the ladder would lend credence to the story he planned to tell later. He put the shoes back on the dead doctor's feet. He hung the little clock saying 'Doctor Is Out' on the outside of the apartment door.

"He had taken the watch and the identification cards from Phil's pockets. He now met the nameless man with the bulldog face at an appointed place. He supplied him with the identification cards, took him to the bank, gave him the key to the safe-deposit box and instructed him to remove the contents. He doubtless waited outside the bank until the man joined him. He took the envelope and made an appointment to meet the vagrant that evening in Father Demo Square.

"He rented a car before the time arrived, parked it near the undertaking parlor. I suggest that the old woman was probably waiting near the funeral home also, that when the vagrant appeared she called him by name, lured him across the icy street. The poor vagrant was a sitting duck for the murderer. He was unsteady on his feet anyway. The street was slippery. Snowy had the motor running. He roared down upon the befuddled bum, crushed him beneath the wheels, sped away. He may have simply ditched the car, or he may have returned it to the garage. Caselli's identification cards were found on the body. The old woman claimed the body as the remains of her nephew. Snowy had supplied her with money from the envelope the bum had taken from the box. She paid the undertaker, had the corpse embalmed and laid out."

Tommy sipped brandy.

He continued, "You can see what Snowy had accomplished by murdering the vagrant. He had sealed his lips. He had made sure that the police would find Phil Caselli's identification cards on him and he knew that eventually the police would connect the name of Caselli up with that of the murdered doctor. His motives were much deeper, though. He thought that the death of a boxer once as prominent as Phil would attract wide attention, that someone would see through the hoax, would know that the body in the mortuary was that of an impostor. When that occurred, the natural conclusion would be that Phil had persuaded some man to impersonate him, that he had killed the man in order to establish himself as legally dead. That would indicate he had murdered the doctor and disappeared with the cash from the safe-deposit box. Snowy was determined to have Phil tried and convicted. He would have produced him in time, helpless and unable to answer questions coherently.

"But he did not realize there is nothing so dead as yesterday's headlines unless it is the people who made them. Fighting Phil Caselli was forgotten by the crowds who once cheered him. No one at all came to the funeral parlor to pay their respects. The unidentified man was about to be buried under the name of Phil Caselli, even before the old doctor's murder was discovered. Snowy had counted upon me visiting the funeral parlor because of my long and profitable association with Phil in the heyday of his fame. But I was in California. Snowy lurked outside the funeral home. He followed several persons in, no doubt. Finally Soldier came along. Snowy followed Soldier and heard him ask where the Caselli remains were laid out.

"From that point on, he had to improvise as emergencies arose. He dashed past Soldier, ran into the room where the impersonator was laid out, fired a clip of .45 bullets into the head of the corpse. He told the old woman to order the body cremated and to meet him at her house later that night. He threatened Soldier and others with his gun, made his getaway. It is quite possible that he suspected Soldier was my emissary. He probably thought it doubtful that a man of Soldier's age would have known Phil, who had been out of the public eye for so many years. But there was one sure way to attract attention to the corpse—by blowing its head off. That would make it obvious that someone wished to conceal the true identity of the corpse. It would, of course, incriminate him, but he is a man who stresses his peculiarity by wearing white clothes even in winter. We are dealing here with a unique murderer—a man who actually *planted* clues to cast suspicion upon himself. He knew that I was an old friend of the doctor's and the executor of his will. He knew that I had been Fighting Phil Caselli's friend and manager. He knew of my interest in criminology. He thought it inevitable that I would concern myself with this case. He had a story ready to explain his mad act. I knew him as perverse, irrational at times, emotional, addicted to marijuana. He thought I would swallow the story he told Soldier the next day. He said that he had been overcome with rage when confronted with the corpse of the man who had murdered his friend, that he had been so blinded with fury he had hardly noticed the embalmed corpse resembled Phil only superficially, and that he had emptied his gun without considering the consequences. He thought I would consider that explanation entirely compatible with his character, and I might possibly have accepted it except for the bump on the doctor's head.

"Later that evening Snowy went to the hotel, saw Eddie, learned that Soldier and Jenks were in the doctor's suite and that the murder had finally been discovered. Now another idea occurred to him. If the parrot's cage were discovered beside the unconscious Caselli, it would be further evidence of his guilt. He instructed Eddie to obtain the cage, bribed him with marijuana, went outside and rang the switchboard so that Eddie could have an excuse for calling Jenks and Soldier away from the doctor's flat. When he talked to Soldier on the phone, he added to the confusion by stating that he was Phil, and thus implanted the idea that the real Caselli might be alive.

"After Romano and the others left the hotel, Snowy returned, went to the basement and obtained the cage. But Soldier interrupted him, just as he was leaving, there was a brief scuffle, and he dropped the parrot. He then went to the old woman's tenement on Bleecker. It was urgent she be kept away from the police, now the murder was discovered. He learned that Soldier had obtained the old woman's address. He brazenly showed himself to the superintendent, asked him to help him with a trunk. He had odds and ends of clothing in the apartment and he purposely left a pair of his sneakers in the closet. He reasoned that when I concerned myself with the case, I would deduce that if Phil had hired a man to impersonate him he might also have hired a man to don a white suit and impersonate Snowy in an attempt to frame him. Impersonating Snowy would be no difficult task. A small man, a pair of thick glasses, a white suit were all that was required.

"Snowy must have rented another car. Police investigation should establish this fact. In any event I doubt he took the waiting taxi all the way to the house Phil owned in Congers. He had taken the keys to the house from Phil. He told the old woman to hide out there. He might even have remained overnight himself. He had probably intended to kill the old woman right along. But I doubt he killed her that night. The next afternoon Snowy visited

Soldier at his office and told the story through which he inadvertently convicted himself. He thought he could predict my reaction to it, my thought processes. He did not think I would believe that any guilty man, who had left no traces whatsoever of his presence at the scene of a murder, would wilfully confess that he was there and had tampered with evidence. Snowy did a quick-change act from a white raincoat and hat to a black raincoat and hat and left the building unnoticed. But he lurked about and followed Soldier to Ginny's place. It was not difficult for him to locate the right apartment after he saw Ginny and Soldier leave. Soldier's name is on the bell, alongside Ginny's. He rang the superintendent, flattened himself against the wall in the hall, slugged the man when he poked his head outside the door. He obtained the passkeys. He knew I would not consider it illogical for a dope-fogged man who was committing assault and burglary to drop his watch. So he left Phil's watch in the super's apartment. Then he obtained the parrot's cage from Ginny's place and took it to the flat beneath the Brooklyn Bridge. He put the envelope containing the bonds and the remainder of the money the derelict had removed from the deposit box in the bottom of the cage, to be found when Phil was discovered. The watch and the cage would establish the fact that Phil was not unconscious or doped, as he might claim, during the time of the murders.

"That night Snowy came to Tarrytown. He climbed a tree outside my window, planted the fragment of cloth on a limb to convince me further that someone was trying to frame him. He fired at me through the window, and was careful to miss. He did not want me dead. He was relying upon me to argue his innocence and to convict Phil. He crossed the river to Congers and hanged the old woman by the neck. Perhaps she brought matters to a head by demanding more money or making threats. He probably had an old pair of glasses, since weak eyes are subject to frequent change.

He crushed them and left them beside the hanging woman, more evidence that he was being persecuted. He had fired at me with a .32. He planted that and some marijuana cigarettes, which might also tend to involve him, in the baggage in the hall."

There wasn't any use in my keeping my hands on Snowy any longer. There seemed to be no resistance in him. Romano must have been thinking the same thing. He moved away from the albino.

Tommy drank, said, "A very large red herring then appeared in the case. Jenks presented it unwittingly. He is unable to speak, but he has written a statement. His mother was Dr. Mulholland's favorite relative, but the old man disapproved of her husband and broke off all relations with his niece when she married. He carried over his dislike of the father to the son. He would not aid Jenks financially when he was broke and desperate, but he did relent to the extent of securing him a job in the Suffield on condition that the nephew would not reveal their relationship. When the old man was murdered, Jenks thought he was entitled to his money. He suspected that Snowy might be involved in the murder. He consulted a lawyer who engaged the services of a private detective. The detective had underworld connections. He learned that Snowy was frequently at the C-Note Club, picked him up there one day and followed him to the flat beneath the bridge. He gave the lawyer the address and the lawyer gave it to Jenks. Jenks went to the address as soon as he was off duty. Eddie, who had overheard the telephone conversation and was not above turning a dishonest dollar, followed him. Jenks knocked on the door of the flat but was not answered. He went out on the fire escape, entered the room through a window. He tried to rouse Phil. He picked up the bottle of whisky and examined it. Eddie had also gone out on the fire escape. He saw Jenks, with the bottle in his hand, and he saw the man on the bed. He thought Jenks had murdered the man. Eddie kicked over a flower pot and fled. He returned the next day, peered through the window, saw Phil still lying on the bed. A short while later Jenks came down to the flat to see if Phil had revived. This time his knock was answered. Snowy was in the room. Snowy once more flattened himself against the wall, slugged Jenks as he entered. He then strangled Jenks, knowing that when he revived and found Phil there he would rush to the police and accuse Caselli of the assault upon his person.

"Snowy was 'disguised' in black clothes at the time. He had the white linen suit he had shed in the flat. It occurred to him that he might kill two birds with one stone, involve Jenks as the little man who had impersonated him. He stripped the unconscious Jenks, put the white suit on him, made off with Jenks's clothing.

"Late that night, when Snowy was on his way up here, Soldier went to the flat. He found both men unconscious, revived them. Even men who are doped have moments of lucidity. Such a moment came to Phil when the strong coffee roused him to semi-consciousness. He realized suddenly that his friend Snowy was the villain in the piece. His drugged gaze fell upon a little man in a white suit sitting in a chair. He thought it was Snowy and attacked him. Later, on the way up here, he revived again. The blanket had slipped down from the shoulders of the little man in the white suit who was sitting beside him. Phil attacked again. When Jenks fled through the snow, with Soldier after him, Phil crawled into the car, managed to get it started, pursued Jenks and Soldier, bent upon destroying them. To his dazed mind, they were his captors and the murderers of his friend.

"I think," said Tommy Twotoes, "that is all, and that Lieutenant Romano can take over. And, Polvo, please refill our glasses."

At that instant, Snowy rose suddenly. I grabbed for him and so did Romano. But he slipped away from us. With the surprising strength of the demented, he swung the unwieldy serpent above his head and hurled it at Tommy. Something catapulted through the air. The something was the midget, Colonel Finger. The midget plummeted into Snowy, knocked him off his feet. The serpent sailed over Tommy's head, crashed into a marble statue of the "Discobolus" and sent it sprawling.

"The ole Flying Filly!" chortled the little Colonel.

The cops led Snowy away—in handcuffs.

Ivan, the timid Great Dane, was so emboldened and inspired by the example of his tiny master that he came out from behind the sofa, roaring like a lion. He knocked Montmorency, the arrogant gander, halfway across the room with one swipe of his huge paw and bounded after him like an oversized retriever. He lifted the gander by the neck and shook him as if he were a feather duster. Feathers flew through the room like snowflakes in a windstorm. It reminded me of the annual Vassar-Wellesley pillow fight. The screaming Madame Eden finally rescued her pet gander, and he was no longer arrogant.

Snowy Sylvester died quietly soon after he was committed to an asylum for the incurably insane. It was only fitting that Tommy should employ the services of the talented mortician, Mr. Dinwiddie, to make the hideous albino as comely as possible in death. For the first and only time, the pallid little monstrosity had roses in his cheeks as he lay in his coffin at the funeral parlor where I first had seen him.

As you probably are aware, the Twotoes Television Varieties, with its orchestra of ancient instruments, is now the only video attraction that rivals Uncle Miltie and Howdy Doody in popularity, and Colonel Thomas Finger has succeeded Buzzbomb Nussbaum as midget wrestling champion of the world. Terry Bob Rooke, Investigator, is the only private richard in New York who gets advertised on television.

Jenks and Phil came to an amicable agreement through which they split Dr. Mulholland's estate. Each made a substantial donation to Eddie's Church of the Sanctified Soul.

Ginny also benefited from the old man's legacy. Tommy gave her Quasimodo, the parrot, and she uses him every night in her act at the Triangle Club. She says she is bringing Quasimodo up carefully and is teaching him not to curse.

Old Quasi is a very smart cookie. He learns fast. He has already added two brand-new words to his vocabulary.

Both are decidedly profane.

ABOUT THE AUTHOR

David C. Alexander (1907-1973) was born in Shelbyville, Kentucky, and raised in Louisville. He attended the University of Kentucky and Columbia University to begin a career in journalism with the *Lexington Herald*, soon focusing on horse racing. After serving in the Army during WWII, he continued writing columns for various publications, but his attention also turned towards writing mystery fiction. To gain a better grasp of his subject, he attended the New York Institute of Criminology in 1950, going on to write fifteen mysteries by 1962. His first two mysteries, published in 1951, are included in this volume. His most popular series detective, Bart Hardin, would first appear in *Terror on Broadway* (1954).

COACHWHIP PUBLICATIONS
COACHWHIPBOOKS.COM

SAMUEL ROGERS

YOU'LL BE
SORRY!

YOU LEAVE
ME COLD!

COACHWHIP PUBLICATIONS
CoachwhipBooks.com

THE
SARA ELIZABETH
MASON
MYSTERIES

MURDER RENTS A ROOM

THE CRIMSON FEATHER

COACHWHIP PUBLICATIONS
COACHWHIPBOOKS.COM

THE QUINNY HITE
MYSTERIES
CHINESE RED · HERE LIES THE BODY

RICHARD BURKE

COACHWHIP PUBLICATIONS
CoachwhipBooks.com

THE
BEACON HILL
MURDERS

THE
BACK BAY
MURDERS

THE ROGER SCARLETT MYSTERIES
VOL. 1

COACHWHIP PUBLICATIONS
CoachwhipBooks.com

THE SERGEANT HARTY MYSTERIES
JOEL Y. DANE

MURDER CUM LAUDE
1
THE CABANA MURDERS

DEAD
WEIGHT
ADDISON
SIMMONS

COACHWHIP PUBLICATIONS
CoachwhipBooks.com

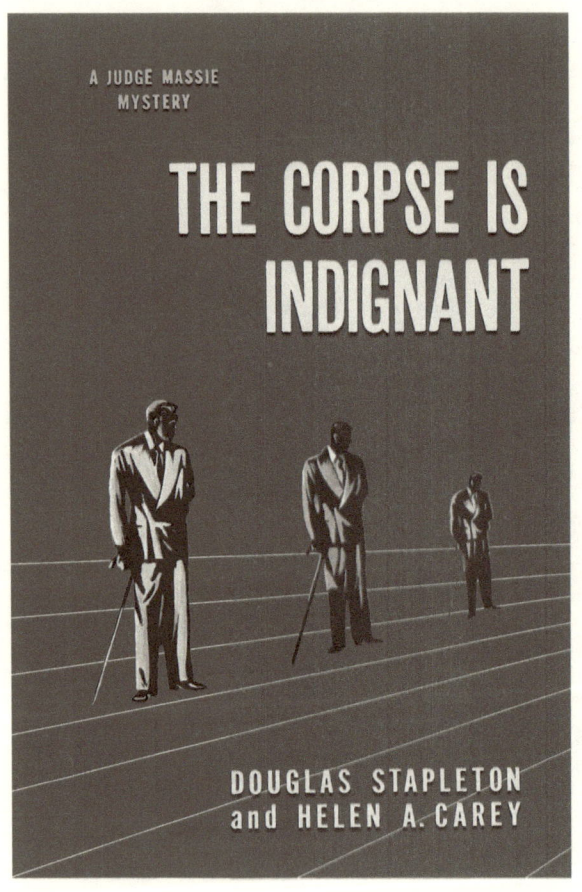

A JUDGE MASSIE MYSTERY

THE CORPSE IS INDIGNANT

DOUGLAS STAPLETON
and HELEN A. CAREY

COACHWHIP PUBLICATIONS
CoachwhipBooks.com

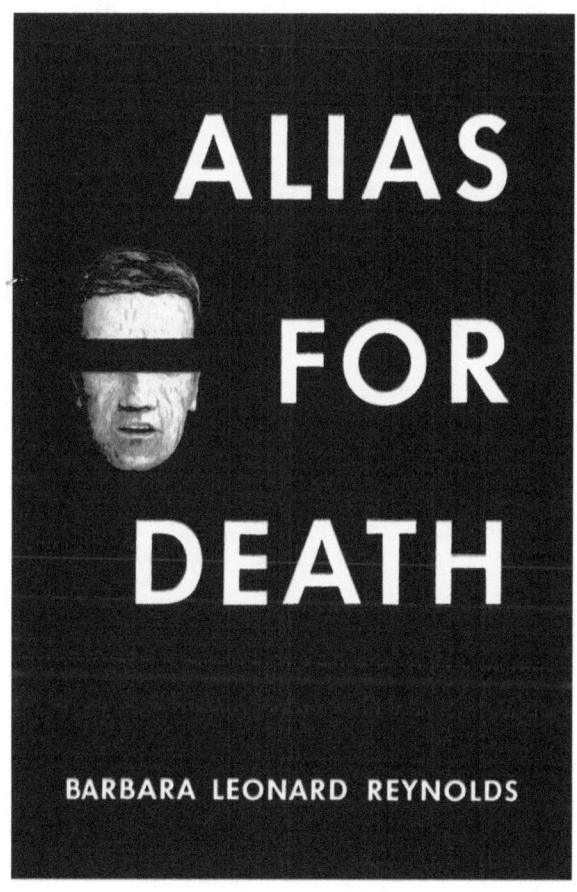

ALIAS FOR DEATH

BARBARA LEONARD REYNOLDS

www.ingramcontent.com/pod-product-compliance
Lightning Source LLC
Chambersburg PA
CBHW030629020726
47493CB00006B/1628